LIBERATION

LIBERATION

Imogen Kealey

GRAND CENTRAL
PUBLISHING

New York   Boston

Grand Central Publishing
Hachette Book Group
1290 Avenue of the Americas, New York, NY 10104
grandcentralpublishing.com
twitter.com/grandcentralpub

Originally published in Great Britain in 2019 by Sphere

First U.S. Edition: April 2020

Grand Central Publishing is a division of Hachette Book Group, Inc. The Grand Central Publishing name and logo is a trademark of Hachette Book Group, Inc.

The publisher is not responsible for websites (or their content) that are not owned by the publisher.

The Hachette Speakers Bureau provides a wide range of authors for speaking events. To find out more, go to www.hachettespeakersbureau.com or call (866) 376-6591.

Map by Viv Mullett

Library of Congress Cataloging-in-Publication Data has been applied for.

ISBNs: 978-1-5387-3319-6 (hardcover), 978-1-5387-3320-2 (ebook), 978-1-5387-5322-4 (Canadian trade paperback)

Printed in the United States of America

LSC-C

10 9 8 7 6 5 4 3 2 1

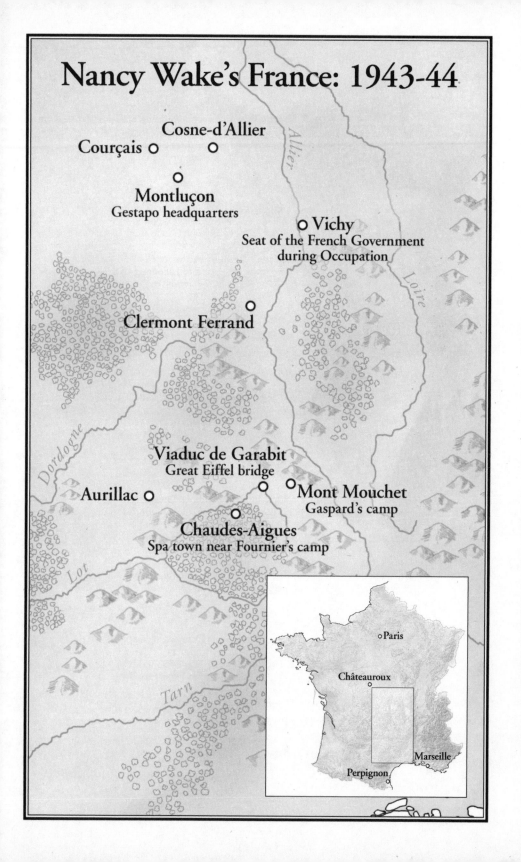

PART I

MARSEILLE, JANUARY 1943

1

This was a bad idea. A very bad idea. Damn it.

Nancy closed her eyes for a moment as she crouched behind the remains of a blasted wall and took a deep breath. The smell of burning buildings was clawing at the back of her throat, the smoke stinging her eyes, and squeezed into her narrow hiding place her muscles were beginning to cramp. She could hear the voices of the approaching German patrol clearly now.

"Auf der linken Seite." On the left side.

The wall she was hiding behind had yesterday been part of a house, a home. Just one of the thousands of narrow tenements in this corner of Marseille, where the city's less respectable inhabitants had for years brawled, grifted and bargained their way from one day to the next.

Now she sheltered in the remains of a small dirty room in her second-best coat and third-best high heels. The bloody things were pinching. The cloudless winter sky was visible through the remains of the upper story, but this room had only one door. She'd made a stupid mistake when she ducked in here to avoid the German patrol. They were swaggering through the ruins while their colleagues continued the business of setting explosives higher up the hill, chasing out the former residents of the Old Quarter from their holes. Going from house to house. And this house was next. Dull crumps and the rumble of falling masonry, together with occasional bursts of gunfire echoed dryly from higher up the hill.

"They have found more rats, boys," said an older voice, probably the officer.

"But I want a mouse," one of his men replied, and they laughed.

Most of Nancy's wealthy friends wouldn't have dreamed of coming to this part of town, even before the war. Too dangerous. Too strange. On her first day in Marseille, though, five years ago, Nancy had found her way into the steep narrow streets of the Old Quarter and she had fallen for it and the sinners and drinkers and gamblers she'd found there. She loved all its angry, messed-up color and contrast and dived straight in. It was her talent for going to places she shouldn't, of course, which meant she could earn a living as a journalist in France. And she knew that being Australian, she could get away with things most French women, so careful of their reputations, wouldn't dream of doing. In the years since then, Nancy had moved through these twisting roads and alleyways without fear, sharing cigarettes with the corner boys and trading foul language with their bosses. Even when she got engaged to one of the richest industrialists in the city, Nancy didn't stop going wherever the hell she liked. And it had worked out OK. When the war began and supplies started to dwindle even in Vichy territories, Nancy was already good friends with half the black marketeers in the city.

"It's empty, Captain!"

"OK, on to the next, lads."

Then the Nazis arrived in the city with their ugliness and casual violence, and the fiction that any part of France remained unoccupied fell apart, and then the Nazis decided the way to deal with the provocateurs, smugglers and thieves of the Old Quarter was to burn their homes to the ground and shoot anyone who didn't make a run for it.

So crouched behind the wall, with the patrol coming ever closer, Nancy had to admit it, reluctantly, even to herself: coming here on one last mission while SS troops rooted through the rubble for survivors and escapees was a bad idea, and coming here when the one person the jack-booted sadists really wanted to find was the Resistance courier and people smuggler known as the White Mouse, and you, as well as being Miss Nancy Wake, former journalist and pampered princess of the Marseille upper crust, *were* the White Mouse, made it a really, really no good, not clever at all, bad idea.

Not that she'd had a choice. Every mission she went on was important, but this one was vital and had to happen today, even while the Germans tore the world to shreds around her. She'd left the luxurious villa she shared with Henri determined, slipped past the patrols, tracked down her contact, bullied the tricksy twitchy devil into holding up his side of the bargain and got what she had come for. The package was secure under her arm, wrapped in more Nazi-loving bullshit from the Vichy press. It had cost her a thousand francs and was worth every centime—*if* she could make it back alive.

She had to get out of here. Now. No way was she going to reach her next appointment in time if she got picked up and questioned, even if they fell for the "What me, officer? Oh, I took a wrong turn on the way back from the spa. How smart you look in that uniform. Your mother must be so proud" act. God knows she'd winked and flirted her way through plenty of checkpoints in the last two years, a dash of rouge on her lips, with secret communiqués and radio parts for the Resistance sewn into the lining of her handbag, or strapped tightly to the inside of her thigh. But she had to, *had* to, make that appointment.

Two men from the patrol were already in the hallway. Double damn. If she could get them out onto the street again she could make a dash through the back of the building. It was that or shooting her way out.

She reached into her handbag, fished out her revolver and wet her lips. No time to fret about it. This thing just needed doing. She lifted her head and peered over the edge of the shattered window frame and looked right and left along the street. The house on the other side of the road and to the east still had parts of its second floor standing. Somebody being stingy with the TNT. Nancy could see a table, a vase placed carefully at its center in a room which no longer had walls or ceiling. The single blown rose it held shifted in the breeze made by the sucking currents of the fire. Excellent.

Nancy snapped open the cylinder of her revolver and emptied the bullets into her palm, then hurled them overarm across and along the narrow street. One of the soldiers on the street twisted round with a frown, sensing movement. Nancy flattened herself against the wall again and held her breath. One. Two. Then a sudden crack as the fire found the first bullet, then another.

"Return fire!"

The two soldiers in the hallway turned back out into the street and started firing into the burning building. Nancy could smell the cordite on their clothes as she slipped out of the room and made a dash for the back of the house. The patrol was still firing at ghosts. She pushed open the back door, ran through the narrow, rubble-strewn yard and plunged into the maze of nameless back lanes until she tumbled out into the relative peace of Rue de Bon Pasteur. Empty. She ran straight down the hill with a whoop of victory, her package still under her arm, and one gloved hand holding her elegant straw hat in place, trying hard not to laugh and skidding into the square like a kid freewheeling on a bicycle.

Straight into another patrol. Or almost. They had their backs to her. She threw herself back against the nearest wall and inched slightly up the hill. From the upper window of a house opposite a cat watched her, and blinked.

Nancy looked up at it and held her finger to her lips, hoping the creature couldn't tell at this distance that she was more of a dog person. Two feet east of her she saw the shadow of an opening in the blank and empty street. An alley, hardly big enough to walk down and silted up with God knew what rubbish.

She reached it and slipped in sideways, trying not to let her coat touch the walls, which looked suspiciously greasy. So did the cobbles beneath her feet. God, the smell. Even the drains of the fish market in mid-summer didn't stink like this. She breathed through her mouth, deafened by the thud of her own heart. She hoped her maid would be able to save her shoes, even if they did pinch. She could hear the voices of the patrol again. They had grabbed hold of some poor bugger, and she listened to them yelling at him, and his softer replies. He sounded desperate, afraid.

"Don't show them you're scared, mate," she whispered between clenched teeth. "It just gets their blood up."

"To your knees!"

Not good. Nancy looked up at the narrow strip of bright blue sky above her and prayed. Not that she believed in God, but maybe the Frenchman did, or the German with a gun. How many people were hiding in the houses around them now, listening but too frightened to move? Maybe they were praying too. Maybe that would make a difference. Maybe not.

She heard the click of a rifle bolt being slid into position, then a yell and running feet coming up the hill toward her hiding place. The idiot was trying to make a break for it. The crack of the shot echoed off the high walls. She heard the guttural gasp, very close, as the bullet hit, and looked sideways in time to see him fall, arms out in front of him, parallel with her hiding place in the middle of the steep cobbled road. His face was turned toward her. Christ, he was just a kid. Eighteen at most. She stared at him and it seemed he saw her. His skin was the smooth olive of a boy born under the Marseille sun, deep brown eyes, high cheekbones. He had on the collarless linen shirt all the working men of the area wore, thin with washing but kept blindingly white by a devoted mother. Lord, his mother. Where was she? The blood was pooling under his chest, and trickling down the slope between the high curved stones. His lips were moving, as if he was trying to whisper some secret to her. Then her view of his face was blocked by the boots of a German soldier. He looked back toward the square and shouted something Nancy didn't catch. A short reply.

The soldier unslung his rifle from his shoulder, worked the bolt and lifted it. He took a half step back so Nancy could see the lad's face again. The world narrowed to this patch of cobbled road, the yellow plaster wall opposite startled with sunlight, the movement of the dying boy's lips. *Crack!* Blood and brain matter fountained across the road. His body twitched and went still, the light in his eyes suddenly, absolutely extinguished.

Nancy felt a plume of rage lift through her. Lawless, murderous bastards. She put her hand in her purse and closed her hand around her revolver, before remembering with a bitter lurch that it was empty.

"Ah, shit!" the soldier said quietly, wiping away a smear of blood from the edge of his tunic. He'd been standing too close. He'd know better next time. He looked up at the window where the cat had been, then right and left along the street. Nancy had nowhere to go. One moment more and he would see her and there was nothing she could do, and if she couldn't kill him she'd have to talk her way out of it. She began to prepare her excuses and blandishments. Should she play the frightened girl? Or perhaps the outraged French housewife, intimidating even the SS with talk of her husband's wealth, her high-ranking friends? Attack can be the best form of defense. Just to scream in his face would be a pleasure, even if it got her shot in the end.

Another shout from the square and the soldier turned away. He walked back down the hill, slinging his rifle over his shoulder and leaving the White Mouse, shaking with rage, in her hiding place.

LIBERATION

She had to wait, so she counted to fifty and watched the dead man's face. One. Hitler speaking in Berlin, Nancy standing in a small group of journalists, not understanding the words but feeling the wild, ugly enthusiasm of the crowd. She had glanced round at her friends, all foreign correspondents based like her in Paris, all like her in Germany to see for themselves what this funny little man was up to. They were to a man older and much more experienced than she was, but they looked, all of them, as scared and sickened as she felt. Two. Vienna, thugs in the brown shirts of the Sturmabteilung, smashing the windows of Jewish businesses, dragging the owners out into the streets by their hair and whipping them in front of their neighbors; the neighbors turning away; the neighbors laughing and applauding. Three. Poland invaded, the declaration of war and the months of waiting which followed. Four. Cramming refugees into her ambulance as France fell. Five. German fighters strafing the lines of fleeing women and children with machine-gun fire. Six. Henri returning from his stint at the front heart-sore and humiliated by the speed of France's defeat. Seven. The day that Paris fell.

The images came in an orderly procession. Nancy clenched her fists. She'd sworn on that day in Vienna that if she ever had any chance to do the Nazis harm she'd take it, and everything she'd been through since only strengthened that conviction. She fed off her hatred for them. She delighted in every tiny victory. She believed that Hitler was a mad man, and that smashing himself on the great rock of Russia would end him. She would do anything she could to bring the collapse of his vicious, hate-filled regime a moment closer. She knew she was supposed to be afraid, stay quiet, keep out of trouble, and wait until Hitler and his foul crew imploded, but she was too angry to be afraid, and she didn't hold with keeping quiet.

Fifty. This man. This boy, caught up in the occupation and destruction of the Old Quarter of Marseille casually murdered by an invader with a rifle. The light leaving his eyes. Nancy

9

stepped back out into the street and walked down to the market place without looking at the corpse. She would never forget him. She unlocked her bicycle from the railings by the water fountain and, putting her package in its wicker basket, wheeled it out of the quarter.

When she reached the seafront, the glittering Mediterranean jewel-like under the cool winter skies, she took off her glove, leaned forward and ran her perfectly manicured nail down the edge of the newspaper wrapping, slicing it open, neat as a knife. The package held a bottle of Krug 1928, the champagne and the vintage Henri had ordered the night they first met in Cannes. Nancy turned the parcel so the tear wouldn't show and pushed off on her bicycle toward the smart end of town, where Henri and she had lived together since war broke out. The shock of seeing the man die was fading now. She lifted her face to the sun and let the breeze cool her skin. Damn the Germans. As the White Mouse the Germans had already put a price of a hundred thousand francs on her head, so she must be doing something right. A hundred black-market bottles of excellent champagne. She'd drink to that, but now she was going home to dress for her wedding.

2

Henri Fiocca was watching from the window of his dressing room as Nancy came up the path. He felt his heart lift and the familiar sensations of wonderment, fear and anger. Even on her wedding day she had to head off on some mission. Letters for the Resistance probably, false papers for another refugee desperate to leave France, radio parts for Resistance cells in Marseille itself, Cannes, Toulouse. Nancy was always on a train risking her life to take money and messages to some shadowy friend of a friend. He hated that. The loose, improvised nature of the Resistance network forced her to trust strangers, and these days one couldn't trust one's own family. Henri was a patriot—he loathed the Germans with a white-hot rage which equaled Nancy's, and so he shared his wealth and his table with anyone who could do the enemy harm. But he still wished to God he did not have to share his wife-to-be with them. Nancy seemed to have been born without fear, but Henri knew what fear was. His love for her had taught him that lesson.

He put his hand on the window pane as she disappeared into the house and said her name under his breath. She had blazed into his life like a meteor, this girl, and scattered light and magic and chaos in equal measure in her wake. He had fallen in love with her at once, absolutely, the first night they met. It had been like stepping off a cliff edge and into the shocking embrace of the ocean, but he was unsure what she wanted from him. He was so much older than her, and his life, for all its luxury, was so dull compared to hers. After a year he discovered she didn't care about his money. Oh, she enjoyed spending it, just as she enjoyed every fresh pleasure she could find, but she did it with the delight of a child. Slowly, he learned about Nancy's early miserable years and her flight from Australia to America and London at sixteen; her desperation to put an ocean, half a world, between herself and that unhappy childhood had turned into an animal appetite for pleasure and a fierce self-reliance. After another year, Henri realized that even Nancy needed someone to lean on from time to time and she had chosen him.

She had chosen him.

Pride flared in his chest.

Tonight, he would be able to call her his wife. He knew she wouldn't stop draining his wealth and running insane risks to help the Resistance just by marrying him—he had no illusions about that—but today and tonight at least, he would know where she was, know she was his own.

"Perhaps *I* should talk to Nancy," a voice behind him said, narrow and nasal. "If she can't be on time for her hairdresser on her wedding day, maybe she doesn't even want to get married."

Henri looked over his shoulder. His sister was perched on the edge of his bed like an elderly crane. She had been a pretty girl when she was young, even with that long face and thin lips, but somehow even with all her wealth she had managed to turn sour, and that, he believed, had made her ugly. She had insisted on accompanying him upstairs when he'd said he was going to dress, desperate to make one last attempt to get him to call off the wedding.

"You may try if you wish, Gabrielle. But she will just tell you to go away and leave her alone. And remember she is not constrained by brotherly love. I may not throw you out of the room, but she will."

Gabrielle ignored the hint, broad as it was. Her voice continued, high and whining as a mosquito. "I will say this for her, she can curse in French like a sailor in the last hour of his shore leave. Where on earth did she learn such language, Henri? It's disgusting."

Henri smiled. Hearing Nancy let rip in her adopted language was one of the great pleasures of his life.

"She is a natural linguist, Gabrielle."

"Stuff! No dowry! She refuses to become a Catholic! Does she even believe in God?"

"I doubt it."

The whine pitched a little higher. "How could you, Henri, how could you pollute our family with this foul little Australian whore?"

That was too far; even brotherly love had its limits. Henri lifted his sister by her shoulders off his bed and propelled her firmly toward the door.

"Gabrielle, speak to me of my wife in that manner once more, and you will not set foot in my house again. If I had to trade my money, my business, my dear family for an hour of Nancy's company in the lowest bar in Montmartre I would do it without a moment's hesitation. Now get out."

Gabrielle realized that she had gone too far and her tone became beseeching. "I am thinking only of you, Henri," she managed as he shut the door in her face.

Thank God she does not know about Nancy's work for the Resistance, Henri thought. She would go tip-tapping her way to the Gestapo in an instant, a mix of hatred of Nancy and greed for the reward making her eager to bloody her claws.

He returned to the mirror and smoothed down his hair. His friends told him he was looking younger since the war had begun. He didn't want to tell them it was just that they were aging at a faster rate. He didn't want to offend them, loyal as they were in their way to their own wives, by pointing out that

13

Nancy, a teenaged runaway from the other side of the world, had given him purpose and hope while they staggered with shock at the defeat of France, the flight of the British soldiers from Dunkirk and then the horrific bombing of the French fleet at Mers-el-Kébir on the coast of French Algeria, ordered by none other than Churchill himself. Over a thousand Frenchmen killed by British bombs. That had shaken his country-men, and so many had retreated into their homes in the face of it that the Germans now thought that they owned the whole country. They did not. France would rise in the end. Nancy made him believe that. What would life without her have been like? He shivered. Hellish, gray.

And then of course Nancy also seemed to be best friends with every black-market operator on the Riviera. Their table was always laden with fresh meat, and so they shared with their friends who had neither connections nor money. Henri did not think he'd eaten a meal alone with Nancy in their home for a year.

He heard a tap at the door.

"What?" he said gruffly, thinking his sister might have gathered her courage for one last assault.

Nancy slid in like a cat. She could only have been in the house for ten minutes, yet there she was, her hair curled and piled high to frame her heart-shaped face, her full lips cherry red against her white powdered skin, her blue dress sweeping and skimming over the full curves of her breasts and hips.

"Is that how you'll greet me every time I knock on your dressing-room door from now on, Henri?"

He walked toward her, a glimmer in his eyes, but she held up her hand.

"Don't disarrange me, you monster! I just wanted you to know I'm all ready to be made an honest woman, if Gabrielle didn't put you off." She winked. "Though I just spotted her sniffing into her hanky in the hall downstairs, so I guess she failed."

LIBERATION

He put his hands on her hips, feeling the blue silk of her dress move over her skin, but did not try to kiss her.

"How could you go out today, Nancy? In the middle of all this hell. On our wedding day?"

She put her hand up to his cheek. "I'm sorry, but don't growl at me, Old Bear. It was important, to me at least. I'm home now."

"Have you seen the new posters, offering one hundred thousand for the White Mouse? It seems your stunt breaking out the prisoners from Puget has not gone unnoticed."

"Worth it," she said, gently removing his hands from her hips before his grip did damage to the delicate—and extremely expensive—silk. "Those men can do something now. Though that British airman was an arse. Complaining about his food and how cramped the safe house was like we hadn't all just risked a firing squad to save his sorry butt."

Henri took a step away from her. Gabrielle was always talking about the other women he could have chosen to be his wife, beautiful, elegant, obedient, French girls. They would have kept careful accounts, stayed quietly at home. But every other woman in the world disappeared when he thought of Nancy. The fire of her, her brutal tongue. The refusal to be cowed. She went up against the world toe-to-toe like a prize fighter. The clash of images in his mind, the bruised hulk of a boxer, and this beautiful young woman in blue silk and red lipstick made him laugh and she looked at him quizzically.

"White Mouse is a bad name for you, Nancy. You are a lion. Now, shall we marry?"

He shrugged on his dinner jacket, and she came close to him again to adjust his tie. He caught the scent of Chanel on her warm skin.

"Yes, Monsieur Fiocca. We shall."

*

The party at the Hotel du Louvre et Paix was a complete triumph. Not even the sour stares of Henri's family could chip away at the perfectly joyous victory of the thing. If anyone wondered how the new Madame Fiocca had managed to get her hands on such a profusion of luxuries, they kept their doubts to themselves and launched themselves headlong into the serious business of pleasure.

Nancy was fiercely happy. She knew that the party would be the talk of the city and that she had done Henry proud. Every hour spent debating and arguing with chefs, florists and dressmakers had been worth it. Take that, Marseille. She slipped her hand into his under the table at the head of the gilded ballroom. He was turned away from her, trading jokes with one of his managers at the shipworks, but he squeezed the tips of her fingers and rubbed the inside of her palm with his thumb in a way that made her shiver.

"Madame Fiocca," said a voice at her elbow. It was Bernard, maître d' of the hotel and one of Nancy's favorite friends. He stepped back to allow one of his underlings to set the silver ice bucket at her elbow and fresh glasses in front of Nancy and Henri, then lifted the chilled bottle out of the ice, showed it to her, and at her nod opened it. It sighed open under his practiced hand and he poured for them both.

Henri turned from his friend, saw the label and vintage, and laughed out loud. "How did you manage this, Nancy?"

"I told you I was on a very important mission today, Old Bear."

He shook his head, but took his glass from Bernard with a reluctant smile on his lips.

She got to her feet and tapped her full glass with a fork. Out of the corner of her eye she saw Gabrielle, sitting with her equally unfriendly father, Claude, stiffen. A bride giving a toast at the wedding? Shocking! Hell yes, Nancy was going to give a toast.

She waved her hands in the air. "Quiet now, you devils!"

The band leader cut off his musicians in full flight and Nancy's friends silenced each other in a chorus of shushes and giggles. Nancy lifted her glass.

"Thank you! Now, my father couldn't be here today, but he sends his regards from Sydney." Nancy was guessing on that one. She hadn't seen him since she was five. "And my mother wasn't invited, which if you knew her, you'd realize was my present to all of you." That mean cramped woman in her mean cramped house, a Bible in one hand and her stick in the other. Let her rot. "So I shall try and give a proper toast of my own. I am toasting my husband this evening"—she paused for cheers and whistles—"with a 1928 Krug, because that was the vintage he ordered the night we met, when France was still free. But war or not, Nazis in our streets or not, I say to you this evening, while we are free in our hearts, France is still free. Henri, I know I am a difficult, expensive, troublesome sort of wife to have, but you are my rock and together we will build a life worthy of this vintage. I swear it."

Henri got to his feet and touched his glass to hers and for a moment, as their eyes met, they were the only people in the world.

"Madame Fiocca," Henri said, and sipped his champagne.

Someone in the crowd sighed loudly and even Nancy felt the prick of sentimental tears behind her eyes. No. Tonight was a party.

"To hell with propriety," she said, and drained her glass, then turned and gave her audience her best, her widest, her most impossible-to-resist smile.

They cheered, a full-throated roar of delight and defiance. The band leader caught his cue and launched into a fast-paced version of "When the Saints go Marching In." The waiters began to clear tables and move them out of the way for the dancing to begin, helped with stumbling enthusiasm by Nancy's most disreputable friends.

Henri set his glass on the table and kissed her. Out of the

corner of her eye Nancy noticed Gabrielle dabbing at her eyes with a linen handkerchief, and so she kissed him back, hard, and tipped herself forward into his arms like a swooning Hollywood star. The applause and whoops were loud enough to be heard up and down the seafront.

3

It was another hour before Nancy had the chance to talk to Philippe and Antoine about what she had seen during the destruction of the Old Quarter.

Antoine, dark-haired and thin but with a wiry strength in his narrow shoulders, was one of the most successful people smugglers in the south. He'd worked with Nancy, a Scotsman named Garrow she had never met and a Belgian Resistance man called O'Leary, all of them guiding escapees to isolated safe houses and arranging guides to take them over the Pyrenees into the relative safety of Spain a dozen times. Philippe, shorter in stature with a square, tanned face, who always looked like he'd just come in from the field even when he was dressed in a dinner jacket, was an excellent forger. Near faultless passes, residence cards and travel permits emerged from his basement workshop day after day and carried those lucky enough to find friends in the Resistance along the winding train tracks and on rural busses into anonymous obscurity, or from safe house to safe house across France until they found their way onto a ship for England.

"They just shot him dead," Nancy said. "Right in the middle of the fucking street. There's not even a pretense of legality anymore." The image of the fatal shot, the spurt of brain matter and blood flickered behind her eyes and she downed the rest of her glass. Close behind them a champagne cork popped noisily and Antoine stiffened, then shrugged.

They are too worn out even to be angry any more, Nancy thought, and held out her glass. I must hang on to my rage.

A passing waiter saw her and she heard the champagne fizz into the glass. It sounded like the hiss of her own blood in her ears when she thought of that dead boy. Gray. Red. Yellow. The blue of the sky. She would feel every second of it.

"I'm worried," Antoine said. "Three times last month my guides had to turn back because of increased patrols, just when we had people to move. Perhaps we should go dark. Suspend operations, slow down for a while. Someone is talking. Or someone is being careless."

Nancy felt his gaze. "Don't look at me! I don't even tell you where those steaks you eat at my table come from. I am the soul of discretion." She winked at him over the rim of her glass.

"Antoine has a point though," Philippe said gruffly, his large hands holding his champagne flute as if he thought it might explode between his fingers any moment. "Nancy, there is a new Gestapo spy hunter in Marseille. A man named Böhm. He destroyed the best network we had in Paris in a matter of weeks. Hardly anyone made it out. He did time in the east too and now he is here. He is coming for the White Mouse. For you. We must be careful."

Careful. Everyone wanted Nancy to be careful, polite, sit on the edge of her chair with her knees together and her hands in her lap and never look anyone in the eye. Fuck that.

"Oh, relax, boys. He's not going to find me. Everyone knows I'm just a girl with expensive habits and a rich husband. Who is going to see the White Mouse when they see Madame Fiocca out shopping?"

"Nancy, take this seriously," Antoine said. "We are not playing a game. And even if the Gestapo don't suspect you, what about the men in your life? You think that Henri can keep funneling half his fortune into our cause without attracting notice?"

That stung. But Henri was a grown man and could make his

own decisions, she told herself. Yes, he kept warning her to be careful too and she kept pushing and pushing but...

"The only way to beat a bully is to punch him in the nose," she said. "Anyone who's ever been in a schoolyard knows that," she added, a sullen and dangerous flicker in her eye. She felt a touch on her shoulder and turned. Her husband. How did he manage to look so cool, so calm after the fountains of champagne they had drunk? Every other man in the room looked flushed and awkward next to him. Her anger was forced out of her by a sudden surge of pride.

"Nancy! You promised me! No talk of your work today." He looked at Philippe and Antoine. They shuffled like schoolboys.

"We have been urging Nancy to be cautious, Monsieur Fiocca," Antoine said.

Henri smiled at them. "Good luck, I hope you have more success than I. Darling, shall we dance?"

Nancy took his hand, then waved at Antoine and Philippe over her shoulder. Caution be damned. Henri was a hero and could look after himself, and she was never going to slow down if she had the chance to bloody the Nazis' noses just one more time.

Their guests moved aside to give the newly-weds room to dance a waltz. Henri was a divine dancer. Nancy could just let go, allowing herself to be guided by him over the polished wood floors. She leaned back against his encircling arm; it was like flying. When she opened her eyes, he was gazing at her steadily, but in a way that put her on her guard.

"Are you going to scold me?"

His hand tightened slightly round her waist. "I think I must. Spending your wedding reception with members of the Resistance. Risking your life for a bottle of Krug."

She widened her eyes. They were still on the edge of playing, of finding it all terribly amusing: the war, the danger, him as sage and wise husband shaking his head over the excesses of his

21

young wife. "They are my friends, and I got the Krug for *you*, my darling."

"I don't need champagne, Nancy." He wasn't playing any more. "I need you."

He brought her closer to him. A hiss outside, like the first hint of the summer mistral wind, and then a dull cramping explosion. The chandeliers shook and a thin shiver of plaster dust whispered from the ceiling.

Henri released her waist, held her hand and lifted it high. "Bernard, *mes amies*, more champagne and *Vive la France!*"

The crowd re-gathered its bravery and cheered. The band launched into a fast, frivolous dance tune and the dancers kicked away the dust as they spun around the floor. Nancy laughed out loud, her head thrown back, and let herself be carried away by the lights, the drink, the feel of Henri's hands.

Even after four hours of dancing, Henri would have no argument. He would carry his wife over at least one threshold this evening. He picked up Nancy in his arms and carried her into the bedroom, then set her gently down on the thick carpet.

"Henri," she said, putting her hand on his chest. "I have something very important to ask you. I need your help."

He frowned. This was Nancy's way, to find her moment and then ask for something outrageous and dangerous. More money. Using their home in the Alps as a refuge for prisoners. Using his business to smuggle arms and men. A bond to buy one more Jewish family safety in England. She watched him prepare for the onslaught and grinned before turning round.

"I can't reach the zipper…"

He laughed softly and very slowly reached for the delicate catch and unhooked it, then eased down the zip, tracing her exposed skin with his knuckle. He came close, kissed the back of her neck.

"Henri, I'm not going to apologize for who I am. You knew who you were marrying," she said, leaning back against him.

"I wouldn't ask you to, Nancy." His words were muffled, his voice low with desire. He ran his hands around her waist, pressing his palms against her stomach.

Nancy felt the need for him, an ache under his fingers.

"I'm sorry. I'm sorry I can't be like those other wives. The thought of hurting you is awful, but so is the thought of letting those bastards win. They cannot win. So I'm not going to lie to you and promise to quit. I can't."

He sighed and turned her round to face him. "Promise me only that you will try to be careful. Can you do that?" His voice was warm, indulgent again.

She nodded.

He led her over to the little sofa and table in the corner of the room by the windows and sat her down beside him.

Nancy twisted in her seat and hitched up her skirt so she could sit astride him. She lifted her hands to let her hair free of its diamond clasp and let the silk slip down her body to pool at her waist.

"Henri Fiocca, I fucking love you."

He put his hands in her hair, pulled her toward him and kissed her. Hard.

4

Major Markus Fredrick Böhm replaced the telephone receiver into its cradle. The call had been to tell him the final reports of the clearing of the Old Quarter would be waiting for him at his office in Rue Paradis in the morning, but it was clear the operation had been a success.

Before Böhm's arrival in Marseille, it seemed every day the German occupying forces were losing men in that rats' nest. Follow a suspect in there and you left, if you managed to leave at all, empty handed or covered in shit poured from an upper window to the delight of the loitering workers in the street. Böhm had listened to the reports and complaints of the men, and the excuses of the French authorities, then issued his orders.

Perhaps half of the inhabitants of the Old Quarter gathered together their blankets and pots and left when the official notices of eviction were posted up on the walls. Most of the rest found themselves arrested and loaded onto trains for processing at the camps. The large number of foreign or French Jews discovered still living in the Old Quarter provided final proof, as if any were needed, of the slapdash way the new laws had been enforced in the preceding months. Those who fought or ran or hid were shot. Böhm was a Hercules who had cleansed the shit out of the city in three days.

He glanced into the mahogany-framed mirror above the telephone table and smoothed his hair. Behind him in the reflection he saw the door to his daughter's room was ajar. He crossed quietly to it, and looked in.

The telephone had not woken her. Sonia was curled under the blankets, a stuffed rabbit cradled in her arms, still dreaming. Her soft, pale features wore an expression of light concentration, the same expression she wore sitting at the dining table in the quiet hour before dinner as she drew, or wrote letters to her friends back in Berlin in her huge looping handwriting. The fragile innocence of a child. He took the risk of waking her and stepped into the room, smoothed her whisper-soft hair behind her ear and kissed her forehead. That she might be safe, that she might live protected and at peace.

He closed the door as quietly as he could and returned to the drawing room. On his arrival in Marseille, he, his wife and his daughter had been billeted in this neat apartment close to the Gestapo headquarters in Rue Paradis, and it was a luxury to be savored after the conditions he had endured in Poland. The little family shared five comfortably furnished rooms, a tribute to his successes smashing the foreign spy rings in Paris and enforcing some discipline on the *Einsatzgruppen* in the east and, he was not afraid to acknowledge, to his wife's excellent connections in the party.

In the low light, sitting by the fire, at work on some elaborate piece of embroidery, his wife looked almost a child herself. She put her work aside as he came in and went to the dresser to pour him a drink. He took his seat in the armchair on the other side of the fireplace, admiring her slim figure and shapely legs in comfort.

"Captain Heller asked me to apologize for calling so late, Eva. He hopes he did not disturb us."

She brought him his whisky, bending down to kiss him as he took it. "That is very good of him, but I do not mind at all. You know that."

Her voice had been the first thing about her that he had fallen in love with; it was low and tuneful, confident without being brassy. He caught her hand and brushed her slim fingers lightly with his lips.

"What are you smiling at?" she asked as she returned to her place and picked up her workbasket.

"I am grateful that providence has sent me such a helpmate." He tasted his whisky. Drinking it was a habit he had picked up while studying for his doctorate in England. Its flavor took him back to his college rooms, the late night conversations with his peers.

"Me or Heller?" She looked up at him under her eyelashes.

He raised his glass toward her. "You in this instance, my dear."

She nodded, pleased with the compliment, then looked suddenly thoughtful. "Heller is a good deputy though, I think."

Böhm considered his deputy as he sipped his drink. Heller wore little round glasses but was otherwise a healthy-looking young man. Clear skinned, and well muscled without showing a tendency to run to fatness. Böhm had been working with him since his arrival in Marseille, and he had so far proved extremely competent. Heller had learned excellent French studying the law in Grenoble and was, naturally, a staunch believer in the Nazi cause. His little round glasses gave him a scholarly appearance, but he was a fierce and inventive interrogator. Böhm admired that—a man who could seem so mild, yet had a well-spring of violence within him. The surprising discovery that this slight bookish young man could cause such terrifying pain had shocked some captives into talking, perhaps even more than the pain itself.

"He is. Very good."

Eva snipped a thread and shook out the embroidery she had been working on. It was, he saw, an image of a little farmhouse with chickens in the yard and a backdrop of layered trees and hills. It reminded him of the landscape around Würzburg. Perhaps, after the war, if he did not return to Cambridge, he would complete his research there and take just such a modest home for Eva and Sonia.

"We should do something for him, don't you think?" she said. "I'll write to Uncle Gottfried, mention his name." She realized her husband was looking at her handiwork. "It's Sonia's latest masterpiece, I'm just neatening it up. She is going to put it in a frame and give it to you, so remember to look surprised."

"I shall."

She began tidying away her work, and her voice took on a slightly hesitant note. "I had a letter from Gottfried today, as it happens. He says there is no hope for the Sixth Army at Stalingrad. You should see what he writes about their sacrifice. It's terribly moving."

Böhm drained his drink. What a terrible sacrifice it had been. He set his empty glass down on the polished side table. But Böhm had no doubt that the war would be won in the end. The British would eventually understand that their only hope of defeating communism would be to join with Germany against Russia. Any military setbacks in that vast and savage country could only be temporary. The Slavs were beyond redemption with nothing but a capacity for suffering to recommend them.

"Do you think it's wrong of me," Eva said, still not looking at him, "to be very grateful we are together in France, and not there?"

He felt a fresh affection for her. "No, my love. We can honor their sacrifice, without wishing to share in it."

"Would you like another drink?"

Tempting. "No, thank you. I must keep a clear head, there is still so much to be done."

He said it with a smile in his voice, but it was true. The clearance of the Old Quarter was an excellent start, but he knew the roots of the Resistance ran deep and wide in this city. Perhaps the French were not beyond redemption, but they had undoubtedly grown decadent and corrupt. The Germans had absorbed the wisdom of the Far East, and used it to fully comprehend their destiny, but the French had collapsed into luxurious visions of the orient—sensual, feverish dreams which had rotted them from within.

"Your supper will be ready. Do you think you managed to catch your mouse?"

That legendary mouse who had led so many escapees and refugees to Spain, nibbled so many holes in the net that the Germans had cast across southern France.

"Perhaps. Only time will tell."

5

The moon silvered the sea. Nancy hadn't had much choice about the "when" of this operation, but they'd been lucky. It was a clear night with just enough moon to follow the path to the beach without waving their torches around.

Antoine had brought them the message from a contact in Toulouse. A British submarine would creep along the coast, ready to take a crop of escaped prisoners off their hands by sea. The submarine could take up to fifteen men and would row to this beach to pick them up on this date, at this time, give this signal, wait for this response.

Then it was a matter of trust. That the message was genuine and hadn't been garbled, that they had the right place, time and codes, that no one Nancy had spoken to as she contacted the men to be rescued and gave them their instructions on where and when to meet her had talked.

Oh, and that when the British said they could take up to fifteen men, they'd left a bit of wiggle room. Waiting in the dark at the edge of the beach with Nancy were twenty men who needed to get the hell out of France. They were British mostly, and a couple of American airmen, Iowan farm boys with an infectious sense of humor which made Nancy love them. Three of the Brits had been stuck in a safe house outside Montpellier for a week, talking in whispers and trying not to move around the apartment in case the neighbor, a definite Vichyist, heard them. Most of the others had broken out of a transit camp to the northwest. Nancy, Philippe and Antoine had expected six men through the wire, but news had got out in the camp and the rest insisted they get their chance too. The last man they'd picked up from a safe house in Marseille itself, though none of the houses seemed that safe since this man Böhm had arrived in town. The prisoner was called Gregory. He was a Brit with a French mother, and the English had parachuted him in behind enemy lines to help out the loyal French or something, but the Gestapo had grabbed him off the street in his second week. It turned out his contact in town had come to an understanding with the authorities.

He'd been a guest of the Gestapo for a month, until he'd taken a mad chance during a round of questioning, throwing himself from a first-floor window in front of his astonished guards. Somehow he'd managed to escape into the market crowd, and they saved him. One man gave him his cap, another his long blue coat which most of the farmers wore, another the clogs from his feet. The Gestapo officers who poured out of their headquarters in pursuit found their way blocked, accidentally of course, by confused stallholders, a fight over a heavily laden cart. The news of his escape got to the members of the Resistance still at large in the town, and he was scooped up and dumped in Nancy's lap.

Gregory had mumbled this story out to her through broken teeth. Normally they would have sent him on the route out over the Pyrenees, but he didn't have a cat's chance in hell of making the walk. He was missing all the fingernails on his right hand, his ribs were cracked and his wrist broken. Every inch of him was purple with bruising. Nancy had no idea what to do with him other than feed him and keep him hidden until the message about the Royal Navy pickup came in. Praise the Lord. She fetched him herself, and they had strolled along the streets of Marseille, arm in arm, his broken face wrapped up in Henri's scarf, his thin frame bulked out by one of Henri's coats, peering out at the world from under the brim of one of Henri's hats. They took the bus toward the coast to join the others and he thanked her. Quietly. Sincerely. Then he didn't talk much.

Nancy checked her watch in the moonlight. Bloody Royal Navy were late. Not disastrous, they-are-definitely-not-turning-up late yet, but still late. How long could they wait here? How could she get all these men into safe houses before dawn if the British didn't arrive? The coast here, east of Marseille, was rocky and steep, mostly limestone, which looked ghostly in the darkness. This small beach, fringed with wild sage bushes and pines, was one of the few places a boat could come in. She hoped nothing had gone wrong. If all had gone to plan a submarine was out there now, half a mile off shore, dark and silent, waiting to whip these men through the Strait of Gibraltar and back to Britain to rearm, regroup and re-join the fight.

"They're late," Antoine said softly at her shoulder.

"They'll be here," Nancy said firmly.

There was a rustle in the darkness and Philippe joined them. "Any sign yet? They are late."

Jesus.

"Are you certain about the signal, Nancy?" Antoine asked. "Should we signal them?"

"Hold your nerve, guys, for fuck's sake," she whispered. "We're not standing on the beach flashing torches at any German patrol which passes by. They signal *us* first."

"Maybe the message was fake," Antoine breathed. "What if the message was from the Germans? Easy for them to pick us all up then, prisoners, us and the famous White Mouse. All just sitting here on the shore like we're having a moonlight picnic. God knows, the message came just when we needed it! Was it too good to be true?"

It had crossed her mind, of course it had. They'd all heard the rumors: Germans stealing radio sets and sending false messages back and forth to London and then scooping up Resistance

31

fighters, prisoners, supply dumps, casually as kids scrumping apples in the orchards.

"If it were the Germans coming," she said clearly now, and with angry precision, "they'd have bloody well been on time."

Philippe grunted, but she could almost see his swift, reluctant smile.

"Fine, Nancy," he said. "But you can't tell me things aren't getting harder. Major Böhm has picked off a dozen men I know about. How long until he picks up someone who knows about us? There are too many people involved now. That man Henri told me to talk to at the factory, Michael—I don't like him. Too hot."

"You're complaining now the French are finally getting their shit together and fighting back?" she said. He was pissing her off now. "If Henri told you to talk to him, he's fine."

"Henri is a good man, but he's romantic," Philippe persisted. "He thinks every Frenchman is a Resistance fighter at heart. He doesn't want to believe we have fascists of our own. One of those gendarmes we've been using your husband's money to bribe is going to say something eventually. We shouldn't have paid them to keep the road above us clear tonight. It would have been better to risk the police patrols."

Antoine tutted, but Philippe was right. Which didn't help. Antoine had made the decision and paid the bribe without even telling them. He swore he could trust the man he paid, a true French patriot, but if he was that much of a patriot why did he need paying in the first place?

"Nancy!"

She looked out into the darkness and saw it: the flash of a torch about a hundred yards off shore. Three quick flashes then one longer one. She clicked on her torch and pointed it out into the dark. Two longer flashes. She clicked it off again. Waited.

It seemed to take forever before she heard the shiver of the water, then the quiet shift of gravel on the beach as a wooden boat was pulled to the edge of the gentle surf. She went forward alone. The crew consisted of two oarsmen and a man she assumed to be an officer, all wearing the woolen trousers and canvas overalls of the local fishermen.

"Ready for the parade?" she asked.

"Mother sent balloons," he replied. "God, are you English?"

"Australian. Long story."

He nodded. It was not the ideal time to chat. "How many packages?"

"Twenty. One special delivery from the Gestapo, and Auntie sent extra from the camp. Can you take them all?"

He hesitated. Then spoke firmly. "We'll manage. And sorry to be late, patrols have stepped up all along the coast. This route is not going to work in the future. Navy can't risk a submarine here now to pick up escapees."

She turned and waved the men in from their hiding places round the edge of the beach as she replied. "Bastards have made the Pyrenees route almost impassable too. Just hurry up and win the damn war, will you?"

"We'll do our best."

He nodded appreciatively as the men emerged in orderly fashion from their hiding places among the low undergrowth above the high-water mark and were helped into the boat.

"Good show, my dear."

It seemed to take forever, the men coming two at a time. The officer was looking at his watch every five seconds. His men were shuffling the boys about in the rowing boat to make space for the last three escapees now. Gregory went in last, grabbing Nancy's hand and squeezing it as he passed her. The crew men were hauling him in over the side when a light hit them from the coast road, a searchlight. Full beam. Then excited shouts in German above them.

"Time to go," the officer said smartly.

One of his crew jumped lightly into the surf and he and the

officer shoved off, forcing the overloaded boat back onto the water and into the darkness using their shoulders, their feet digging up great banks of wet sand and shingle.

Bullets started to sing and zip into the water beside them as they flung themselves in, the officer ordering them to pull hard.

Nancy turned tail for the woods as the edge of the search beam hit, praying it wouldn't track her. It didn't, thank Christ. They were after the rowing boat. In the shadow she caught sight of Antoine, lying on his back and firing up toward the searchlight.

Shit, was that barking? Please do not let them have dogs.

She dropped into a crouch among the wild sage bushes and twisted round to see how the navy were doing. They were still caught in the beam and at least one figure in the boat was slumped unnaturally in the stern. They were sitting ducks.

"Come on, Antoine," she muttered between gritted teeth, watching him, not daring to move yet. Could she climb back onto the road? Get behind the patrol and take out the searchlight with her revolver?

Antoine exhaled slowly and squeezed the trigger. Glass shattered above them and the light faded.

"You little beauty!" she said aloud. "Now let's get out of here, shall we?"

Not a moment too soon, as she could hear the shouts of the soldiers as they crashed down the slope toward them. They'd have rough going of it if they couldn't find the path which twisted and zigzagged down to the water. Sharp falls and thorns. She hoped they broke their sodding necks.

Philippe grabbed her arm. One path was open to them going east along the shore and the three of them ran, heads down, hunching forward. Nancy could feel the terrible pulse of excitement in her blood. This was better than flirting her way through checkpoints. Her feet seemed to find their way along the narrow track without her needing to think. The bullets tearing past her in the dark really did make a sort of mewing sound, like tiny kittens. The thought made her giggle.

The patrol—it could only be an army patrol chancing this way rather than a trap or they would all be dead already—were still concentrating their fire on the retreating rowing boat, even though they couldn't see it now, the idiots. She guessed only two guys were crashing through the tough grasses, juniper and laurel. Then the light of a torch swept across them from above. A shout and a shot. Nancy heard Antoine gasp, and she spun around as he crumpled onto the needle-thin track, only kept from rolling off the low cliff and into the water by a tangle of undergrowth, his hand on his side.

"Philippe, help me!" she hissed into the darkness, and she saw his shadow returning.

"Here! This way! They are getting away!"

The man on the path above them was answered by his colleagues. Philippe aimed at the voice and the light, pulled the trigger. The torch went out, clicked off neatly to prevent Philippe from finding his target, and the man called for his friends again. He sounded giddy with excitement.

Antoine pushed her away. "Go, Nancy!"

"Like hell, I will."

She bent down to get her arm round his shoulders as Philippe shot blindly toward the voice again.

"Help me get him up," Nancy said to him, but Antoine was too quick for her. He pulled his revolver from his jacket, a revolver Henri had paid for, a revolver Nancy had given to Antoine herself, put the barrel into his mouth and fired.

It happened so fast that Nancy could not even begin to understand it. She was still, too surprised to scream. Philippe howled and shot again into the darkness. More torches were approaching along the path above them. Then Philippe grabbed hold of her arm again, hauling her to her feet, and shoved her forward in front of him, loosing a couple more shots into the dark behind him. She stumbled. Suddenly her feet didn't know what to do after all. What had Antoine done? That gun wasn't supposed to be used on him. She'd given it to him to kill Nazis, not himself, stupid boy. She'd give him such a talking to.

"Move, Nancy!"

She carried on, her thoughts fractured and muzzy. How strange to be here at this time of night. How did she get here? How pleasant and terribly British that officer had been. Shouldn't they wait for Antoine? Philippe jostled her forward until at last her thoughts began to reconnect, make sense. She began to run and she ran on until the sounds of pursuit faded and the only sounds she could hear were her own panting breath and the chirruping song of the cicadas.

They didn't stop until the night became thick and silent around them.

6

Nancy stayed in bed the next day, only getting up to wash and dress when Henri was due home in the evening. If Claudette, Nancy's maid, had noticed the blood on her clothes, she had not mentioned it. Nancy opened the hall cupboard on her way to the drawing room to meet Henri and saw her camel-hair coat hanging neatly on its padded hanger. It was spotless, but a patch on the side, a patch she was sure must have been smeared with Antoine's blood, was slightly damp to the touch and smelled of vinegar.

Henri talked to her about the usual sort of thing: his day, his workers and, after they had hunched over the radio listening to the evening news on the BBC, the progress of the war. Hitler had lost an army at Stalingrad, the Allies were winning in North Africa. Only when they had begun to eat did Nancy tell him about the previous night.

"We could have got him out," she finished, staring at the plate.

Henri filled her glass. "Eat something, my love."

They still ate in the dining room whenever they were at home, and whatever they had, they ate off the best china. Since the arrival of Böhm and the destruction of the Old Quarter they had been having dinner alone more often. Friends not in the Resistance asked too many questions, and friends in the network kept apart from each other when they could.

Claudette had managed to create a sort of *parmentier* with some black-market mince Nancy had got hold of. I can't let it go to waste, Nancy thought, staring at her food, and then she saw Antoine putting the gun in his mouth just as she put the fork of potatoes and mince into her own. If Henri hadn't been watching her, she'd have spat it out onto the plate again. She managed to swallow.

"If he hadn't seen Gregory, that man the Gestapo had...It was just bad luck," she said.

Henri picked up his wine glass. He was trying, dear Old Bear, not to stare at her as if checking to see if she were mad, but she still felt as if she was under a magnifying glass.

"I'll see his family is taken care of, you know that," he said.

"Thank you, Henri."

She put her fork down and covered her eyes with her hand. "We could have got him out."

Henri took her other hand and held it. "My dearest Nancy, isn't it time to listen to Philippe? To be more careful?"

She pulled her hand away. "No, I told you! It was bad luck! No one betrayed us, it wasn't a German trap! We got those men out and then some sharp-eyed Boche must have caught sight of the boat in the moonlight." She stared at him. "They are *here*, Henri. They destroyed the Old Quarter. They have sent the men off to fucking work camps. They are rounding up the Jews! Any pretense that France is independent is gone. We are under the jackboot. You can't ask me to stop fighting. You can't stop fighting." She began attacking her food again. "It has to be faced. It has to be fought. And I won't sit back and let other people do my fighting for me."

He put his elbow on the table and rested his cheek on his palm. He always shaved before dinner as well as in the morning, even now when getting decent soap was a battle. How did she end up married to a man so proper in his habits? Luck. Luck she didn't deserve.

"But the Germans can't even win any more! Why can't they just sod off?"

Henri laughed at that, and she flashed a reluctant smile.

Then he became thoughtful. "A wild beast is at its most dangerous when it is wounded," he replied.

She put her knife and fork together and took his hand again. "Are we both at home this evening?"

He nodded, lifted her hand to his lips and kissed her palm. How strange to still ache with love for a man she woke with every morning, lay down next to each night.

"Invent me a cocktail," she said. "I intend to win your entire fortune from you over cards and far too many drinks."

"You may try, wife of mine. You may try."

Nancy ended the night in happy oblivion, more deeply in his debt than ever.

7

M ajor Böhm's office was lined with books. When the
packing cases arrived in Rue Paradis, three days before the
major, the corporal who opened them thought at first there must
have been some sort of mistake. Yes, the upper ranks of the
Gestapo tended to be reading men—university educated, a lot of
lawyers—but they didn't have this many books. He was about to
report the delivery as an error when he found, taped to the third
crate, a set of typed instructions as to how the books were to be
arranged in the major's office. It was precise. That was more like
a Gestapo man. The corporal followed the instructions, very
carefully indeed.

Böhm had other reasons to be content as he sat down
behind his desk that morning, spending his first hour or two
moving steadily through the pile of papers, arrest warrants,
requests for information on his desk. There was better news
from Russia, gains were being made in Kharkov and the decision had been taken to liquidate the Jewish Ghetto in Krakow.
It was necessary work, but brutal and inelegant. He had felt
even his mind begin to coarsen during his service in Poland.
Some of the lower ranks had shown themselves to be lacking
in the necessary moral fiber, only managing to get through the
business of the day by being drunk, or hyped up on the "vita-
min" pills given out like candy by their officers. Böhm listened
then with interest to the rumors of more efficient methods of

40

disposing of undesirable peoples and trusted their use would make the difficult role of cleansing the Reich less difficult for the men.

The Slavs were, like the Jews, irredeemable. The only humane course of action was to wipe them out as quickly and efficiently as possible. Eastern Europe was a place where one had to work as a hammer; here in France the work was better suited to a scalpel, and that was what Böhm was. A thin, very accurate, well-trained blade.

He looked up as Captain Heller knocked on the door and then opened it.

"Yes?"

"Sir, I wanted to show you this."

Heller placed a sheet of cheap writing paper on Böhm's desk, and he glanced down at it. All in block capitals, a clumsy attempt to hide the identity of the writer, it said: "HENRI FIOCCA IS SPEANDING HIS PROFITS ON GUNES, NOT HIS WORKERS. EVERYBODY KNOWS IT."

Böhm did not touch the sheet. "Who wrote this?"

"A man named Pierre Gaston, sir. Dismissed from Fiocca's factory last month for persistent drunkenness."

Böhm sighed. It was pathetic how many of the French citizenry tried to make use of the Gestapo to carry out their own petty revenges. But that last phrase, "Everybody knows it." That was a telling choice of words.

"Have you questioned Monsieur Gaston?"

Heller nodded. A twitch in his cheek suggested the process had been unpleasant, not because violence was something he found distasteful, only that he regarded with contempt the man on whom he had used it.

"A drunk and a fool, but he stuck to his story," Heller said. "He told me there is a lot of seditious talk in the factory. He came upon his fellow workers several times, quietly boasting that their boss was working with the Resistance."

41

Böhm studied Heller. He clearly had something else to add, something which pleased him.

"And? Out with it."

"Sir, as you suggested might be advisable in these circumstances, I cross-referenced the names he gave me with our records, and found a man with black-market charges on his sheet among those Gaston named as suspicious types in the factory. We took him up very quietly, and he was keen to be of assistance when I made the alternatives clear. Fiocca is certainly providing funding to the Resistance in the area, and Michael, my source, has given us a couple of names from the wider network. Those men are being followed now. Michael claims they are part of the White Mouse group. He also says Fiocca specifically financed the escape by boat of twenty prisoners from the beach east of Marseille last week."

Böhm was impressed. With further training Heller could go far. He was an excellent example of the sort of man on whose shoulders the Thousand-Year Reich would be built.

"The transcript of your interrogation with Michael?"

Heller placed a manila folder neatly above the anonymous letter, like a cat placing a mouse at its mistress's feet. This time Böhm picked it up and began to read, nodding from time to time.

"And no one knows we are speaking to this Michael?"

"No, sir," Heller said. "Unless he has talked."

"Excellent work, Heller."

The captain glowed. "What are your orders?"

Böhm set down the folder and smiled at Heller, the benign teacher. "What would be *your* next move, Captain?"

Heller blinked rapidly behind his little glasses. "Well, sir. I wouldn't want to show our hand by arresting the men we are following immediately, but we could take Fiocca in for questioning, let it be known it is because of the tip-off from the drunk, and see what we could squeeze out of him."

"Very good. I think I need to stretch my legs, Heller. Bring the car round and we shall go and fetch Monsieur Fiocca together. Oh, and have the reports of that escape sent to my office for our return. I would like to look at them again."

Böhm put out his hand and Heller handed him a form authorizing the arrest of Fiocca and the seizure of his records. He signed it with a flourish.

8

Henri had been working quietly in his office since 7 a.m. It had been his habit since he first took control of the family business some ten years ago to spend his Friday mornings clearing the paperwork that had accrued like sediment on his desk during the week. He would have translated a satisfying proportion of it into notes for his secretary, Mademoiselle Boyer, copies for filing, questions for his lawyers and accountants even before his men began to fill up the workshops which lay to the rear of the offices, and the silence of those first hours was slowly replaced by the ringing of telephones, padding footsteps and the rattle of trolleys in the corridors of the offices. It comforted him, that swelling noise of business being done.

So much of his business involved travel up and down the coast, meetings with other businessmen in hotels, factories, lawyers' offices, that he clung to this quiet morning every week where any little problems could be thought out and smoothed over, so the wheels of industry could run uninterrupted. He saw no reason to do any differently in wartime, though, it was true, his wife was not free for lunch after his morning's work as often as she had been before the fall of France.

It was unusual then to hear his secretary tapping at the door while his coffee was still warm and the paperwork unfinished. He called her in.

"Monsieur Fiocca," she said. Her thin body, normally held

ramrod straight, seemed to shake. She clutched the door handle as if for support.

He took off his reading glasses and smiled reassuringly. "What is it, Mademoiselle Boyer?"

"There are...men here."

He stood up quickly and went to the window, breathing in sharply. Three large black cars had drawn up outside the building. One of the drivers was standing on the pavement, not taking his ease or smoking his cigarette like an ordinary soldier, but with his hands clasped loosely behind his back, staring ahead. Gestapo.

Mademoiselle Boyer was still clinging on to the door. "Monsieur Callan just came and told me. They are already questioning the men on the workshop floor. Others are going through the files in the contract room. What shall I do?"

Henri lifted his eyes from the cars and stared out over the port of Joliette, the steamers and docks, the great hazy blue of the Mediterranean beyond.

"Go back to work, Mademoiselle," he said. "I'm sure they will get to us eventually."

He returned to his desk and the young woman retreated, closing the door behind her. Henri finished reading the contract he had been examining and signed both copies, then examined his signature. No one would suspect his hand was shaking. He placed both copies on the pile for Mademoiselle Boyer.

Henri then began to read a request for some slight changes in an order from one of his suppliers to accommodate "unfortunate shortages in the present time." He could feel the change in the rhythm of the building. A phone was ringing unanswered, the footsteps outside were hurried. The distant clangs and hisses which floated up from the workshop had stuttered. He waited, trying to read but seeing nothing. The door opened again and a tall German man in the gray-green tunic and collar patches of an SS major walked into the room. A captain followed respectfully in his wake. Behind them Henri could see Mademoiselle Boyer, on her feet, her mouth a little "oh" of shock.

Henri got to his feet again. "Thank you, Mademoiselle Boyer," he said clearly, as if his guests had been properly introduced.

The major glanced over his shoulder, as if seeing the woman for the first time, then looked back at Henri with a smile. "My name is Böhm, Monsieur Fiocca," he said in excellent French, but did not extend his hand. "This is Captain Heller. We are sorry to burst in on you unannounced."

"Not at all," Henri replied with a bow. "Do take a seat, gentlemen. How may I be of assistance to you today?"

Böhm ignored his offer of a seat and wandered over to the window, admiring the same view Henri had just been drinking in.

"No need, Monsieur Fiocca. And I shouldn't bother sitting down yourself. We have few questions for you. Get your coat. We'd like you to be our guest in Rue Paradis for a little while."

Henri straightened his back. "Ask any question you have. Talk to my secretary, my bookkeeper, but I am afraid I am too busy to waste my afternoon with you."

Böhm was still studying the view. "We shall, of course, be talking to both of them. But I'm afraid I must insist you come with me now, Monsieur Fiocca."

So quickly. How strange when something you've been expecting for months happens, and it still feels sudden. But surely his reputation, the reputation of his family still counted for something in Marseille? Henri stood his ground.

"Why come here yourself if you mean to question me at your headquarters? My understanding is that the Gestapo normally send a nameless group of thugs with a warrant card when they want to talk to someone. And normally at night."

A pointless little flare of defiance. Henri breathed slowly. He would use the law, he would use his money and influence and if it came to it he would use his body to shield his people, and shield Nancy from these men. Major Böhm did not seem to take

46

offense at his question. He finally turned from the window and approached the desk, glancing at the papers before replying with a polite nod.

"Like you, Monsieur Fiocca, I have been at my desk for some time. I needed to stretch my legs." He was reading one of the letters that Henri had written that morning upside down on the table. "Have you ever studied psychology, Monsieur Fiocca? I did. In Cambridge before the war. I have often thought the skills I learned there, understanding men, their behavior and motivations, could have been of great use in business. I suppose you must have learned those skills too, to enjoy the success you have done even in these trying times. Yes, I think we shall have a great deal to talk about."

Their eyes met and Henri felt something cold in his blood. He knew in that moment that the law, his money, his influence would not be shield enough.

9

Nancy marched up the steps of the handsome villa on Rue Paradis, her heels striking the curving marble steps. She was giving herself a run up, letting her fury build and blossom. One thing she had learned since she started working for the Resistance was that even Gestapo officers thought twice when confronted with a French housewife in a virtuous rage.

What do they know? What do they know? Perhaps they'd just heard rumors about the money pouring out from Henri's bank accounts and, seeing the Resistance well funded, had put two and two together. Mademoiselle Boyer, who had phoned her with news of the arrest, had heard that a drunk, sacked a few weeks ago, had been spreading rumors and swearing revenge. Miss Boyer had also assured her that the company books "were correct, Madame," with nervous pride but a slight tremor in her voice. If Henri Fiocca, one of the most respected and respectable businessmen in the city, was being held solely on the basis of the word of a vengeful drunk, there was a chance she could shame the evil bastards into releasing him. But what if they knew more? Worst case—they had been told Nancy was the White Mouse and were using Henri as cheese to bait the trap. Fine. She'd deliver herself to them with a fucking bow around her waist if that got him out. But until she knew for sure, she was playing outraged Society Lady.

She threw open the doors and strode across the marble

flooring, looking neither right nor left. She had a vague impression of men and women waiting on the benches set round the edge of the room, all looking shit-scared or sick with worry, and a couple of uniformed Germans by the door. The rich, arrogant, innocent French wife of a powerful man would have ignored them all, so that's what Nancy did. By the time she reached the desk, which looked like the reception to a better class of hotel, she was convinced that was exactly who she was.

She bore down on the blond, slick-looking clerk. He was sneering at a nervous-looking older man, a square-bodied fellow in his sixties wearing the overalls of a manual worker. He held the photograph of a young man delicately in his massive hands. The care he was taking of the snapshot almost stopped her in her tracks. Was the boy missing? Shipped off to work in Germany, in prison, a hostage? The poor kid had probably been caught with an anti-fascist leaflet in his pocket and been disappeared.

Enough, Nancy. Outraged Society Wife does not care about the fate of some worker's boy. Focus.

She slammed her very expensive little handbag onto the counter top and the worker withdrew meekly to one side.

"How dare you arrest my husband?" she said in her most carrying voice. "Are you completely mad? Good God, he is a close friend of the mayor! I demand you release him at once and I want an immediate, written apology."

The clerk flicked his eyes toward her, then back down to the form he was filling in. "Take a number from the clerk at the door, Madame," he said in passable but heavily accented French.

The clerk at the door had followed Nancy meekly across the foyer, and tried to hand her a cloakroom ticket with an obsequious smile. Nancy looked at him as if he were offering her his used handkerchief.

"I most certainly will not! Do you have any idea who I am?"

She leaned across the polished counter top, her palms flat on the polished rosewood.

"Take a number, and I shall find out in due course," the clerk replied, continuing to write.

Nancy reached over, plucked the pen from his hand and threw it over her shoulder. It skittered and spun across the tiles.

"Look at me when I speak to you, young man!" He did. "I am Mrs. Henri Fiocca and I demand to see my husband at once. Do not—do *not* make me ask a third time."

He was obviously older than her, truth be told, but it felt right.

"That is impossible, your husband is being questioned…"

"Questioned? How dare you question him!" Nancy shouted.

"Madame!"

"Henri!" She yelled his name loud enough to make the windows rattle.

The clerk looked over her shoulder and she heard the sound of the polished boots of the guards approaching. Had she overplayed it? Well, in for a penny, in for a pound. If they dragged her out and threw her down the steps she could charge around the city showing off her laddered stockings and outraged virtue to every official in town. It would be a nightmare for the Gestapo and they'd have to release Henri and send him home. Perfect. She sucked in her breath ready to really make a show of it.

A door to the right of the desk opened and an officer walked slowly out into the foyer. Nancy could never follow these ranks, but he was obviously someone important. The approaching footsteps behind her came to a sudden halt and the slick fellow behind the desk shot to his feet. The officer waved away the guards, then nodded to the clerk who sat down and selected a new pen from one of the little drawers in front of him.

"No need for hysterics, Madame Fiocca," the officer said, again in French. "Major Böhm, at your service."

Nancy blinked at him. He was in his early forties perhaps, slim in build. If he weren't wearing that disgusting uniform, he'd be handsome. And he'd just taken the wind out of her sails, the bastard.

"My husband?" Nancy said, looking down her nose at him.

He bowed. "I shall take you to him at once. Follow me."

He turned back through the door and held it open for her. Nancy picked up her bag, straightened her shoulders and followed him. She'd lost her audience now. Damn. Böhm led her down the corridor away from the foyer with long smooth strides. Nancy's skirt was fashionably tight, and between it and her heels she could only take little steps. She had to trot along behind him like a toy dog. Time to regain the initiative.

"Major Böhm, this is utterly disgraceful, how dare you cart Henri off like some common criminal? I can only imagine what the mayor will say."

Böhm didn't reply, just came to a halt outside an ordinary-looking door and opened it, inviting her in.

She stepped inside. A clean, orderly little room. Probably the office of one of the senior household staff before the Nazis had taken over the building. The window was shuttered, but the afternoon light still filtered into the room. The walls were painted a pale green and hung with engravings of the coastline in simple black frames. The old furniture had been removed though, and in the center of the small space was a rough wooden table and a pair of rickety-looking metal fold-up chairs. On one of them, his back to the window, sat Henri.

He lifted his head and smiled at her gently, sadly. He looked, for the first time since Nancy had met him, old. Her heart felt as if it had been squeezed suddenly dry. She was aware of Major Böhm in the doorway behind her. *Play the role, Nancy.*

"Henri, what on earth is this nonsense? Mademoiselle Boyer called me from the factory sounding as if she was about to drop in a dead faint, saying these monsters had marched you out of your own office. It's an absolute scandal."

He lifted his hand, palm out, shook his head. "My dear, do not distress yourself. My lawyers are on their way, and you know they are the best that money can buy. All good friends of the Vichy government."

"What are you charged with?" This was better. She was getting back into her stride.

"Some misunderstanding, I'm sure. Do not worry yourself." He was staring at her, drinking her in even though his words were light and ordinary. That scared her.

She spun round to Böhm, who had stepped into the room and closed the door behind him. "What are the charges against my husband, Major?"

Böhm made her wait, nodding as if she was still speaking for a moment, and when he answered his voice was calm and reasonable.

"One of your husband's employees alerted us to a conspiracy at Fiocca Shipping. It seems a large sum of money is missing."

Nancy lifted her chin. "I'm sure Henri has nothing to do with *that*."

Böhm's expression shifted to one of polite interest. "Then I take it that you're familiar with his finances?"

"I do not appreciate your tone," Nancy said, channeling Henri's awful stuck-up sister and grateful for the first time ever that the woman existed.

"Because we have reason to believe that this money has been funneled to the Resistance—"

"That's absurd," Nancy said with a toss of her head.

Böhm observed her, his head on one side, as if amused at being interrupted.

"The only thing my wife knows about my money is how to spend it on herself," Henri said with a sigh.

Nancy turned away from Böhm and looked at him again, into his eyes.

"Go home, my dear," he continued. "Let the major and me sort this out between us like gentlemen."

If that was how he had decided to play it, she had to go along with it. He didn't want her to be the enraged matron, but the frivolous society wife, too foolish and pretty and spendthrift to know anything of her husband's business. She managed a slightly sulky pout.

"You know best, Henri."

Major Böhm cleared his throat. "Just one more thing, Madame Fiocca. Please don't leave Marseille—I may have questions for you too."

He opened the door again, ready to show her out. No. Too soon. She couldn't just leave Henri here.

"You think I'm the type of woman who takes a holiday while my husband's being railroaded by the Gestapo? Henri, I'm not going anywhere without you."

It gave her the chance to look at him again. Her rock. Her refuge. Her husband. Her Henri. He smiled at her, warm and encouraging. "Of course not, darling."

OK. He knew what he was doing. She had been fretting unnecessarily. Henri had a dozen lawyers and oodles of cash to bribe his way out of anywhere, up to and including the Gestapo headquarters. She began to walk toward the door.

"Nancy?"

She turned back. The darling man. She would cook him dinner tonight all by herself, whether he liked it or not. And she still had some decent wine in the cellar.

"Tell my mother not to worry."

No. Not that. That was what they agreed would be his code if...Not good. Very, very bad. Panic seized her. She couldn't move. She thought about screaming, about confessing, about spitting in these bastards' faces...oh, but she knew seeing her dragged off by these apes would kill Henri. After everything else she'd done to him, she couldn't do that too. This was his choice. But no, no, no. *This can't happen; this isn't happening.* Her voice sounded hoarse in her throat.

"I'll tell her you love her."

For one, two, three beats of her heart they looked at each other, tried to tell each other everything that could be said, share and celebrate a lifetime, to make their promises and keep them. One, two, three.

"Madame Fiocca?" Böhm was waiting.

She walked past him and out into the corridor. He followed her, closing the door behind him. If he said anything to her as he led her back to the foyer, she didn't hear him.

10

Nancy's maid was waiting for her when she opened the grand front door with her latch key. She was standing in the middle of the hall, her small cardboard suitcase next to her and already wearing her good coat.

"Madame Fiocca, I . . ."

Nancy peeled off her gloves. She couldn't look at the girl.

"Of course you must leave, Claudette. You'll go to your mother in Saint-Julien?" Nancy took another key from her bag and opened the drawer of a small bureau in the hall. Henri always kept a smooth leather wallet there, fat with banknotes. Nancy peeled off a couple of thousand francs and handed them to the girl.

Claudette stared at the money, shaking her head. "I cannot, Madame. Not when I am deserting you."

"Yes, you bloody well can," Nancy snapped. "Just take it."

Claudette shyly pulled the money from between Nancy's fingers and murmured her thanks, tucking the notes into the inside pocket of her coat.

"Go through the back gardens, Claudette. And keep your head down."

"Good luck, Madame. I have very much enjoyed working for you."

Nancy managed to look at her at last. No, whoever had betrayed Henri it was not this girl. She felt she should give her some advice, say something brilliant and clever Claudette would remember all her life, something which would make her into a better person, something she would tell her children and grandchildren. Something inspiring. She had nothing. She just needed a drink. Well, no one had said anything inspiring to her before she ran away from home. Blame them.

"I am glad. Now on your way, dear."

Claudette picked up her suitcase. "Your friend Philippe is in the kitchen, Madame Fiocca."

"Thank you."

Claudette walked away to the back of the house, leaving Nancy standing in the hall, still wearing her camel-hair coat, her patent-leather handbag hung over the crook of her arm. Fresh flowers on the table, the wooden banister polished to a high gleam, oil paintings of Marseille and ships at sea hanging in orderly lines from the picture rail. She'd never even noticed them. Paintings were Henri's thing. She marched into the drawing room and went to the dresser, picked up the decanter and poured a large brandy into one of the heavy crystal glasses. She tossed it back, then grabbed an extra glass and the decanter and headed for the kitchen.

Philippe got to his feet as she came in. She set the glasses and decanter on the scrubbed wood of the table, poured the drinks, sat down, shrugged off her coat and crossed her legs. Drank off the drink. Philippe was still standing.

"Sit down, for fuck's sake," she said, reaching for the decanter again. He flinched. "What? Never seen a woman drink before?"

He sat back down, carefully, but the scrape of his chair against the slate tiles sounded like a scream.

"I'm so sorry, Nancy."

She started shaking. Was it anger or guilt? She had no idea what she was feeling, but whatever it was was making her muscles quiver and her teeth rattle on the glass. "It's my fault. He always told me to be careful, but I kept pushing, asking for more and more money." Guilt, then.

Philippe cradled the glass in his hands and shook his head. "Henri made his own choices. Don't take that away from him, Nancy."

"But..."

"Now it's time to make yours," he said. She knew what he was about to say, and didn't want to hear it. Shut up. Shut. Up. Her hand was trembling so hard, she could hardly get the glass to her lips. He didn't shut up. "We have to get you out. Now."

"I can't just leave him here, with them!" She slammed her glass onto the table, making the cutlery in the drawers tinkle. "I'll set myself on fire on their steps. I'll shove a grenade up their arses. I'll walk in and shoot the clerk. Henri can't make me leave!"

Philippe set his own glass back on the table, a click like a bullet loading in the chamber.

"I know you're not afraid to die, Nancy. But you have to go. If not for you, then for him. They'll force him to watch you suffer, and you *will* suffer. They'll take you alive and they'll torture you both until the whole network is blown. I know he'll keep quiet as long as he can, but I also know he'd tell them anything to save you. So for all our sakes, get out."

She closed her eyes as if she could hide from the truth of it. "He has lawyers. Expensive lawyers. Maybe they'll get him out..."

Philippe dropped his gaze, answered quietly. "And when they do, we'll get him out of France. Send him to join you. But you have to go now."

She blinked back her tears. "Do you swear?"

"I swear I'll do everything I can, Nancy. Is that good enough?" he replied.

At last she nodded. It was the most he could promise, she knew that. "This was my first real home."

He finished his drink. "Be ready as soon as it gets dark, Nancy. They've put a watch on the front and back of the house already, but we'll provide a distraction. Head out the front.

Take the last bus for Toulouse. You know the address of the safe house there?"

She only nodded, afraid that if she said anything else she wouldn't be able to hold back her tears.

11

Böhm would have liked Fiocca if they had met in peacetime. He was obviously a man of taste and sophistication, a man with whom one could discuss modern ideas, and that was rare in Böhm's experience. He had held up to the initial stages of interrogation well, answering all the basic questions calmly and quietly, not volunteering additional information, or floundering when asked for information about specific dates, simply saying he could not remember, but would be happy to explain anything if he could see the relevant records.

It was a pity, really, that none of that calm intelligence would help him in the hours to come.

The workload was pressing. The weak and vacillating Vichy leadership had allowed French terrorists, communists and Jews to operate throughout the south of France. The people, originally obedient after the shock of their complete military defeat, had grown restive. Now they pinned their hopes on the Americans and were sneaking out of the woodwork like vermin when the farmer has neglected putting down poison on their trails. One mouse in particular.

Böhm did not approve of handing out these names to enemy agents as if they were badges of honor. To him, the White Mouse was simply Operative A and he insisted he was never referred to by any other name in this building. He had hoped that destroying the rat runs of the Old Quarter would have forced him out into the open, but rumors of activities only increased. Prisoners and airmen who had been shot down disappeared along routes of safe houses, collecting false papers on the way, and reappearing in Spain or in England, or in North Africa. His detector vans picked up the coded squeals of a dozen radio sets whispering to London and Algiers, and this man seemed to be able to carry it all—papers, messages, radio parts, prisoners—through every checkpoint they set up.

At first he had assumed him to be a peasant or fisherman who knew the coast and the back roads. But perhaps he had been wrong.

He began to read through the reports Heller had left on his desk of the escape from the coast. The terrorist who had been killed had been identified as Antoine Colbert, a lawyer whose father's firm had been arranging the finances of the wealthy in Marseille for years. For a moment Böhm had hoped they had, by some stroke of luck, caught their mouse. In the days which followed, however, Colbert's family had disappeared too smoothly and efficiently for it to have been the work of an organization panicked by losing its head.

The White Mouse was still out there.

He read the reports again. The sharp-eyed private who had seen movement on the steep and rocky shore and insisted his patrol leader turn on the searchlight; the boasts, almost certainly exaggerated, of the number of escapees they had shot while they huddled in an overloaded rowing boat until their light had been shot out; the scramble to find the shore party who had helped the escapees. Then he saw it, a line in the middle of the account of the man who had winged Colbert, causing him to shoot himself. He saw two other persons with the dead man, and thought one, judging by a glimpse caught in the swinging beam of a torch, might have been a woman.

A woman? Surely not. Women did not fight among men. Radio operators, the occasional student painting slogans on the wall, yes, but surely the Resistance had not sunk so low as to put a gun in a woman's hands? But then again, he had himself interrogated a number of female radio operators in Paris and some had shown a certain unwomanly enthusiasm for the fight. He began to reconsider. What if the White Mouse was a woman? Would Frenchmen take instructions from a female? Unusual perhaps, but not impossible. The ease with which the White Mouse made his—or *her*—way through checkpoints and railway stations, disappeared from rendezvous, melted like mist into the streets looked a lot less like magic if you considered his searchers had been looking for a man of fighting age, not a woman.

He leaned back in his chair, pressed the tips of his fingers together and remained motionless, staring straight into the air in front of him until he knew what it was he really wanted, then picked up the heavy handset on his desk.

"Captain, come in please."

He came at once. "*Heil Hitler!*"

"Heller, the files we hold on the civilian population of Marseille. I want you to look again at all the women we've heard even the vaguest rumor about. Especially those known to frequent the black market. Exclude all those with children under ten years of age, and those who are themselves over fifty. I want reports of each of them on my desk, arranged in order of their family's wealth."

Heller blinked behind his glasses. "Of course, sir. May I ask why?"

Böhm was happy to explain his theory and pleased to see Heller's eyes light up with intelligent appreciation.

"And why you are concentrating on the wealthier women?"

A sensible question.

"Because, whoever she is, she operates with great confidence and freedom. We had thought that to be the confidence of the lower orders, untrammeled by a civilized education and a freedom born of a familiarity with every rat hole in this city. But what else gives a woman confidence and freedom, Heller?"

Heller hardly hesitated at all. "Money."

Böhm nodded. "The files please, Heller."

"Of course." But the man didn't move; his mouth simply opened and closed like a fish.

"What is it?"

"I shall fetch the files at once. Only I think...sir, I think Madame Fiocca's file will almost certainly be on the top of the pile."

Böhm frowned. She had seemed every inch the spoiled French housewife. Loud, showy, confident. His voice became sharp. "Tell me what you know of her now, if you please."

Heller spoke quickly. "Born in Australia. Ran away from home and worked as a journalist in Paris for Hearst Newspapers. Known to use the black market frequently and supply her friends from her stores..." He faltered. "Travels frequently, and used to regularly visit a prisoner in Mauzac, before he escaped."

Böhm's mouth had thinned into a straight line.

Heller stared into the space above his head and continued. "She had her husband send her fifty thousand francs to the inn where she was staying near the prison. Naturally it was investigated as a possible bribe after the man escaped, but she told the local police it was used to pay her bar bills and complained about the gross abuse of confidentiality to the Post Office. They issued her a formal letter of apology."

Böhm was not used to feeling rage, but he felt it now, running white hot through his bones. "Where is she?"

"We put a car on her, sir. When she left here. She went straight back to their home."

Böhm gritted his teeth. "Get her. Get her now."

Heller saluted and withdrew, and as the door closed behind him, Böhm stood up quickly, then leaned forward on his desk.

He should have known. She had been high-handed when she arrived, then sulky and girlish in front of her husband. But he had been watching Henri, not her.

When Philippe left, Nancy was expecting to break down, but she did not. She took her glass and walked through the empty house, looking at each room, trying to fix it in her memory.

The drawing room had elegant, minimal furnishings and a crop of pre-war fashion magazines on the low coffee table that she had ordered from Paris. Henri used to tease her by putting his feet up on it when they came home in the early hours of the morning from a club.

Henri's study was much more old-fashioned. She called it his Bear Cave, book-lined and with an oak desk where he would sigh over her bills from the dressmaker's while she smiled at him sweetly from one of the red leather armchairs by the fire. A photograph of his mother stood on his desk, next to one of Nancy herself. Madame Fiocca the elder had died the year before she and Henri met. He had always said his mother would have appreciated Nancy. It was a sweet thing to say, but Nancy thought it was good that they'd never had to test that theory. She undid the back of the photograph and found two sets of false identity papers, one for her, one for Henri. She put hers into her pocket and carefully replaced his so they'd be there when he needed them.

Upstairs she lingered on the landing before at last going into their bedroom. The bed was made, her makeup arranged neatly on her dressing table, all those lotions and potions, cold creams and colors, her silver-back hairbrushes and ivory-handled powder puffs. She glanced at the door to her dressing room. No point going in there. She couldn't pack a suitcase like Claudette; she could take nothing with her which wouldn't fit into her largest, but not suspiciously large, handbag. She put on two silk blouses but couldn't risk two skirts, a scarf that could act as a shawl, her camel-hair coat and shoes that while stylish enough she also could walk in comfortably. She needed cash of course, and gathered up a pearl-handled penknife, jewelry, face cream, a comb and her genuine papers. She tucked the false papers into the lining of her bag. What else? A wedding photograph? No, it would arouse suspicion. Or one of the notes Henri had left her when he went to work in the morning, reminding her to pick up the dry-cleaning or that a business acquaintance was coming for dinner? One of those would be innocent enough, surely, and that way she would have something he had touched to hold until they met again. She found one in the drawer of her dressing table, signed as they all were, "With all my love, Henri."

She slipped it into her bag, then returned to the hall, leaning against the wall in the shadows. Through the stained glass and metal grill of the door she could see one of the fat black Gestapo cars drawn up across the street. What was Philippe planning? The light was fading from the sky and the last bus to Toulouse left in forty minutes. She hoped to hell he was going to hurry up. She counted her breaths. One. Two. It was a trick a fellow passenger on the boat from Australia to New York had taught her when she was sixteen, alone and panicked by her sudden freedom. She thought about those first weeks in New York, the first friends she had made, her first apartment and job, her first taste of bathtub gin. Her decision, on seeing a smartly dressed woman on the steps outside the court house asking questions of some dark-suited lawyer without apology or deference, to be a journalist. Come on, Philippe. She had her hand on the door. Could she just run? Risk it? She wouldn't stand a chance.

There was just a wisp of smoke at first—Nancy blinked to make sure she wasn't seeing things—then the upper window of the fishmonger's shop on the other side of the road was thrown open and a great belch of black smoke billowed out into the evening. Madame Bissot came running out, hammering on the side of the Gestapo car, pointing into the shop. Two men got out. One followed her in, the other stood leaning on the open passenger door, looking up at the lick of flame. Nancy opened the door and shut it behind her, and walked down the path to the gate as quickly as she could, staring at the Gestapo man's back. Her heart was in her throat. Through the gate. Had it been open or closed when she came to it? Think! It was only a moment ago. Open. Henri always scolded her for leaving it unlatched, and she had been the last one coming in from the street. But then Claudette would have closed it when she'd left. No, she'd gone out the back way. Nancy left it half-open, turned back toward the shop, sure the Gestapo man would have turned round by now and already be crossing the road toward her. No. He was still staring up at the fire. She walked quickly east along the road. Each footstep sounded in her mind like a gunshot and it felt as if she had a searchlight trained on her back. How long was this damned road? She allowed herself to quicken her pace a little, then she couldn't help herself, she ran, took her first right, then the next left, then stopped and peered round the corner to see if they were coming. The rumble of an engine made her heart stop. But no, it was just a jeep rattling along the main road, then the street was empty.

When Heller arrived outside the Fiocca house he knew at once something was wrong. The remains of a fire were being doused at the fishmonger's shop, and though one of the men he had sent to keep an eye on Madame Fiocca was still sitting in his car staring solidly at her front door, the other was helping to put out the last embers.

Heller ignored the man helping, and rapped his knuckles on the window of the car. The man inside paled and rolled down the window.

"Well, Kaufman?" Heller said.

"No movement from inside the house," Kaufman said hopefully. Then he pointed at an angle across the street. "Bauer is watching the back gate from there, and hasn't spotted anyone coming out either. Anything wrong, sir?"

"When did the fire start?"

"About half an hour ago. Nasty blaze. We thought the whole building was going to go."

"And while you were watching it, who was observing the front door?"

Kaufman was silent, his eyes widening. "I was...I only stepped out of the car to see about the blaze for a minute. Less than a minute."

Heller closed his eyes. "And did it not seem strange to you, that while the house opposite was going up in flames, neither Madame Fiocca nor her maid ever came out to their front door to see what was happening?"

The man blinked.

Heller felt a sickness in the pit of his stomach. Then he began to walk toward the house, shouting over his shoulder. "Kaufman, follow me! Bring a crowbar for the door!"

She was gone. Of course she was gone.

12

Train stations were too risky, but the Gestapo were always slow to get to the busses, and as they were mostly used by the poorer classes and the French-Italians, it was unlikely they'd look for Madame Fiocca there.

Nancy felt naked as a newborn as she bought her ticket and found a seat in the back by the window next to a very elderly lady bundled up in a dozen shawls and her granddaughter, a pretty, ringleted child of about six years old.

Surely the bus was full. It had to leave. She looked at her watch and the grandmother noticed her and shrugged.

"Old Claude drives this route on a Tuesday, Madame. He's always late. Still getting his last cognac in at the station bar, I bet. And then he'll need a piss."

"I would like to get away," Nancy murmured.

The old lady gave her a slow appraising look. "Would you now? Traveling alone, are you?" Then she glanced past Nancy and out of the window. "Not those shit-heads!"

Nancy glanced by her. Two men in SS uniforms were interrogating the ticket girl by the gate to the yard and glancing over at the row of busses waiting to leave. Hell. It wasn't even as if she could get out and make a run for it. Every inch of floor space was crammed. The old lady next to her sniffed very loudly.

"Julie!" The ringleted girl turned away from the counting game she was playing on her fingers. "Sit on this lady's lap and sing her a song until we get going."

With a short sigh as if this was a habitual, if slightly irritating request, Julie clambered up onto Nancy's lap and began to sing her a quiet, semi-improvised version of "*Alouette.*" At first Nancy was going to protest, then she realized the old lady was offering her a disguise. If the Gestapo were looking for a woman on her own they wouldn't notice a mother and her daughter.

Out of the corner of her eye she saw the Gestapo men approach with a fat and red-faced man in the uniform of the bus company panting alongside them. Some heated discussion followed, and then the two Germans began walking up and down the outside of the bus, peering in at the windows. Nancy lowered her head over the child. A sharp knock on the window and she looked up over Julie's ringleted head blinking into the eyes of an SS man. Was it one of the ones who had been in the foyer this morning? He looked at her confused.

The old lady leaned over her and banged her fist on the window. "Sod off!" she shouted. "My daughter's been up with the baby all night and now when she gets five minutes to have a doze you have to bloody wake her up! Sod off, I say!"

It wasn't clear how much the German understood. But he got the general idea, so with a mumbled apology moved away. Moments later the engine spluttered into life and with a metallic groan the bus pulled off.

"Back on the floor with you, Julie," the old lady said, and the child slipped away from Nancy.

"Thank you," Nancy said. "That was wonderful of you."

She opened her purse and withdrew a note, the old lady looked at it and sniffed again.

"You done these shit-heels damage, my dear?"

"Yes."

"You mean to do them more?"

"Too bloody right," Nancy replied.

The old lady nodded sagely. "Then we're square. Now keep an eye on the little one, I'm getting some sleep."

Marie Dissard, the woman whose flat they used as a safe house in Toulouse, gave her a good welcome. It was a tiny place, four small square rooms, three of them without windows, in one of the narrow alleys in the center of the city. Nancy knew the place and her host well. Marie was in her sixties, subsisted on coffee and cigarettes and had a large black cat called Mifouf and nerves of steel. They got on well enough, hunched over the radio listening to the BBC then talking about what they had heard. Marie didn't ask Nancy about Henri, didn't dwell on what might be happening to him, and Nancy didn't ask about her nephew, banged up in a POW camp for three years now. They talked about the war, about when the British would pull their fingers out and invade France. Any day now. Had to be.

Three times Nancy said goodbye to her and took the train to Perpignan. There she sat in a little café on the edge of town, staring up at the distant peaks of the Pyrenees and trying to wish away the storm clouds she saw gathering. If there was a chance of starting the journey through the mountains, her contact in town, Albert, would put a geranium on the windowsill of his flat. No flower appeared.

After the third trip she got a message from Marseille from a courier, a young girl with freckles and pale eyelashes who gave her name as Mathilde, that Albert had been picked up by the Gestapo—and worse, so had Philippe.

"When?" Nancy asked, her skin growing cold in the warm safe-house kitchen. "How?"

The girl was drinking Madame Dissard's coffee in tiny sips, as if she wanted to make it last as long as possible. "The day after you left, Madame."

Mathilde had huge eyes and an air of utter simplicity. No wonder they'd sent her. German soldiers might stop and stare at her, but they'd never believe she was a spy. *The best disguise we have is the assumptions other people make about us.* Nancy knew that better than anyone.

Thank God. For one foul moment she had thought that perhaps Henri had...but no. The arrest had come too soon for Henri to have been the source of the Gestapo's information.

"Who betrayed him? Do you know what happened?"

"I was there, Madame." The girl caught Nancy's frown. "At the next table. I had details of a prison escape to give to Philippe, but he must have seen something. He did not give the signal to approach. Then a man came and sat with him. A Frenchman, he called him 'Michael.' They spoke for a minute or two and then the men from the table behind Philippe got up, pulled out guns and took him away."

"But they didn't take Michael?" Nancy said quickly.

"No, the little shit just sat there grinning and finishing his wine." She threw out her words. "I know the girl in the café, Madame. She is a good French girl. She will spit in his food every time this Michael eats at her table."

Nancy shook her head. Still, it was something. "I know him," she said. "He worked for my husband."

Mathilde nodded sadly.

Marie ground out her cigarette in the ashtray and lit another. "Has anyone else been picked up since?" she asked.

"Just Albert, on the same day."

Nancy glanced at Marie and caught the older woman's small nod of satisfaction. They knew what that meant. Neither Philippe nor Henri had broken yet. Nancy's stomach twisted and she had a flash of Gregory's broken hands. Jesus. What were they doing to Henri? She looked away, drank her coffee.

Marie cleared her throat. "What about the prison break plans, Mathilde?"

The girl smiled at her. "They are to go ahead. Tonight. That is why I am here. You should expect them sometime overnight and then they can go with you, Madame Fiocca, to Spain."

"Albert was my contact in Perpignan, Antoine is dead," Nancy replied. "Who do I go to for a guide?"

Mathilde rubbed her eyes and yawned before she replied. "I'll give you a rendezvous, a café on the edge of town."

"And a fallback?"

The girl shook her head. "We have run out of them."

Mifouf jumped up heavily into her lap and yowled in sympathy. Mathilde stroked him and he began to purr.

"I worked with a Scotsman named Garrow," Marie said. "He had to run last month, but we went together to Perpignan once. I have an address. No passwords, no names, but an address. That will have to do as your fallback, Nancy." She took another swig of her coffee and tapped her fingers on the table. "With Philippe gone, we'll have to use another forger to make papers for the prisoners. He's not so good."

Nancy thought of the men she'd collected from prison breaks in the past.

"Their clothes will need washing too," she said. "At least it's something to do."

The men, seven of them, arrived at 2:30 a.m. How the hell they'd made it through Toulouse in their condition Nancy had no idea. Their clothes were in rags, their faces gaunt, and they stank. Nancy was for once grateful for Marie's smoking habit, but still, the reek of them.

Once they'd told the story of their escape—drugged wine, a bribed guard, a hay truck and a three-mile walk with a map drawn on the back of a cigarette packet—Nancy ordered them to strip, dump their clothes in Marie's bath and wash themselves down. They returned to the kitchen one by one, wrapped in old sheets and blankets, pink and scrubbed. The sirens started at dawn. The gendarmes, the Milice and the Germans were pulling the city apart looking for the cast of *Julius Caesar* now huddled in silence in Marie's kitchen.

"Dear lady," one tall English airman said to Nancy as the patrols went back and forth outside. "I can't face the Gestapo in a sheet. Any chance of getting my trousers back?"

"Nope. Sorry, Brutus. Not until they are clean," Nancy said. "And then they'll take at least a day to dry—we can't hang them anywhere near the windows, can we?"

"Brutus?" He glanced down at himself. "Oh. Yes. Quite."

He adjusted his grip on his sheet and shuffled awkwardly back to the kitchen.

They split up on the train. Four of the escaped prisoners spoke French pretty well, the rest did not. Nancy divided them into groups, gave them times to turn up at the rendezvous point in Perpignan and drilled them through a series of nods, shrugs and odd words which might get them past a casual checkpoint. The papers wouldn't stand up to any closer scrutiny than that.

Now she was in a crowded second-class carriage with her handbag on her lap praying for good weather over the mountains. Two of the English were with her, the man who wanted his trousers and a redhead Nancy had taken a dislike to. He'd turned his nose up at the food Marie had offered him and complained that Nancy hadn't managed to get all the stains out of his shirt. She almost throttled him with it. They'd taken the evening train. True, it meant when they got to Perpignan the streets would be emptying, but they'd still have a couple of hours before curfew to get to where they needed to be going. If their luck held.

Their luck didn't hold.

13

Half an hour before they were due to arrive in Perpignan, as the dusk was deepening over the countryside, the conductor stuck his head into the compartment.

"Move," he said, looking straight at Nancy. "The Germans are stopping the train. Full search."

She didn't have time to thank him or work out how he knew she needed the warning. He was gone as soon as he finished speaking.

"Shit, now what?" the redhead said in English.

One of the French passengers in the compartment crossed herself as if she'd heard the devil himself speak.

Nancy pulled down the window.

"You've got crap papers," she said. "We have to run, or you'll be back in prison before dawn. If they don't just shoot you."

The other Englishman, Brutus, was squinting out of the window next to hers. "There's a hill, mile or two off, with a copse up top. Meet there."

He certainly had a bit more authority now he had his trousers back on.

Nancy reached for the door handle, just as the train lurched against its brakes and began to slow. The door swung open and she fell forward. The world filled with the churning thunder of the wheels. She hung in mid-air by some miracle just long enough to grab the other side of the door frame with her left hand. She pulled herself back in, panting. An elderly Frenchman squeezed into the corner of the carriage had grabbed on to the edge of her coat and saved her life. She caught his eye, nodded her thanks, tried to control her breathing. The train had slowed to a walking pace.

No time to wait for it to stop completely. No time to think. That was a blessing anyway, looking at the drop below her. Thank God she wasn't in her high heels today.

"Come on!" she shouted to the others, and jumped.

Nancy landed OK, then slipped on the gravel and slid down a steep embankment into the darkness.

Two figures leaped out behind her, carried farther down the line and silhouetted by the lights in the carriage as the train finally came to a rest. Farther up the train she saw another door swing open and another group of figures jump one by one into the shadows. Then shouts, as another shape appeared in the open door and lifted a rifle. The shot popped in the silent countryside, a sudden punctuation mark as the hot metal of the wheels above her clicked and cooled.

Soldiers were climbing out of the train now. Shit. Time to run.

She scrambled over the low stone wall at the bottom of the embankment. It was a vineyard. Jesus, that was lucky. Paths to run along and foliage to hide behind. If they'd been on pasture land, the soldiers could have just mown them down like wheat.

Fast or slow? If she went slowly, moving between the shadows, they might never spot her, but if they sent enough men into the field they might pick her up while she was still creeping about. If she ran they'd be more likely to see her. She was still hesitating, just inside the rows of vines, when she heard for the first time the deadly rattle of a light machine gun.

Fast then.

She ran straight and hard between the rows of vines, keeping as close as she could to the shadows. Behind her she heard the shouts in German, and the barking of dogs. Bullets thudded into the dry soil behind her, sending up little clumps of earth which sounded like rain as they landed among the leaves.

To the east of her she heard more shouts, more excited barking. They'd got someone. Sons of bitches. Go faster, Nancy. The ground began to rise. Torches to her west, she spun east, forcing her way between the vines, then went north again. She knew she was bleeding now. Was it from a vine scratch or a bullet? Did it matter? Keep on. Would they shoot the men they recaptured? Maybe. They'd certainly shoot her. The acid burn in her legs was excruciating and she couldn't pause and catch her breath.

Keep going. Follow the rise.

She ran out of the vineyard, floundering into a wire fence and falling forward across it into a square, sloping field of grass. She turned over and lifted herself up on her elbows, looking back down the hill for the first time. Torches bobbed through the lower part of the vineyard near the embankment like fireflies, but they didn't seem to be coming up the hill as yet. Above them, on the tracks, the train still waited.

She lay there on the cool ground for a second, staring up at the moon and panting. Then she dragged herself to her feet and followed the fence east to the far corner of the field. The wire turned north, and she followed it, with woodland on her right and climbing again.

She'd never liked walks in the country. She was a city girl to the core, and when her friends had told her, smugly, about the joys of tramping through the beautiful French countryside with a sort of religious conviction she was pretty sure they were mad. The countryside was where food and wine came from, but there were no shops, no cafés, and how excited could you get about looking at the same view for hours, or weeks? She was in no mood to change her mind now.

She reached the top of the hill. This seemed to be the hill the

Englishman had pointed out. Total silence. She sat down on the edge of the little copse and looked down again. The lights were still there, bobbing around in the vineyard, but as she watched they retreated toward the train and blinked out, and then, finally, the lit windows of the carriages were on the move again. She let out a long sigh as it disappeared toward Perpignan.

It was then she realized she'd lost her handbag. It came as a cold feeling in the gut which spread upward and closed her throat. Her papers. Her money. Her jewelry. Her engagement ring. *Her fucking engagement ring.* She'd worn it through the whole occupation, but it was too fancy to wear around Marie's flat, so she'd tucked it into the lining of her bag. Oh, the note! She'd been so careful, taken so little, but even that scrap of Henri's writing was gone now.

For the first time since the Germans had turned up in France she burst into tears. The cold, the exhaustion. Her ring. The note. How could she have dropped it without noticing? Shit shit shit shit shit.

A rustle in the undergrowth startled her and she half-turned to see Brutus and the redhead approaching her carefully. The redhead held back, but Brutus knelt down beside her and offered her a handkerchief.

"You hurt, Madame?"

She shook her head. "No. I'm fine. I'm sorry. It's stupid. I lost my bag, it had my engagement ring in it. All my papers."

"Shall I go and look for it?" he said quietly.

"Don't be a sodding fool," the redhead whispered fiercely. "The Germans will have left a platoon down there. Just because they've switched their torches off doesn't mean they are gone. If the silly bitch wants it, let her go and look for it herself."

Brutus ignored him. "I'm happy to do it."

Nancy wavered, then shook her head. "It's too dangerous. We need to get moving."

She wiped her eyes with the back of her hand. "I'm more tired than I thought, that's all. We walk tonight, find somewhere to lay up during the day and then go into Perpignan when it gets dark."

"We haven't any food! Any water!" the redhead protested.

"If you are missing prison rations, just hand yourself over to the Gestapo," Nancy snapped.

Brutus patted her awkwardly on the shoulder. "Of course we should only travel by night. We'll get there."

14

Nancy knocked at the door again.

"Come on, come on…"

It opened, just a crack, and a thin sliver of light fell onto the roughly cobbled road.

"My name is Nancy Fiocca," she said. "Marie Dissard sent me; she worked with Garrow. I worked with Antoine. I've two men with me and we need to get out over the mountains."

She had nothing but hope. Hope that the right man would open the door, hope that he'd know the names and help.

It had taken two days to make it this far. They only dared to move at night, spending the daylight hours in deserted barns or huddled under hedgerows. Every day they'd seen patrols passing by them, inches away one time, but they hadn't been spotted. Once they'd walked straight into a local farmer heading out to his fields before dawn and just stared at him on the track, too surprised to run, until the old man had taken his pack from his shoulder and given them his lunch of bread and cheese and a flask of watered wine. It was the only food they'd eaten since they'd left the flat in Toulouse.

When they got to the outskirts of Perpignan they'd discussed their next move. The redhead, whose French turned out to be fluent, went first, like the raven out of Noah's ark, to see what the chances were of meeting a friendly face at the original rendez-vous point. He came back thin-lipped and discouraging.

LIBERATION

The word in the café was their contact had gone dark. Three men from the train had been recaptured or killed. Their contact had now skipped town and headed over the mountains himself with the two remaining escapees. They had managed, cunning buggers, to double back to the train during the search of the vineyard and retake their seats as if nothing had happened. They had wanted to wait for Nancy and the others to reach them, the redhead reported, his voice dripping with sarcasm, but the contact was spooked, and insisted he wasn't hanging around waiting for the Gestapo. He forced them to choose and they chose to leave with him.

Now it was Nancy's turn, going out to find a safe perch, like Noah's dove, on the basis of a half-remembered address and hoping whoever looked at her face would know, somehow, that she wasn't lying.

The door opened a little wider. She didn't know the man who greeted her, and he looked afraid, but he also looked like a friend.

"You'd better come inside."

Nancy was counting again. Her steps this time. The route was steep, heading over the highest peaks because the dogs the Germans used on the lower slopes couldn't smell them through the thin air at this altitude. The track was so uneven that it was impossible to get into a rhythm, one two...one...two. She missed the bloody coal truck that had taken them out of Perpignan and into the special zone that extended twenty kilometers into France from the Spanish border. Funny that. She hadn't been a fan at the time, but even jolting along the back roads under one coal sack and lying awkwardly on another had been bliss compared with this.

She needed a holiday, she thought idly as she counted, then giggled. She could see it so clearly: Henri waiting round the next bend in his car, ready to whisk her away to some health resort. She could imagine falling into his arms, complaining about what a terrible time she'd been having. Washing prison clothes in a bathtub, shot at, starved, thrown in the back of a truck. She could imagine his sympathy, his warm chuckle of laughter, his promises to make it all up to her.

She started telling him the story in her head, making it big, comic, ridiculous, pouting and swearing her way through the tale until he made her stop because his ribs ached with laughing so hard.

"What are you so fucking happy about?" The redhead.

She didn't bother replying. She missed Brutus. He'd shipped out of Perpignan a day before them. His clothes were in better shape and his shoes were still in decent nick. The redhead and Nancy had been forced to wait until the last shreds of the Resistance network in Perpignan could gather warm clothing for them.

The redhead took her silence as an invitation to talk. Not talk so much as complain. They were going too fast, this was a stupid route to take, why hadn't the Resistance managed to get him more socks? Two pairs wasn't enough.

Nancy ignored it, tuned him out and listened only to the sound of her internal voice, counting. He didn't seem to notice.

"We rest now," Pilar said.

Pilar and her father were their guides. They didn't talk much, and didn't rest much either. Ten minutes every two hours, and that was it. The paths twisted and snaked over the peaks, and sometimes in those ten-minute pauses, Nancy looked around her in wonder. They were caught among the snowy peaks like travelers in some fairy tale, like pilgrims, staring out over this exuberant feat of nature, the endless parade of mountain tops disappearing into the bluish spring air. And it seemed Pilar wanted to make sure they climbed every damned one of them.

Onward again, up tracks only Pilar was able to see. This was mountaineering, not walking. Nancy saved her breath and kept moving. The redhead wittered on. Now he wanted to know why they hadn't brought more food, how they were expected to keep going through the cold as the snow began to deepen around them. His voice became shrill.

"I can't go any further. I won't." He stood stock still on the track.

Pilar broke her usual silence, turning to Nancy and muttering under her breath. "Tell him to shut up and keep moving. Doesn't he know how far sound travels up here?"

"What's she saying?" the redhead said plaintively. "Tell me."

Nancy did. The redhead didn't budge.

"I can't go any further today, and no one is going to make me."

And that was it. The pleasant warming dreams of Henri disappeared, Nancy had lost count of her steps, and both Pilar and her father were looking at her with unmistakable "Deal with this shit, will you?" expressions. So she did.

She pushed the redhead, hard, so he stumbled backward off the path and into a fast-running stream of ice-cold mountain water that drenched him up to his knees.

"What the hell?" he shrieked at her, scrambling back out onto the snow. "You crazy bitch!"

He didn't make a move to strike her though. Probably knew the old guy would knock him on his arse if he did. Pilar grinned.

"It's your choice now," Nancy said very calmly. "If you stay still you'll freeze to death in half an hour. So walk. And shut up."

"Bitch," he muttered again, but he kept walking. Nancy started to count again.

They reached the border the next morning. Pilar pointed them down a clear and steeply sloping path toward Figueras, shook hands with Nancy, and then she and her father simply turned round and headed back into the mountains. A Spanish patrol picked them up an hour later, and Nancy thought them the most delicious human beings she had ever encountered in her life. She was out.

15

Arriving in London unnerved Nancy. The city was so different to the one she had known before the war, scarred by the bombing it had endured. You'd turn a corner and find a sudden blank where you knew there had once been a house, or an apartment building. It was a city of absences. And the people! Most of the men were in uniform and the women moved a lot faster than they used to, unless they were in hopeful queues, baskets over their arms and ration cards clutched in their hands. There were women driving the trams and punching tickets; posters urging the populace to save food and keep their nerve were pasted over old advertising. Mostly everyone gave the impression they had somewhere they needed to be, and needed to be there five minutes ago. Everyone except Nancy.

To be fair, it had taken a lot of time to sort out her paperwork, and before she could do anything useful she needed papers. When the Spanish police found them wandering down off the mountain, she'd told them she was American. That meant she got separated from the redhead, which was a blessing. Then she told the Americans she was a Brit, and then told an exasperated and skeptical Brit at the embassy that she was technically Australian, but had money in London and wanted to go and spend it. Also, she was Nancy Wake, aka the White Mouse, and the Gestapo were very keen to speak to her.

He phoned Henri's lawyer in London, who confirmed after a

long and expensive exchange of telegrams that yes, it probably was Madame Fiocca and yes, she had sufficient funds in the UK to sustain herself and pay back His Majesty's Government for a ticket and a cash advance so she could buy something respectable to wear on the voyage home and food so she wouldn't starve before she got there.

Henri's lawyer, Mr. Campbell, met her on the dock and shepherded her through customs. Nancy had met him once before when she and Henri had made a visit to London together and taken tea in his paneled offices while they talked business. She had been a bit bored at the time, impatient to get to the theater, the cafés and nightclubs of the West End. It turned out now that the conversation was the saving of her. Henri had opened an account with a London bank and made a healthy deposit.

"He managed to get a message to me just before your marriage," Campbell said, as he guided her out of the customs building and into a first-class carriage of the London train.

"How?" Nancy asked. She was in such a fog after the journey that she couldn't really take it all in—the comfortable seats, the attentive waiter. Campbell ordered her a Scotch.

"A Spanish smuggler he knew in the city, I believe, who was on his way to Brazil at the time. The message was sent from there, anyway. We had to pay a lot of postage on it—seems the man didn't use anywhere near enough stamps." He looked away. "I'm sorry to say we haven't had any news of Mr. Fiocca since."

The waiter set down their drinks and Nancy knocked back the full measure. Campbell blinked, then swapped his untouched glass with her empty one and called back the waiter for another round.

"Anyway, Mrs. Fiocca, the letter was quite clear. Henri is punctilious about his business. It was properly witnessed and dated, and instructed us that if ever you were to find yourself in need, we were to make available to you all the funds in the account and offer our assistance." He lifted his fresh whisky to her, having blandly ignored the waiter's slightly suspicious stare. "Which, naturally, we are delighted to do."

Definitely a nice old stick. Nancy leaned back in her seat with a sigh. No Gestapo breathing down her neck, no flying bullets. All she needed now was word of Henri, that he had reached Spain, and she would be in heaven.

It was typical of Henri to have thought ahead like this, putting some money in England even before war broke out. She'd only ever thought of one day at a time, of throwing herself in to the Resistance work, and if she was alive tomorrow or next week, so much the better. Henri, though, had made plans, including plans of how she could escape alone if she needed to.

She tried to sip her drink this time. Campbell was still talking. He looked like a caricature of an Edwardian lawyer: the high collar, white hair, the cream waistcoat with a gold watch chain across it. She looked again. His clothes were very slightly too big for him, and she thought she could spot signs at the seams that his waistcoat had been taken in at least once already. So even the rich were beginning to slim down in England. They didn't mention that on the radio.

She tried to listen.

"...sufficient at least for you to live in comfort for three years or so, and of course we are all sure the war won't continue longer than that! Since we received news of your arrival in Gibraltar, we've had a nose around and found some quite charming little houses in the smaller provincial towns where you'll be safe from the bombings and may wait the war out in peace."

What? No. Wait out the war in peace? Like hell.

"Mr. Campbell, I'm not just going to sit around drinking tea with a bunch of provincial ladies until Henri makes it over to join me."

He frowned. "But your safety, Mrs. Fiocca. And you have already done so much. Surely your nerves must be in pieces. A few months' rest!"

Oh, sod sipping. She downed the rest of the Scotch. "I don't think I have any nerves, Mr. Campbell. And trust me. Three weeks in the provinces with nothing to do but take tea and I'll blow my brains out in front of the vicar and ruin the doilies."

He stared at her, then the corner of his mouth twitched. "Well, yes. That would be unfortunate. In that case, Mrs. Fiocca, I have a friend who is looking for a tenant for his flat in Piccadilly. Does that sound more the ticket?"

"Can I take it today?"

16

Nancy looked at her watch. They were making her wait. It had taken twenty-four days to get all her paperwork sorted out, twenty-three days more than she needed to get bored of her new freedom and start working out how to get back to France.

Henri had not made it out and to London yet. She made sure the flat was ready for him when he arrived, complete with his favorite brandy and a bottle of champagne in the cupboard. And a pair of slippers and a decent shirt. All of it was black market of course, and horribly expensive, but she wanted him to be comfortable as soon as he arrived. But she couldn't wait for him. Couldn't sit there doing nothing but stare at the four walls.

She had arrived at the Headquarters of the Free French Forces in Carlton Gardens at 9 a.m. precisely, having walked briskly from her flat in Piccadilly in her best heels and a well-cut suit, which showed off her curves without looking like it was supposed to show off her curves. Batting her eyelashes at the guards had got her as far as the waiting room, or rather a chair in the marbled hallway under the eye of a Frenchwoman with reading glasses. The old trout scowled at Nancy, but she had an obsequious smile ready for any man in uniform marching through the hall with a fistful of papers in his hand and a self-conscious "here I am, saving France" look on his face.

Nancy looked at her watch. Then at the woman. Then at her watch again.

"Madame..." Nancy said.

The woman was too wrinkled and slow to be a trout. The woman held up her hand, and Nancy decided she looked more like a tortoise directing traffic.

"They know you are waiting, Madame"—she adjusted her reading glasses and looked down at her notepad—"Fiocca."

"But..."

"Do you have some other urgent appointment?" the tortoise said, opening her eyes very wide.

Nancy crossed her arms and slouched in her chair. No, she didn't, and that was exactly the damned problem. After months of every moment being packed with danger and activity, she had exactly nowhere to be at all.

"Madame Fiocca?"

Nancy looked up. A thin, olive-skinned man in a lieutenant's uniform was hesitating in front of her. His shoes were as polished as the marble floor. She nodded.

"If you would follow me."

The office he led her into must have been the cupboard where the charlady stored her mops in peacetime. Still, the officer had managed to squeeze in an oversized antique desk and a good chair for himself. Nancy got a metal folding chair which squeaked when she sat on it. The shelves where the char used to keep her dustpans and polishing cloths were packed with rows of manila files. She stared about her.

"I thought there was a paper shortage," she said.

He ignored the remark and continued reading the file he had open on the table in front of him. Her file.

"I'm right here, you know," she said after five minutes. "If you want to know what I did in France, you can ask me."

He glanced up. "Yes, we've had reports you were quite helpful. The Gestapo even gave you a pet name. How charming."

"Charming? You think that's charming?"

He smiled at her. Big mistake. The frustration that had

been building as she had waited and waited and waited burned loose.

"Do you also think it's charming that the Gestapo are holding my husband? Do you think it's charming that I risked my neck and his a thousand times in Marseille, that I have three years' worth of experience dodging the Nazis while you've been arranging your paperwork? When was the last time you saw action? *I* was outrunning bullets last month and I need to get back out there. Now. So sign me up and I'll leave you to your filing."

His smile froze. "Madame, the Free French Forces do not accept women. You are by nature unsuited for warfare, it's a scientific fact."

For crying out loud, she thought. "You're a scientist too? Amazing. I just told you, I've *been* at war ever since the Nazis rolled into France, so I guess science is wrong."

"But your womanhood—"

"By which you mean what? My vagina? Does my vagina mean I can't hold a gun? Run a safe house? Smuggle money, men, ammunition? Trek across a mountain range? All my vagina means is I've learned to do all of that and more in high heels."

He leaned backward in his chair and put his fingertips together and looked down his nose.

"I am sorry, Madame. The operations of the Free French Forces can't be compromised by a person so obviously emotionally unbalanced, the way you speak of your..." He flushed to his roots.

"Vagina, vagina, vagina—it's a scien-fucking-tific term!" Nancy shouted.

He glanced nervously around him as if expecting the walls to collapse in shock and tried to rally. "Given your knowledge of anatomy, perhaps you should be a nurse, give succor to our brave fighting men."

"I'd succor them if I could *find* any brave fighting men!" She sprang up, knocking her metal chair backward and pulling open the door to the marble hall. The officer flinched. "And I'd gladly take a scalpel to your balls too, but I suspect they've already been removed!"

Her voice echoed in a satisfying fashion in the high hallway and she slammed the door behind her. The tortoise was staring at her open-mouthed.

"Keep his bollocks in your drawer with your pencil sharpener, do you?" Nancy said, and she swept out onto Carlton Gardens, round the corner and into St. James's Park without looking back.

After an hour of walking round the park in tight miserable circles, past the show allotments and the anti-aircraft guns, she started to see the funny side, so she strode into the Red Lion off Duke Street, halfway back to her flat, bought drinks for every man in uniform and told the story. She did it well. Every new arrival had to hear the tale again, and the barmaid kept giggling along at the new bits Nancy added as the story bloomed. As the lunchtime rush reached its height, the tortoise lady had become a terrifying gargoyle and the officer a quivering wreck of a man with sweaty palms and a nervous twitch in his eye.

"Then he called it my *womanhood*!" Nancy said, lifting her glass.

"Beginning to think that's where you store all your booze," a sergeant muttered, trying to light a cigarette with the swaying flame held out by one of his friends.

"I volunteer to scout the territory," a fresh-faced American said with a brave attempt at a wink.

"What are you, nineteen?" Nancy replied, blowing out the wavering flame and offering the sergeant one from her own lighter with a steady hand. "You wouldn't even know where to plant your flag."

The men cheered and thumped the American on the back

until he choked on his beer. Nancy looked at the lighter in her hand. She'd never smoked—she'd been too afraid when she was living on a journalist's wage in Paris of burning holes in her one good dress to start—but she always carried a lighter. It gave you a chance to talk to people. Something about taking that offered fire, bent over your hand, meant they were more inclined to talk to you, take you into their confidence. Henri had laughed hard when he'd told her that, called her a witch and the next week given her a gold Cartier model engraved with her first name. She'd lost it with her other jewels and papers escaping from the train.

She heard him now, his laugh, among all the cheers of these strangers and wondered what he'd think of her interview in Carlton Gardens. Oh, he'd have laughed too, done himself an injury and then boasted about his impossible wife to his friends, no doubt. But he'd have understood, too, her frustration, her rage at the narrow stupidity of these men. How useless and angry she felt right now.

"Then what, Nancy? You got to hear this, George," the sergeant said. "George, he said she should be a nurse, can you fucking imagine it? Isn't that what he said, Nancy?"

Nancy looked at their faces, saw Henri, saw Antoine and Philippe. They waited, a little unsure as to what was coming next. She beamed at them.

"Damn right, he did. Mildred?"

The barmaid set down the glass she was polishing. "What can I get you, Nancy?"

"Champagne all round! We're drinking to my medical career!"

The crowd cheered again.

The pub was supposed to close between two and six, but no one wanted to go home and once they'd got one of the local bobbies in to warm himself up with a brandy no one tried to make them. When Nancy staggered out into the shadowy dark she had made at least a dozen more lifelong friends and felt lonely as all hell. Not that she took up any of the offers, chivalrous or hopeful, to see her home.

The London night air felt cold and damp on her face—not the salty tang of Marseille, but a swampy, coal-soaked damp that would get into your bones if you let it. Behind her a figure moved between the shadows, keeping her in sight. She missed her footing on the curb, pulled herself upright and set off across the square, looking at the paving stones in front of her, swinging her handbag, then sauntered down the shortcut in the side alley, singing a song the Scottish sergeant had taught her.

The man following her quickened his pace, keen not to lose her in the growing dark. He stepped into the alley and paused. His quarry had disappeared. Then he froze, feeling the cold sting of a blade just below his Adam's apple.

"You've been following me since Carlton Gardens," Nancy whispered in his ear. "Now who the hell are you?"

"You really can take your drink, can't you?" he said. He had a Scottish accent. "That little stumble was just a show for me, was it?"

Nancy pressed the blade into the throat, not quite enough to break the skin, but close. "I asked you a question," she said. "Why have you been following me all day?"

"Madame Fiocca, I've been following you all week," the man said calmly, then stamped down hard on the top of her right foot. The pain shot up her leg and at the same moment he grabbed onto her forearm and bent forward, throwing her over his shoulder. She landed awkwardly on her hip, and the knife spun out of her hand and across the alley.

"You utter bugger, that's ripped my stocking!" Nancy gasped as soon as she had breath to speak again. She pulled herself up on her elbows.

The man laughed and put out his hand. "My apologies. My name is Ian Garrow."

She stared at his shadow hard for a moment, then took his hand, and he hauled her to her feet.

"I know you," she said, rubbing her hip. "You worked with Marie. You made it out then?"

"I did," he replied. "And just in time. Last I heard, Marie is still safe, but a lot of the network has been rolled out. Very few are getting through now." He paused. "I was told about your stunt pushing that lad into the river. Apparently Pilar told several people. Pretty remarkable given she rarely says anything at all."

"He whined."

Garrow took out a cigarette and waited a moment. Nancy didn't offer him the use of her lighter, so he struck a match and in its brief flare she saw his hollow cheeks and long nose.

Nancy felt a burst of hope in the middle of her chest. "Any other news out of Marseille?"

"Some, but nothing about your husband, I'm afraid."

Suddenly Nancy was sore and tired and miserable again. Maybe it was drinking all the bathtub gin in New York after she'd first left Australia, but for some reason Nancy could never stay drunk for long. The champagne buzz from the bar, the thrill of the laughter and chat, even the excitement of the brief and humiliating fight with Garrow had left her.

"Mrs. Fiocca," Garrow said quietly, "do you really want to fight?"

"Dear God, I think I'll go mad if I can't, Garrow," she replied.

He put his hand in his pocket and drew out a card and passed it to her. It felt like a business card, though she couldn't read it in the darkness.

"Come to that address, tomorrow, say three o'clock?" Then he put his hand to the brim of his hat and walked away from her into the shadows.

17

The card led Nancy to a rather dull-looking office building above a shuttered car dealership. There were a number of buzzers, as if for flats. Only the bottom one had any label on it. A little metaphysical plea. "Please ring."

She did and waited and waited. God, this was going to be like the Free French Forces all over again. A sudden buzz and she pushed open the door. A narrow flight of shallow steps led up to a wide lobby. It might have been a rather smart art deco block twenty years earlier, but everything looked a little shabby now. And it was quiet. Just walls of pale oak paneling and an elevator door with an "Out of Order" sign on it. No strutting officers. Nancy couldn't decide if she thought this was a good thing or not.

The woman behind the desk this time was younger, though, and grinned at Nancy in a madly cheerful manner. Her lipstick was a very fetching scarlet.

"Purchase war bonds, madam?"

Nancy passed the card she had been given and the girl immediately pressed a discreet buzzer on her desk.

"I love your lip color," Nancy said. "But as to why I'm here, I haven't the foggiest idea."

"Such is the human condition," a male voice behind her said, and Nancy turned to see Garrow opening a door discreetly hidden in the paneling. He put out his hand.

She turned up her chin. "Forgive me if I don't shake, Garrow. A strange man assaulted me last night, so I'm feeling shy."

"Good," Garrow replied, inviting her into the office with a courtly bow. "Then we won't have to hear about your vagina today."

The girl at the desk snorted with laughter and tried to disguise it, badly, with a cough.

"Thank you, Miss Atkins," Garrow said, and ushered Nancy into the room.

The office he took her through led straight into another corridor. He turned right and they walked along a further corridor, which seemed impossible given the shape of the building she had stepped into, and up another short flight of stairs. He knocked at a door, then, without waiting for an answer, opened it and showed her in.

The room was windowless and its walls were plastered with maps of France. It was bigger than the rabbit hutch she'd been interviewed in at Carlton Gardens at least, though the desk facing the door was just a rough trestle table and all the chairs were metal-and-canvas fold-up horrors. Where the hell did all the decent chairs go when war broke out?

The only person in the room was a tall, narrow man with a thick mustache sitting behind the desk, a teacup in one hand. A trolley with a teapot, another cup and saucer and a sad-looking plate of biscuits sat in the gap between him and the wall. He was studying a file and glanced up briefly to look at her. He didn't invite her to take a seat. The air stank of stale tobacco.

"Garrow, I told you I needed recruits, not a battered drunk."

Nancy blinked.

"War's killed off all the decent ones, sir," Garrow replied. He went over to the trolley and poured himself a cup of tea. How did the British drink so much of the stuff?

"Not as pretty as her photos either," the man behind the desk said, turning a page.

"You guys are such a blast," Nancy said and smiled sweetly.

"Perhaps we can salvage her as a secretary," the desk man said with a sigh. "Can she still remember how to do shorthand?"

He flicked over another page. It annoyed her. The file annoyed her.

Nancy plucked the lighter from her handbag and walked up to the table, leaned across the desk, the same sweet smile still plastered on her face, and set fire to the bloody thing. The man holding it stared at it in alarm for a good three seconds, which allowed the flame to catch nicely, before throwing it on the floor in front of Garrow. Garrow stamped on it, then picked up the teapot from the trolley behind him and doused the smoldering pages. The tea leaves slopped onto the floor with a pleasing splat.

There was a long silence as both men stared at the sodden and charred remains. Nancy slipped her lighter back into her bag and clicked it shut.

"Never had anyone do that before," the man behind the desk said. He stood up and put out his hand. "Madame Fiocca, welcome to the Special Operations Executive. I'm Colonel Buckmaster, head of the French Section."

"Then France is lost," Nancy replied. "And I think as Henri is a guest of the Gestapo at the moment, I shall go by my maiden name for now. Wake."

"I think we've hurt her feelings, sir," Garrow said, and Nancy thought she could detect a hint of a laugh in his voice. "Nancy, take a seat."

She hesitated, but then did so, because what else was she supposed to do?

"Garrow tells me you want to fight," Buckmaster said, sitting down again. "Is that true?"

"Yes."

"Good." Buckmaster pulled a pipe from his pocket and began to fill it. "Because unlike the Free French Forces, we might give you the chance. Churchill wants the SOE to set Europe ablaze, and given that little demonstration, you might fit in rather well."

Nancy said nothing.

"So you have lived in France since the age of twenty…"

"I was a reporter with Hearst Newspapers."

Buckmaster waved his hand. "Yes, shabby prose, but you obviously traveled around the place. Then you used the wealth of your husband Henri Fiocca to establish a network in Marseille and called yourself the White Mouse."

The fact that her file had been reduced to a damp mess on the floor didn't seem to cause Buckmaster any difficulty. Nancy had the uncomfortable feeling he had memorized the whole thing before she had arrived.

"I didn't call myself the White Mouse, the Nazis did."

"Ever kill anyone, Miss Wake?" Buckmaster interrupted.

"No, but—"

"You need to learn how to, Miss Wake. You need to learn a great deal. What do you think fighting in France consists of? Giving the Nazis a nasty talking to?" He sighed, an infuriatingly sad smile on his face. "If you get through training…"

"And that won't be easy," Garrow added.

"Indeed it will not." These two were a regular double act. "*If* you get through training we'll be sending you to work with one of the Resistance cells in France. For the brief period you manage to survive you will have to get your hands bloody and watch others die horribly without being able to do a damn thing to help them. Now, are you quite sure you wouldn't like to be a secretary?"

Did he really expect her to back off now? Start quivering in her shoes and leave it to the men to fight back? The Nazis had torn her life apart. It was a life she had fought hard to make and she loved it, and France and Henri, with her gut and her soul. They wanted her just to sit there and wait for someone to fetch it all back for her while she kept herself busy with a bit of typing?

She thought of that boy in the Old Quarter, Antoine with the gun in his mouth.

"I'll be more use in France."

"To whom, Nancy?" Buckmaster dropped the friendly tone and turned raging demon on her. He brought his fist down hard on the table, making the teacup rattle. Nancy did not flinch. "To me? To England? Or to your husband? This isn't some fairy tale rescue mission. It's a vicious fight to the death."

Christ. You just can't get through to some people.

"You don't have to tell me that, you patronizing son of a bitch," Nancy said with calm precision. "I was there. I know France, I know the French and I know the Germans. I know what it feels like to watch a man die and wipe his blood off your hands then get on with the mission, and I also know you need agents on the ground more than you need a new secretary, so stop giving me the runaround and let me get on with it."

He studied her for a long moment and for the first time Nancy thought of the men and women who had sat in this chair before her, saying what she was saying. Did he have a tally somewhere saying how many were dead, how many lived, how many had just disappeared into the fog of war? But then the corner of Buckmaster's mouth twitched. Back to Uncle Bucky again.

"OK, Nancy. You're in." He picked up another file from the stack next to him and began to read.

Garrow pushed himself upright. "Come on then, Nancy. Let's get started on the paperwork."

And that was that. Nancy followed Garrow out of the room and to his office near the front door. He selected another of those bloody manila folders from his desk and produced half a dozen typewritten sheets. She picked up her pen and signed where indicated, without reading any of them, while he talked.

"Officially, you'll be signed up as a nurse. You'll get the papers at your Piccadilly address, and you can expect to be leaving London within the week, so don't make any plans."

Then he tapped the papers together and all but shoved her out into the drab little hallway. As he was shutting the door in her face Nancy noticed him give a tiny nod to Miss Atkins at reception. Whatever it was she had meant to say, which of the thousand questions or witty comebacks she was sure were rattling around in her head somewhere, she never found out. The door clicked shut, and slightly dazed and with no idea what else to do, Nancy headed for the stairs.

"Hey, Nancy?" She turned. Miss Atkins threw something toward her and Nancy caught it. A tube of lipstick. "It's called V for Victory, Elizabeth Arden. Welcome aboard."

PART II

ARISAIG, INVERNESS-SHIRE,
SCOTLAND, SEPTEMBER 1943

18

The first day of training was the worst because she'd been so damned pleased to get here. The weeks since her interview with Buckmaster had been torture—more waiting, jumping on the post and afraid to go out in case the telephone rang.

Eventually the papers—more papers—arrived. She packed a bag according to instructions, filled out the travel chit and, having sent a note to Campbell giving her new contact address as instructed and telling him to keep the flat on, she left for Scotland.

Arriving had been fine, and the instructor who had met her at the station and driven her through the long dusk of late summer in Scotland to the training camp seemed decent. The camp was some aristocrat's hunting lodge on the edge of a loch, surrounded by great peaks, blue in the haze, and the sunset—pinks and purples smudged across the sky—had been magnificent. She was the only woman in this group, the instructor told her, looking at her sideways, and she'd shrugged. She was used to being the only woman in a group of men after working as a correspondent in Paris. She understood men. She tried to protest when they showed her to an empty bunk room though, but they weren't budging. There was no way she'd be allowed to muck in with the blokes.

Still, the next morning when she reported for her first training session in her PT kit at 6 a.m. it had been with a glad heart. Then she saw him. The redhead. And he saw her. One or two of the men shook her hand or nodded to her in a friendly enough way, but before the sergeant who would lead them on the run had wandered out to join them, the redhead had gathered a little group around him and they were shooting looks her way and laughing.

The redhead was rubbing his eyes as if crying. "Ooh, I've lost my handbag," she heard him saying in a high whine. "Please will you fetch it for me?" Then he made more fake sobbing noises and they all laughed.

She should have gone and smacked that grin off his face right there and then, and told them all what a whiny little shit he'd been during the crossing, but just as she was balling her fists the sergeant arrived. Do it anyway? No, they'd kick her out before she'd even got started. She'd have to go back to Buckmaster and beg for a secretarial job and that would kill her. *Patience, Nancy.*

"Mr. Marshall, if you are quite ready?" the sergeant said, and the redhead grinned and stood at ease. So that was his bloody name.

Nancy had known the run was going to hurt, but she had no idea how much. She thought all the traveling around, the bike riding with radio parts and messages would have toughened her up, but half these guys were in the services already and had been doing PT runs for years. She just managed to keep up, in the final third of the group—never last, but near enough to it to hear the sergeant bullying the stragglers just behind her. He was an odd, square little man three inches shorter than Nancy, but apparently fashioned by God to run up hills like he was having a gentle stroll down the high street. How did the man have that much air in his lungs?

About twenty minutes in, or it may have been three, or an hour and a half—Nancy lost her sense of time pretty quickly when she couldn't breathe—she noticed Marshall, who had started off at the front of the pack, dropping backward, letting others overtake him. Soon he was running alongside her. He flashed her a quick grin and for a stupid moment, Nancy thought he was going to apologize.

"So your name's Nancy?" he said. "You doing OK?"

"Fine." It was a struggle to speak, but she managed that much.

"Just, it must be so hard for you..." The bastard wasn't even panting. "After all, you have to carry those big bouncing titties with you."

He said it loud enough to draw glances and grins from the other men around them. He had his hands in front of his body now, cradling imaginary breasts with a look of sorrow and struggle on his face, tongue sticking out, making his fake tits bounce.

"Fuck you," she said. Not original, but it was short.

He stuck his foot out sideways, catching her mid-air and sending her sprawling into the mud. She landed hard, face in the filth and the air knocked out of her. She lifted her head and saw him easily moving back through the pack to lead it again. The other runners flowed past her.

"Get up, Wake!"

The sergeant was standing over her. Running on the bloody spot.

"I..."

"Just get up!"

She pushed herself up to her knees, then onto her feet. Her T-shirt was black with mud and clung to her. Her hair was plastered to her face and she could feel blood on her cheek.

The sergeant looked at her critically. "You'll live. Now run."

And she did. She finished last, of course. No way could she make up the time she had lost, and then because she had to shower, she was late to her first class. She apologized to the instructor and went to find a seat. Marshall and his newly formed crew of grinning sycophants gathered round him were all rubbing imaginary tears from their eyes.

*

105

That set the pattern—the assault courses where someone accidentally shoved her off the balance bar, or stood on her hand as they scrambled over the rope net. The sniggering became a constant buzz in her ears that followed her from the mess hall to the training grounds to the classroom. She gritted her teeth and took it.

After her third run, and she made it through that one without getting slathered in mud, the sergeant called her aside and handed her a role of bandages from his pocket and a couple of safety pins.

"Had a wee lassie who was blessed in the chest area here last year, Wake," he said. "She bandaged herself up before the runs. Said it gave her more support than just a brassiere."

He flushed to his ears when he said brassiere, but he was right. It helped.

The room had been stripped of all its pre-war furniture. Pale spots on the wall showed where paintings had hung in those unimaginable days. Henri would have liked it then, probably stuffed with leather armchairs and old books. Now the only furniture was the usual metal table, folding metal chairs and a pair of gunmetal-gray filing cabinets. And this guy. Holding up a messy inkblot and staring at her over it. Pale blue eyes and thinning hair. Dr. Timmons.

"What do you see?"

"An ink blot, and you staring at me," she answered, putting her hands in her pockets and stretching out her legs in front of her. It wasn't very comfortable, but she wasn't going to sit up straight like a good little girl in the schoolroom for this man. A psychiatrist. Trick cyclists they called them here. Even the instructors called them that.

He released one edge of his inkblot sheet to write something down.

"Now you're just throwing good ink after bad."

She turned to look out of the window. A group of men were being hurried across the driveway in their PT kits. God, she'd rather go with them all the way up a mountain in the pissing rain than this.

"This is a test, Nancy," he said. "Mental health is just as important as physical. Perhaps more so, in your field. What do you see?"

"A dragon."

He smiled without warmth and set the paper down. "You are the third recruit from your section to say that. Haven't you the imagination to come up with something else?"

She shrugged and crossed her ankles.

"Very well. Let's do this the old-fashioned way. Tell me about Australia. Your childhood."

She blinked. All those times the instructors had gone on about knowing your cover story in the field, and she'd completely forgotten to prepare one for this guy. Bugger. She was there again, in her mother's house. Her older siblings had left home, so it was just the two of them. Not speaking. She couldn't remember one conversation with her mother. Just the lectures. How Nancy was ugly, stupid, sin in human form.

"I was perfectly happy."

"Lots of friends?" Timmons asked, still making notes.

"Oodles," Nancy replied. She could feel the heat of the sun as she walked home, moving more and more slowly the closer she got to the ratty clapboard house. Her mother would be waiting when she got there. Not with love, or warmth, but with another monologue of complaint and accusation, salted with Bible quotes. Everything was Nancy's fault and Nancy was God's punishment, though Mrs. Wake couldn't understand what she had done to deserve such an ugly, unnatural, disobedient child.

"And what about your parents?" Timmons had his head on one

side, like the macaw in the pet shop on the way to school. Nancy had always thought it was judging her too.

"Terribly, terribly happy," Nancy said in her best upper-class English accent.

Timmons sighed. "Why did your father run out on his wife and six children then? You were, what, five years old? Have you seen him since?"

"She drove him out," Nancy said sharply. "The others had left home and she was a bully and a bigot and he couldn't take it any more."

"So it was her fault?"

What did this have to do with anything? All that training to shoot instinctively and from the hip was working. She was itching to shoot this bastard; she could feel it in her fingertips.

"Of course it was her fault. Daddy was a prince. He was funny and kind and he absolutely adored me."

That was true. She had felt that love, and the memory of it kept her sane until she met Henri.

Timmons was writing again. "Not enough to take you with him though." That hit her like a punch to the gut. "He stayed until all the other children had left home, but couldn't do the same for you, could he?"

One. Two. The double tap. The little sandy-haired balding bastard. She said nothing.

"You flew the proverbial coop at sixteen, persuaded your family doctor you were eighteen so you could get a passport and run away. So you were an enterprising little girl, good at twisting men around your little finger."

How the hell did they find this shit out? So what if she had? And she'd made a success of it too. Made friends, learned her trade and had a ball, then fallen in love with Henri, the cherry on top of her life.

"Only a fool would have stayed in that house to be bullied."

He linked his hands behind his head, pushed his elbows

backward to stretch his back. His throat was totally exposed, and his sides. With what Nancy had learned over the last few weeks she could kill him in a moment, and that sad weary sigh could be his last breath.

"Yet here you are, Nancy."

"What?"

"Half the men hate you and you are continually bullied. And yet you persist."

She swung her legs back under her and leaned over the desk toward him.

"Because I want to see those fucking Nazis punished. It's that simple. I've seen it. In Austria. In France. They are scum. They need to be wiped out, I need to wipe them out." She tapped his notebook with her finger. "Now, erase the 'fucking,' add a bit of pomp and patriotism, jot it down, we're finished. *Happy?*"

He met her gaze steadily and Nancy withdrew.

"*You* need to wipe out the Nazis, do you, Nancy? Well, I'm sure we'll all be terribly grateful. But you are part of a team, part of an army, part of a country."

He sighed again. Damn it, that was irritating.

"You might be a good agent, Nancy. Section D needs independent thinkers, but you also need to realize you are part of something larger than yourself. It may come as something of a shock, but the war isn't about you."

Oh, enough already.

"You think I'm doing this because I'm angry Daddy left and Mummy thought I was some black toad squatting on her life?"

He glanced sideways at the inkblot. "It does look a bit like a toad, doesn't it? Interesting." He wrote something else down. "Nancy, listen to me. I think you *feel* like you need the suffering here and the suffering that is in all likelihood waiting for you in France, maybe not consciously, but you do. That you deserve it. That you are the monster your mother told you you were."

Nancy clenched her fists in her pockets. She could feel the muscles tightening in her jaw. "They actually pay you for this?"

When she was little and things were very bad, she'd hide in the crawlspace under the house and read *Anne of Green Gables* by the fierce sunlight filtering through the wooden boards of the porch until the pain and anger bled out of her. It was still her favorite novel. The only novel she really liked, actually. She'd put down her book and leave it all there, the rage and fear and self-loathing, under the house. She was sure it would blow up the whole place one day; all those foul feelings she'd left stinking under the porch would ignite, and BOOM! All gone. Then she reached sixteen and out of the blue an aunt sent her a check, and she decided she couldn't wait for the explosion any longer, so had left all that crap behind instead. Now she took everything Timmons had just said, tied it up in brown paper and stuck it down there too.

She wet her lips, then spoke quietly, reasonably, as if she and Dr. Timmons were discussing bus routes at a London cocktail party. "Ever thought of getting out from behind your desk and fighting yourself, Dr. Timmons?"

He raised one eyebrow. "Like that, is it, Nancy? Very well." He wrote again, sighed again.

"Just do me one favor, Nancy. Do try and prevent your self-serving bullshit getting anyone killed, won't you? Dismissed."

19

She walked out of there with her chin up, of course she did, but she felt hollowed out somehow for the rest of the morning. She had her head handed to her by an instructor she thought had liked her when she misidentified the rank insignia of a German tank officer. Worse still, the instructor took her mistake as an opportunity to point out to them all how mistakes like that could cost them their lives. She hardly kept it together as he banged on and on about how he expected more of her, how they all did, and about the grim and protracted deaths that could await her and anyone who worked with her if she ever made an error like that again.

At dinner she sat alone. Marshall dropped a sheet of paper beside her with a crude childlike drawing of a man in one of the officer's caps of the Gestapo with an arrow pointing to it and the words "NAZI BAD!" in block capitals. Cheap little arsehole. She screwed it up and threw it at him and he and his little band of brothers giggled. The whispering, the laughter, the long stares. She longed to gouge out his snake-green eyes. She turned back to her food. An apple core caught the side of her head and splattered into the cold gravy of whatever it was they were eating. The slop in this place. She spun round, but Marshall and his merry band were already leaving. Instead a tall, slightly older man was sitting on the bench behind her and shrugged at her as she turned.

"I think they throw apples because they're still cross about Eve." He put out his hand, and she shook it. "I'm Denis Rake, but my friends call me Denden."

No snide remark, no suppressed laughter, no leering stare slithering its way from her head to her toes. Good.

"Fancy a drink, Denden?"

Nancy had been surprised at how easy it was to bring alcohol up here, and how easy it was to get more. It took her until her third week up north to realize the instructors were trying to get them all drunk to see which ones would talk. Fine by her.

She took Denden back to her dorm and fetched out the good bottle of French brandy the barman at the Café Royale had sold her before she came up north. Denden stared up and down the empty dorm.

"At least you get some privacy with your isolation, dearie. I suppose they thought the boys couldn't control themselves if you bunked with them."

"That's about it," she said, and fetched a couple of water glasses from the bathroom. "The billets officer went pink to his ears when I said I wanted to stick with the men, mumbled something about the showers."

"Yet he expects me to control myself!" Denden rolled his eyes. Nancy frowned slightly. He was a good-looking man, thin and wiry, but then they all were after six weeks of forced marches and runs in the Highlands and those bloody assault courses. He watched her with quiet curiosity for a moment. "Yes, I'm queer as a coot. That's why some of the boys don't like us, because we both like cock. Unless you are a lover of lady parts?"

Nancy had met a fair number of queer men in Paris, thought they were good company by and large. And a homosexual was the only person in the world Nancy's mother hated more than Nancy herself.

"Only my own. Come on, let's find a nicer spot to drink." At the door she stopped and turned round again. "Denden, how can you be so...? I mean, I can't hide the fact I'm a woman, but you could hide."

"Yes, I could, but if I can't be who I am the goose-steppers already have their jackboot on my throat. Besides, I mean, all that worship of the masculine nonsense, half of those leather-clad krauts are queer as I am."

She laughed, and realized it was the first time she had done so in weeks. A real laugh, not a playing along, fake it till you make it laugh. It felt good.

They went out into the grounds and after some debate and a couple of wrong turns, clambered up onto the high bar of the assault course, then, wrapping their legs around the rope net for security, started doing their drinking seriously.

Denden was a hell of a mimic, his voice swelling with aggression as he repeated the mantras of unarmed combat, oozing weary disdain in the nasal cockney of the sabotage trainer, giving a worried twitch to the long Norfolk vowels of the King's Game-keeper at Sandringham who taught them how to poach rabbits and game birds.

"I'm really not sure what King George would make of this," he said, catching the man's voice and head shake so perfectly Nancy almost fell off the bar.

"You should be in the theater, Denden!"

"Oh, I was," he answered, taking a swig from the bottle— they'd never got round to using the glasses. "Well, the circus actually. Tightrope, clowning."

"You're bullshitting me."

He unwrapped his legs from the netting and in a single movement lifted himself until he was standing on their wooden perch, still holding the half-empty bottle of brandy in his left hand. Then he lifted his arms above his head and pirouetted in place, before leaning forward, one leg lifted straight behind

113

him, arms out, and held the pose for one, two, three seconds. Nancy could hardly breathe. Then he threw the bottle up in the air, making it spin. Nancy yelped, but before she knew it he was sitting next to her again just as he had been and had snatched the spinning bottle out of the air without spilling a drop.

Nancy whooped and applauded. Then, as he bowed, she grabbed the bottle off him.

"How did you end up in the circus?" she asked and drank deep.

"Mum didn't want me around," he said, staring out into the silvery darkness. "She knew there was something different about me from the age of four, so when the circus rolled through town she handed me over to the ringmaster saying, 'He's a freak, he belongs to you.'"

Nancy took another pull at the bottle.

"Thank all the saints she did," he went on. "They were good to me at the circus. Taught me to do tricks but made sure I could read and write too. The palm reader taught me history and the trapeze artists taught me French and Spanish. We toured a lot in France. Spent half my winters there since I was eight years old."

Nancy felt a bubble of jealousy pop in her bloodstream. Denden yanked the bottle out of her hand again.

"Much good it will do me," he said as he released it. "Not sure this lot are going to let me go back to France."

"Why not?" Nancy turned to him.

"I hate guns. Won't use the damn things. That's not too bad, I'm excellent on the radio if I do say so myself, but Timmons is the real problem. Says I'm not fit because I refuse to hide my 'homosexual illness.' He's sure to fail me out. Thanks, freak, but no thanks. Piss off back to the Molly house."

The burn of her own interview rose in her throat. Bastard trick cyclist. "Denden, want to do something foolish?"

*

If they really wanted to keep the files secure, they wouldn't leave them behind two pretty simple locks in a house full of students they'd been training to slip through security a lot tighter than this. That was what Nancy reasoned, anyway.

Once in Timmons's office they drew the heavy blackout curtains, switched on the desk lamp and made themselves comfortable. The filing cabinet was locked too, and Timmons had even had the sense to place scraps of paper into the drawers which would fall out if they were opened. Denden collected them up to pop them back in later, then he pulled out their files.

"I get excellent marks in combat, tactics, explosives, *lockpicking*..." Nancy read off her marks with a certain pride from Timmons's chair.

Denden was leaning up against the cabinet. " 'Rake's among the best radio operators we've seen, but—' Christ. A one in marksmanship."

"Well, I got a two on the jump training," Nancy said, the pride draining out of her voice.

"Bugger that," Denden said, and set his file on the desk top next to hers, then examined the pens, laid out in a little neat rank on the right-hand side of the desk. "Yes, you'll do," he said, picking up one of the pens.

"Denden?"

"What?" he said. "They sent me on a forger's course too. I'm just having a little practice."

With a casual flick his one in marksmanship became a seven, and Nancy's two in jump training was magically upgraded to an eight.

Nancy offered silent applause and Denden grinned shyly, and turned the page.

"Wonderful. The report of the good Doctor Timmons himself. 'Rake's shameless perversion is a danger to troop cohesion.' Not at all. I bring men together."

She giggled and looked at her own, reading it aloud with a

breathless, eyelash-fluttering intensity. " 'Wake is extraordinarily motivated to return to France…' "

"Bless, I think that's his version of nice," Denden said. "Do we have any brandy left?"

"Shush, Denden. I'm not done. '…but this bravado masks deep insecurity. The guilt over her husband's…her husband's capture…' " And just like that it wasn't funny any more. Not a bit. Where was Henri? What was he feeling right now? " '…coupled with childhood trauma, compounds the danger of grave instability.' "

Denden put his hand on her shoulder.

"Come on, ducks, that's enough." It was, but she couldn't help herself. She shook him off.

" 'It is my judgment that she is not fit for command and for all her commitment could put herself and her men at risk in the field.' "

The room felt very quiet and outside in the grounds an owl hooted at the moonlit shadows.

"Psychobabble horseshit," Denden said firmly. "Whatever happened to 'anything that doesn't kill you makes you stronger'? And, for the sake of all holy fuckery, you are *supposed* to be putting people at risk in the field! You have to be able to send men out to sabotage Nazi factories, ambush convoys! Do they think blowing up a train under enemy fire is risk free?"

It was a good speech and kind of him, but it was no good. They were going to wash her out and she'd be stuck in some typing pool, dying inside every day and drinking herself to oblivion every night while the Nazis did what they pleased to France, to her friends, to Henri. And worst of all, they might be right to keep her out of the way, where she could do less damage. She blinked.

"Denden, what are you doing?"

Denden had lifted down Timmons's portable typewriter from the top of the filing cabinet and set it on the table, then found his blank report forms in the top drawer.

"Budge up, my pretty, and take a quick peek in the corridor will you, in case anyone's lolling about? I think it's time we told our own stories."

Twenty minutes later, Nancy was feeling a lot better. A thought occurred to her.

"Denden," she said, tucking the slips of paper back into the filing cabinet drawers so Timmons wouldn't spot someone had been rifling through his business, "got any plans for tomorrow night?"

20

The lock rattled open and Henri looked slowly round. The pain never stopped now. Whippings and beatings hour after hour, day after day, his injuries never allowed to heal, meant his only emotion for weeks had been exhaustion and a longing to be done. Hope had gone, and in the bright white light of the pain sometimes so had love and faith and his own self.

Sometimes something Böhm said reminded him he had once been Henri Fiocca, a rich and happy man with a beautiful wife living day after day in sunshine and luxury. It was just a dream. The door swung open. Henri was expecting the rat-faced torturer with the glasses at the door—astonishing how the man managed to ring fresh waves of pain out of him, out of the rag of a man he had become—but it was Böhm.

"Monsieur Fiocca, you have a visitor," Böhm said in his careful, English-accented French.

Böhm had studied psychology at Cambridge before the war, Henri remembered, and had waxed lyrical about the great buildings and great men he had encountered there from time to time during their chats. Böhm was never in the room for the whippings which left the skin hanging from Henri's back. He'd just come in afterward.

A visitor? That meant the world outside these walls still existed. How strange. He thought of Nancy. If they caught her, would they be cruel enough to bring them together? Yes. They would torture her in front of him. No doubt Böhm's studies had taught him a meeting like that might break him at last. If Böhm had Nancy, proved that he did, Henri would give him the names of every Resistance member, every escapee who had eaten at his table, every safe house bought for cash at the beginning of the war, to save her a moment of this pain. They would not release her, of course not. They had worked out she was the White Mouse. Böhm had made that clear in their chats. But if Böhm brought Nancy in and said, "Tell us everything you know and we will simply shoot her, no torture, no rape," Henri would take that bargain.

Böhm brought a pair of fold-up metal chairs in from the corridor and set them by Henri's cot.

"My apologies, Monsieur Fiocca, I should say two visitors." He looked over his shoulder. "Monsieur, Madame…"

A shuffling of feet and Henri's father and sister edged into the room. Gabrielle gave a little shriek and put her handkerchief over her mouth and nose, then edged toward him with her hand outstretched. His father hung back next to the door, his jaw slack and his shoulders trembling.

"I shall leave you to catch up," Böhm said with a warm smile, and closed the door behind them.

Henri could not move, did not feel like speaking.

His sister tottered to his bedside then collapsed to her knees with a wail. "What has she done to you? Oh God, have mercy on us!"

His father collapsed heavily onto one of the chairs. Henri studied Gabrielle with his remaining good eye. She lifted her hand again and managed, briefly, to touch his shoulder. Henri was not sure if he was clothed or not. They always stripped him before they beat him, sometimes they redressed him afterward, at other times they did not. He'd long since ceased to care.

"Tell them what you know, Henri." That was his father's voice, a cracked version of it anyway. "Böhm says he has already

captured most of the Resistance network in Marseille. He just
wants you to talk about Nancy, where she might be, what you
know of her plans."

"Then he will let you go!" Gabrielle squeaked. "He will let us
take you back to the house and nurse you. God, Henri, haven't
you suffered enough for her?"

Henri licked his lips, finally understanding. They *blamed*
Nancy. They thought it was her fault that he was lying here,
barely conscious, torn by the whips, his fingers broken, his fingernails gone and his face hardly recognizable. They thought
it was her fault. How could he have sprung from such people?
The Gestapo had done this to him. The power lust of a group of
deluded zealots who had somehow managed to poison their own
nation, then spread that poison abroad. The Nazis who had used
fear and flattery to hold France, his beloved glorious France,
under their jackboot.

He did not have the strength to explain this to them. He'd
leave that task to other men and women, or to God.

"Leave me alone."

Gabrielle twisted round to look at their father. She looked
half crazed.

"Papa! Make him see! What does it matter anyway now that
whore has run away?"

"Henri, you must think of your family," his father said.

She had escaped, then. Henri had not been sure when Böhm
had told him she'd slipped through his net. He thought it might
have been a trick to make him talk, tell him Nancy's secrets. And
God knew, he did want to talk about her. But Gabrielle could
not have played a trick like that, she was not an actress. Nancy
was free.

The pain was still there, but Henri felt something else. Peace
perhaps. Yes, that was it. He had never been much of a one for
religion, and Nancy loathed any mention of God, but Henri
sensed *something* beyond his pain now, a place cool and quiet

which would welcome him when the time came. And perhaps that was close enough.

"You are not fit to touch the hem of my wife's skirts," he said. He hoped that was what he said—it was getting harder and harder to form any intelligible words. "Now leave me, both of you, leave me in peace."

Gabrielle cried, his father raged and pleaded, but it meant nothing to him. He observed them from a great height, their words muffled and meaningless.

He closed his eyes, and when he opened them again, they were gone. Böhm was sitting on one of the metal chairs, staring at him.

"Disappointing!" he began. He was leaning forward, elbows on his knees. "Your family, I mean. I had hoped they'd manage to break you down at least a little. I told them to talk about the soft bed waiting for you at home, how Nancy would want you to talk to me, what harm can it do now? She's escaped after all."

Henri's eyelids flickered, hungry for any crumb of news.

Böhm wrinkled his nose. "Yes, she made it to London. I hear she's been recruited by a bunch of amateur saboteurs and criminals. Her official job is with the nursing auxiliary core, but she sounds like just the sort of woman the British army is sending over here to do their work for them. Dirty terrorists." He sat back in his chair and crossed his legs. "Are you smiling, Monsieur Fiocca? It's difficult to tell. I wouldn't be pleased if I were you. Do you know what we do to the female spies we capture? They are begging to be shot in the end. I have seen it myself, many times."

He stared at the blank wall above Henri's cot as he spoke. "They last a few weeks behind enemy lines at the most, cause us at most a slight inconvenience, then we pick them up and squeeze them until they vomit up their secrets. That is what will happen to your Nancy."

The last words came out too fiercely, too much venom. For a moment the mask cracked and with distant interest Henri observed the man behind it. Böhm hated Nancy, hated her for what she did, who she was, what she represented. A woman who did what she wanted and what she thought was right.

Nancy.

Böhm leaned forward eagerly, too hungry, too eager.

"What was that, Henri?"

"I said," Henri managed to articulate each word with great care, "that you'll have to catch her first."

Böhm stood up so fast the metal chair was knocked over and collapsed behind him. This struck Henri as very funny.

Böhm strode to the door and called into the corridor. "Heller! Monsieur Fiocca is ready for you!"

That struck Henri as funny too, so he was still laughing through his broken teeth when Böhm had left and two of Heller's men had picked him up off the cot and dragged him along the corridor to the cellar. Some of the other prisoners must have heard him, because behind him faint and croaky he heard a voice starting to sing the Marseillaise, then another, then another.

Heller grew red in the face. "Silence! Silence all of you!"

The voices continued, raw and ugly as drunks when the bars closed and just as unstoppable, and Henri laughed again. He could still hear it as they slung him into the yellow room. He lay on the blood-washed tiles, still laughing, and listened to them, the voices of his ragged angels.

21

Nancy was back in Baker Street. God, was it only six months since she'd been in this bare room trading barbs with Buckmaster? She had not been offered a chair this time. Denden was in uniform standing "at ease" with his hands clasped behind his back. Nancy was wearing the FANY uniform, hands at her side, eyes front.

" 'Wake is popular with her peers. A born leader.' " Buckmaster was reading from a fresh manila file on the fold-up table in front of him. Honestly, Nancy thought, they could get the man a proper desk.

"That's what her file says," Buckmaster continued, looking over to Garrow who was in his usual place, leaning against the wall. "Funny thing, though: we employ Dr. Timmons to find flaws, not praise. Then, of course, there was that unfortunate incident in Scotland before Wake and Rake—God, you sound like a poor Vaudeville act—left to complete their training at Beaulieu."

"Yes," Garrow replied with a sigh, "a very promising recruit named Marshall discovered at reveille, naked and tied to the flag post outside the main offices. Quite overset him for a while."

"The names of these two were mentioned in the report, weren't they?" Buckmaster inquired politely.

Garrow raised his eyebrows. "Yes, quite wild assertions as I recall, of attempted seduction and being clubbed over the head."

"Poor man."

Nancy managed not to smile. The memory of Marshall tied to the flag post was a bright, shining light in her memory. It was only a bit of a bump too—he'd been so pissed he practically fell over at the slightest touch. And it had been a mild night.

Garrow lit a cigarette. "Perhaps we've been duped, sir."

He exhaled, watching as Buckmaster got to his feet and walked round the edge of the desk.

"Just think, Garrow. If a German spy were to penetrate the SOE, he, or perhaps *she*, would attack our best men, not to mention covert access to our records."

Oh shit. They were busted. Perhaps altering the files had only seemed like a good idea after a bottle of brandy. And what the hell was this? Buckmaster was drawing his side arm. He couldn't really think...

"I'm only going to ask nicely once: whose idea was it to break in?" Buckmaster was so close to Denden that his breath made him blink. "Was it you, Rake?"

For a long second both men stayed absolutely still, then Buckmaster lifted and swung his revolver at Denden's head, tearing the skin from the edge of his eye along the cheekbone. Denden staggered sideways into a crouch, then stood up again.

"Answer me! Did the Germans send a queer spy into our midst?"

Denden didn't even look at him, just clasped his hands behind his back again and stared at the wall. Nancy swallowed. Was it a test? They'd all been dragged out of their beds at Beaulieu from time to time and made to answer questions on their backstory, still befuddled by sleep. Even when they recognized the instructors, the confusion of those moments was enough to panic some. But they'd never been violent—rough maybe, but not this. Did he really think they were spies?

Buckmaster moved behind her, making her skin creep, then stood directly in front of her and placed the barrel of his revolver against her forehead.

"Or did they send a woman?" He had gone mad. Why wasn't Garrow intervening? This was insane.

"Who was it? *Who?*" She watched as he cocked the pistol and began to squeeze the trigger. "LAST CHANCE! WHO?"

Nancy stared straight at him. Click.

And the world didn't end. They were still in the room. The gun was empty. Buckmaster nodded and holstered his side arm again.

"Good show," he said lightly as he returned to his seat. "Do sit down, both of you."

Jesus mother-fucking son of a bitch. Nancy wasn't sure if she sat down or fell down. Garrow stepped forward and gave Denden a handkerchief. Nancy couldn't be sure, but it looked as if Denden wasn't just wiping the blood off his face but making sure the handkerchief was thoroughly ruined in the process.

"Silence can work for men. The Gestapo will assume a male foreign agent has plentiful strategic information, so may keep you alive long enough for you to manage an escape. But, Miss Wake, the Nazis aren't as forward thinking about the use and capacities of females as we are. Neither are the French, come to think of it. They will kill you or send you straight to the camps. A woman must ingratiate herself. Play the part, grovel, cry, sleep with them if you have to. Swallow your pride because the bullets will be real and you are no use to me dead."

Nancy nodded, because he was waiting for her to nod. She wasn't above flirting her way through checkpoints and fluttering her eyelashes at men she'd cheerfully murder, but there were limits, for God's sake, and playing the fuckable princess was beyond that limit. Her limit.

"You have a mission for us then, sir?" Denden said, handing the handkerchief back to Garrow who looked at it with distress.

"Yes. And as you seem to have decided you are a team during training, we're sending you together. You'll share the rank of captain, but as your radio man, Rake will report to you, Nancy. Garrow, the map, please."

Garrow laid it out across the table. It was the sort of map tourist guides printed for motorists before the war, but this was scattered with "X"s, each followed by a short numerical code.

"Each 'X' represents an active SOE operation," Buckmaster said, a certain pride creeping into his voice. "Smuggling in Paris, foundering U-boats in Cannes. Even got a team who blew up a munitions factory in Toulouse last week."

"Where are we going, sir?" Nancy asked.

"You're assigned to the Auvergne," Buckmaster said, studying her face and seemingly pleased at what he saw. "Not far from Vichy, teeming with Germans. Harsh weather, rains all the time, impossible terrain, befitting the Resistance who operate there: the Maquis name themselves after scrub brush because they're so hard to kill, or control. Your first mission is to establish command over the largest band of Maquis in the region. They're led by Major Gaspard."

"Who is a puffed-up, one-eyed prick," Garrow added.

"And he despises the SOE," Buckmaster continued smoothly. "Fears that once we clear out the Boche we're planning to keep France for ourselves. Last thing he wants is to work with you, but he's also low on supplies, so that's your carrot."

"What if he doesn't take it?" she asked.

"Make him. You'll bring him to heel or die trying. He's tactically sloppy. Brave, but he'll waste his men and our money without a firm guiding hand. That's you. The Auvergne is crucial for moving resources throughout France. We must make it impossible for the Germans to get their men and machines through the area quickly."

"We'll be sabotaging the transport routes?" Denden asked, perky as a spaniel again.

"Exactly," Buckmaster replied. "The key to the success of this invasion is preventing the Nazis from resupplying their men on the new front. We're working damn hard to make sure they won't know which direction we are coming from, but once we land they'll scramble everything to counterattack. That means we have to slow them down everywhere and the Auvergne is crucial to that. Take out the railway bridges, knock out communications, make them scared of their own shadows and you'll be doing the work of the angels."

The excitement shivered through Nancy. She was going to be there. Finally.

"When do we ship out?" she asked.

"In a week," Buckmaster said. "Until then you'll be in one of our London safe houses studying the maps of the area and plans of the major targets until you can draw them in your sleep. And you're not shipping out, Wake. Why do you think we bothered training you to jump out of airplanes? Rake, you're flying into the outskirts of Montluçon on a Lysander. There's a burned-out operator we need to pick up, and you'll be using their radio. Nancy, you're parachuting in nearer Gaspard's group. One of our men in the area, Southgate, will be in the reception committee and he'll get you to Gaspard. Charm him until Denden gets there with the radio." He looked at Nancy again. "Something wrong, Captain Wake?"

Nancy swallowed. "No, sir. Only, I haven't really enjoyed jumping out of perfectly good airplanes."

Buckmaster opened his eyes wide and blinked. "Really? But you scored *so* well on your jump training."

22

That last drink at the Astor had been a mistake. Or maybe it was the one before that. Perhaps the error was switching to whisky. The Liberator lurched as the ack-ack burst in the air and the pressure pushed the plane sideways. What happens if you throw up in an oxygen mask at fifteen thousand feet? Nothing good. Nancy swallowed hard and groaned, knowing that at least no one would hear her in the thundering noise of the plane and the exploding air. The Spam sandwiches and coffee before take-off—that was her mistake right there. She could feel them churning in her stomach. What the hell did they put in Spam anyway and why were the British so bloody proud of being able to eat it? She grabbed at the ribs of the fuselage as it dropped and bounced. Yup. Definitely the Spam sandwiches' fault. Another burst, closer this time, and the plane seemed to fall hard and fast, uncontrolled. Her eardrums sang and her chest tightened. The engines whined and then roared, and suddenly they were climbing again. She slid forward and scrabbled for purchase with her feet against the riveted panels. Sharp roll right and another deafening bang as if God himself had thrown his fist against the side of the plane. Not now. Not before she even got to France. Please. Her hip slammed against metal and she gasped as the pain shot through her. Then the plane began to level out and the engine noise lowered in pitch. The explosions were more distant. She took long, slow breaths, slowly released her grip on the rib. Her hand was cramping. It looked strange to her without her wedding ring. They'd insisted she take it off for the jump, and it was the first time she'd done so since Henri put it on her finger. The pale skin looked like a scar.

The dispatcher came through to check on her and tapped at his watch to show they were half an hour out from the drop zone. She checked the straps of her parachute and the bandages wrapped round her ankles. In the pocket of her camel-hair coat her fingers brushed the smooth metal of the compact Buckmaster had given her. A nice little parting gift that, the sweetie. Catching herself thinking fondly of a man who had held a pistol to her head only a week before made her shake her head, and the plane began to drop at the same time. She tasted Spam in the back of her throat and swallowed again. If ever there was a time she'd be willing to jump out of a fucking plane it was right now.

She'd told the dispatcher to give her a shove, and he took her at her word. One minute she was in the rattling whirring belly of the plane, staring out of the Joe hole at the flicker of the signal bonfires and the discreet flashes of a torch, and the next she was out in the cold and falling.

The parachute snapped open and she felt the fierce tug of the straps on her shoulders and waist and across her thighs. Relief first, then a moment of calm. The moonlit landscape lay below her, the rise and fall of the mountains, the steep silhouettes against the sky, the peace of it, the fires and... oh Christ, all the trees.

The earth was approaching pretty bloody fast.

She yanked on the cord, trying to aim for open ground. Nearly there, and then a casual whip of a breeze pushed her south and back over the tree line. Time up.

She pulled her knees to her chest and tucked in her chin as she felt the top-most branches grabbing at her in the darkness.

Gravity took the chance to make it perfectly clear who was boss in the end. Nothing she could do about it now. The brittle hands of the trees grabbed and jabbed at her till the chute caught, the harness jerked her again and she was stopped dead.

She opened her eyes, one at a time, to find herself dangling in the air, like a fish on the end of a lucky angler's line. She could smell the smoke of the signal bonfires, but even twisting on the end of her cords, she could see nothing but pinched and branching darkness.

"A parachute, over there!" a French voice said.

"*Merde*," she hissed. Strange how even her mind switched back to French as soon as she took a lungful of the air of her adopted home. A light was approaching up the track. Friend or foe? She reached into the side pocket of her coat and closed her fingers around the grip of her Webley revolver. If it was a German patrol she was dead, but she'd take at least one of the bastards with her. Still, the voice sounded pretty relaxed. Maybe a German patrol happening on a landing site would sound a bit less…casual. Whoever was coming up the track seemed to be coming at an easy stroll too.

The torch paused under her tree and she heard a low laugh. A French laugh.

"The trees in France bear beautiful fruit this spring," the voice said. Very funny.

"Oh, just cut out that French shit and get me down," Nancy said, releasing her grip on the gun. The torchlight panned down from her feet to the forest floor. Less than ten feet. She sighed and pulled the chute's release mechanism, managing a landing which didn't snap her ankles or roll her into a thorn bush, at least.

The man with the torch shone it toward his own face briefly and Nancy saw a youngish man, good looking in that classically French long-nosed, high-cheekbones sort of a way. He put out his hand and helped her to her feet.

"My name is Tardivat."

"Nancy Wake." Tardivat's grip was firm and cool. "Is Southgate here? I was told he'd be picking me up."

"One moment."

As soon as Nancy was on her feet, Tardivat passed her the torch and clambered into the lower branches of the tree. He moved easily, pulling himself up from branch to branch until he could get to work on the cords of her parachute.

"Shine the torch here," he said, and began to gather the silk into his arms, taking care not to tear it or leave any telltale scraps of cord in the branches. The night seemed very still, and Nancy could smell the soil in the thin high air, the fresh growth of the spring pushing through the rotting leaves of last year.

"Southgate was picked up by the Gestapo a week ago," Tardivat said.

"Betrayed?"

"Only by bad luck," he continued. "He was caught with forged papers. Once we have doused the signal fires, I am to take you to Gaspard, he's the head of the Maquis here."

"Yeah, I've heard of him."

He gathered the parachute under one arm, then jumped lightly to the ground, his fingertips brushing the soil as he landed. "What have they told you about him?"

Nancy examined his face in the glow of the edge of the torchlight. Maybe she'd not tell him exactly what Buckmaster had said.

"A good fighter, but arrogant."

Tardivat nodded slowly. "True. Did they tell you he hates the English too?"

"Well, I'm Australian."

He snorted. "I don't think he'll see the distinction, Madame."

He opened his pack and began to stuff the parachute inside. She took a step toward him.

"Hey, we have to bury that! And it's Captain."

Tardivat carried on. "Forgive me if this is just more 'French shit,' but I was a tailor before the war, Captain. I will not bury silk like this. I shall make something pretty for my wife so I can remember the days before the Germans started taking everything fine and handsome for themselves."

Hell. She'd only landed on French soil five minutes ago and here was trouble already. It was driven into them every day through training—bury the parachute, bury the parachute. But on the other hand, if Southgate was in the Gestapo cells and Gaspard was as much of a bastard as Buckmaster had said he was, Nancy was going to need as many friends as she could get.

"Fair enough. How do we get to Gaspard?"

"We'll have to walk. The trail is about eight kilometers and rough."

Nancy sighed and began to unwrap the bandages from around her ankles; under them she wore silk stockings and high heels.

Tardivat began to laugh. "My God, you jumped into France in those?"

Nancy fished a pair of walking shoes out of her backpack and carefully wiped the forest mulch off the polished leather of her good pair before slipping them into the pack and doing it up.

"And under this stupid tin hat, my hair is very nicely styled. Now shall we get going?"

They went in darkness. Tardivat extinguished his torch as soon as they were sure they'd left no sign of Nancy at the drop site. At first Nancy was just getting used to being off that damn plane, then she began to feel the thrill of having French soil under her feet. Not that this steep path through the woods was much like Paris or Marseille, of course. But it still felt like home, somehow. An image of Henri turning from the windows in their bedroom in his white dinner jacket flashed into her mind so strongly it was as if she had seen a ghost.

"What's the news here?" She spoke in a whisper.

It was too dark to see it, but she could hear the shrug in Tardivat's voice.

"People are beginning to feel their blood and courage rise. We French have always known what happens to armies who try to invade Russia. The Germans are starting to learn that lesson at last."

That had been the moment, Nancy thought. She remembered when she heard the news, crouched over the radio, Henri's hand squeezing her own in excitement. Every kid in France knew what happened to Napoleon when he tried to take Moscow, but apparently no one had told Hitler. The day he launched his surprise attack on the Soviet Union in the summer of 1941 was the first day anyone in France dared to hope. It also meant all the French communists were finally free to pick up their weapons and start fighting back.

Then the Führer lost an army at Stalingrad.

"We have gained many men this year," Tardivat said. "The young men who refuse to work in Germany come to us. It is good, but it has made problems too."

"What problems?"

"We are many. At first there were enough abandoned barns and farms for everyone. Now it is harder to find a place, and to keep moving so the police cannot find us."

"What else?"

"We fight, but we fight among ourselves too." Tardivat sighed. "There are feuds between villages and families here that go back to the Revolution. Some use the Gestapo to attack their enemies, some use the Maquis. Not all the scores being settled are against the invader."

Great. Politics. Not Nancy's strong point.

"And Gaspard lets this happen?"

"He lets his men raid the farms of his enemies." Tardivat paused in the darkness, then, as if guided by some invisible hand, headed off again. The path got steeper and narrower.

"That's not going to happen while I'm here," Nancy said firmly. Perhaps all that bloody physical training had been a good idea after all. It sounded better, saying stuff like that if you weren't panting.

They reached the edge of the tree line and the first light of dawn showed shadows in gray and silver as the night retreated.

"We'll pay for what we take," Nancy said. "And this is a military operation now. That means rules. We're not the Germans. We're the good guys and we're going to act like it."

Tardivat sighed. "Whatever you say, *Captain*."

Nancy turned away from the view. He could have his parachute, but she was damned if she would let him take that tone with her. She breathed in, ready to explain that to him in short, sharp sentences. Too late she saw his eyes flick up as he caught a movement over her shoulder. She began to turn, then something struck her across the head and everything went dark.

23

Not dead. That was her first discovery. The dead felt no pain, and Nancy was in agony. She opened her eyes. She could see a little light and she smelled straw and chaff. Someone had put a feed bag over her head. She tried to move. No joy. She was sitting upright on some sort of chair, and her hands were tied behind its back. It was the pain of the howling muscles in her arms that had woken her. Her ankles were bound too and they'd taken her shoes; under her silk stockings she felt a hard earth floor. She lifted her head and breathed in slowly and carefully. Cool air. Wind in the trees. So she was still in the mountains, still in the countryside, and this was a barn, the outbuilding of some farm, not Gestapo headquarters in Montluçon.

Voices outside, echoing as they entered. Men, of course, and more than one, though only one was doing the talking—the rest were just laughing and agreeing.

"Looks like our little guest has woken up." He spoke in French, his voice low and rasping.

OK. Nancy. It's show time.

The bag was ripped from her head and she found herself looking up at a smooth-shaven, round-faced man. He wore an eyepatch.

"What a pretty little bitch they've sent! Much better looking than that shitbird they're beating in the cells right now." Does he know about Henri? No, get it together, Nancy, he's talking about Southgate. "They're hoping your tits will save your neck, are they? Come to try and make us Frenchmen scurry around and do England's bidding, cunt?"

She looked him up and down. Some of the men behind him shifted uncomfortably.

"That's right, Gaspard." She kept her voice cool. "They even told me to fuck you if I thought it would help. But you know, I can't decide between that and the cyanide pill at the moment."

A couple of the men grinned. Whatever they'd been expecting from a woman sent by the English, it wasn't that sort of language coming out of her pretty mouth in fluent demotic French. Gaspard—yeah, this was Gaspard all right—twitched. Time to press home her advantage.

"But I can offer you support from London. Honest aid. Guns, money. Whatever you need to win your country back."

"Bullshit. You want our land. You want us to dance to your tune."

"You can trust me."

"A deal with the devil. You're worse than the Germans, you lying cunt."

He leaned over her and she could smell his sweat, the sour smell of unwashed clothes. She let a sneer creep into her voice.

"Christ! That's your favorite word, isn't it? Does it give you a bit of a thrill? Not seen the real thing for a while?" Some of the guys behind him were smirking now. "If you can get your head out of my crutch for a moment and listen, I'm telling you I'm here as an ally. Guns. Money. Help for your families and intelligence from London. As to the rest, you're looking at the White Mouse of Marseille and as fierce a patriot for France as any one of you...bastards."

The blokes behind him were ready to burst out in applause, she could feel it. She could work this crowd. She watched their reactions out of the corner of her eye and felt the corner of her lips twitch. Big mistake.

The second she took her eye off him, Gaspard kicked the leg of the chair out from under her and she went down, heavy and hard on her shoulder. The air was knocked out of her lungs and the pain blossomed in her side.

"Lying bitch! I know about the White Mouse of Marseille. Got her men shot while she pranced around spending all the money she got from her rich old husband. No one in Auvergne is going to pay for you to get your hair done and play at soldiers."

She tried to breathe. "My husband is a hero, you sack of shit." She didn't have breath to say it loud enough.

Gaspard was looking at something in his hand. He crouched down and showed it to her. Her wedding ring.

"So why is this in your bag and not on your finger?"

"Give it back!" Now she sounded like the kid getting bullied in the playground. "I took it off so I wouldn't get my finger ripped off jumping from a fucking plane, you moron."

She kicked out hard, but he saw it coming and stepped aside, kicking away the upended chair at the same time. She was on her back now, her hands still tied behind her. She pulled her legs up, ready to push herself up onto her knees, but he straddled her, his weight heavy over her hips. She blinked. She could feel a warmth on her face. Blood. From that blow she'd taken over the head earlier. It ran into her eye, blinding and stinging.

He leaned in close, holding her wedding ring between thumb and forefinger. "What's to stop us just killing you now? We can take that nice stack of francs sewn into the lining of your hand-bag, bury you under the floor and say you never made it. Looks like you brought a nice fat wad with you. We might even send this ring back to Marseille. If your poor little husband survives maybe he'll find someone even prettier to give it to."

He shifted his weight and she felt the flesh of his thighs pressing against her hips. She drew in her breath and spoke loudly enough for his men to hear.

"It would be the last money you ever get from London if you

do. They know I landed safely, I signaled from the ground that I'd made my rendezvous. If you want guns, if you want more than the loose change I carry in my handbag, you'll have to deal with me. Now, why don't you just fuck off and let me do my job? If your men don't want machine guns, army boots and more cigarettes than they can smoke, I reckon there are others who do."

He glanced up, looking at someone she couldn't see.

"Is that true? Did she signal the plane?"

Damn. Tardivat was in the room. He knew bloody well she hadn't sent a signal. He'd been with her every second since she'd landed in that sodding tree.

"She was signaling when I met her." Tardivat's voice sounded neutral, bored.

"Bitch," Gaspard said. She saw him pull back his fist. She could not defend herself. Another explosion of pain, then silence.

Tardivat was there when she woke up. They were still in the barn, but the daylight had faded. She noticed old packing cases and broken furniture round the walls. So this was the place where broken and useless things went to die. Someone, Tardivat probably, had untied her wrists and ankles and put a blanket over her. When he saw her eyes open, Tardivat handed her his canteen and she drank greedily. She thanked him and passed it back. He took it with a nod then reached into his top pocket and took out her wedding ring.

Nancy put out her hand and he dropped it into her palm. It had taken a fight with a beardless lieutenant and a hatchet-faced secretary to bring it with her. Thank God Henri hadn't got it engraved or bought anything too flashy. Her engagement ring, swollen with emeralds, she had lost escaping from the train. But this plain gold band she had kept on her finger. She remembered the touch of his long cool fingers as he slipped it over her knuckle in the town hall at Marseille, that look of affectionate amusement in his eyes. She put it on again. Perhaps they shouldn't have married. In the early days they had lived together, and she had been Madame Fiocca to their servants and acquaintances. They had said they'd wait until the war was over at first, then they had become impatient, set the date and arranged the party. Why? They were listening to the BBC reports about the ferocity of the struggle in Russia, and she'd just had a near miss carrying papers from Toulouse. They hadn't dared wait.

"I can get you to a farmhouse where they can give you a bed for the night," Tardivat said. "And I know of a radio operator in Clermont-Ferrand. He should be able to get a message to London for you. Arrange your escape."

She shook her head. "I'm not going anywhere, Tardi."

"They're just going to kill you some other way, Captain Wake. Make up another story—yes, she got here, but she was murdered by a patrol or something."

"Call me Nancy. Where's my pack?"

He nodded toward it. She got to her feet and fetched it. It had been ransacked and roughly repacked. Her handbag was still there and so was the money. Strange. She guessed Gaspard wanted to work out his new plot before he did anything. She took everything out then carefully repacked again: two embroidered nightdresses, a red satin pillow, then the usual changes in underwear, a simple outfit suitable for an Auvergne housewife of moderate means, her high heels for if she needed to take a train or go into one of the local towns, her hairbrush and makeup. She began to make herself look respectable. A bit of water from Tardivat's canteen and her handkerchief got rid of the blood. The cut on her forehead was long but shallow, and just under the hairline. No need for stitches.

She was applying her V for Victory lipstick with the aid of Buckmaster's compact when she noticed Tardivat was at work at the silk of the parachute.

"Making something for your wife?"

He nodded.

"Do you feel guilty, leaving her alone while you fight?"

He didn't look up from his stitching. "This is the second world war in twenty years. We are all guilty."

She lifted her chin and bared her teeth to check for lipstick. All in order. "How do you suppose they mean to kill me?"

"They know you are trained. Probably they will pretend to be friendly and kill you in your sleep." His voice was conversational.

"Are there other groups of Maquis near here? Another leader I could talk to?"

"A man named Fournier, up on the plateau near Chaudes-Aigues. The other side of the valley. He and Gaspard are not friendly. But he had only thirty men and they live wild up there."

Nancy rolled her shoulders. Her arms still ached and she could feel bruises coming on her side. Her brain felt sick and swimming. Sod them.

"Will you take me to him?"

"Now?" he said, and began to pack up his sewing.

"In a minute. I want to have dinner with my hosts first."

Around a hundred Maquis were gathered around a central fire pit, bent over billycans of some sort of foul-smelling stew being served from an improvised cauldron. Gaspard was sitting in the firelight, perched on a packing crate, while his men gathered round him like disciples. He saw Nancy at once, and gradually all other eyes turned toward her too.

One man got up from his crouch at Gaspard's feet and fetched a plate of the stew from the cook, then brought it across to her. He was a good-looking man, twenty-five perhaps, huge brown eyes and an athletic build. He presented the plate to her with a flourish, a low bow.

"Madame, forgive our rudeness. We have been so long in the wilds we hardly know how to treat a lady."

140

Nancy could see Gaspard watching, grinning.

The good-looking young man continued. "This slop is not fit for your lips, the talk of this company not fit for your ears."

Nancy still did not take the plate, but she smiled, a warm grateful V for Victory by Elizabeth Arden smile, looking up slightly from under her eyelashes.

"Thank you...?"

"Franc, Madame."

"Franc! How very kind of you." She touched his arm.

"I have managed to find a bottle of decent wine, perhaps that might make the food a little easier to swallow. Let me entertain you in privacy in my tent."

"How kind!" Nancy said in a murmur, then raising her voice just a little. "The new plan being to lull me into a comfortable snooze, strangle me and then steal my money?"

Franc blinked.

"Madame, I..."

"Then tell London if they come asking that I wandered off into the forest and got eaten by wolves like Red Riding Hood? God, you're stupid." She grabbed the bowl out of his hands and upended it over his head, then threw the tin plate at his feet.

He gasped and tried to wipe it out of his eyes. "Bitch."

"Too bloody right, but while I am here you will call me Captain Wake, because that is the rank I've earned while you lot have been playing in the woods."

She turned toward Gaspard. "Where are your escape routes? Where are your lookouts? I've seen girl guides run a better camp. You've got too many men here out in the open and not a damn clue what to do with them other than sheep stealing. You here to fight the Germans or what?"

They stared back at her, silent, resistant.

She walked up to Gaspard on his packing crate. He stared at her, his thick jaws still chewing at his slop.

"I'm going up to the plateau. Fournier's men are going to be the best-armed, best-trained fighting force for fifty miles within a month. You are, and will always be, a bunch of amateurs." She raised her voice again. "When you are done starving and screwing about down here, come and join me. Until then, go fuck yourselves."

She spat a satisfyingly solid mass with just a little blood in it into Gaspard's stew, then went back to the door of the barn, picked up her pack and headed off into the darkness without looking back, following the rising ground. Under the treeline she stopped and rested her head against the trunk of a young birch tree. It shivered behind her. Footsteps. One man. A match flared, and she saw it was Tardivat, lighting his cigarette.

"This is the wrong track for the plateau, Captain," he said softly.

"I thought asking for directions might have ruined my exit," she replied, trying not to let too much relief creep into her voice.

"You may be right." She could feel the smile. "*Tant pis*, it will add only a mile or two to the walk. Are you ready?"

"I am ready."

24

E va Böhm was certain she had been cheated. The woman who sold her the two trunks she was now packing for her return to Berlin with Sonia had just had that French look, surly and superior at the same time, which Eva had encountered again and again when the residents of Marseille heard her German accent and schoolgirl French. She had been overcharged. Without doubt. It would be a relief to get home.

She felt a little spasm of guilt. It was wrong to feel relieved when her husband had to remain in France among these peasants and swindlers. News had arrived a week ago that he was being transferred to the Auvergne where thousands of young Frenchmen had been allowed by the corrupt authorities to flee into the hills rather than do their duty and go to Germany to work.

Now the trunk wouldn't close properly. She fiddled with the catch, caught her fingernail on it and was overwhelmed with a sudden desire to cry.

It was all so unfair.

"Mummy?"

She twisted round to see Sonia standing awkwardly in the doorway, her toy rabbit cradled in her arms.

"What is it, darling?"

"We won't forget Pumpkin, will we?" It was Markus who had named the rabbit Pumpkin and every time her daughter said it,

Eva felt her love for both of them swell in her chest. She opened her arms and Sonia tottered forward and dug her head into her neck. She smelled of lemon soap and pine trees.

"Of course not, sweetie. We'll take good care of him. You sleep with him tonight and then when the car comes in the morning, he'll sit beside us on the back seat all the way home." Her daughter mumbled something. "What was that, my love?"

"I don't want to leave Daddy. Please can we go with him?"

She wished they could, but they would be safer in Berlin. Or at least she hoped they would. The letters from her family and friends were growing increasingly dark. The bombing raids in Berlin, only bad news from Russia, the pathetic failure of the Führer's allies. Her faith in Hitler remained pure, but even she was worried that the weight would be too much for any man to bear, even him.

"Please? I shan't make noise or bother him when he needs to work."

Eva squeezed her again. Markus had snapped at her the other day for interrupting him when he was reading reports at home, and she remembered it. Of course she did. Markus doted on her, and Eva couldn't remember a time he had raised his voice to either of them before.

"Darling girl, I promise you Daddy would love to have both of us with him all the time. You must believe that. He was very sorry he was cross. He said so, didn't he?"

She felt Sonia nod. Her daughter was holding on to her hard, and Eva shifted her position so she could lean against the trunk and stretch her legs out a little on the thick pale carpet. So French to have these pale carpets, so impractical.

"That's right! But your father is a very important man, and the Führer has asked him to do a very important job for him, so we must be brave and go home and wait for him until it is done."

"Indeed."

Eva looked up. Markus was leaning against the door, watching them. Sonia detached herself from Eva and ran toward him, dropping Pumpkin the rabbit and throwing her arms around his legs. He picked her up then put out his hand to help Eva to her feet. She would miss him terribly.

"Can you have supper with us, Daddy?" Eva asked.

He kissed her, then his daughter. "That is why I am here! I could not miss having supper with my wife and little girl before I go off to do the important job!" Sonia giggled. "And also I wanted to introduce you to a new friend. He's going to go to Berlin with you to keep you company while I am gone."

He stepped back out into the hall and Eva followed. There was a cage by the door with a German shepherd puppy in it. It wagged its tail and yapped.

Sonia struggled out of her father's arms and launched herself forward, opening the cage door and receiving a liberator's welcome from the puppy in the form of yaps, licks and more tail-wagging.

Böhm put his arm around Eva's waist as they watched.

"Markus, really? A puppy? Now?"

"He's house-trained, I promise!" His face grew more serious. "He's the pup of one of the guard dogs. Look after him. Teach him to distrust strangers."

She laid her cheek against his tunic, drew a long slow breath. "I shall, darling."

25

Tardivat was silent as they walked, and Nancy was grateful for it. The climb was steep and the adrenaline which had powered her through the last few hours was fading. The ache in her head was making her sick and the bruising on her shoulders and side seemed to grow more painful with every step. She had already failed. Buckmaster had told her to turn Gaspard's troops into a decent fighting force, and she'd walked out on them within twenty-four hours of dropping into France. She had one ally, won at the cost of a parachute, and God knew how long he was going to stay with her. What did she have to offer to this Fournier anyway? Some cash, true enough, but that was obviously as likely to get her killed as anything. Where the hell was Denden?

They must have been walking for a couple of hours when Tardivat stopped and leaned against a low stone wall, overgrown with lichen.

"We rest."

Stopping was almost worse, every muscle in her body shook.

"I need my radio operator," she said at last. "He was landed near Montluçon and was supposed to meet me at Gaspard's camp."

Tardivat said nothing for a moment, then sniffed. "I can send a message in that direction. Tell him where we are going."

She looked at him sideways. She could just make out his profile in the darkness, but could not read his expression.

"What do you mean, send a message?"

"The Germans have few friends in these hills, and yes, Gaspard's men are sloppy and careless, but because of what they do, the Germans keep to the main roads. Messages are passed in the same way they always have been round here, from one farm hand to another, between the women. They will already know you are here and why. We shall ask them to watch for a stranger and tell him which way to come." He grinned. "Most of the gendarmes in the region would give him directions."

"Good." She stood up, and her body swayed. Only Tardivat's arm under her elbow stopping her falling entirely.

"No more walking tonight," he said firmly. "There is a cowshed over the next rise. We shall camp there tonight and I will send my message."

"I want to get to Fournier."

"Captain, it would be better, I think, if you met him when you are not about to collapse. First impressions, yes?"

She held out her hand in front of her. Even in the pale shadows of the moon, she could see it shake. He was right.

"Very well."

The cold when she woke up in the morning was sharp. She shrugged the blanket up over her shoulders for just one more second of warmth. It stank of smoke and animals. She opened her eyes. The building Tardivat had nominated for their camp last night was a low stone barn. Nancy rubbed her hands together under the blanket, and pins and needles shot up her arm. She thought of her bed in Marseille, the ironed linen sheets and silk pillows, the coffee and croissant waiting for her, Claudette twitching back the curtains and opening the shutters so the Mediterranean warmth and light could flood into the room. While Nancy drank her coffee, sitting up in bed, Claudette would draw her bath, ask about her plans for the day and for her instructions. Henri left every morning for the office before she even woke, but she would always put her hand into the hollow his body had left in the mattress, wishing him good morning.

And now she was filthy, sore, in a cow barn and so bloody cold she'd have welcomed the cows back in just to warm the place up a bit. Tardivat appeared in the doorway, a bundle of firewood under his arm. She decided it was perfectly reasonable to pretend to be asleep until he got the fire going, then once it looked like it had caught she "woke up" with a theatrical yawn, took the red satin pillow out from under her head and dusted it off.

Tardivat grinned. "Good morning, Captain."

"Good morning. Is there anything to eat? I could swallow that mutton slop Gaspard was eating last night now. I'm famished."

He sat cross-legged in front of the flames and opened his bag to reveal a half baguette and a wedge of deep gold Cantal cheese which smelled of summer meadows, and, god love him, two bottles of beer.

"You owe me forty francs," he said as she shuffled toward him and the fire on her bottom.

"You're kidding!"

He shrugged, tore off a share of the bread and cut the cheese with his knife. "You want the right people to know a British agent with money is here and intends to pay for what she needs, overpaying for your breakfast is a good way to spread the news."

Reasonable point. Nancy didn't reply until she had her share of the bread and cheese in her hand, and the bottle of beer propped up against her thigh.

"You Maquis have no sense of security, do you?"

He shrugged. "The people here won't tell the Germans anything. If they did their animals might all suddenly get sick and die overnight."

Nancy tried to chew more slowly. The food was good and particularly welcome after the miserable day yesterday, and the freezing night. She felt like her old self was beginning to stretch and wake up inside her shabby shell.

"You don't know what they're like," she said at last. "They've left you alone up here until now, but I think that's going to change. When they really get a grip on a place, the Germans go mad somehow. The farmers might stay quiet if they think they're going to lose their cows, but they'll start talking if someone puts a gun to their son's head."

Tardivat paused in his chewing and stared at her, seeming to weigh her words.

"I'm just saying, Tardi, be very, very careful what you tell folks from now on. If they don't know where we are, or what we're doing, they won't have to lie when that happens."

He shrugged, but Nancy reckoned he'd taken the point.

"Have you lived here all your life?" she asked, once the worst of her hunger and thirst was dealt with.

"Most of it," he said. "Apart from my time in the army. My father was a tailor in Aurillac; I learned my trade from him. My wife was born into a farming family and when we were first married we'd spend some weeks each year on their land. It is good land. Worth fighting for."

She watched him eat and realized she'd never enjoyed a lobster and champagne supper more than she was savoring this bread and cheese. But then it was a long time since she had been really, truly hungry. Perhaps she could fight for this France too, the France of Tardivat and his family, the farmers and villagers, as well as her France of sophistication and bright lights. Perhaps.

The purr of a motorbike. Nancy pointed to the underbrush and Tardivat nodded; they skipped over the wall at the edge of the track and kept their heads down. Nancy shifted until she could see through the gap where it had crumbled a little. The thrum of the motor became a throb. It wasn't until the bike had passed them that she stood up and whistled. The bike stopped and the man riding pillion turned round. Then he waved and hopped down from the seat.

"Denden! My God, I'm glad to see you."

She chased up the path toward him.

"Nancy! You look an absolute fright."

He flung his arms around her, and Nancy shut her eyes and squeezed him hard, drinking him in. He chuckled then pushed her away, holding her by her shoulders at arm's length.

"Now, who is that rather dashing man lurking in the hedgerows?"

"His name is Tardivat. He found me in a tree."

"Obviously a lucky fellow, but tell me everything. All I know is that security here is an absolute joke. A peasant with a face like the arse end of a sheep flagged us down on the road, and said, calm as you like, that the other British agent is trekking up to the plateau to join Fournier. There I was with all my pass phrases and cover stories gaping at her like a trout pulled fresh from the stream."

She laughed. "I know, Buckmaster would shoot the lot of them. I'll tell you everything. How did you manage to get a lift on a motorcycle?"

The man on the motorbike had turned his machine round. He passed them with a curt nod to which Denden replied with a wave, and blew him a kiss. The rider frowned and accelerated away from them.

"Oh bless his cotton socks, he's gone shy," Denden said. "Obviously I've been making friends, doing a rather better job of it than you by the looks of things."

Tardivat watched the motorbike retreat down the hill, then approached them. Nancy made the introductions.

"Delighted, I'm sure. Now carry this, will you?" Denden thrust a canvas bag, square-edged, into Tardivat's chest, who held on to it with a look of skepticism and surprise. "It's the almighty radio, Mr. Tardivat, and our lives depend on it, so be a love and don't drop it. Now lead on, and Nancy and I will trot along behind you and have a bit of a catch-up."

26

The miserable camp on the edge of the plateau made Gaspard's shit-covered field look like a paradise, but Nancy had been here ten minutes and no one had knocked her over the head yet, so on that score at least things were improving.

Tardivat beckoned them over to a lank-limbed man in his forties with a heavy brow and a rifle over his shoulder. Fournier. Nancy had counted thirty men with them and spotted two barrack buildings hidden under the trees and well covered in foliage. An enemy plane could buzz over at a hundred feet and not spot them. That was an improvement too.

"When's the next London transmission?" she muttered out of the side of her mouth.

"Ten minutes, ducks, but there won't be anything for us on it! We'll have to tell them we haven't been eaten by wolves before they'll send us anything. Not to mention they'll need coordinates for a drop site. They won't be listening for my signal until tomorrow at three."

"Can you get the radio together in ten minutes? I want to make a point."

He looked at her then sighed. "It'll be ready and buffed to a shine."

Nancy went forward and put out her hand to Fournier with a smile. He shook it, but did not smile back.

"I'm Captain Nancy Wake," she said. "And London wants

me to give all the weapons I can to Gaspard and his men. But Gaspard and I did not get on. Would you like them instead?"

He looked her up and down, a cool assessing look. "Perhaps. What have you got to offer, Captain Wake?" He stressed her rank, making it sound as contemptuous an insult as anything she'd heard at Gaspard's camp. She had a sudden picture of herself trekking around the Auvergne until hell froze over, looking for a group of fighting men who could get over themselves long enough to take what she was offering with a polite "thank you."

No time for that.

"I'd be happy to explain," she said.

The Maquisards watched as Denden put the radio receiver together and Nancy sat on the grass next to the set, watching them. Undernourished the lot of them, and it didn't look as if they were taking proper care of their weapons—not that they had many. Mostly they were very, very young. Early twenties. They should have been chasing girls in the villages and annoying the graybeards, not rotting up here in the forest, dodging the Germans trying to draft them into factory work in the Reich, or preparing to sacrifice themselves to drive them out of France. Nancy once more felt that wave of anger she had felt in Vienna and Berlin rising in her throat. The world was already a broken, violent place; why did the Nazis have to make it worse with their poison? That rally she had witnessed in Berlin—the wild abandon on the faces of the people in the crowd as they screamed their enthusiasm for the unreasoning hate spilling from the stage.

"It's time, Nancy," Denden said.

She pulled herself out of the clamor of that sweating auditorium and into the heavy peace of the Auvergne forests. "Switch it on," she said.

A hiss of static, then a voice broke through. "This is London," the voice said in French, and the men lifted their heads, Fournier turning toward them. "The French talking to the French. But first some personal messages. Jean has a long mustache. There is a fire at the insurance agency." The Maquis exchanged bemused glances. "The frog croaks thrice." A couple of them laughed.

Nancy grinned. "This isn't gibberish. It's code. London confirming with agents like me across France that parachute drops are coming tonight. It can bring you canned meat and juice. Chocolate and cigarettes."

"French cigarettes?" one of the Maquis asked.

"Son, you look too young to smoke, but yes, French cigarettes." The boy blushed. "And French tents to protect you from the French rain and boots to tramp through the French mud." They were all grinning at her now. Well, all except Fournier. "Best of all we can supply you with arms, plans and intelligence. Sten machine guns, plastic explosive, timed detonators, grenades, revolvers, a target list so we know exactly where to hit the Germans where it will hurt most, and plans on how to take them out."

Fournier lit a cigarette and blew a thin stream of smoke out of the corner of his mouth. "And you just give us this, yes? Out of the kindness of your English hearts?"

Any more of a sneer and he'd pull something. Bloody Frenchmen, Nancy thought. Sure, she'd married one of them, but en masse they were the most pig-headed, touchy...

"There's no charge, Fournier," she said, meeting his eye, "if that's what you mean. You won't have to sell your best pig to get hold of a case of machine guns."

"That's not what I mean, and you know it."

She nodded. "All requests to London go through me. And I've seen how the English are sweating and bankrupting themselves to get you this stuff, so no bloody way I'm going to see it wasted. I'm going to train you in how to use these weapons, I'm going to insist on proper security measures and I'm going to rain merry hell on anyone who can't keep up. You'll launch no attacks without the nod from me, and remember this is all about getting ready for when the Allies invade and liberate France, so no settling scores or pursuing vendettas. We coordinate."

"We're not your bitches," Fournier growled.

"And I'm not yours. We work together. That's the deal. Now tell me what you need and let us deliver you...salvation."

The men all looked to Fournier. He didn't smile, but he did nod. The men relaxed. Fournier pulled a neat black notebook out of his top pocket.

"I have a list of things we need, *Captain*."

He still managed to say her rank as if it hurt him to make the sounds, but it was a start and hey—still not knocked out or tied to a chair.

"Let's go through it then," Nancy said, then twisted round to Denden. "Think you can put your box of tricks away for now. Go make friends."

"Ooh good, you can be strict Mummy and I can be Daddy who spoils his pretty French children." She flinched. "What did I say, darling?"

"Nothing. Get going."

27

Buckmaster raised his eyebrows when he saw the message from Nancy. Garrow recognized the gesture as the equivalent of some men going into full cardiac arrest.

"At least she's alive, sir."

"Yes. There is that. Though of course I sent her to establish links with Gaspard, and she's holed up with the dregs on the plateau. Southgate taken too. That is a blow."

He continued to stare at the paper.

"I'm sure, sir, with this list she is aiming high. She can't possibly expect us to drop all of this for a ragtag group such as Fournier's. Let me revise it to something more in keeping."

Garrow reached out to take the decoded message back, but Buckmaster gave a tiny shake of his head.

"We don't second-guess our men or women in the field, Garrow. Not unless we have good reason. Perhaps Captain Wake is overreaching, but it is just as possible that she intends to put on a show for her new friends, and possibly for Gaspard too. She certainly knows how to make an impression."

"For Gaspard, sir?"

Buckmaster laid down the sheet and started carefully stuffing his pipe. "You read the reports Southgate managed to send before he was taken. They all know which of their rivals have taken a shit before the privy door has banged. If we make this drop..." He paused stuffing his pipe to point the stem at the paper in front of him. "Gaspard and all his crew will know about our munificence by breakfast. Give her all of it. And add her care package."

Garrow retrieved the message from his table with a nod. Then cleared his throat.

"Yes, Garrow?"

"May I impress on her the time factor, sir?"

Buckmaster held a match to his pipe and inhaled in short little huffs until he had the tobacco burning as he wanted. "Yes. Tell her to knock them into shape quickly. By whatever means necessary. She has six weeks to make those men into a useful fighting force."

Garrow left the office with a spring in his step, or something like it. For the first time since he had escaped France he felt a surge of excitement. The invasion of France was coming. Soon. Six weeks wasn't a number Buckmaster had just pulled out of the air. He glanced out of the window. Below him Baker Street was stirring into life. He looked at the sandbags, the tape on the windows, and wondered what the street would look like when the war was done—the lights on, men in suits rather than uniform, women like Nancy back to shopping for dinner parties rather than queuing for necessities, and Hitler and all the hate and misery he stood for nothing but a memory. He wished he was out there again, but though his French was good, he still spoke it with a Scottish accent. He'd spent those months in the south running escape routes, having languished for a year in a prisoner of war camp. It had been an accident, and he'd got away with it only through the winking negligence of a few officials and sheer luck. When the Germans had arrived in the south the friendly officials had begun to disappear and his luck had dried up. Still, at least his knowledge of the country and the language was of use in "D" section, and he understood what Nancy and agents like her were up against. And soon, very soon, all the plans they had been making, all the people they had smuggled in behind enemy lines, would be put into action.

"The game's afoot," he said to himself with a wry smile. "Now what the hell do I put in Nancy's care package?"

"Talking to yourself, Captain?" said Vera Atkins as she climbed the stairs, her handbag over one arm. "First sign of madness, you know."

"I would have thought the first sign of madness was working here, Miss Atkins. Now, I need your advice."

28

Nancy was having a shitty night. A brilliant, victorious, glorious, but still epically shitty night. The landing site on the flank of the plateau was perfect for a drop, and she'd managed to shriek and bully Fournier and his men until they got the signal fires built and lit. The exchange of torch code with the aircraft had gone fine, and the moonlit sky had filled with a gratifyingly large number of parachutes. Tardivat would be able to sew his wife a ball gown or seven out of this lot. Fournier was impressed. Surprised, impressed, if not a bit shaken up by the success, which was exactly what Nancy wanted. So of course he had to prove he was top dog, even while his men were still staring up at the sky like shepherds watching the angels announce the holy birth.

Nancy was coordinating the men, removing the parachutes and carrying the heavy containers to the two waiting carts. Fournier strolled into the middle of the landing site as the last parachute was deflating and opened the container right out in the open. He fished out a carton of cigarettes, waving them over his head, then tore out a pack, fished out a fag and lit it, all in the time it took Nancy to cross the pasture behind him. Out of the corner of her eye she could see the other men—no way to hold them back now, splitting open containers and handing round the contents. Damn it. Some of them had found bottles of brandy and were already working out the corks.

"You're dead, Fournier," Nancy said. He turned and found himself looking into the barrel of her revolver.

Another Maquis, one of the former members of the Spanish freedom brigade now fighting alongside Fournier, wandered over to see the fun, and handed Fournier the bottle of brandy. He took it and swallowed a good pull then took another drag on his cigarette. A long inhale and exhale.

"Then at least I die happy."

Nancy's trigger finger itched. "You think the Germans don't notice our planes coming over? They aren't as thick as you. We've got an hour, maybe two, to get all of this stuff out of here and cover the fire sites or we're blown. And you're having a cigarette out in the middle of a sodding field."

He inhaled again and blew the smoke right in her face, then yawned. "Just enjoying our new friendship, Captain." Then he turned away again. "Right then, lads. Let's get this shit home."

And that was that—they were taking orders from him again now. Nancy remembered what one of her instructors in Beaulieu had told her. Never pull your gun unless you are going to use your gun. Shit. She holstered the weapon and got her hands under the container, great metal tubes six foot long and heavy as all hell. The Spaniard looked confused: a well-brought-up lad wouldn't want to see a woman struggle with something heavy on her own, but he couldn't work out the power play. Fournier gave him a nod and he took the other end. Nancy raged in herself. These men. At least she looked better carrying the gear rather than just watching while Fournier ordered the men around, but he'd won this round. And so easily, while she had to be perfect every moment not to slither back down in their opinion.

Denden brought her the care package while she was sulking over a fire on the edge of the encampment just before dawn. He approached with exaggerated care, which would have made her laugh normally, but not today. Fournier's men were gathered under the edge of the tree line, working their way through the brandy and fags. At least the guns, explosives and ammo were safely stowed and Tardivat had commandeered the parachute silk. As the men drank, a few of them glanced toward her. She could tell by the muddled, schoolboy laughter that they were talking about her. Denden caught her eye as she looked up, her face warm with the firelight, and dropped the pantomime creep.

"Present from Baker Street for you," he said.

She took it, a square package wrapped in thick hessian and string, with her code name, Hélène, on a rectangular postcard. He sat down on the ground next to her and pulled a bottle of brandy from under his coat, took a long pull then offered it to her. It was good brandy, but it burned her throat and seemed to chill rather than warm her.

"Open your present, then let's get smashed," he said.

She didn't bother smiling, but cut away the string and undid the wrapping. The note she shoved into her pocket; it was too dark to read it anyway, but the gift made her smile. Cold cream, a Parisian make, very expensive, just what she would use to remove her makeup after a night out with Henri in the clubs of Marseille. She unscrewed the lid and held it to her nose. Just a subtle suggestion of rose and lavender. She was there for a moment, in their bedroom, her silk dressing gown whispering around her as she left her dressing table and walked toward Henri in bed, in their warm soft bed, looking at her with love, with hunger. Her throat closed and for a moment she was afraid she was going to cry.

"I'm beginning to think," Denden said, his words slurring just a tiny amount, "that Buckmaster might have been a bit off sending a woman and a queer to beat these horrible boys into shape." He hiccupped. "Not that I'm unwilling to give it a go."

"How come they get to laugh with each other, get pissed and

fight together, they can even cry together, damn them," she said, "but me, no. If I slip for one second…"

She took the bottle again and drowned the curl of self-pity in her belly.

"Give that back, you witch," Denden said and grabbed it out of her hand.

"They can't decide if they want to murder me, sleep with me, protect me or worship me, Denden."

"Isn't that always the way between boys and girls? They want your body, but they are scared of it too." He passed back the bottle. "You're going to have to be their sister, somehow. None of the other roles available to you will work."

"Roles?"

"Darling, I've been in theater all my life. Everything's a role, a mask. Just remember we are so busy hiding behind our own masks that we are generally crap at noticing everyone else is just a bad actor in their own story too."

Nancy stood up, hating everyone. "I'm going for a swim."

"That's the spirit," Denden said, his voice growing sleepy. "I think I'm drunk enough to pass out now." He pulled his jacket around himself and settled onto the ground. "Thank you, Buckmaster, for one night's rest at least."

Fournier's camp was cold, wet and, until tonight at least, poorly equipped, but camping up here did have one big advantage. At the base of a slope ten minutes downhill was a pool, fed by one of the hot springs that gave Chaudes-Aigues its name. Dawn was just creeping up the valley as Nancy pulled off her loose combat trousers and unbuttoned her shirt. Then she stepped out of her knickers and unhooked her brassiere. Every stitch made in France, and any English laundry marks cut out by the staff at Baker Street. She stepped cautiously into the water. The surface was cold, but just below it she found a warm current.

It worked its way around her muscles, those new sinewy muscles she'd developed in the weeks of physical training. For a moment she laughed. When war was declared in September 1939, Nancy had been staying at the Savoy in London, on her way to a health resort in Hampshire to lose those extra pounds she'd accrued eating lobster in butter sauce and drinking champagne with Henri.

Would he recognize her now? He might like this new figure, she thought. Still a good pair of tits, but her hips were narrower, the soft pillow of her belly had gone, leaving it flat and hard to the touch, and her arms were sharply defined. Dressed as a French housewife, she looked like a young woman who'd been living on short rations for four years; naked, she looked like an Amazon.

She dived down into the water, let it take her weight and felt the tension ease slowly out of her bones. She considered her conversation with Denden. What did she need to be in these men's eyes to lead them? A sister to tease and protect, a lover to defend or a goddess to worship? Goddess wouldn't work. Too remote. She needed to trust and be trusted. A lover? What if she did take one of the lads off into the woods? Perhaps she could find a potential lion among Fournier's men and seduce him into becoming her champion. She dived again, testing herself to see how long she could hold her breath. No. She might gain one ally that way, but she'd lose the rest. And the idea of any man other than Henri touching her...No.

She broke the surface and filled her lungs with the morning air. The dawn was upon her now and she looked around at the steep wooded slopes of the mountains, the clearing sky and the shivering leaves with wonder. She swam lazily over to the rock where she had left her clothes, then she saw a shiver in the undergrowth where no breezes reached. An animal? There were wild boar in the forests, but she hadn't seen any of their trails near here and nothing else living in the forest was big enough to shake the bushes that much. Except men. Could a German patrol have come this far into the woods? A villager? But there wasn't a farm or hamlet for a mile.

Still in the water, she snatched her revolver out from under the towel and pointed it toward the movement, her free hand gripping on to the high rocks around the pool.

"Show yourselves!" The bushes stayed still. Had she imagined it? A couple of nights of bad sleep and she had started seeing things. Then she remembered that schoolboy laughter around the camp fire and suddenly she understood. "Now, you little shits, unless you want to risk a bullet!"

She let off one round, aiming high. It thwacked into the bark of a young oak with a satisfying punch.

From the bushes, three men emerged. The Spaniards—three of the men who had actually had fighting experience. She had thought better of them. They held their hands above their heads.

"Rodrigo, Mateo and Juan," she said, enunciating their names very clearly. "You stupid bastards. Let me get this straight. You boys survived a civil war in Spain, came all the way here to fight the fascists, and I could've shot you dead—*for what?*"

She stepped out of the water, still keeping her gun on them and moving slowly. No way was she going to slip. They flushed, stared, their eyes fluttering all over her flesh, those muscled arms, the swell of her breasts, the dark brown fur between her legs. She let them look, felt them suck in the sight of her. Then, as she remained there, still silent and with a revolver pointing right at them, she felt them growing confused. Their eyes finally returned to hers and their shame flared in their faces.

"Yes, I have a cunt. You think that makes me weak? That I'm a little girl who will run away at the sight of blood? Juan!" She shifted her aim to the oldest of the men. "Is that what you think, Juan?"

"No, *señora.*"

She kept her aim, her hand steady as a rock. "Mateo, hand me my towel."

164

He ran past her to grab it and put it into her free hand, trying very hard not to look at her at all, then returned to his place between his two compatriots and lifted his hands again. Nancy managed to suppress a smile.

"No, *señora*," she said. "That's right. Because I'm a grown woman, aren't I, Rodrigo?"

Rodrigo was staring fixedly at a point six inches above her head. "Yes, *señora*."

"And do you know what that means, Mateo?"

He shook his head.

"It means, you idiots, I've been bleeding half my goddam life." She studied them, one after the other, all of them looking into the clouds.

She uncocked the pistol and let her hand fall to her side, then started to dry her hair, still not making any attempt to cover herself. They still kept their arms raised.

"Now, when you address me, you address me by rank. I am Captain Wake to you, got it?"

"Yes, Captain," they chorused. She didn't even bother looking at them.

"Good, now sod off."

They ran for it, back up the slope toward camp and, shivering in the chill, Nancy dressed.

She climbed the path slowly after them. Most of the men had snatched some sleep where they lay, others were finishing the last of the brandy even as they started boiling water for their breakfast mash of oats. Nancy saw the three Spanish men, away from the others, looking sullen and guilty. Fournier was still swilling the last of the brandy from his bottle by the embers of his fire. He saw her and leered, his eyes traveling from head to toe.

"Did you give our boys a good show?" he said.

She didn't plan it. Didn't think. She went straight at him,

165

covering the ground between them at a run, then smacked him across the side of his face with the back of her hand, knocking the cigarette from between his lips and making him drop the bottle into the embers. He scrambled to his feet, a good six inches taller than her, and raised his fist. Then hesitated. She spat into his face. He struck, knocking her sideways to the ground and started to turn away. She struck out with her boot, catching him square on the shin and making him yell. He fell on her then, punching into her sides, while she held her arms up to defend her head. She didn't make a sound.

With a roar of rage, Fournier got to his feet and started to walk away. Nancy could feel the blood on her lips, but she couldn't feel the pain yet. She rolled onto her feet and grabbed his smoldering fag from the ground and launched herself at him again, landing her full weight on his back so he fell forward onto the earth, the breath coming out of him in a sudden grunt, and she drove the smoldering butt into the side of his cheek, then got her arm around his neck in a choke hold. He grabbed at her wrist but he couldn't get purchase, thrashing and trying to throw off her weight. She could feel him beginning to weaken.

"Captain…" said one of the French fighters, keeping a careful distance, softly. Pleading even.

She dropped her hold and stood up, then walked away toward the high path. Behind her she could hear Fournier choking and cursing and the murmurs of the men helping him up.

Well, they weren't fucking laughing now.

29

They watched her. Not with smirks on their faces any more, but there was nothing friendly about the looks she got either. The day after her fight with Fournier, Nancy kicked them out of their sleeping bags as soon as it was light and ordered them into ranks. News of the drop had brought two other groups of men who had been hiding in the hills all winter to join them. There were forty of them now. Not enough, nowhere near enough, but enough to make a start. All local lads apart from the Spanish boys.

Fournier was in the front row, at the far right, staring, but saying nothing and giving no hint to the men about which way to jump either. Below them the patchwork of trees and pasture flowed down into the valley, in a million shifting greens, a land to love, but not their land any more. Not while one German in uniform was within France's borders. They knew that. Their families knew that. Then she realized she had the key in her hand to unlock their stubborn hearts.

She chose her words carefully, but kept it simple. No more brandy and no more cigarettes until they had learned to handle the weapons that had been dropped, planned escape routes from the camp and started on a full program of marksmanship and physical training. But she had something else to offer them.

"The liberation of France is coming," she told them, her voice raised and clear. "And we need to be ready when it does. You don't want us and our guns and our gold, fine. Your funeral. You can stay up here and be slaughtered by the first company of SS soldiers they decide to send up here after you. I'll take my treasure somewhere else. But do the training, and it won't be just you who gets British help. Any of you have family, wives, children, mothers struggling on their own while you're up here?"

A few of the men nodded.

"I'll give them fifty francs a day, every day you train. First weapons session is in an hour. If you want your family to eat, be there."

Who was going to leave their people to starve for the sake of their pride? Not these men. For the next week they did what they were told. Sort of.

When she briefed them on tactics, they stared over her head and yawned. When she showed them how to put the Bren guns together, they chatted to each other in undertones. When she sent them on PT runs, they rambled. On Sunday afternoon they practiced marksmanship, and as Nancy was demonstrating the double tap, a bullet bit into the bark six inches above her head.

She shot at her target and struck it before she turned round. Fournier was holding his rifle loosely in the crook of his arm. He smiled at her for the first time since their fight. It was not a nice smile.

That evening she gathered addresses from the men and told them they'd get half the money promised. They swore at her, but under their breath.

"Shall I tell your mother you said that?" she asked one Maquisard from Chaudes-Aigues.

He looked startled. "No, Captain." He scratched behind his ear and grinned. "Not unless you want her up here trying to take it out of my backside."

She dismissed him with a nod, then went back to her usual

spot at the edge of the tree line where Tardivat was working at his silk supply and Denden was setting up to listen to the BBC transmissions. She flopped down onto the grass next to him.

"What do you think, dearie?" he murmured. "Shall we chuck it all in and pop up to Paris for a cocktail and a show? I'll take you dancing."

She turned onto her stomach. "I would, if I didn't know perfectly well you'd ditch me for the first handsome Frenchman we met."

"I do love a Frenchman," he said musingly.

"How can I get these bastards to pay attention to me, Denden?"

"Just do your job, respect yourself and don't give a crap what they think. It's their funeral."

Nancy felt a black rage swirl in her gut. "That's exactly the point, Denden. If they don't train, if they don't listen, they are going to die. The odds are against us anyway. If they try and fight the Germans as they are now, they are going to get slaughtered. And they'll die without doing any damage. I hate the Boche, but they are well trained. These boys…they are going to be wiped out."

"Well, yes, that would be a shame," Denden said as he twitched the dial. A sudden burst of speech, French and very clear, came tripping out of the speaker.

"The Germans are our friends, the true enemy of every Frenchmen are the traitors who undermine their efforts for peace." Denden put his hand to the tuning knob again, but Nancy stopped him. "We know these vagabonds and criminals who steal the food from your mouths and attack our allies on orders from communists and the treacherous English are not the real French. Remember all it takes is a word to one of our friends and they can be scrubbed from our beautiful land. Wives and mothers of France, daughters of France, these men leave you to battle on alone while they hide in the shadows. Let us defend you. Let us protect you."

"Weasly sods," Denden said, turning down the volume. "And these guys are almost as bad as the propaganda says they are."

Tardivat looked up from his sewing. "With respect, you have delivered guns, yes, but these men came to fight. You want them to go to school."

"They'll be no bloody good in a fight without training," Nancy snapped back. "And we need them for the actions *after* the invasion. Can't risk wasting lives and weapons taking them on a little field trip just for the fun of it."

Tardivat snipped a thread and gave one of those French shrugs that seemed to communicate more than should be possible. "*You* have training. Show them what you can do with it and perhaps they'll want to learn then. Fournier's a good man, he was a soldier before the war, but he's never trained for anything but leading a hundred men into a field to shoot at a hundred other men in different uniforms."

"Give them a taster of what we might get up to when the invasion kicks in you mean?" Nancy said. "Whet their appetites?"

Tardivat smiled at her. "An *amuse-bouche*, a salty snack of an attack."

"You can't risk it, Nancy!" Denden huffed.

"But if I took a small group..." She sat up again. "Denden, where is this shit transmitting from?"

"Close, I'd say. Chaudes-Aigues would be my guess."

"I might have a look around while I'm in town handing out disbursements and picking our next landing site tomorrow." Denden pursed his lips, but didn't argue. "Tardi, you haven't given me your address. I want to drop off your pay to your wife."

He shook his head. "That is not necessary."

"I won't blunder in saying, 'Hello all, I'm a British Agent, you know.' I can be discreet."

He still didn't look at her. "That is not the point, *Capitan*. My wife has everything she needs."

"Fine." Nancy lay back on the ground. She was growing used

to the earth of France as a bed, even if she hadn't slept much since she'd jumped out of that damned plane, but as she lay there, thinking about that voice on the radio, what Tardivat had said about an aperitif to sharpen the appetite, she began to feel a plan forming, and thought that perhaps tonight she might sleep very well indeed.

30

By the time Nancy was halfway through her trip handing out money to the dependents of the men in Fournier's band, she was glowing. For one thing, riding a bike along the forested tracks had given her time to think, and for another—and my God what a blessing it was—she had had the chance to spend some time with women.

She had been greeted like an old friend in hamlets and villages all the way to Chaudes-Aigues and back. She told all of them their son or husband was a credit to them, a brave fighting man, vital to the fight for liberty, and was rewarded with smiles and hugs; they touched her arm or held her hand as she walked to the door. It was the war—no French countrywoman would be so affectionate with a stranger in peacetime—and Nancy knew she was a proxy for the missing men, a connection with the boys in the woods. Still, she took comfort in it.

She learned something useful about almost all the men up on the plateau. This one had a weak chest, that one was in love with a girl in the next town who didn't want to be the wife of a farmer. Another loved birds, the feathered sort, and another was a superb fisherman. Jean-Clair loved to climb, and before the war would spend all his pay from the garage where he worked traveling in the Alps. She counted out little piles of notes into the hands of these hungry families, played games with the children and flirted with the old men and young boys still trying to do the work on the farm.

By the time she reached Chaudes-Aigues she was sure she had something on most of them. She had two families to meet in the town, and the second was the elderly mother of the lad who had sworn at Nancy only the day before. The old lady introduced herself with a dry, light handshake as Madame Hubert, and led Nancy into the kitchen with a faltering step, but Nancy noticed as they chatted the woman seemed to drop a dozen years.

"You will be careful in town, Madame Wake," she said, examining Nancy over the rim of her teacup with a sharp eye. "I think the Germans are beginning to pay more attention to us here."

"Why do you say that?" Nancy said carefully.

"The mayor is not brushing his coat, and the local gendarme is drinking too much. They are growing nervous. More cars are going through town, running on petrol, and with men in them I do not know, uniforms I do not recognize. Nervous men, petrol and strangers—I think that means Gestapo, don't you?"

"No one else has said anything, Madame," Nancy said.

Madame Hubert waved her hand. "Pfft, they do not sit at their window all day looking out into the square with their knitting on their lap as I do."

Fair point. "Thank you for telling me." Nancy studied Madame Hubert's calm, lined face. "Most people are afraid to speak of the Gestapo, Madame."

Madame Hubert shrugged. "I am too old to be scared; my son is too young. It is the men of the town here—a little too old to fight, a little too rich to lose everything—they are afraid. They bluster about the Boche in the café in the square, then take a little trip to Montluçon, perhaps to whisper in a friendly Nazi's ear, do them a little service. Like Pierre Frangrod. His mother, God rest her soul, would be ashamed of him. He gifted the Germans a field she left him to build one of their radio transmitters so it can broadcast that...shit into our homes. And it is a good piece of land too. They got his soul into the bargain."

Nancy had spotted the transmitter on the way in. Felt her mouth water when she saw it too.

"Madame Hubert, the saints have brought us together. I would like to do something about that transmitter. How well do you know the land?"

When Madame Hubert got up to fetch paper and pencil there was nothing faltering about her walk at all. She was grinning as she sketched the terrain and the tracks and roads leading to and from the station.

"I walk past it every day. It is just on the edge of town. Always at least six men on guard. Wire fencing, searchlights here and here. It is a strong signal; they have their generator there."

Nancy studied the map on the carefully polished table. "Madame Hubert, you are a gift from God."

The old lady looked pleased and straightened the crochet doily between them. "Would you like to meet my cousin Georges? He helped build the transmitter building and he hates the Germans. You can trust him."

If the Gestapo were circling the area it was not a time to make new friends, but Nancy liked this woman, liked her very much.

"Yes, please."

"Come tomorrow afternoon then, Madame Wake. He will be here. He is sad he is too old to join my Georges on the plateau with you. It will cheer him to help you."

Nancy looked around the neat, modest home again. "Are you sure you aren't afraid for your boy?"

Madame Hubert stopped smiling. "I would rather be afraid for him and proud, than know he was safe and despise him. That is why I am glad my friend"—she tapped the map—"died in thirty-seven before she was forced to realize her boy was a coward."

Nancy scouted the land, and Georges turned out to be an absolute treasure. On the ride home the following day Nancy made her plan. They would go tonight. When she got back to the camp, she stowed her bicycle in the broken-down hay barn in the corner of the field and then went to find Fournier's men, hunched over their dinner. They looked bored.

"I need five men."

"What for?" one of the men asked.

"It's not a menu, Jean-Clair. I'll tell you what for when you've volunteered."

The silence stretched until Nancy could feel it in the air.

"I'll come." Tardivat, bless his parachute-stealing soul.

"So will we." It was one of the Spaniards, Mateo. "We owe amends." He led his brothers with him. Nancy was surprised—they had kept away from her since that moment by the springs and she hadn't been to Spain and given money to any of their families. She put out her hand and Mateo shook it; Rodrigo and Juan did the same.

She raised her eyebrow. "Any other *Frenchmen* want to fight the Boche?"

That got them. There was a shuffling among the men, but Fournier moved before the others.

"I'll come. Let's see what you can do, Captain." Nancy looked him up and down. "I assume you meant to miss me in the forest?"

"Of course." She put out her hand and he shook it, but as if he feared some sort of contagion. She put her hand on his shoulder. "Your little sister told me yesterday you can shoot a swallow out of the sky. You are our sniper."

She pulled them aside and took them through the plan, then showed them Madame Hubert's map and Cousin Georges's plans. "Each one of you will be able to draw the map of the compound from memory before we leave. Fail, and I won't take you. You'll just have to stay at home with the other little boys. One hour."

She dropped the plan in the grass at their feet. Mateo bent down and picked it up as she stalked off to put her own kit together.

Denden strolled over to join her. "You don't want me to come, Nancy?"

She shook her head. "You're too valuable."

"Good, because I hate all that running about and shooting." He gave a theatrical shudder.

"If it all goes tits up," Nancy went on, "get a message through to London and go back to Gaspard. You might get on with him better than I did."

"Hardly think that's likely. But I'll try." He rocked against her, his hands in his pockets. "I'd rather you didn't die though."

"I'm touched."

She stood up and checked her watch. Time to get something to eat and maybe sleep for twenty minutes before drilling the men.

"Nancy, how did you know the Spaniards would volunteer?" Denden asked, looking at her with his head on one side. "Tardivat was always going to. He seems to have adopted us, the funny old stick. Fournier would never stay here, he'd lose too much face. But the Spaniards?"

She shrugged. "They owe me. But what are you getting at, Denden?"

"I'm getting at the fact that you are, dear girl, something of a trick cyclist yourself. You are taking with you the only five men in this group who have some military experience, but you made it seem as if it all just happened by accident."

31

Rain. Rain. Rain. Sometimes the Auvergne felt more like England than France given the weather, and this was only the start. As the daylight faded they could all see the thunderclouds forming above the extinct volcanoes like the memory of ash clouds, the flickers of lightning flashing the sunset. Water gurgled through the thin soil of the pine forests, and roared and plunged among the mixed sections of oak and beech.

The men had learned the map and knew the plan. None of them had had much experience with explosives, other than Nancy back in Britain. She handed out the blocks of TNT and the time pencils to fire them, and took them through the basics. They were certainly paying attention this evening. Even Fournier—though as a sniper he didn't get to play with the explosives—couldn't resist shuffling closer to listen as she explained how to crush the tip of the pencil to set it going, and where to place the charge.

The minute they were out of sight of the camp, something changed. A feeling in the air and in Nancy's blood, that at first she couldn't place, couldn't recognize. She thought of that last night in Piccadilly, heading out with her makeup and best dress on, knowing she'd be spending the next hours with her friends, drinking champagne and causing as much trouble as she could manage. That was it—she was excited. And the men around her were too.

The light had almost faded from the sky when they turned off the main path to make their way quietly through a dense patch of woodland. The compound was on the edge of the town, and there was always a chance of running into someone in the woods the nearer they got, though in this weather Nancy reckoned most people would stay home.

The rain had soaked her hair and she could feel the chill kiss of it on her neck, but the forest floor was slick, not muddy, and the constant smatter of rain on the leaves covered the sound of their approach. The world smelled fresh, full of vegetable growth. Nancy lifted her hand as she spotted the lights of the compound through the trees. She had bicycled past here twice since her chat with Madame Hubert, both times in her disguise as an ordinary French housewife with her string bag over her handlebars, exchanging smiles with the guards.

Her informant certainly had keen eyes. As she had said, there were six guards: two at the gate, two patrolling singly around the perimeter and two taking their ease inside the building. The tower itself, a lacework of steel bars needling into the sky, was anchored in three places with steel guy ropes fixed in reinforced concrete blocks. The single-story main building was roughly divided into three: the generator room, the main transmitter room and then a couple of offices with a garage round the back.

The six of them stood in the rain, looking down on it.

"Are you ready?" Nancy said.

"Yes." They each said it, no sarcasm, no rolling of the eyes. Like greyhounds straining at the leash.

It was a simple plan. Fournier would take a position Nancy had scouted out for him a hundred yards down the road, splitting his role between watching their backs during the attack and disrupting any reinforcements coming from the barracks building in the town. If things went well, he'd just sit on his arse, wet and uncomfortable in the branches of an oak watching them take out the whole place. They'd be back into the woods before the

Germans knew what was happening. A nice idea, but unlikely. Nancy's instructors had drilled it into her head often enough: things never went that well.

Mateo, Rodrigo and Juan were in charge of taking out the guards patrolling the perimeter and placing the charges on the three concrete blocks holding the transmitter tower in place. Nancy and Tardivat would take the guards on the gates silently, then either sneak into the building and plant charges or smash the windows of the transmitter and generator rooms and chuck in grenades to destroy the equipment. What could go wrong?

Everything. But this—this was what she had trained for. This was what she wanted. She thought of that nameless Jew she'd seen whipped through the streets of Vienna; the boy, his brains scattered over the cobbles of the Old Quarter in Marseille. This was for them.

"Get into position, Fournier," she said.

He slung his rifle over his shoulder and disappeared into the darkness. Five slow minutes passed, then they heard a low whistle—his signal he was in place. Nancy lifted her binoculars and watched the patrolling guards pass the main gates. You could tell their mood from their walk, rain capes hanging sodden round their shoulders, collars up, heads down, casting envious looks at their two colleagues protected from the thundering rain by their guard boxes either side of the gate. They walked slowly, bored, miserable and deafened by the rain. Good. They passed out of the lights at the main gate.

"Mateo, go!"

The three Spaniards melted into the darkness.

Nancy waited. Five minutes she had told them. Five minutes to take them out, and cut the links of the chain fence. Then she and Tardivat would take the two guards out front. Her heart pulsed hard as a flash of lightning in the mountain behind her cast a wash of light over the compound. A long roll of thunder bounced off the hills behind them.

179

"Time to go, Tardi," she said.

He headed to the north edge of the compound, she to the south. The storm was helping them. The darkness seemed even thicker after every flash of lightning. As the thunder crashed, she ran across the road, keeping low and keeping her eyes on the soldiers at the main gate. A cry, short and suddenly cut off from the west. No gunfire. The guards on the gate had heard it though; they raised their rifles, stepping out of their pillboxes. Nancy was at the very edge of the darkness now. She could see the face of the guard nearest to her, the rain running down his pale cheeks, the blond hair darkened with water just visible under his helmet.

"What is happening?" he called into the night.

Nothing answered him but the sound of the storm. He stared out into the darkness, blinking, and Nancy moved low and quick to get behind him, her knife in her hand.

On the north side of the gate Tardivat reared out of the darkness, got his arm around the neck of the other guard and sliced his throat. Nancy came forward fast, but some instinct made the guard in front of her turn her way.

She hesitated, staring into his dark blue eyes, then charged. He used the barrel of his rifle to block the knife blow, jarring her wrist. She used her left to punch him hard in his jaw, but he grabbed at her as she went down, dragging her under him. He had his weight on her, his hand grasped around her knife hand, forcing the blade toward her neck. He was winning, she could feel the blade beginning to press. Another flash of lightning and she looked straight into his eyes. She realized that he was more frightened than she was, registered his shock as he saw he had his knife to a woman's throat.

The thunder came again, and before she had even heard the crack of Fournier's rifle she felt the German's limbs go slack, and a spray of blood hit her full in the face.

She shoved the body off her and was on her feet again before Tardivat reached her side. They ran through the gates and into the compound in a low crouch, heading toward the main building across the grass. The main door opened, they flattened themselves against the rough concrete wall.

A German officer stared blinking out into the rain, his hand on his holster. The lightning flashed, and Nancy saw him jerk forward as he saw the bodies of his guards. He turned back into the building.

"We're under attack! Call for reinforcements!"

There was another crack from Fournier's nest, not disguised by the thunder this time, and the German fell backward into the hallway. Nancy swung away from the wall, stepped over his body and through the door, going left into the generator room.

Ugly thing. A mass of iron, painted dark green, bulging with thick tubing which looked like muscles, chuntering away to itself with a low chugging rhythm. She closed the door behind her and felt a twitch of pleasure. It stank of oil. They'd shown her exactly where to place the charges on beasts like these during training. She used three of her one-pound blocks of TNT, jamming them close to its soft underbelly, selected a time pencil that should give her four minutes to get clear and pinched the top of the tube to get it going.

Just as she did, she heard a crump outside which no one could mistake for thunder. The percussive blast, the sounds of shattered concrete thrown up into the air and against the rear of the building, a deep metallic groan which shook the building as the huge transmitter tower shifted.

On the other side of the door she could hear orders being screamed into telephones, and shots from inside the building. She lifted her head to glance at the entrance, dragged a chair over from the desk in the far corner and forced it under the door, then smashed the window.

She still had three minutes.

As soon as she broke the glass a bullet flew through the opening and ricocheted off the metal carcass of the generator. She ducked, covering her head, and heard the bullet bury itself in the wall above her.

She switched off the lights in the room and took her chances, using the thick wool of her sleeves to protect her palms from the glass as she vaulted out of the window under the thin whine of another bullet.

There was a second explosion outside, and that metallic groan again. Two of the three concrete anchors of the tower were gone. The lightning flashed as she twisted round to see the tower lurch forward, held now at only one point, to the rear of the building. Time to get going. She went south, heading for the gap Mateo was supposed to have cut through the fence.

Two minutes.

Lightning flashed. She saw the neat slice up the wire in front of her and raced toward it, but was tackled from behind and brought down full length. She kicked out, twisting. Another guard, older and heavier and all muscle by the feel of him.

She reached for her knife, but he struck out hard and fast enough at her wrist to send it flying.

One minute. Fuck.

He sprawled on top of her, got his hands around her throat and reared out of reach as she tried to go for his eyes. The pressure on her throat increased. Black spots appeared in front of her eyes. *Fight, Nancy.* She tried to punch him in the stomach, but his heavy coat was protecting him.

The block of TNT in the generator room exploded with a force that shook the ground under them.

Nancy's guard slackened his grip and the force of the blast made him bow over her. He was in reach. She did not hesitate this time.

The side of her hand caught him exactly where it was supposed to, crushing his windpipe. He didn't even have time to cry out, just a rattling gasp and a look of shock and hurt on his face. She pushed him off her. Another charge exploded—Tardi's

TNT in the main transmitter equipment room. Smoke poured from the shattered windows and she could see flames flickering through the remains of the roof.

An engine roared behind her and she spun round to see an old army bus careening across the grass, straight at her. She pulled out her revolver.

"Captain! Come on!" A Spanish accent.

Arms reached out for her from the passenger side. She caught a glimpse of Tardivat in the driver's seat. She didn't need to be asked twice. She grabbed Mateo's wrist, stepped up the wheel and let him haul her in.

Tardivat ground the gears and swung out of the main gates heading north as bullets struck the sides of the bus. He flicked the headlights then switched them off and put his foot down.

Another massive crump as the last charge exploded behind them. Nancy ran through the bus to the back window and watched as, with a final tear of metal, the transmitter tower fell forward, bursting apart the flaming ruin of the building and crashing across the road behind them.

Tardi slowed the bus to a crawl and flicked on the headlights again in time to catch Fournier as he charged down the slope, his rifle held above his head, yelling with delight. They hauled him in, Tardivat sped up and they disappeared into the thunderclouds.

32

The bus had taken damage as they fled. It sighed, groaned and near the camp at the base of the upper slopes, it gave up completely. They shoved it off the road and cut brush to camouflage it, then hiked the rest of the way back to camp. The storm had passed and the men were waiting up under their dripping tarpaulin shelters like anxious parents.

"We're home, you fuckers!" Fournier said. "All of us!"

They cheered. His excitement drove the damp and fear out of the place. Denden flung his arms around Nancy, nearly squeezing the life out of her. Handshakes, back slaps, punching the Spanish guys on the arm and mussing their hair. They looked happy. Then Fournier produced a crate of wine from some secret stock of his own, and under the dripping covers on the edge of the wood he told and retold the story of the raid, and the others sat goggle-eyed with excitement as they listened.

Nancy drank and watched Fournier, his surging delight. He was a bloody good storyteller.

"I saw her through my sights, boys. But too many trees, too much movement not a thing I could do about it." He mimed peering through the dark, wiping the rain out of his eyes. "I'm there thinking, shit, she's going to get throttled. Just when I thought I might be getting to like her, that fat kraut's going to choke her to death." Pause for laughter. "Then BOOM, right behind her the generator blows. Kraut's a bit surprised, and

BOOM. She strikes like a fucking cobra, I'm telling you. Right hand to his neck and he is DONE!" The men cheered. "She killed that big German bastard with one blow. I thought his head was going to pop off and just bounce along the ground…boing, boing…boing…"

More laughter. Fournier put out his arms, bottle in one hand, and looked right to left. They all leaned forward and he lowered his voice.

"I thought this was rough." He pointed to the burn scar on his cheek, then lifted his voice to a roar like a music hall comedian. "Turns out it's just her version of a little kiss!"

The men hollered now, started twisting round toward Nancy. Fournier lifted his bottle toward her.

"So do your homework, boys! Captain Wake!"

They all raised their mugs and mess tins and Nancy lifted her half-empty bottle in acknowledgment.

"Hey, Denden. Think we'll be able to get Radio Londres a bit more clearly now?" she asked.

"Oh, I should think so!"

He switched on the set. Crystal clear. And God bless 'em, they were playing the new anthem of the Maquis. Half of the lads sprang to their feet linking arms and spinning each other around. Nancy couldn't tell if they were dancing or wrestling. They probably couldn't either.

She watched for a minute or two, then ducked out from under the tarpaulin back into the peace outside. The thunderstorm had left the air cool and fresh and the moon hung above them, a thickening crescent. She looked down at her hands.

"That was your first kill, no?" It was Tardivat, like her, pulling away from the crowd.

No point in lying to him. And she owed him. He brought her here after all, lied to Gaspard to save her neck, volunteered for the mission.

"Yes, it was. You know, when I was in Marseille my husband

used to take me to get my nails done every Monday. He wouldn't even recognize these hands."

Tardi blew a cloud of smoke into the pale moonlight.

"Were you afraid?"

She had to think about it. "No. Not even when I thought I was going to die. I was glad somehow...to be actually fighting. It all happened so fast, and I was angry at myself. Angry for dropping the knife, for hesitating with the first guard. But not scared. Thrilled." Yes, that was the right word. Jesus. "It was thrilling. That's not normal, is it, Tardi?"

Another of those shrugs. "We are at war. Nothing is normal. Normal will get you killed. Normal will make a man a collaborator. Normal is no use to anyone." He seemed to catch himself and took a long breath. "Your plan was good. Setting the charges on the blocks like that so they would draw the guards out of the building, then the last charge dropping the tower across the road. A good plan. We should all be grateful you enjoy your work."

She wanted to protest. Yes, planning and executing the mission was...great, no doubt, but the killing...she wanted to tell him she did not *like* the killing at all. She was glad to survive, yes, and it had been exciting, but what sort of person takes pleasure in killing? Only the sort of person she wanted to wipe off the face of the earth. Her head spun.

"NanCYYY!" Denden stumbled out into the darkness, a bottle in his hand, and Tardivat melted off into the forest before Nancy had a chance to say anything at all. "NanCYYYY!!"

She stepped forward. "I'm here, you idiot. No need to bring the whole bloody German army down on us."

He came toward her stumbling a bit and giggling.

"A total victory, darling." He put his arm around her. "Want to do something foolish?"

*

She had to trust him, but up on the promontory west of the camp, with a length of rope wrapped around her forearms, the other end tied around a chestnut tree twenty feet back from the edge, the idea looked not just foolish but completely insane.

"You want us to lean out over the edge of the cliff?" Nancy said.

Denden was tugging at his own rope. "Darling, I swear by all that's holy, *you* want to lean out over the edge too, you just don't know it yet."

Satisfied with his knot, he took her hand and led her to the very edge of the drop. The rope behind her still seemed pretty slack. Even in the almost moonless dark he must have caught her expression.

"Nancy Wake, I have set up the ropes for a thousand trapeze acts and tightrope walkers while you were swigging cheap champagne in cheap bars. Trust me. Just walk until your toes are on the very edge, then lean backward as far as you can. It's utterly delicious."

He demonstrated, his whole body hovering above the deep dark, just his hands on the rope, his boots resting on the cliff edge.

Oh, why not? Nancy turned, set her feet apart and leaned back. And felt it. The pull of gravity on her back, on her head, the comfortable tug on her arms as the rope tightened and held. This did feel good. She let a little more of the rope out, leaning farther back and bending her back—then laughed, a great burbling laugh that came from the soles of her feet and shook loose her whole body. Behind them the void pulled at them and the breeze whipped her hair across her face, but the void could go fuck itself. Captain Nancy Wake commanded gravity.

"I never drank cheap champagne, you horror," she said. "But you were right, Denden, I needed this."

Beside her, Denden let go with one hand and took one foot off the edge, swinging from side to side.

"Best trick I learned in the circus. Whenever I hated my sinful self, which was every time I got hot for another boy, which was every goddamn day, well, I'd hang off the trapeze. No net. Made me feel alive again, being on the edge."

"It's a 'sod you' to the universe, isn't it!" Nancy said, then whooped, hearing her voice echo and bounce into the darkness below, and giggled.

"It is! Don't feel bad about destroying those bastards, Nancy. Even if you have to do it with your own hands. Use it! Use that feeling of being out over the edge to live. Sure I like shagging boys and people tell me I shouldn't, and people tell *you* you should sit at home and let the men get their blood rage on. Well, screw them. Use your rage and never let them shame you for it."

"Thank you, Denden." He got it. He got how it was to be her. She released one hand too, felt the lurch, re-found her balance and felt a surge of pleasure. "But you know you sound a bit like Dr. Timmons when you talk like that, don't you?"

He howled. "You monstrous witch! I've never been so insulted in my life."

Their laughter echoed down into the silence.

33

S he could have sworn she'd barely closed her eyes, having stumbled back to camp exhausted and triumphant, when Denden woke her.

"Nancy, there's trouble! Come on!"

She struggled clumsily into her clothes and boots. Not that she was hungover—no, lacking sleep, sir, that's all...something in her eye made the light look a bit too bright. It was quiet in the camp, too quiet. What the hell?

"Nancy!"

"Jesus, I'm coming!"

She stumbled out of the tent to see Denden was already deeper into the woodland in the direction of the hot spring, beckoning her on. She checked her side arm, then followed him. Perhaps Fournier had picked up a spy, and they wanted her help interrogating him. Or Denden thought it was time for the interrogation to stop...The thoughts chased themselves round her sodden head as she made her way down the path. She could hear men talking now, but although she couldn't hear the words she could hear the tone. Relaxed, happy even. So what the...?

She turned into the clearing and saw the old bus they'd stolen last night.

"We left it at the bottom of the slope! How the hell did it get up here?"

Most of Fournier's men were here along with Fournier

189

himself, the Spanish brothers and Tardivat. They were all dirty as sin and looked extremely pleased with themselves.

"We pushed it up the hill, last night!" Jean-Clair said eagerly.

Fournier took a cigarette from his mouth. "Thought you could do with some privacy, Captain. We've fixed it up a bit for you."

It was the first time he'd called her Captain without making her rank sound like an insult; first time he'd done so sober anyway.

"Thanks," she said, meaning it.

They were waiting for her to go inside. She did and the men peered through the windows while she examined their work. Several rows of seats had been pulled out and the remaining ones rearranged to make a living space. Up front by the cab, a packing case table was surrounded with seats arranged in a U, like a meeting room. Against one side of the bus a couple more cases had been arranged on top of each other into shelves and one of the silly buggers had actually picked flowers, stuck them in an empty tin can and put it on top. Down the back of the bus, two more rows of seats had been shoved together to make a sort of cot. A nightdress, fashioned out of long panels of silk, was laid across it, along with a pair of folded blankets.

She picked up the nightdress, felt the sheerness of the fabric, and put it across her arm before she went outside again. The men looked up at her, eager as puppies.

"Bloody hell, guys. I love it!"

They cheered and started slapping each other on the back again.

"Right—breakfast now, I think," Denden declared, rubbing his hands together. "Let the captain get settled in."

Grinning and shoving each other like kids on the way home from school, most of the men started drifting back up to the main clearing.

"Tardi?" Nancy said.

Tardivat disengaged himself from the back of the group

and came back to her, his eyes lowered. She held up the ivory nightdress.

"This is from my parachute. Tardivat, it's perfect... But it's for your wife."

He looked up as she held it against herself and ran her hands down its liquid folds. Then he smiled, a craftsman glad to see his work appreciated.

"As is everything I create, Captain, but she can't wear it. She died in forty-one. She'd want you to have this, I'm certain."

Nancy felt her throat close up. "Thank you," she managed.

The sun coming through the forest canopy pattered his face with light and shadow. "My pleasure, Captain."

He turned and walked away up the slope without waiting for her to say any more and Nancy watched him go. She had them now, Fournier and his men. They would follow her, they would listen, and when the invasion came she'd be able to provide London with a group of trained and disciplined fighters and saboteurs.

The victory should have tasted sweet, but she could still feel something dark in it. She realized she was holding the fabric of the nightdress tightly in her hand and remembered the moment her training had taken over and she'd struck the blow across the German's throat. She closed her eyes. Enough. It was necessary. If she wanted to fight alongside these men she had to live with the consequences. Still, it had been easy to shout about killing Nazis in London. It was harder than she had thought to do it with her own hands. Damn it. The thing that made her hate the Nazis was their contempt for human life, their brutality, and now she had to learn to have contempt for *their* lives, to not care that the guard she had killed, or the one whose blood Fournier had splattered all over her face with his bullet were, perhaps, just ordinary men with mothers and wives, caught up in something they didn't really understand. But what was the alternative? Offer them tea and understanding? Send them to their rooms for being naughty murderous invaders? No. She needed to take on some of that brutality. Needed to sacrifice...what? Some corner of her soul. OK. She would take that deal.

34

Major Böhm was reading a letter from his wife when Heller knocked and entered his new office in Montluçon.

Eva was well, and his daughter and the puppy were playing in the garden of their comfortable new house on the outskirts of Berlin. She was delighted to be out of France and among her own people and said all the proper things about her admiration for his work and her desire to welcome him home when it was complete. He felt a twinge of envy. Montluçon was a fresh challenge, but the character of the people was more like the Slavs he had seen in the east than the sparkling, mercurial terrorists of Marseille. He could not quite decide if the people were as stupid as they pretended to be. Questioned about the roving gangs of Maquis, they offered nothing but a cow-like blank expression. No, they'd never heard anything about that sort of thing, sir. The officials blinked and promised they'd do everything they could to assist the major, but somehow the papers and reports he requested were painfully slow in coming.

Heller set a knife on his desk and Böhm studied it.

"I thought you might wish to see it, sir. It was dropped during the raid on the transmitter at Chaudes-Aigues."

Böhm set down his letter. "Were there any witnesses?"

Heller shook his head. "Two survivors, but they never saw the team which staged the raid."

"They used TNT?"

"Yes, sir."

Böhm picked up the knife, testing its weight. "This, Heller, is a Fairbairn-Sykes knife. Standard issue for British agents dropped into France to encourage and coordinate the rabble in the hills."

Böhm practiced a slash and thrust in the air and nodded his approval. It was a well-made weapon.

"I think, Heller, it is time to show the French populace that our patience is not without limit."

35

Sometimes there were moments when Nancy could forget the war. Just moments, but they existed—strange glimmers of light when she was so tired her brain switched off and she was freewheeling on her bike on a lonely back road with the scent of late spring in the air and the sunlight patterning through the trees hypnotizing her.

The parachute drops were coming every night when there was enough moon, and every day more young men arrived at the campsites dotted across the plateau, in abandoned farms and patches of forest. She trained them, trained them to teach each other, distributed supplies and weapons, established escape routes and fallback rendezvous points, and gave a quiet nod when they approached her with plans for small-scale ambushes, thefts and plans for minor sabotage. She would not risk large actions, but she had seen the benefits of on-the-job training, and thought London would just have to trust her not to fuck up before D-Day. Then there was all the pastoral care. Money to be handed out, news to be exchanged. And every day someone asked her when the Allies were coming, and every day she said "soon" and hoped to God it was true, though she knew that landing would only be the start, the moment their work could begin in earnest. Until then, it was all preparation.

The track curved and she slowed down, coming back to herself reluctantly. Tardivat had said he thought these fields south of the Maleval River would make a decent drop site, and she wanted to see them for herself. She hid her bike behind the hedge near a likely candidate and began to scope it out. Promising. Yes, this one would do, if the farmer who owned it was willing to turn a blind eye. She paced it out. Roughly seven hundred meters square. Spot-on. And no telephone wires or cables anywhere near. Decent cover, but it wouldn't hide the signal fires from the approaching planes. So far so good. But to the west the ground sloped sharply upward between here and Chaudes-Aigues. Not steep or high enough to be a problem for the planes, but she'd have to hike to the top of the hill. If there were easy tracks up there from the town and the Germans spotted the planes coming over, they could trek up there, then launch an attack on Nancy and her men while they gathered in the parachute containers. If, though, the forest between the town and the top of the slope was densely wooded, it would be worth the risk. She'd just make sure they posted lookouts up here to watch for torches or signs of activity in the town below.

She headed up the slope. She could feel the sweat trickling down the small of her back as she went. Did she need to find more locations to conceal the goodies they already had? Some of their stashes were turning into Aladdin's caves of arms and ammunition. She needed to send the Spaniards out scouting for fresh places to conceal arms in the woods, perhaps along escape routes they'd worked out. Or, better still, a few totally remote locations known only to a few, so that if the Germans ever managed to deal them a severe blow, whoever survived would be able to find a gun and a bullet.

When the gradient leveled out, she walked south for a thousand paces and, seeing no easy access for the Germans that way, turned, retraced her steps and continued north till she came to a point where the slope fell hard and fast under her toward the town. No easy route from here either, which was perfect, and from this point she could look directly down into the center of the town. A lookout standing where she was now would be able to signal to the reception committee in the field if things started getting lively.

A movement below caught her eye. Not the usual comings and goings of the townspeople. Something different.

She lifted her field glasses and trained them on a group of gray uniforms clustered at the top of the market place. They parted, and she saw they had a man and woman in civilian clothes on the ground between them. Nancy tightened her grip on the binoculars. Some of the soldiers dragged the two civilians to their feet. The woman twisted in their grip and she saw the heavy swell of her belly. The man struggled hard. Nancy could hear nothing but the stir of the leaves in the woodland around her, but she could see the man was screaming, his body bent double. She swallowed. She knew them both.

The man was one of Gaspard's. He'd been in the barn when they pulled the feed sack off her head. She recognized the woman too. When she was in town a week or so earlier, the pregnant girl had approached her. Said she knew she wasn't due anything because her husband wasn't one of Fournier's men, but if Madame could perhaps help with something for the baby? The baby had swung it. Nancy had given the girl fifty francs and a couple of bars of chocolate, knowing it would piss off Gaspard if he found out she was giving charity to the families of his men. Elisabeth, that was her name. Her husband was Luc.

The soldiers lifted her onto the base of the market cross and were tying her hands behind it. SS men. Luc was on his knees now, begging at the feet of an officer in polished boots and the cap of a major. He lifted his hand. One of his soldiers unslung his rifle and fixed his bayonet. Nancy tasted something bitter and acrid in her throat.

She spoke out loud. "No. No. They can't..."

The major dropped his hand and the soldier presented his weapon, but rather than a direct stab into the bound woman's belly, he swung the blade sideways, under the curve of her pregnancy. Nancy dropped the glasses and turned sideways throwing up her guts into the grass.

She didn't want to see any more. She wiped her mouth with the back of her hand. She had to. Someone had to see this. She lifted her glasses again. The woman's front was soaked with blood, and there was a purplish slop at her feet. Her dress had been pulled from her shoulder and Nancy could see the whiteness of her neck. She was still alive, twisting her head from side to side in rolling arcs.

"Just die," Nancy whispered. "Please, sweet girl, just die."

Luc was at the major's feet, his hands together, pleading. The major had a pistol in his hand and was pointing it upward at Elisabeth's head. He was saying something.

Luc dropped his arms to his side. The officer appeared to be listening.

The major's hand twitched. Nancy heard the echo of the shot a second later, quiet as a twig snapping underfoot. Elisabeth slumped forward. Luc was still on his knees staring at her. He didn't react, didn't move at all as the officer walked over to him and shot him through the back of the head.

Then the major turned and looked out into the hills, and Nancy saw his face for the first time.

Major Böhm.

He was looking directly at her, smiling that same pleasant, slightly patronizing smile he had worn when he showed her out of the Gestapo headquarters in Marseille the day he arrested Henri.

She lowered her glasses and started to walk down the slope toward her bike, then her legs went out from under her and she was sitting at the base of a mountain ash, her breath coming in short tight pants, her chest tight, her head spinning.

Stop it. *Stop it.* Slow down. Don't think about it, think about what it means. What did Luc say to Böhm? What did he trade to end the torture of his wife?

She shot to her feet. Rage, pure rage took her down the slope, across the field and onto her bike. Rage carried her up the flank of the valley and into the hills. Rage carried her over every one of the twenty miles to the first of Gaspard's sentries as they blocked her path on the track on Mont Mouchet.

"Madame Wake, such a pleasure," the Maquisard said.

"Drop the pleasantries, you little shit, and take me to Gaspard. Now!"

If she'd had time to think, she might have realized this wasn't going to go well. Gaspard would have heard that Fournier's men now had Brens and TNT and plastic explosive and were having fun practicing with them from Clermont-Ferrand to Aurillac. Their victory blowing up the radio tower would have put his nose out of joint too, and none of that would put him in the mood to listen. She didn't have time to play nicely though.

She told him what she had seen.

"You have to leave here," she said into the sickened silence that followed.

Gaspard was sitting on a crate by the fire pit. They had a tarp rigged above it so the smoke wouldn't give them away to the occasional air patrols, though that and the lookouts along the roads seemed to be where their security measures stopped. At least seventy of his men were enjoying the sunshine in the open space around them. There were probably two or three hundred more in the immediate area.

Gaspard looked at her as if she had suggested popping into town and sorting it all out over a drink with Major Böhm.

"No."

Pig-headed, stupid arsehole. Deep breath. Explain it in terms even he can understand.

"Luc was here," she said. "He told the Gestapo where you are.

What else would they want to know? You have four, five hours at most, Gaspard." Nancy spoke clearly and firmly. "Böhm will call in an airstrike on your position and follow up with ground troops. They are coming now. You can't wait. If you had properly prepared escape routes—"

"I said NO!" Gaspard slammed his heavy hands onto his knees with a solid thwack. "I did not lead these men into the mountains to run from the Nazis at every alarm. And I have known Luc for ten years. He would never betray us. Never. We are as safe here today as we were yesterday."

Nancy balled her fists. "You didn't see it! You didn't see what they did to her! He would have said anything to spare her a second more suffering—so would I. They cut her belly open."

Gaspard stood up. Now they were both on their feet, eyeball to eyeball.

"Then he would have lied!" Gaspard shouted in her face. "The Boche will waste their bombs and men on some ruin miles from here."

"You don't know that! Böhm has broken dozens of men."

He sliced through the air with his hand. "Bullshit. I'm not giving up this place, this camp, because you think Luc might have given away its location, Madame."

She grabbed his arm and tried to control her voice. "What would it cost you? You could spread your men further out in the hills. Leave here for two, three days and if it turns out Luc managed to give them a false location or none at all, you can come back."

He gave her a look of complete contempt. "I do not understand why Fournier's men listen to you, little girl. How am I supposed to lead my fighters if I keep telling them to run and hide every time there is a rumor the Germans might be coming? Are we men or rabbits? We are here to fight."

The urge to scream in his face was almost overwhelming. "When the time is right! When the Allies land in France we'll need every man to harry the Germans behind their lines. Now we need to arm, prepare, train and survive until we are needed."

That was a mistake.

"I am not the pawn of a bunch of British imperialists in London! I say how I will fight for my country, not them!" The men around him were nodding in agreement. "You will not turn me into a good little English soldier with a handful of bullets and a slab of chocolate. Now piss off back to your little band of rabbits in the hills."

He walked away.

"Luc told them, Gaspard!" she yelled after him. "They are coming! For God's sake, do something!"

He kept walking.

36

The second Nancy got back to camp, she dragged Fournier, Tardivat, Mateo and Denden to the bus and told them the whole story.

"Screw him," Fournier said, lighting another cigarette. "If he won't listen, then let the Boche have him."

Denden shook his head. "If it was just Gaspard, I'd say, go for it. Let this Major Böhm chew him up for breakfast. But he has hundreds of men spread around those hills. We can't let Böhm polish them off for lunch."

Fournier sniffed, then leaned over the map spread between them. "So you want us to do something? What?"

Nancy pointed out the routes up to Mont Mouchet. Strange to think these places were just lines on a map a few weeks ago. Now she could see every road, the villagers in every house, recite the name of every friendly peasant, every suspected collaborator.

"We can't risk getting destroyed ourselves. The Germans will have air support so we are going to stay hidden from the bombers and Henschel's, but the ground troops? We can do something about that. There are no good roads leading to the summit from the east, so I reckon the Germans will send in their men from Pinols, Clavières and Paulhac then try and complete the encirclement of Mont Mouchet from there. Those are the troops we can slow down. Give Gaspard's men a chance to hold them off till nightfall and then disappear off the mountain into the woods or through Auvers before the Germans can fully close the trap."

Fournier tapped the map on the road north of Mont Mouchet. "That road I know well. A few booby traps, I think."

"Good," Nancy said. Delaying tactics rather than full-pitch battles—Fournier was thinking like a guerrilla at last.

"I'll need to take the *gazogène* to make it in time," Fournier added.

They only had three of the chugging charcoal-burning trucks, but he was right. She hesitated. Made a decision.

"OK. Take it. But hide it well and come back on foot. The roads will be crawling with troops for the next week."

She held his gaze until he nodded, then she turned to Mateo.

"We'll take the road from Clavières. Then we'll need guides in groups of three along these paths toward Le Besset to take Gaspard's men out of the fight."

She looked at the men around her. They nodded.

"Spread the word among the farmers. Tardivat, you coordinate the rescue parties and can you arrange for the reception of whoever makes it out? Cover in the woods, get some supplies into the farms above Chavagnac. And you're in charge of improvising any other small-scale ambushes on the smaller roads. Take the chance to let some of the new boys have a taste of action, but keep them safe. Denden, whatever happens, don't miss your transmission. Tell London we want extra medical supplies and plastic."

She rolled up the map.

Denden downed the last of the tea in his mug. "Marvelous. Let Operation Ungrateful Bastards commence."

Mateo and Nancy took a dozen men, including Juan and Rodrigo, down the valley to the Clavières road. She had hopes of finding what she needed about two miles from Mont Mouchet, where the pasture lining the roadside was dotted with mature trees. She kept glancing at her watch. She was sure Böhm would advise the military to attack Gaspard's position at once, before news of the horror in the market place and its implications had time to spread. How long did it take to make the final preparations for an attack like this? Brief the officers, assemble the vehicles and weaponry? She spent half the hike to the road trying to work it out, and half swearing she would not think about it again.

They emerged onto the road as the sun reached its zenith, and in twenty minutes found a place for the first stage of the operation. When Nancy saw an oak tree tall enough to block the road she planted a kiss on its wrinkled bark, then told Mateo to take it down with a ring of plastic explosive. Then she sent a couple of scouts toward Clavières to keep an eye on the road and warn away any locals. The scouts she picked were two of the younger lads, and as they set off Nancy noticed Mateo watching them until they disappeared round the bend of the road.

"Worried about them, Mateo?" she asked, handing him the plastic from her pack and watching as he made a neat ring of charges around the thick trunk.

"No. Just, I am twenty-three years old, and they make me feel like a grandfather."

"Why?"

He plunged a time pencil into the charge and crimped the copper top. "Fire in the hole!"

They scrambled to a safe distance in the roadside ditches, heads down.

"Because," Mateo said, as if their conversation hadn't been interrupted, "I picked up a rifle at sixteen and have been fighting ever since."

"You should have tried picking up a girl instead," she said. He grunted. "Maybe Jean-Clair will give you lessons. His mother told me he left broken hearts in every village in the Alps. Seemed pleased about it."

His reply, in Spanish and probably obscene, was lost in the sudden crack of the explosion, then the tear of wood and storm in the leaves as the great tree fell. The impact made the earth shudder. Nancy lifted her head. Perfectly done. The oak had fallen right across the width of the road.

She clambered out of the ditch, unslung her pack and pulled out one of their precious anti-tank grenades. How many men would the Germans send? A vision struck her, as if carried by the breeze, of Gaspard's men clustered round the old farm buildings caught unaware by a wave of artillery fire, the fountains of earth, the scream of the shells, the blood and confusion.

Nancy felt the spring wind on her face, and remembered this sensation, a fizz in her blood, from their attack on the transmitter. Not fear, but a strange heightening of her senses. There was something dangerously delicious about it.

"Jean-Clair! Stop staring down the road and watch what Captain Wake is doing!" Mateo said sharply. Jean-Clair jumped and Nancy almost dropped the bloody mine. "The scouts will whistle when they see something," Mateo continued. "You watch and learn."

Watch and learn indeed. Nancy wanted to find the sweet spot under the fallen trunk. The Germans would have to use their heavy vehicles to shift this monster out of the way, and when it started to shift, the grenade would go off—if they didn't spot it first. She lay on her front and crawled under the branches, the spring leaves catching in her hair. It was a Hawkins grenade, impossible to throw far, but fierce, adaptable devils with about a pound of explosive in them. They used a chemical igniter, triggered by pressure, so grenade or not, they were perfect to use as mines for booby traps like this. She pushed it in front of her, using her elbows to drag herself under the twisted limbs of the oak along the gravel road, looking for a curve in the main trunk. Just a little farther. She looked right and left, judging the distance to the roadside, the cover above her. This would do, tucked under the main body of the tree, and far enough forward so the trunk wouldn't take all the force of the blast and leave the vehicle pushing it undamaged.

She removed the retaining pin, then heard the crack of a snapping branch as the trunk jerked toward her. She snatched back the Hawkins with her fingertips, scrabbling to pull it clear as the trunk settled forward into the very place she had just put the damned thing.

A sudden thumping rush of blood made her hand twitch. She waited to see if she were dead.

"All good, Captain?" she heard Mateo ask.

"Peachy," she replied through gritted teeth. Then she took a long, slow breath and very carefully repositioned the Hawkins. She slithered back through the branches, every nerve taut and singing now.

Mateo pulled her to her feet and she ran her hand through her hair, shaking out the twigs. The countryside seemed unnaturally quiet, or maybe she was just listening too hard. She caught the sound of one of the scouts thudding toward them.

The boy was sprinting up to the roadblock like he had Hitler himself on his heels.

"Tree's mined!" Nancy shouted at him, and he skidded to a halt in the gravel and skirted round, keeping his eye on the giant oak as if it might rear up and fight him.

"Well?" Mateo said gruffly as the boy reached them.

"Two kilometers out. I think...I think...a thousand men. I think artillery too," he panted.

Mateo lit a cigarette. "They weren't going to come to the party with balloons and streamers, kid."

Nancy shot him a look. "Let's get into position, shall we?"

They left Juan in the forest near the fallen oak, then headed east for a mile and split the team. Rodrigo took his squad onto the northern slopes while Mateo and Nancy set up basic tripwires with two of the French boys, Jean-Clair and Jules.

"I wish we had more time," Mateo muttered to Nancy as she dug into her pack again.

Jean-Clair and Jules watched them. She didn't reply.

Mateo took a pair of hand grenades from her and a roll of industrial tape, then bound the first grenade to the slim trunk of a sapling at the roadside at waist height. He didn't speak again. Nancy tied off the cord on another sapling on the opposite side of the road, then came back to watch Mateo tie his end to the loop of the firing pin. He made a neat job of it.

"Jean-Clair," Nancy said, "you and Jules take the other grenade, set it up like this one, twenty meters further on."

Jean-Clair took the grenade, cord and tape and the two boys trotted up the road.

Nancy watched them tie the tripwire at just the right height for the front of a troop lorry. Even knowing where it was, Nancy could barely see where the thin gray cord stretched across the road in the dappled shadows. As Jean-Clair and Jules came back Nancy noticed their drawn, concentrated expressions, and where their fingers gripped their Bren guns, she saw the telltale slick of sweat on metal.

She spoke quietly. "Boys, you've been trained for this. You'll be fine. Get into position."

They nodded, their Adam's apples bobbing up and down as they swallowed down their fear and excitement, then scrambled up the shallow slope to the south. Trained, my arse. Two or three weeks in a class of fifty with Nancy yelling at them was not exactly Sandhurst.

"You'd better be right about this, Captain," Mateo said as he climbed over the low stone wall that separated the road from the field.

There wasn't great cover on this side of the road, just a drainage ditch on the upper edge of the field, then the woods beyond that.

"Why?" she asked as she followed him.

"Because if you are wrong about this attack, I'm going to have to defuse Jean-Clair's first booby trap."

It was meant as a joke, but she was too strung out to laugh now.

"I'm not wrong," she said, walking up the slope away from him. Then she stopped, feeling the ripple in the air before she even heard it. An explosion rolled toward them up the road.

37

The two hours they spent waiting for the convoy to finish clearing the oak and reach them was a delicate torture. Nancy wanted it done, needed to move, to fight, but every moment the Germans spent looking for further booby traps was another moment for Gaspard to prepare his defense and start getting his men off the plateau. She glanced at her watch. Only four hours of daylight left. If they could keep the Germans from overrunning Mont Mouchet till dark, most of Gaspard's fighters might make it off the mountain.

She put her head back, leaning against the back wall of the ditch, counting her breaths, then her head snapped up as she heard a rattle of machine-gun fire to the west. Minutes later came the throaty detonations of mortars and the snap of rifle fire. It was the second part of the plan. As soon as the road was cleared, Juan was ordered to fire into the convoy then run. With any luck, the Germans would waste another hour looking for him.

Juan dropped panting into the ditch beside them twenty minutes later. Mateo embraced him, a brief fluttering sigh the only sign he'd found the waiting for him hard.

"Well?" Nancy asked.

"Kid was right," Juan replied. "Thousand-odd infantry with artillery in support. Your mine took the track off the tank they sent up to clear the tree; they had to repair it before they could move. All very orderly. When they looked like they were nearly done, I gave them a little blast." He mimed spraying his machine gun. "They had mortars on my position within two minutes. So I scarpered." He sounded grudgingly impressed. "They're Waffen-SS. Haven't seen troops that good in this area before. Only the best for Gaspard."

Nancy cursed fluently under her breath. That was all they needed. Crack troops and plenty of them. She could smell wild garlic, gun oil, the mineral tang of the soil, sweat. They would be coming soon. She twisted round in the ditch and put her hand on Jean-Clair's arm.

"Kid, our job is not to stop these guys, it's just to slow them down. We want them to waste time chasing us. We're going to make some noise, then disappear like smoke, OK?" She spoke low enough so only Jean-Clair could hear her.

"OK," he said.

The minutes crawled by until Nancy heard the rumble of engines in the distance, then lifted her voice. "Anybody fires a shot before I give the order, and I'll kill you my goddamn self. Clear?"

"Yes, my captain..." they murmured.

The throaty roar of the diesel trucks grew distinct. Nancy peered through the long grasses which lined the ditch. A light tank upfront was followed by two half-track vehicles towing howitzers. Damn it. The grenades wouldn't make a dent. She watched the heavy vehicles pass, shaking the valley as they went, then saw the mass of infantry coming up behind them, four abreast. As they passed below her, less than thirty yards away, she could see the individual faces. Men, not boys. Fit, well-fed masters of the universe, their lines orderly, marching in time. Farther west along the road they became a green snake crawling up the valley. Her valley.

She gripped her Bren, feeling its metal, warm from the spring sun against her fingers and prayed, not to God, but to whoever back in Britain had made that pair of grenades and hoping they had managed to get some extra magic in there; or that the breeze, the moisture in the air, the million little movements of the world would mean one of them would roll under one of the half-tracks before it exploded. Knock out an engine, force the Germans to leave one of those howitzers useless on the road rather than drag it up the mountain and train it on the boys in Gaspard's camp.

The first grenade went off, a short vicious explosion, which shivered up the valley and sent a flock of game birds into startled flight behind them. Then the second one went half a minute later. The sound was different—a muffled, doubled explosion which shook the ground, not the air. Nancy pressed herself against the ditch, watching for the smoke. *Yes.* A column of it, black and unctuous with engine oil from the first half-track.

She felt Jean-Clair move beside her.

"Wait your turn, Jean-Clair."

A clatter of machine-gun fire, echo tripled by the high slopes above them, poured down on the Germans from the woods opposite Nancy's position as Rodrigo and his squad engaged. The rattle of the light machine guns and the thud of the bullets into the scudding gravel mixed with the sharp urgent orders shouted in German, the cries of men already injured, then a hollow boom as the fuel tank on the injured half-track went up, the stink of it washing over them. The SS-men reacted fast, taking firing positions behind the remaining vehicles. Nancy's knuckles whitened on the stock of her Bren as she watched four groups of three infantry set up mortar positions on the northern verge, where the low stone walls edging the road gave them cover, and began finding the range on Rodrigo's position. Nancy could taste the adrenaline, bitter in the back of her throat.

"Captain," Jean-Clair said, his voice desperate.

"Wait!" she hissed.

More orders, swiftly given in German and small groups of men, rifles held across their chests, began to run up the northern slope to the west of Rodrigo's position, ready to flank him and his squad from above.

Time to mess things up.

"Now!"

Mateo and Juan sprang to their feet and hurled grenades from the ditch across the pasture and into the road among the rifle men behind the half-track, as Nancy, Jean-Clair and Jules concentrated their fire on the mortar teams. Time moved very slowly and way too fast. She could feel each bullet from the Bren as if on her own body as it pierced the heavy tunic of the corporal steadying the mortar, one two three across his back in a diagonal from shoulder blade, spine, kidneys, throwing him forward. The tube went over sideways sending its charge into the slope and a great plume of earth and rock was driven up into the air.

That shook them.

"Go! Go! Go!" Nancy screamed, and followed Mateo and Juan west along the ditch in a low crouch while the Germans were still trying to work out where the new attack was coming from.

She grabbed another grenade from her belt as she ran, pulled the pin with her teeth and threw it underarm across the field. It exploded against the wall, sending a blast of rock fragments spinning into the troops.

Rodrigo's men had stopped firing, melting into the depths of the woods the second Nancy's squad had piled in. Jules turned back and fired his Bren again, then staggered back, his arm over his eyes as a mortar round exploded at his feet. Jean-Clair grabbed hold of his jacket and dragged him, blind and shrieking along the drainage way. It was deeper here, better cover but muddy as hell, and Nancy's boots began to stick. The bullets whipped past her head, then they were in cover again, a thin copse between them and the woods.

"Break for the trees!" she shouted. Jean-Clair was trying to lift Jules in his arms. Mateo shoved him aside and lifted the blinded boy over his shoulder.

LIBERATION

"Captain! To the west!" Mateo yelled as he turned.

Nancy spun round to see a squad of Germans clambering over the wall on the far side of the copse, trying to outflank her now.

She fired short controlled bursts as Juan threw the last of his grenades and it exploded in a haze of earth and blood in the first team.

"Go on!" She shoved Jean-Clair hard in the back until his stupor broke, and he and Juan dashed up the slope to the tree line. She followed them at a sprint. As they threw themselves into the shelter of the dense foliage, Nancy heard the sound of the first German bombers rumbling overhead toward Gaspard's camp.

38

Denden had made his transmission and was helping to treat their wounded when Nancy and her squad got back to camp.

Mateo had carried Jules, stunned and bleeding, for a mile through the forest, but he had managed the rest of the trek back to camp on his own two feet, a rough bandage round his eyes with Jean-Clair at his elbow to guide him over the uneven ground. Nancy sent off the rest of the squad to eat and rest, then led Jules into the tent, a structure made of pine logs and tarpaulin that was serving as their field hospital. Denden was there, preparing to receive their wounded, and Nancy noticed a look of shock and fear flicker across his face as he recognized Jules, and then it was swiftly concealed.

Denden led Jules to a cot and Nancy followed.

"No word from Fournier yet," Denden said over his shoulder, as Jules sat down. Nancy nodded; they couldn't expect him back before nightfall. "But two of Tardivat's patrols managed to panic a convoy with grenades and Brens into an hour of immobility at that bottleneck near Paulhac-en-Margeride."

"SS troops?" Nancy asked, watching him unwind Jules's bandages. The boy flinched, and Denden rested his hand on his shoulder.

"No! You ran into the SS?" Denden said.

"A thousand of them, Denis!" Jules said, with deep satisfaction. "Captain Wake took out a tank!"

Denden snorted, and gently examined Jules's eyes. "Yes, with a nail file and a stern talking to, I'm sure. Now shush."

"I used a Hawkins and an oak tree, as it happens," Nancy said. "Any news from Mont Mouchet itself?"

Denden began to wash the earth and gravel from Jules's eyes. "A little. Whatever he said to your face, Gaspard must have done something to prepare. I keep hearing the words 'fierce resistance.'" He lifted Jules's chin. "You're going to be OK, my lad. Soon you'll be able to see my handsome face again."

Jules's shoulders relaxed.

"Nancy," Denden said. "Go and rest. We won't know any more until tonight. I'll look after Jules."

She was tired to her bones come to think of it. She squeezed Jules's shoulder. "You did well, Jules," she said. "You and Jean-Clair."

Then she went in search of a corner to sleep in. It was nearly dark already.

The next twenty-four hours were a blur of reports, orders, lightning raids to harry the German troops as their attack continued. Fournier found her in the bus at 2 a.m. and talked for forty minutes straight about his successes on the northern approach, then they worked through a half-bottle of brandy, making their plans for the next day. The Germans had pulled back as darkness fell, but they pushed back up the slopes of Mont Mouchet as soon as dawn broke, slowed by booby traps and the occasional burst of machine-gun fire from Nancy's men in the woods. When the Germans reached the summit, only the dead remained to greet them in the smoldering ruins of the camp. As the afternoon light began to soften, Jean-Clair found Nancy with the news that Gaspard himself had escaped and Tardivat was bringing him to camp.

Gaspard had asked, not demanded, to see her, Tardivat said,

so she gave orders for him to be shown into her bus and treated with every civility. Then she made him wait. She'd have made him wait anyway, but she still had wounded men to see to and informers to talk to. She made sure that Gaspard's men saw her, moving among them, and her Maquis made sure every one of them knew that Gaspard had been warned, that they owed their lives to Nancy's Operation Ungrateful Bastards and that the brandy they were drinking and the food they were eating were her gift.

It was clear Gaspard's men had fought like lions though. She wouldn't take that from him, or them. She learned that after her visit he had set up booby traps, doubled patrols and sent scouts toward the town, so they had had some warning. The planes shot up their camp ground, all their comfy barracks and stores, but the men were already in position in the woods. Their evacuation had been slow and improvised, but they'd retired in good fighting order and reached the guides and the safety of Fournier's camps. They were bloody, tired and ragged, but they'd made it. Most of them. Seventy men were dead, and fifty others injured too badly to be of use in the fight to come for a good few weeks. The scouts told her more than two hundred SS men had been killed, and they would be busy all tonight and tomorrow carrying the dead and wounded down the slopes.

Tardivat was waiting for her by the bus, and followed her inside. Gaspard was sitting awkwardly among the cushions. Tardivat sat next to him, and leaned back, the picture of masculine ease and a vague smile on his lips. Nancy didn't sit or speak; instead she picked up her hairbrush, balanced her compact on the shelf and arranged her hair, then took her lipstick from the pocket of her fatigues and carefully painted her lips. She'd never be allowed into the Café de Paris in these shoes, but her face would pass.

Only when she was good and ready did she sit down opposite Gaspard.

"Do you know the real difference between men and women, Gaspard?" She smiled. "And please don't say tits."

"Fuck you," he hissed.

Tardivat dealt him a single blow backhanded across the side of his head. He stared daggers at him, but didn't return the strike. That told her everything she needed to know.

"See?" She kept her voice soft. "Men solve problems with violence. The Germans were violent to you, which brings you here. And you were violent to me, which makes my men want to hang you from the highest tree."

Tardivat snorted in agreement, and Nancy could see a flicker of doubt on Gaspard's face.

"But lucky for you, Gaspard," she continued, "I've been thinking about how women solve problems. We do it by talking—talking about our dreaded feelings. Right now, you feel fear. Anger, of course. Pride in your men too, and rightly so, but beneath that, *shame*. We both know that acid churn. Exactly as you feel now, you made me feel. And I could've stayed in your camp, puffing my chest, until some man murdered me. I could've died of shame. But that would be a shamefully stupid way to die, don't you agree?"

Gaspard licked his lips, nodded.

"Good. Because D-Day is imminent, and I need every fighting man I can get. I have instructions from London on what to hit and when. I need your men to carry out those missions. I need you. Together we're going to stop the Germans moving their troops and give the Allies coming into France every chance we can to gain a foothold and push in. That's our role. That's the part we—you and me—are going to play in liberating France. Not pitched battles, no heroic stands. Clever, surgical sabotage. Because this isn't about us. This is about the whole fucking war."

He didn't say anything. That was a good sign. Now to lock it up nice and tight.

"All you have to do is accept that I'm now your commanding

officer. Since you're a major, let's say I'm…colonel? Do what you are told, and you will get all the guns and ammo you need. Enough plastic to blow every bridge and railhead within twenty miles and enough money to feed yourselves like little kings while you do it. Now, do we have a deal?"

He stared at her, and Nancy wondered what he saw. Yesterday, when she had gone charging into the camp, he had seen her just as he had on her first day in France—a girl, an English amateur playing games over his country. Now he had to see that she wasn't that girl. She'd killed a man with her bare hands since then, won the faith and loyalty of a band of fighting men just like him, and planned and led the operation which had saved his men.

"Yes, you have a deal."

He didn't look her in the eye and she didn't like that. She got to her feet and grabbed the hair at the back of his head, yanked hard, so he was staring up at her with his one good eye, reading her crimson lips.

"Say that again, you son of a bitch. And say it better."

The fight left him. "Yes, *mon colonel*."

She released him, smoothed his hair back into place and patted him on the shoulder before returning to her seat. She thought of the reports she'd heard of how he'd fought, inspired his men. She needed him to do what she said, but she didn't want to knock all the fight out of him.

"Then I think we should celebrate, don't you?"

39

The party was to mark their escape from the SS, honor their fallen comrades and affirm the union of Fournier's and Gaspard's men. Booze and food was funded by Uncle Buckmaster and the Bank of England. The SS men had returned to barracks in Clermont-Ferrand, so the teams who went out through the villages paying over the odds for booze and bread and whatever cheese they could get their hands on were also sending a message to the locals that it would take more than the SS to dislodge them. With that confidence and with wads of Nancy's francs in their hands, they were greeted like heroes, and came back stumbling under the weight of their purchases.

Nancy slept on her satin pillow in the bus for a couple of hours, and when she emerged into the dusk of the evening she could hear the laughter and chat of the main camp from the bus. She brushed her hair, put on her lipstick and walked up the hill. They cheered her. The Australian Angel, Mother Nancy, Voice of God, and my colonel, my colonel, my colonel greeted her from every side.

The day's battle had already grown in the telling, and changed from a near defeat to a total victory. You'd have thought Nancy and Gaspard had been working together the whole time to draw the Nazis into a trap.

Fine. Believing that did them no harm, and if Gaspard's men

decided she was some sort of tactical savant, the witch and soothsayer at Gaspard's side, that could work for her.

She took her place at one end of the banks of tables between Denden and Tardi, with Gaspard down the other end, but once someone had put her drink in her hand, she stood up and called for quiet.

"Enjoy, lads, because this may be your last supper." They laughed. "I drink to the men who didn't make it off the mountain! Sons of France!"

She raised her glass and they toasted with her, but she stayed standing and they hushed down again quickly enough.

"Very soon, we'll get our orders, and we'll begin the real fight to take back our home. So I suppose, in a way, that makes us family."

"To family!"

"But remember, boys, just because I'm a bitch, doesn't make me your mother, so if I ever hear one of you calling me Mother Nancy again, I'll shoot you myself. To victory!"

"Victory!"

Damn, the drink was rough. Toasts rippled round the fires, then there was singing, then more toasts. The fires seemed to have been banked very high. Someone put down a bowl of meat and vegetable stew in front of her, and when she tasted it she was surprised to discover it was actually pretty good. Tardivat saw her expression and laughed.

"Tardi, who made this?"

"Look over there."

In the gloom beyond the firelight she could see figures moving round the cook house. One was in the pristine whites of a chef.

"We've got a real cook?"

"He's a cousin of Gaspard's. He volunteered to be 'kidnapped' for the evening to make us something worth eating."

She shook her head and took another spoonful of the stew, savoring it.

"Everything's changing, Nancy. The people are with us now," Tardi said.

She grinned. "It's helped that you've stopped stealing their chickens."

The drinking went on after the food was finished, the chef unkidnapped himself and his helpers and the fighters congregated round the fires again. Nancy went into the woods for a piss, and by the time she got back, humming the song of the Partisans under her breath, something new was going on. The men were beating out a rhythm on the rocks and Gaspard was standing by the fire, his shirt open to the waist and a heavy knife in his hand.

"Why don't they just fuck already?"

Nancy glanced round to see who had spoken. Denden of course, glowering at them all in the darkness.

When she turned back, Gaspard was cutting a line across his bare chest; it beaded immediately with blood and he roared. The rhythm of the stones increased as one after one the men approached him, wet their fingertips with his blood and painted it in stripes across their faces, whooping as they did. Those not drumming on the rocks were on their feet now, dancing in a stamping, staggering, wide-legged roar of a dance, each shouting their own war cries.

"Now that's just nasty," Denden added, then he saw Nancy moving toward the fire. "Nancy? What the hell?"

She ignored him, and stalked across to Gaspard, pushing a waiting acolyte out of the way so he stumbled into the grass. Gaspard grinned and Nancy wet her fingers with the fresh blood seeping from his wound, then she painted a line across her face and, eye to eye, face to face, they screamed at each other. The men whooped and hollered in chorus, the rock orchestra increased in tempo and volume. Nancy grabbed a

221

bottle out of the hand of the man nearest her and spun out into the dark again.

She saw Denden watching her and tried not to notice the expression of disgust and surprise on his face.

PART III

JUNE 1944

40

Whatever had gone before was forgotten. The returning moon meant more drops responding to Denden's flow of requests tapped out and transmitted from the high places around the base on the plateau. The bounty of London knew no bounds, but Nancy had to balance the scale of her requests with the time it would take to gather in the packed cylinders and disappear with them into the night before the German patrols caught up with them. Then the guns had to be degreased and Gaspard's men trained to assemble and strip them. Denden helped teach the men on how to use the explosives and Tardivat tested the new time pencils and pronounced darkly about their reliability. The list of targets to be attacked on D-Day was regularly updated by London, and Nancy sent messages back via Denden's quick fingers, suggesting changes and additional targets.

The men weren't content to wait though. Gaspard's men in particular wanted to avenge their friends killed in the SS raid, and Nancy could see she'd have to give them some release or waste all her energy holding them back.

So she continued to sanction regular raiding parties, small groups of men traveling in one or other of the little charcoal-powered trucks they now had stowed in barns and stables across the region, who lay in wait for isolated patrols. Tardivat trained the men to run tripwires between the trees along the road when they knew a patrol was approaching. The explosion would take out the first vehicle, then the group would fire down on the rest of the patrol with their brand-new Bren guns before melting back into the endless countryside.

They came back from each successful outing wild with victory, and the Germans stayed clear of the back roads.

Nancy slept when she could, feeling the temperature of the air change around her.

On the first of June, Denden shook her awake after she'd had twenty minutes of the deepest, most perfect sleep, dreaming of her bed in Marseille. She threw her satin pillow at him, but he caught it, damn him, and threw it straight back at her.

"Hold your temper, witch! We've got the call!"

"I don't care. Tell the Germans to come back tomorrow, I have to sleep."

She put the pillow under her head again and closed her eyes. Denden crouched down beside her and whispered to her.

"Les sanglots longs des violons d'automne."

Nancy's eyes snapped open again and she sat up. "Seriously?" He nodded.

"At last, Denden! They are coming. Within two weeks?"

Any thought of sleep left her. The lines of the Verlaine poem, their cue that D-Day was almost upon them, acted on her like eight hours of sleep and a cold shower.

Denden laughed. "I still think they should have used your code poem to tip us that the invasion was coming. Bit more fun than that dreary Verlaine. What was it again?"

Nancy was wriggling out of her nightgown and grabbing her shirt.

"You're not supposed to know it. That's the whole bloody point of a code poem."

"Seriously, dearie, you didn't think when every other agent was choosing Keats, or schoolroom crap about nobility and sacrifice, no one would let slip one of the female agents had chosen... let me think... 'She stood right there, in the moonlight fair, And the moon shone through her nightie. It lit right on, the nipple of her tit...'"

"'Oh Jesus Christ Almighty!'" Nancy finished, tugging a brush through her hair. Then she shrugged into her new leather jacket. A week ago Fournier had led a raid on the factory that made them, and gifted her one of his prizes. Nancy thought it suited her rather well. Denden was laughing hard now.

"Leave it, Denden. It's just a bloody limerick!"

"I know, but just imagine the announcer on *Ici Londres* reading it."

She did, and it was funny. Suddenly so funny that there were tears running down her face. Within two weeks! Two weeks and there'd be British and French and American army boots on the ground in France again. She needed to up her reconnaissance of the key targets, check the stashes were still filled with what they needed, firm up arrangements for medical care, find another half-dozen abandoned barns and equip them as hospitals.

She wiped her eyes and checked her makeup in the mirror. "Come on, Denden, let's make some noise."

No one knew where the Allies were going to land, of course, but that was the whole point: catch the Germans with their troops in the wrong place. Then it was up to the Maquis and men like them all over France to make sure they couldn't move their men—small groups of fighters, multiple targets, coordinated strikes. Nancy was on the road twenty-four hours a day, briefing saboteurs on exactly where and when to cut rails and supplying them with the grenades and plastic explosive with which to do it. Telegraph poles and high-tension wires would go down in a blizzard, the heavy machinery factories would grind to a halt and every transmission station in Cantal would be reduced to a shower of sparks.

They didn't even have to wait a week. The next lines of the Verlaine poem were transmitted late on June 5, and Nancy, Gaspard, Fournier and Tardivat gathered their men at dawn the next day.

They had about a hundred of their best fighters on the plateau and another fifty youths primed to head out and give the go order to the other scattered camps. Half wore the leather jackets Fournier had stolen, the rest a ragtag outfit of peasant clothing, British army boots and berets. Nancy climbed up on a log on the tree line and looked down on them. Dirty, scruffy-looking buggers, but every one of them had a revolver in their waistband, a Bren slung over their shoulder and plastic in their pack. And they were straining to be off.

"Men of France!" Nancy called to them. "Today is the day we have waited for. The liberation of France has begun. You know what to do, so do it well. Claim back your country and let's give the Boche the kick in the balls he's been asking for."

They cheered like maniacs, then their squad leaders were leading them off in groups before the echo had died away. Denden offered Nancy his hand, and she took it to jump off the log again with a bounce.

"Positively Churchillian, darling!"

"*Mon colonel?*" It was Mateo, already kitted out and handing her her pack. She took it and strapped it over her back.

"You sure you don't want to come, Denden?"

"No thank you!" He lifted his hands. "Far too many guns involved. Mother will stay home and arrange a decent welcome for you when you get back."

He made a fuss of checking her pack. "Got your grenades? Revolver? Plastic? Rope? Murderous fellow fighters?" He let his eyes drift to Tardivat, the three Spanish fighters and the rest of the men Nancy was taking with her. "Yes, I see you have." Then he smiled. "Play safely, Nancy, and come home."

She blew him a kiss, then led her men down and into the woods.

41

The few guidebooks published on the beauties of the Auvergne in the years before the war all recommended the joys of travel by train. The views afforded to a comfortable traveler in the first-class carriages of the deep gorges, pine-covered mountains and sudden mountainscapes were not, they insisted, to be missed. And, in particular, every traveler should experience that triumph of engineering by the acknowledged genius Gustave Eiffel, the Garabit viaduct. The guidebooks listed the numbers with shivering pleasure: a single span of almost 550 feet, a smooth arch rising 400 feet above the Truyère River in an elegant lace of wrought iron. A wonder. A work of art as well as a miracle of engineering skill.

And Nancy was going to blow it up.

No one used the railways for pleasure now. The tracks were the snaking dark arteries carrying German men and arms north and south through the heart of France, slow, hulking iron troop trains, packed with soldiers and cigarette smoke, now heading toward the allied landing sites. The Allies had managed to keep their plans quiet, however—Nancy had heard of reinforcements being prepared for landing sites in the south and north—and the Germans were forced to wait and see which way to pounce.

Nancy found out which while she was packing her backpack from the warm voice of *Ici Londres*. Normandy. She'd have put her wedding ring on Calais, but no. Far away on the cold Atlantic shores in the fog and surf, thousands of troops were struggling through the sand and now the race was on. If the Nazis could get their men and heavy armaments up to those beaches in the next couple of days, the Allies might be pushed back into the sea. If the Resistance could stop them, gum up the works, block and sever those arteries, then the great German war machine would seize up, bleed out, and the troops on the Normandy beaches might be able to hang on and force their way into France.

Fournier led a crew of men to take out a railhead just south of Clermont-Ferrand; Gaspard would destroy the fuel train heading up from the coast, then the fuel manufactory itself; and Nancy, Tardivat and their team would take out Eiffel's bridge over the Truyère.

It was the main target she'd been given in the days after Buckmaster had held a gun to her head, and he said himself it was a bugger. Crisscrossed riveted iron, complex woven metal, a beautifully balanced beast which could withstand multiple failures at multiple points and still not fail. But it had to go. If the Germans couldn't use it, their networks would snarl. If Nancy's other groups also took out their targets—signal boxes, junction points, bits of the line where the tracks turned in awkward curves—their networks would be choked and the repairs would take months.

The engineers in London, looking at fuzzy reconnaissance photos, old drawings, postcards and the photographs one of them had brought back from a very pleasant motoring tour in the area, said the key point to attack was at the highest part of the arch, where the train line rested on its back, but to be sure, it would be best to blow the charges when a train was crossing the gorge too. The extra weight should make it certain the arch would fall. They were sure. Nancy could imagine them taking their pipes out of their mouths and shrugging round a table in Baker Street. Almost sure.

It had seemed straightforward enough when they told her

about it in London, but when Nancy first saw the bridge, a week after she'd dropped, her heart had sunk. It was a monster. The numbers in the guidebooks meant nothing until you stood below it, craning your neck and seeing it towering above you against the pale blue sky.

The banks on either side of the bridge were almost sheer, so to get to the base of the arch you had to scramble down a brush-covered slope and skirt round the massive stone pilings. You could go at it from the north side, but the more gentle gradient on that bank meant it would make life much easier for anyone with a rifle and a steady hand to spot you before you got there, or send you plummeting off the arch before you got half-way up. In the photographs taken before the war, a metal ladder had led up the side of the concrete piles on each shore, but the Germans had taken those off with a blowtorch.

If you could make it onto the top of the piling, though, a long, narrow flight of iron stairs ran all the way up the curve of the arch. The only problem was, given that pretty open lacework of iron, it would be bloody obvious when a handful of Maquisards ran up it with heavy packs of explosives on their backs.

The Germans knew the viaduct was crucial and they guarded it well. Nancy had watched long enough, sitting in the spring rain for hours at a time with a notebook and a hip flask, to recognize some of the men guarding it. Three patrols were on the move at all times, going up and down the narrow walkways on the top of the bridge. A bell rang ten minutes before a train was due to cross to give them time to clear, and they always did it at a jog. Sensible. Four more patrols went up and down the riverbanks and they'd built themselves wooden guard posts, like lookout towers in a prison camp, on each side of the bridge, with heavy machine guns. Nancy and Tardivat had broken their brains late into the night working out how to deal with them.

Then there was the problem of knowing when the trains were going to cross. One thing of which Nancy was pretty sure was that they wouldn't keep to the regular timetable once news of the invasion hit.

They needed a diversion to cover their approach and ambushes on the northern shore to take out the patrols. Then Nancy, Franc and Jean-Clair would scramble down the slope, climb the piling, sprint up the shallow stairs, lay the charges to go off as the train crossed and scarper back down the way they had come. Simple really.

Setting up the diversion was easy. Easy-ish. A narrow road bridge, a sad flat ugly sister of Eiffel's beautiful arch, crossed the river about 350 meters upstream. It had to go. Rodrigo led that team. The patrols on the banks would be next, then Tardivat, Juan and Mateo would stay in place to keep the men up top distracted. And it all had to happen fast. Sure, they might get lucky and take out the patrols, plant the charges and piss off again without the Germans being any the wiser, but it was a hell of a risk. If they were spotted too soon, the men in the guard towers would warn the train and stop it before it went over the bridge. Even if the charges still blew, Eiffel's bridge might be reparable, and instead of a gut punch the whole thing would just be an irritation. Nancy wasn't in the mood to just be an irritation.

42

A middle-aged man in overalls cycled slowly down the back road from Saint-Georges, the front wheel of his bike creaking on each turn, until he heard a low whistle from the steep bank above him. He clambered off his bike, lit his pipe and waited. As he sent a contented cloud of smoke into the air, Nancy and Tardivat emerged from the tree line and greeted him.

He didn't bother speaking, just handed them a sheet of paper, turned his bike around in the road and set off again. Nancy would have kissed him if he'd only stayed still long enough. He was a train driver who had spent thirty years loving every engine, every sleeper and rail on his patch, and now he did everything he could to help the Resistance destroy them. Just as long as you didn't ask him to get chatty. Nancy was pretty sure she could rely on him, but they had set up this meet the day the first lines of the poem had been transmitted, and she couldn't be certain he'd heard the next lines yesterday evening on *Ici Londres* until she heard that squeak of his bike.

"How long have we got?" Tardi asked as she studied the paper.

"Forty minutes."

They picked up the rest of the team from their cover farther off the road and forded the Ruisseau de Mongon, a fierce little tributary of the Truyère, without being spotted, dodging between the beech trees and pines. Nancy was grateful for every moment she had spent on these tracks now and every hour of PT she'd endured. The climb was fierce; they had to drag themselves up, reaching from one slender trunk to the next until they reached a narrow promontory where they could see both the road and the rail bridge.

Nancy got out her compact and Tardivat raised his eyebrows. "I assure you, *mon colonel*, you look beautiful."

"Grow up, Tardi," she said, then rather ruined the effect by sticking her tongue out at him. She checked the position of the sun, flicked open the compact and twisted the mirror, angling it to give three quick flashes. Far below them on the river, a single flash answered them. Nancy flashed the mirror again, twice this time.

"They'll blow it in twenty minutes?" Tardi said, looking at his watch.

"That's right. Now, shall we get a move on? All clear on the plan?"

Jean-Clair rolled his eyes. "*Mon colonel*, I can draw this bridge in my sleep and every time I swallow I taste steel." He patted his backpack. "Can we blow it up now?"

Nancy felt her lips twitch in a smile, her fingers tingle. This is living, she thought. This is what it is to live.

"Roger that."

Tardi, Mateo and Juan headed out first, then eight minutes later Nancy followed with Franc and Jean-Clair, staying high up the slope where the trees gave them some cover, and looking down on the lower track that the Germans patrolled, winding its way along the line of the river, halfway down between them and the water. Nancy was as close as she could get now without losing the cover of the trees; that left a hundred meters of open ground sloping fiercely downward before they got to the concrete pilings.

"Ready?"

The two men nodded without looking at her, focused only on the base of the bridge. Mateo was clenching and unclenching his fists.

Nancy looked at her watch. "Now!"

A muffled rumbling explosion from the road bridge, then another sharper detonation and Nancy saw a great plume of stone and smoke fountaining up in the center of the river. Franc and Jean-Clair set off down the slope at once; she couldn't resist twisting sideways to see the patrol on the western edge of the path spinning toward the sound and straight into a burst of machine-gun fire from the trees. They crumpled to the floor.

Then she ran.

Jean-Clair had already clambered to the top of the concrete piling twenty feet above their heads, fastened and tied a rope and thrown it down to them. His mother had been right about his climbing abilities and she was right to be proud, he was like a rat up a drainpipe, the darling. Franc, his sister had told her, used to sneak out of their house to visit his girlfriends in Montluçon by climbing out of their bedroom window and over the roofs in darkness. And ever since she'd joined forces with Gaspard, Franc had been terribly respectful toward her, trying to make up for plotting to kill her on day one. They both were confident with explosives now too, handling the deadly blocks with confident attention. So they were her bridge team.

She walked up the wall, leaning back on the rope, and Franc followed her. Jean-Clair gathered up the rope and returned it to his pack, and she checked her watch again.

"Fifteen minutes."

The sound of scattered small arms fire came from the direction of the road bridge. Rodrigo and his team had orders to try to keep the Germans as busy as possible.

Nancy, Franc and Jean-Clair started up the iron steps. *Don't look up, don't look down.* The crisscross ironwork cut the world into impossible shapes. Twisted diamonds of sky and river, bank

236

and woodland. A handrail of some kind would have been nice though. You'd have thought the greatest engineer in France might have considered a banister. No such bloody luck.

The patrols on top of the bridge and in the guard towers would stop staring at the remains of the road bridge soon. She thought in the rhythm of her jogging steps. South side top, blind from this angle. South side bottom, dead she hoped. North side top, blind soon, north side bottom, not blind, not dead. Hopefully still distracted. If they could reach the top of the arch before any of them thought to look up into the ironwork, they might not be seen at all. It felt good, the burn in her muscles, the thrill of doing what she had trained for. Even the weight of the plastic in her backpack felt right.

Nearly there. She checked her watch again, and at the same moment heard the warning bell above her on the tracks. The ten-minute warning. Shit. They pushed on at the final ascent, her legs screaming in protest, and she could hear Jean-Clair panting behind her.

This is it. She looked above her, searching for the right joints where the charges needed to be placed to make a chain of three blocks across the width of the rail track, four pounds of explosive in each block to tear a line slicing through the top of the arch like a hot knife.

OK. Just there.

They spread out, Nancy staying on the walkway, the two men clambering, nimble as monkeys, out across the joists. Smooth, practiced movements, no need to chat. They had both heard the bell too and knew exactly what it meant.

Nancy threaded the detonation cord through the explosive. Jean-Clair was walking, apparently on air, balancing on one of the central cross bars, his packs of explosive already in place. He caught the coil as she threw it, passed it through his own charge, slung it across to Franc. Franc buried it in his own, turned to them and grinned.

"Six minutes," she said.

Now for the pressure trigger. Franc swung across the lace-work, passed Jean-Clair and back to Nancy and took it from her, then hauled himself upward to the point immediately under the rails.

"Jean-Clair," she said, "get over here."

"Just want to be sure it's secure, *mon colonel.*"

Franc reached up, pushing the pressure switch into position where the weight of the train would set off the fireworks. They could get well away from the blast in six minutes. This was almost too...

The shots struck sparks from the iron that flew up into her face and almost blinded her. She fell sideways. Franc cried out, fell heavily onto the walkway and rolled. Nancy grabbed hold of his belt, yanking him back. The pressure switch bounced on the iron and spun into the empty air. Franc's hand shot out, just brushing it as it spiraled out into the river and disappeared. It was too far for them to even hear the splash.

"*Mon colonel...*" Jean-Clair said, and something was wrong with his voice.

She twisted round toward him as another spatter of gunfire sparked and clanged around them. Jean-Clair was gripping one of the central struts with one arm, slumped in the V of a cross-piece. His shirt was already soaked with blood, and Nancy could see the pulse of another wound in his thigh.

She abandoned the walkway and scrambled out toward him on her hands and knees along a foot-wide beam, keeping her eyes on his face.

"Jean-Clair, we can get you down."

"The pressure switch?" he panted, each word an effort.

"It's gone, forget it. The Nazis get to keep this bridge. Give me your hand."

He shook his head. Stared at her. "Give me a grenade, *mon colonel.*"

She understood. A grenade would do nothing to the bridge, but exploded here, right here, it would be enough to set off the charges.

"No."

"*Mon colonel*," he said, "please."

He couldn't say any more. She pulled one from her belt. Put it in his hand, closed his fingers around it.

"Take out the pin."

She took out the pin and brushed his knuckles with her fingertips.

"For France," she said, and he managed to smile, his eyes half open.

"For freedom," he whispered.

"Nancy!" Franc was screaming, reaching for her.

She inched backward across the beam until he grabbed her, dragging her away over the last couple of feet, then shoved her down the walkway in front of him.

There was no need to look at her watch now; they could feel the earth shaking as the train bore down on them. Above their heads they could hear the desperate warning shouts of the guards, but they were lost in the thunderous metallic roar of the approaching train. She ran. The bridge shook as it took the weight of the engine, and she looked up as the bridge became a flashing nightmare of clattering metal.

Franc shouted her name again and she realized they were at the rappel point. Not enough time. Franc had already anchored his rope and started his descent. She wove her rope around her as another burst of gunfire came from the bank, then she stepped out into the air and looked up—the train was already nearing the other side of the bank.

Her fall was too fast, not fast enough, the rope hot and tearing at her fingers. They had fucked it up, the train was going to make it over before the charges...

Everything happened at once. She hit the water hard, and

fumbled to release herself from the rope as the current turned her upside down and above her the charges blew. One, two. One, two. Grenade, middle charge, west side, east side. The world was noise and water. She was deaf and blind, turned over in the river, a wave of heat and light striking her as the rocks and roots grabbed at her legs. Her lungs began to ache. Then she felt a hand pulling at her wrist, hauling her out, and she took a great shuddering breath of air.

Tardi was dragging her ashore. She shoved him away and staggered upright in time to see Franc being pulled out of the water by Mateo. Then they stood there, mute and staring.

The smoke plume began to clear and Nancy saw the rip they had made in Eiffel's beautiful ironwork. The rest of the bridge groaned and swayed, but the train was still there, not moving. Why hadn't it raced away? She rubbed her eyes, trying to clear the river water out of her vision. No. The last carriage had been above the site of the explosion, now it hung between the twisted bars. It was jerking downward, pulling the train back.

Her hearing began to come back, the high whistle fading. Through the shrieking of the metal she could hear other sounds: screams, the screams of the soldiers in the last carriage. Too amazed to move, Nancy watched men from the train still on the bridge trying desperately to uncouple it and the pleading cries of the men suspended in the air who realized what they were doing.

Other soldiers were smashing the windows of the carriages nearer the engine and scrambling out, running north over the bridge, a panicking mass. One fell, or was shoved out of the way, his greatcoat flapping, arms flailing as he struck the water. The train shifted back again, the bridge swayed and more men went tumbling into nothingness.

Then the void won. Slowly, then very fast, the last carriage swung free and the whole train was pulled backward in a rush, the metal work sighed and twisted sideways as if trying to shrug it off and the train plunged four hundred feet into the water.

LIBERATION

Eiffel's masterpiece did not quite fall, but it sagged and twisted sideways, the line cut, the arch pulled low. It groaned, like an animal in pain.

Someone was shouting her name. "Nancy! Now!"

Tardi, shaking her shoulders.

"Fall back!" she said, and they raced together back into the woods, making for the rendezvous point, just as the fixed machine gun on the opposite bank found its range and began spattering the shingle under their feet with bullets.

43

Fournier had organized two field hospitals on the plateau, and half a dozen safe houses where a nurse, or a teacher who had some medical training, or a priest might do what they could to help the injured.

One of Rodrigo's boys had taken a bullet through the shin and Tardivat insisted Nancy drive him up to the plateau hospital and get herself seen to at the same time. She hadn't even noticed her own wound, a bullet straight through the flesh of her upper arm, until she noticed the blood mixed in with the water dripping from her sodden clothes. Tardi would gather reports from the other teams active that day and get back to her. He swore he would as he bandaged her arm.

The boy was pale with loss of blood, and dozed fitfully against the window while Nancy drove. The charcoal-powered cars were painfully slow, but they could take the climb. Three miles from camp, a Maquisard, his Bren across his chest and a cigarette dangling from the corner of his mouth, stopped them. He approached the window with his gun raised, but as soon as he recognized Nancy, dropped it and ground out his fag on the gravel road.

"Colonel Nancy! We have two wounded. Can you take them?"

"Hop in."

He waved his arm and a cluster of men emerged from the woods, carrying two boys between them, one unconscious, the other awake and gibbering with pain. He screamed when they set him down in the back.

"You were taking out the rail tracks west of here, weren't you? What went wrong?"

The man who had stopped her shrugged. "Nothing. Bad luck. Doing the tracks was easy, then we walked straight into a patrol on the way home."

Probably too pleased with themselves to be paying attention.

She didn't say that. "Get in the back. Try and keep them alive until we get help."

He looked like he'd rather go and take on the patrol again, but he clambered up, folded his jacket and stuck it under the head of the man who was screaming. The others they left in the road to make their own way back to their camps.

The field hospital was overflowing. Two doctors, three nurses and anyone who could stand it were helping out where they could. Outside the boys clustered around Nancy, shoving each other aside in their eagerness to talk of their successes—bridges burned, telephone and telegram wires brought down. Inside no one had any time to speak.

Nancy was there for hours, first to get her wound washed and dressed, then to help. She held down one whimpering boy as the doctor pulled a bullet from his shoulder. The morphine was reserved for gut shot and severe burn cases. An older recruit, a farmer in his forties, thought she was his wife. He talked to her calmly about the harvest, then squeezed her hand, said, "I have to go now," and died.

When she finally left the building the plateau was in darkness. Far below them in the valley a church bell was ringing. Gaspard, Denden and Tardi were standing, heads bowed, by a fresh row of graves. The priest from Chaudes-Aigues was standing over them, saying his prayers, his voice exhausted.

Nancy waited a little way off until he had finished, then went to join them. Gaspard's leg was bandaged and he leaned on a pale shepherd's crook—pilfered from one of the abandoned farms, no doubt. Between that and the eyepatch he looked more like a pirate than ever. It wasn't funny.

"The bells are ringing for our victories, *mon colonel*," he said as she approached. "France is rising."

"Victory?" Nancy said, staring at the graves. The gut shot boy in the back of the wagon hadn't made it. He'd stopped screaming about a mile before they reached the plateau. His friend was weeping when they finally stopped. He jumped off, head down, and strode toward the woods without looking at her.

"They knew the risks going in, Nancy," Denden said.

"Brave words from a fairy who didn't even fight," Gaspard spat out.

"The radio is my weapon," Denden said back, his voice haughty.

Oh, not this again. The more she worked with Gaspard, the more Denden seemed to go out of his way to provoke him. Fournier seemed to find their spats amusing and Tardi didn't care.

Nancy brushed the hair off her face with a trembling hand. "Not today, boys. Not here." Then she walked away.

44

The day after the disaster, Böhm walked out onto the stunted remains of Eiffel's bridge, and the guards he had been questioning, unsure what to do, scuttled after him.

They should have sent for him sooner. It was despicable, traitorous even that his superiors had delayed dispatching him to the Auvergne for so long. The fact that half the local mayors and a good number of the gendarmerie were working hand in hand with the Maquis had been clear for months. If they had sent him here during the winter, when the snow made it easier to track the Maquis, when the bare trees allowed them to see their pathetic encampments from the air, then all this could have been avoided. The Führer would have been able to move the pieces of his army at will, and the Allies would already have been kicked back into the Atlantic, defeated and sniveling and begging for the chance to join with Germany against Russia.

He turned to the guard closest to him. "You saw her, didn't you?"

"Only for a moment, sir! As she was repelling down from the bridge."

"Describe her to me."

The boy looked confused. "I don't know...so much was happening, it was just as the train..."

They both looked down into the water where the twisted carcass of the train still lay the bodies caught in the wreckage moving like weeds with the flow of the river four hundred feet below them.

Böhm sighed. "It's understandable that your mind would block such a painful memory. I have a technique which might help, if you are willing."

The guard smiled, reassured. "Of course, sir!"

Böhm came up to him, close. "Very well."

Böhm grabbed his lapels and forced him toward the torn iron at the edge of the bridge, overbalancing him, holding on. The guard's boots clanged on the metal as he struggled to keep them on the brittle bars.

"I won't let you fall. Feel. Please, just *feel*." The man looked as if he was going to be sick. "The Jew Freud theorizes that inducing the emotions of a repressed trauma brings it back. Now think."

The guard nodded and Böhm pulled him back. He staggered sideways and backward till he was on solid ground again. Böhm followed him.

"Now close your eyes and return to the attack. What do you see?"

The guard did much better this time. It was her. No doubt about it. He'd wondered, having heard rumors of a woman leading the Maquis and helping thwart the attack on Mont Mouchet, but now he was certain. Madame Fiocca, the White Mouse, now at the center of all this trouble in the Auvergne. Providence moved in mysterious ways, indeed. If it had been some other agent, Böhm would have needed time, too much time, to get to know his quarry—watch for her hiding holes, learn her habits and weaknesses. But Nancy he knew. All was not yet lost.

He walked back toward the car, where Heller was waiting, polishing his eye glasses. The younger man was unnerved to see his boss was smiling.

45

The blaze of sabotage was a beginning, not an end. London kept sending new targets and the campaign to snarl the Germans as they tried to reinforce their troops at Normandy became a battle to harry them, tie them down, exhaust and demoralize them. That meant more drops, more ambushes and a continual round of regular supply runs to the smaller groups of Maquis dotted around the region, all of them on the move to keep out of reach of the Germans.

The days bled one into another as Nancy catnapped in fields waiting for supply drops, or let one of the Spaniards drive and allowed her head to droop, her Bren still on her lap as they bounced through the back roads. The Allies had gained a grip in Europe, and it was their job to make sure they kept it. Once they had ticked off the lists from London, they made their own, working with railway crews to blow engines and tracks, cratering every road wide enough to carry armored trucks, forcing troops into smaller, more vulnerable wagons and then ambushing them in lightning raids and disappearing back into the woods when the road was ablaze with burning vehicles and filled with the screams of injured men. When the guns were blazing, she was alive, absolutely awake. The moment the immediate danger passed, her body shut down and she went through the intervening hours in a daze.

Reprisals against the civilian population had been talked

about, of course. Long before Nancy had even got back to England, the Nazis' habit of shooting hostages in revenge for covert enemy action was well known. At first they had made a pretense of executing political prisoners, couriers and communists they had on hand in their jails, but now all pretense of order, control or justice was gone. Perhaps the French thought the SS wouldn't behave like that in France. Even when, after the assassination of the Gestapo leader Heydrich, rumors reached them of two Czechoslovakian villages wiped out—men, women and children—they thought no. They only do that in the east.

Now they had their answer. That useless rage the SS men felt when they found their enemy had disappeared into the mountains and valleys was turned on the people, those tied to their land and their families who could not run.

"Shit..." Nancy blinked and lifted her head.

They were traveling down through Védrines-Saint-Loup, and the road was a familiar one. They'd bought supplies from the farm here from time to time. A ragged plume of smoke was rising straight up into the air round the next bend in the road. She rubbed her eyes, peered through the windscreen.

"Shall we go round?" Mateo asked.

Nancy examined the smoke again. "No, if that's the Boyer farmhouse, it's been burning a while and it'll cost us two hours and a ton of fuel to detour. Keep going."

They saw the first body before they turned the corner. An old man, a worker on the farm who'd sold them cheese from the back barn. The Germans had strung him up in one of the chestnut trees whose heavy branches shaded the road. Nancy felt her mouth go dry. Mateo turned the corner, slowing down.

Two more bodies, the farmer and his wife. Boyer had lost an arm in 1918 so had been spared the call up and worked like a battalion to keep his animals fed and his storehouses full. The couple had been hanged side by side from the door to the loft of the hay barn. Their children were trying to get them down.

The girl, twelve maybe, was up in the loft, trying to saw through the ropes with a penknife while their son, a little younger, was waiting below, his arms raised, ready to catch the bodies. Behind the loft the farmhouse continued to smolder.

"Stop," Nancy said.

"Nancy, there's nothing we can do," said Mateo.

"Stop the fucking car, and take Jules and help those kids get their parents down."

He knew not to argue when she spoke in that tone of voice. He stopped the pickup, climbed out and through a sort of fog Nancy heard him giving his orders to the boys riding in the back.

Now two of her men were holding the legs of the man and woman, while another pair sawed through the ropes up top. The bodies fell like ripe fruit. It reminded her of that time Henri took her to see the harvest in Bordeaux, how the thick purple bunches fell into the waiting baskets, full of juice, the dusty purple of their skins.

The boy and girl circled round the men, mewling. The girl was pawing at her dead mother's skirts as the man who had caught her carried her across the yard. They didn't have time to stop and help bury them. Mateo told them to lay them down under the slope of the woodpile. He closed their eyes and worked the ropes off their necks while the girl sat on the ground between the bodies, still keening wordlessly, turning right and left touching them, holding their hands and dropping them, picking them up again.

Nancy got out of the car, took an envelope from her tunic, counted out a fistful of notes. What was a parent worth? Two parents, a home? She didn't have enough for that. Enough for food for a few weeks. Should she give it to the boy? Where was the boy?

He came at her fast, with a roar of hatred, his little pocket-knife, the knife his sister had been using to try and saw through the ropes, held out in front of him. When did he get hold of that?

He was screaming. That it was her fault. That he would kill her. She just watched him come. Didn't move. Mateo turned from the bodies, raised his gun, but Jules was too quick—he jumped down from the gatepost where he'd been sitting and caught the boy with his rifle butt. The kid went down like a sack of oats, his knife spinning away from him across the dry mud of the yard. Jules bent down, examined the boy, then stood.

"He'll live."

Nancy still didn't move. Jules took the money from her hand then jogged across to the girl and gave it to her. She didn't understand. You could see that. Her mind was scattered with the horror of it all. Perhaps it would come back. She didn't even seem to notice her brother laid out on the ground by the gate. Jules pushed the money into the pocket of her pinafore and left her.

Then Nancy's men were back in the car, and she was back in her seat and the farmhouse disappeared back into the folds of the valley.

Back at the bus, after she'd told them the location and timing of that night's drop in a monotone, Mateo handed her a single sheet of paper.

"It was pinned to Monsieur's coat," he said. Then he picked up his rifle and, with the other senior men, ducked out of the bus, leaving her alone with it.

She unfolded it. Her picture. A good likeness too. "Reward for murderous and unnatural English spy, Nancy Wake, aka Madame Fiocca, aka the White Mouse. A million francs." That boy could buy a new farm for that. She knew that wasn't why he had attacked her, but for a moment she was sorry he hadn't managed to get to gut stab her and claim the cash. *Fuck. Get it together, Nancy.* If they were ready to do this, hang a husband, a wife and an old man for her sake, what were they doing to

Henri? She remembered the first time she had seen Gregory after his stay with the Gestapo, and tasted bile in her throat.

The door of the bus slammed open. It was Denden.

"Nancy! Have you sorted out the reception committees for tonight? They are going to rain all sorts of goodies on us."

She didn't reply, just handed him the notice. He scanned it quickly, raised his eyebrows.

"A million francs! My, my! Well, don't let it go to your head."

She grabbed a glass off the table and poured herself a large measure of whatever the hell it was in the clear glass bottle on the shelf. Some sort of brandy. Burned like hell.

"It's not funny, Denden. These sick bastards have my husband, and they know exactly who I am. They'll take it out on *his hide*."

He held up his hands. "Sorry, sorry! Just a stupid joke."

She poured herself another drink and drank it. Closed her eyes and saw the old man's body swinging from the chestnut tree. Who would cut him down?

"Yes, it's all one big fucking joke to you, isn't it?" she muttered darkly to the glass. Out of the corner of her eye she saw Denden flush.

"What did you say?"

"You know, Gaspard has a point." She picked up the bottle and slouched opposite him, took another swig. "I'm responsible for hundreds of lives, but you prance around like you're on holiday."

He lifted his hands. "Here we go!"

"Sticking your cock in every hole you can find…" The corner of his eye twitched, a sure sign he was hurt. She knew that. Remembered it from training. Didn't care.

"Fine, Nancy! Take your guilt out on the queer!"

"We're out there, sacrificing everything…" She could feel the rope in her hands. She saw her own hands tying it round their necks. Saw herself kicking them out of the loft, laughing as the rope squeaked and stretched.

"Yes, come on then, all your self-loathing, lance the boil…"

"And you won't even pick up a gun, because you are *a fucking coward.*"

She took another swig, watching how the words stuck him right between the ribs.

"Apologize, Nancy," he said standing up, his face white.

She looked at him and found she didn't want to apologize. "That's 'Colonel' to you."

He waited, and when he spoke again his voice was cold.

"Message from London, Colonel. You are to pick up a shipment of bazookas and a man to train the Maquis in their use. Tomorrow night. Courçais. Rendezvous is the Café des Amis. Contact is blond, code name René. Ask him the time, he'll tell you he sold his watch for brandy."

She studied him. He hated her at this moment, she could see it. And it felt right.

"Dismissed."

He saluted and left her to the bottle.

Still no proper sleep, and when she did fall into a half-doze, she dreamed of Böhm, his face in the square. It kept flickering in between memories of bomb blasts, of flames. Then, as his smile grew kinder, warmer, the flames engulfed her and she woke hearing her mother's voice whispering in her ears. She came to, finding herself sitting on the edge of a field near Saint-Marc. For crying out loud, she'd been napping in the middle of a drop. The canisters were already coming down, the sky was full of them.

She pushed herself to her feet and Tardivat turned to look at her.

"*Mon colonel,*" he said softly. "Rest if you can, the men can gather these in. They know what to do."

She shook her head. "This is my job, Tardi."

"It is the job of each of us, and the responsibility of each of us."

252

LIBERATION

Nancy didn't hear the last part; she was already striding across the field.

One of the containers had a black cross chalked on the side. A care package for her. Buckmaster must have passed the message to Denden that it was coming, and that was why he had been so cheery about the drop tonight. She remembered the first time one came, including face cream from Vera, it *had* felt like Christmas. She wasn't looking for presents from Daddy Buckmaster now though. As soon as the container was in the back of the truck she clambered up after it and unbolted the latch, ignoring the grumbling of the men who muttered it "wasn't procedure." The cross marked not just the fact that the canister contained a package for Nancy, but also its rough position, so it was the work of minutes to pull it out from in between the packs of plastic explosive. She hopped out of the truck again and leaned against the cab as she unwrapped the bundle. More face cream and a bottle of cologne. The cologne was a decent antiseptic, so she kept that. The cream she would hand over to the first female villager she met. Then there was the letter.

Very sorry to report no news of our friend delayed in Marseille, it said. Typed. She could see Vera at the desk in Baker Street tapping it out while the officers went to and fro in their nice clean uniforms discussing their losses among the agents in France: who was dead, who had burned out, who had ended up in a camp, a cellar. Then a note in Buckmaster's firm hand. *Courage, my dear. The end is coming.*

Fuck him. The nearest he'd got to action in this war was watching his agents clambering over an assault course. Had they even bothered trying to get any news of Henri? Of course they hadn't. They were just pretending to keep her quiet a little longer. Keep her pretty nose to the grindstone until some Nazi sadist smashed her face to smithereens or hanged her from a hayloft. But Böhm knew. Böhm knew where Henri was.

253

46

T he boy stepped into the middle of the road. Nancy had to brake hard and wrench the wheel to avoid killing the idiot. When he ran over to the window, Mateo curled his finger around the trigger of his pistol, but the boy was already talking too fast to notice.

"Madame Nancy!"

She recognized him now. She'd seen him peering at her from the doorway of a room in a house near here. His father had been one of the men killed in the rail attack Fournier led on D-Day. She remembered the speech she'd made to the young widow, one of ten she'd made that week telling families how the men they loved had died for France.

"Relax, Mateo," she whispered. "What is it, son?"

"The Milice are in Courçais. They have sealed up the place," the boy said. He was pale in the evening light. "You should stay away."

The Milice. Nancy hated them almost more than she hated the Nazis. French fascists given weapons and uniforms by Vichy and their German overlords to hunt Resistance fighters.

"You and your mother doing OK? You need anything?"

The boy shook his head. "My father would have wanted me to warn you," he said staunchly.

Nancy managed to smile at him; she knew it was fake, an impersonation of the sort of smile she might have given a boy like this a year ago, when she didn't have blood in her eyes, but it was close enough to being real.

"He would have been proud of you," Nancy told him. "Thanks for the warning."

"You're still going, Madame?" He looked up and down the road.

"I am, kid. People to see."

She started the engine and left him on the roadside.

Mateo cleared his throat. "But Nancy…we can arrange another meet."

She pressed her foot on the accelerator, feeling her heartbeat, steady and slow. "But Mateo, I need a drink."

The square was deserted. The main café was shuttered, but the place they'd been told to meet this René was up a narrow side street and the lamps inside were lit. There was hardly any one about, just an old man passing in the street, his shoulders hunched against the evening chill, glancing sideways at them as the light glimmering through the closed shutters of the café fell across their faces. Nancy pushed open the door. A quiet night, obviously. Only four men. All Milice. And the patron and a girl behind the bar. Looked like their contact wasn't there yet.

Nancy sat down at a table in the center of the room. The girl, stringy, and too young to be working in this place, approached them, her eyes darting everywhere.

"Cognac, dear," Nancy said. "Bring the bottle."

"Shit," Mateo said as the girl went wordlessly to fetch it.

"What?"

"Look above the bar."

Nancy glanced over. Her wanted poster was pinned up on the beam.

Mateo leaned closer. "Let's go, Nancy. While we still can."

The girl came back and poured the first round.

"Sorry, Mateo," Nancy said. "But I really want this drink."

She knocked it back and the girl poured her another.

"What's your name, dear?"

"Anne," she replied in a whisper. Her hair was dirty but combed back carefully behind her ears and her cuffs were clean.

Nancy smiled. "Like *Anne of Green Gables*! That's my favorite book. Have you read it?"

Mateo looked left and right. The other patrons were watching them now.

The girl shook her head.

"But how rude of me." Nancy nudged Mateo, showing him the gun already in her hand under the table. "I should introduce myself. I'm Nancy Wake. That's my poster above the bar."

The girl turned, blinked at it, then back at Nancy. "They are offering a lot of money for your capture, Madame."

Nancy nodded as if considering this question for the first time.

"Yes. Do you know why the Gestapo offer steep rewards for people like me, Anne? It's not to motivate the Germans—no. They'd shoot me or turn me in for free. It's for the French. For French cowards. For men and women who want to lick the shit off Nazi boots rather than stand up and defend themselves. For Frenchmen who say they love their country and claim the people they betray are just criminals, Jews and communists. Clever. These rewards make us wary of friends and neighbors. My husband—one of his spineless employees ratted him out. But here's the thing: collaborators won't get to spend their reward. No, we're going to find them—every Vichy politician, every *Milice thug*—and we're going to hang them by their traitorous little necks."

One of the patrons stood, reaching for his side arm. Nancy spun round and shot twice from the hip just like they'd taught her. The man fell backward, sending the table and glasses smashing to the ground. Anne didn't scream, just fled behind the bar.

LIBERATION

Nancy shot the second Milice while he was still fumbling to get his gun out of his holster.

The third one came at her with a knife. Cowards and bullies joined the Milice, and cowards were no good in a knife fight. Nancy used his momentum to tip him down onto the wooden floorboards, then twisted the knife from his hand and plunged it into his neck in one smooth movement. Like a dance. And she had been such a good dancer. Oh those nights dancing with Henri under the star-spangled sky! The man beneath her spluttered, coughed a fine spray of blood, which she felt on her face like summer rain, and went still.

One, two, three. Mateo killed the last of them as he made a dash for the door. He sprawled in front of it. From man to meat in three seconds. That was the lesson of war. We are all just flesh. Nancy reached for her glass and finished her drink. Good stuff.

She was counting out notes to pay for the drinks, and a bit more for the mess, when the door jangled open and a tall skinny blond man in a black jacket stepped into the room. He saw the dead bodies on the floor, the smashed glasses, Mateo with his pistol drawn and Nancy paying the bill, her hands red with blood, and he laughed, loud and long.

"Hey, this is better than the usual password bullshit! I'm René. If you've had enough fun, you want to come with me and pick up the stuff?"

Nancy and Mateo followed him out back into the darkness.

Heller said a word of thanks into the phone, then went directly along the corridor and knocked on the door of Böhm's office, going in before waiting for a reply. Böhm was working in a circle of lamplight, making his steady way through the pile of action reports on his desk. The volume of them increased every day—robberies, ambushes, anti-German pamphleteering, crude caricatures of the Führer painted on the walls.

"Madame Fiocca has been seen in Courçais," Heller said as soon as Böhm looked up.

"When?" Böhm asked.

"Now. She was seen entering a café with a man not more than ten minutes ago." Böhm got to his feet and Heller watched in confusion as he picked up his greatcoat.

"Bring the car round, Heller. I want a team of our men to follow us from here, and send up three squads from the barracks. I will have checkpoints in place at the mile point on every road out of that village within the hour, please."

"We are going, sir? Now?"

He saw Böhm's face distort, a quick and suppressed glimmer of frustration, but when he spoke his voice was under control.

"Courçais is only twenty minutes away in a fast car. Mrs. Fiocca obviously has business to attend to there. We go now. Too much time has been wasted in this war by men afraid to act independently and decisively, Heller. I will not be numbered among them."

47

M ateo was pissed off at her. Nancy could feel it coming off him in waves as they sat in the cab of the little truck. He disapproved of what had happened in the café and now was shooting her brooding disappointed looks like a maiden aunt who caught you not sitting up straight at a tea party. What was his problem? He hated the Milice, and now there were four fewer of them in the world, and they'd died easily, not strung up in front of their families or tortured into madness in Gestapo cells.

She was so busy being angry at him that she hardly noticed the track René was guiding them along in the chugging truck, out to the west of the village through copses of beech and chestnut. It ended at a two-story barn.

They clambered out of the truck in silence and followed René into the barn. The air was cool and dry and smelled of leather and fresh straw. René hung up his lamp on a nail hammered into one of the struts between the stalls and rubbed his hands together. They watched as he kicked aside the straw and pulled up a trapdoor, chatting as he did. Not the babbling, ingratiating speech of a nervous man, just a low happy burble. Mateo might have disliked the scene at the bar, but René seemed only pleasantly amused by it.

"Southgate arranged for these to be dropped in February but told me to keep them out of the way until D-Day. When I heard the news of the landings my fingers were itching to tell you, but no Southgate, no orders. Poor René! All these lovely toys and no one to play with them."

"The Gestapo picked up Southgate in Clermont in March."

René paused. "That is a shame. A nice man." Then he giggled. "Though he lacked your flare, Colonel Wake."

He unhooked the lamp and lowered it so they could see inside the space dug under the barn. A dozen hessian-wrapped tubes. Nancy hadn't seen a bazooka since training in the Hampshire mud, but she recognized the deadly heft of them, sleeping under the horses.

"How much ammunition do you have?"

"Enough to take out a battalion." He caught the look in her eye and shrugged. "Fifty rounds for each."

"Come on then," Mateo said gruffly, and they began to maneuver each one out of its hiding place and stack them near the door.

Heller had selected an excellent driver and they covered the ten miles to Courçais in just under twenty minutes. Heller struggled to keep his torch steady as they sped up the road, reading to Böhm from his intelligence file on the village and its inhabitants. The last dregs of the fallen brandy bottle were still dripping from the table top into the blood of one of the murdered Milice when Böhm entered the café.

The bar owner stuttered out his account of the woman, the murders and the man who came to meet her. Half an hour later, Heller brought him the news that the checkpoints had been set up and Böhm left the scene of Nancy's madness. All these strange meetings and coincidences. He felt almost sorry for her. If he could only reach her somehow, make her see. Lights were flickering behind the shutters of a dozen of the houses now. Heller followed him into the square and found him staring up into the star-studded sky.

"Set up the loud speaker," Böhm said.

"It will take a little time, sir," Heller replied.

Böhm only nodded. He seemed deep in thought, still looking up into the night.

The bazookas had a thrilling power to them, even in their hessian covers and smelling of straw and earth. Nancy smiled. A round could blow an armored jeep ten feet in the air. If you got lucky, they could disable or destroy a tank. They needed two men to operate them properly, and the guys using them needed to be properly trained or they'd blow each other apart, but it was like being able to carry a cannon over your shoulder.

The door creaked open, and Nancy glanced round.

The girl from the bar. René pointed his pistol from the hip; Nancy held up her hand and he didn't fire. She stepped forward. The girl was shaking.

"Anne? You followed us? You could have been killed, you stupid child," she said.

Anne put her hands out. "Please, Madame, take me with you! I can cook, I can clean. Don't send me back to Maman."

Nancy sighed. "Don't be ridiculous. Go home to your family."

"I want to help fight! My family are Milice, I hate them. I wish my father and brother had been in the bar when you came in."

Nancy looked at René.

"I don't know her," he said. "Or this place. I just use this barn for storage. I don't like this village. Too fascist. I hear they were very sorry when they found they had no Jews to give up here, though they looked carefully in every single cupboard just to make sure."

"And I know a way out of town," Anne said quickly. "A track through my uncle's farm just north of here. There are already Germans in the square, they are setting up roadblocks."

"Thanks to your little escapade," Mateo growled, looking at

Nancy. He peered out of the doorway of the barn. "We have to get moving. Lights coming up from the village."

"Please, Madame!" The girl put her hands together, and she looked like one of those sentimental Victorian adverts of a poor, golden-hearted child praying for her sick puppy. "I do not want to go home."

Nancy could relate to that. "Fine. Let's finish loading, and hurry the fuck up."

A sudden squeal of static booming up from the village made them freeze.

"What the hell?" Mateo said. "Let's get moving."

Nancy put her hand on his arm. "Wait."

The voice curled up from the square. She knew it at once, the exact, slightly accented French of the officer in the Rue Paradis, the man she had seen presiding over the execution in the town square.

"Madame Fiocca? Nancy? I know you are there. This is Major Böhm." He paused for a moment, as if expecting her to answer, then continued. "That was an ugly business in the tavern, Nancy. As if you *want* to get caught. I've seen it before, the guilt has driven you mad. I wonder how your men feel? Do they know that you're leading them to ruin, just as you did Henri?"

She heard him. She felt his voice in her bones. She looked around her. The girl had clambered into the cab of the truck; René had paused to listen, his hand resting on the box of ammunition he had just loaded into the back. Mateo had his shoulders hunched, staring at the ground. He would not look at her.

"Madame Fiocca, Henri is still alive."

Nancy felt her whole body lurch forward into the darkness, felt Mateo's hand on her elbow, steadying her. She strained forward to listen.

"I swear to you he lives. Give yourself up, Nancy, and I shall arrange for his release. It is as simple as that. You know I am in Montluçon. Come to me."

She took a step forward as the voice clicked off, and Mateo's grip tightened on her arm.

"*Mon colonel!*" he hissed, and she shook herself.

"Who is Henri?" René asked conversationally.

"My husband," Nancy answered him. "My husband."

"We have to leave, Nancy," Mateo said. "Now."

He almost shoved her into the cab, as if she were a prisoner, then as soon as they heard René climb into the back, he released the brake and they moved off into the dark.

48

Henri was alive. The idea she could save him made her heart flower and burst. She could see him arriving back in Marseille, see him being greeted by his old friends, even his father and his sister, and the joy she felt stopped her breath. She had not known, had never dared realize, how desperate she was to trade her life for his. She had thought only of helping speed the war to an end, willing him to survive until then. This was so much better. The road passed without registering on her mind; she only realized they were back as the truck nosed carefully up the track to the camp. Something was wrong. Perhaps it was the lack of a reception committee. The men knew they'd been out looking for bazookas and normally the prospect of new kit would make them as giddy as kids waiting for Father Christmas. No cooking fires either. She spotted Juan jogging toward her across the field. The way he carried himself confirmed her fears.

She got out. "Wait here," she said to Anne over her shoulder. "Stay in the truck. Don't say anything to anyone other than René and Mateo."

Mateo had gone to greet his brother, and now they came toward her together.

"What is it?"

"*Mon colonel*, Gaspard caught Captain Rake with a recruit. Fournier and Tardivat are away at the lower camp. Gaspard—"

"Shit!"

LIBERATION

She strode up the hill. Most of the men were staying at a distance, but a group of perhaps twenty were clustered round one of the waste pits, laughing and nudging each other. A couple of them slunk off sideways as they saw her approach, without even bothering to warn their playmates she was on her way. One guy had his cock in his hand and was pissing down into the hole.

At last the pisser heard her coming and half turned, his greasy little face still pink with amusement. She hit him, hard on the side of the jaw, and he went down, getting piss all over his trousers in the process.

"Where is Gaspard?"

The men started backing away. For the first time she looked into the hole. Denden was curled up in the corner of the pit on a pile of shit and animal bones. His hands covered his face, but she could see the bruises blooming on his neck and cheek. They had beaten him first. The impulse to shoot someone was almost overwhelming.

"*Mon colonel.*" It was Gaspard, sauntering out from under the tree line with a fag between his stubby fingers, looking as if he was just out for a quiet stroll.

"Get him out of there," she said.

Gaspard shrugged. "The pervert was discovered corrupting a recruit."

"I imagine the recruit was enjoying it."

Irritation flickered across Gaspard's face. "These men do not volunteer to be the prey of a disgusting deviant."

She spoke softly and clearly. "That *British officer* is the reason you have weapons, ammunition and information. Without that highly trained *British officer*, you are nothing but a bully stealing sheep from the peasants and playing hide and seek with the local collaborators. Now get him the fuck out of there."

Gaspard's gaze didn't shift from Nancy—one, two, three— then he lifted his hand and a couple of the men crouched down at the edge of the pit and put out their hands to haul Denden up.

"No," Nancy said, still quietly, but shifting the Bren across her chest. "You, Major. You get in there and help him out."

The breeze shifted through the trees, and the dappled shade rippled across their faces. Nancy heard Mateo clearing his throat discreetly behind her.

Gaspard blinked. He sat down on the edge of the waste pit, then shoved himself off the side. His boots squelched in the crap and bones as he landed, and she thought he was going to fall face forward into the stink, but he managed to stay upright. He took three uneven precarious steps across the foul-smelling, shifting morass and put his hand out.

Denden grasped it and hauled himself upright. He was covered in filth, and blood trickled from his nose and a cut above his eye. He did not speak.

The men nearest to him outside the pit lay prone on the ground, their faces contorted as they tried to stop breathing in the stench, and put out their arms. Gaspard lifted Denden from below and Denden was hoicked bodily from the pit and rolled onto the grass. He got to his feet and wavered for a second. One of the fighters grabbed on to his arm and held him steady, and when Denden had his balance back he patted the boy's hand and was released, then walked slowly off into the woods without looking at any of them.

Nancy didn't stay to watch them hauling out Gaspard. She went straight to Denden's tent, fished out a shirt and shorts from his pack, grabbed a towel and followed him.

He was waiting for her by the bathing spot and as he saw her approach, began unbuttoning his shirt.

"Gaspard will pay for this," she said as she set down his fresh clothes and helped him pull the sodden and stinking shirt off his shoulders.

"It's nothing," he said.

"It's a fucking outrage."

He turned to let her peel the fabric from his back.

"I said it's *nothing*." His voice was vicious, clear. She was about to insist, then she saw. His back was covered in scar tissue. The thick ropes of whip scars.

"Denden…"

He bent down to untie his laces and stepped out of his boots. "You knew this wasn't my first time in France, Nancy. I was here in thirty-nine. I toured with a circus troop and ended up in Paris, passing information through the network there. Lasted almost three years. Trained to use the radio in the field when one of the other operators was shot. I was one of the agents they picked up when they broke our radio codes."

"The Gestapo?"

He took off his trousers and stepped gingerly from the rock platform into the water. He was as thin and wiry as she was. His arms from elbow to wrist were deeply tanned. She sat down cross-legged on the shore while he lowered himself under the water then emerged, pushing the hair back from his face.

"Who else? They had me for six months then deported me, but I jumped from the train with a couple of others. Made it to the Breton coast. Found a friendly fisherman."

"Why didn't you tell me?" she asked, her chin in her hand.

He poured the warm water over his skin with his cupped palms, working it through his hair.

"Because I shouldn't need to show people my scars to prove I'm not a queer coward."

Nancy flinched. She'd said that. To a man who had survived three years in occupied Paris. To a man who it turned out knew exactly what would happen to him if he were caught. To her friend.

"Denden, what I said…I didn't mean it…"

"Yes, you did." He palmed more of the water, rubbed it across his chest, then more to clean the blood from around his nose. "Everyone thinks queers are cowards. I was afraid they were right; I think that's why I started passing information in the first place." He leaned his head back, feeling the sun on his face, his arms wide. He looked like Jesus being baptized. "You think you're a modern girl, Nancy. But you're still your mother's daughter. All that dreary Bible shit is still in you somewhere, judging us all."

He stepped out of the water and she handed him the towel. He wrapped it round his middle and sat down next to her.

"You might be right. I judge myself too. It makes me a miserable bitch sometimes."

He lay back on the cool stone and looked up into the sky.

"Was it Jules they caught you with?"

"I don't kiss and tell."

Nancy had drawn in her breath, ready to tell him about the Milice, about Böhm, about what she was going to do, but that curt little dismissal caught her own confession in her throat. She'd literally dug him out of the shit, and she'd tried to apologize. She didn't owe him any more than that. Yes, she did. She knew she did, but she couldn't give it to him.

49

The incident was not spoken of afterward, and if anyone had anything to say about Anne's arrival in camp they kept it to themselves. Nancy had most of the day to prepare her notes for Denden and whatever officer SOE sent in after her before Tardi found her.

He slammed his way into the bus. She hid the notes she'd been making under the satin pillow and waited calmly for the onslaught.

"Mateo thinks you aren't going to do it, but you are, aren't you?"

She'd never seen him like this, his face flushed, voice raised. He seemed to take up all the oxygen in the narrow space of the bus, leaning toward her. She let her hand rest on her side arm.

"This German is lying to you!"

"Tardi," she said calmly, "I have to do it. If there is any chance that Henri is alive, I have to trade my life for his. I love him. He would do the same for me."

Tardivat slammed the flat of his palm against the side of the bus, making the world lurch. "Bullshit! You're not in France for him, you're here for us. That's what you said, that's what you swore."

Nancy felt a sweep of cold anger through her bones. "I've done enough for you! God, Tardi, don't panic! There will still be plenty of drops, lots of parachutes. Find some other girl to make dresses for."

He rocked back for a second as if she'd struck him, then came forward again. "We need you! No one man is worth the damage losing you will do."

She stood up quickly, forcing him to back off. "Henri is worth ten of me!" she said. "A hundred of me. You don't know, Tardi, you don't know him. You don't know either of us. My God, if there is any chance... I'd die for these men, but I'd die a thousand times over for Henri." The anger died from his face as she spoke, leaving grief, bewilderment. "You'd do the same for your wife, Tardi. Don't deny it."

She took her hand off her gun and he moved a step back.

"Maybe, *mon colonel*," he said, his voice bitter, "but I thought you were better than me."

Then he left. Nancy sat back down heavily, her head in her hands, and for the first time since she had come back to France, she realized she was shaking.

When Nancy woke the next morning the nest on the floor she had made for Anne had been tidied neatly away. She felt a brief pang of guilt at leaving the child, but Tardi and Mateo would look after her. Nancy pulled herself up on her elbows and looked out of the window. All quiet. She had not seen Tardi again yesterday, and no one else had visited to tell her what she should or should not do. That meant Mateo hadn't told Fournier or Denden about the offer and Tardi had kept her decision to himself. Good. It would be easier this way.

She would sort the men into groups for training with the bazookas and get René to brief the senior fighters on their tactical use. Then, when they were all occupied she would tell one of the junior officers who hadn't heard about Böhm's offer, Jules perhaps, that she was going to search for another drop site closer to Montluçon and be on her way.

She wondered what mood Mateo would be in. Would he

have forgiven her for the bloodletting in the café? Maybe forgive was the wrong word. For him to forgive her she'd have to admit she was wrong—and she wasn't wrong. He'd get over it. And Gaspard would be watching her too, looking for some way to pay her back for the incident with Denden. He'd crow when news of her departure spread round the camp. Couldn't be helped. Fournier would be able to stand up to him now.

At least she had some meat to throw at the buggers. The prospect of big action would focus their minds. Denden had received a message from London last night. They wanted Nancy's group to take a bite out of a German army group forty miles south, to draw off some of the troops and help clear the way for the British to land at Marseille. Thank God they had the bazookas. Time to throw some bones: she'd consult as to strategy, as Fournier knew that part of the country well; Gaspard could pick which of the men they should train with the bazookas. Let them rub that on the sore spots of their egos.

She dressed quickly and went off to relieve herself in the woods, then walked up the track to the main camp.

What the...? Tardivat had Anne by the arm. She was cowering in front of him and his arm was raised.

He saw Nancy and released the girl, throwing her forward onto the ground.

"*Mon colonel*, this stupid child set a fire going out of cover! She was sending smoke signals into the air for hours."

"Stop scaring the kid and put it out then," Nancy said.

"I made bread, Madame," Anne said, pointing at a dozen rolls sitting on a napkin on the grass. "I saw the oven last night and thought I would make a special breakfast for you, to say thank you."

Stupid girl. You don't use up resources to make special thank you meals for officers. What next? Birthday cakes? But poor kid.

271

Nancy remembered her first days as a runaway, and the kindness of strangers.

"OK, Anne. Just don't do it again."

Anne scurried past her, loading rolls into the skirts of her dress and retreating toward the old bus. Tardivat stamped out the cooking fire, swearing fluently.

"Seen any planes?" Nancy asked.

Tardivat shook his head. "But it's a clear day. They could be far enough off and high enough to see the smoke without us seeing them."

Nancy thrust her hands into her pockets. "Tell the guys to keep an extra-sharp lookout. And I need you, Fournier, Mateo and Gaspard in the bus, quick as you like. New messages from London."

He hesitated. "You're still going?"

"Yes. Afraid I'll give away our position?" She couldn't keep the sneer out of her voice.

He looked hurt. "No, I am not afraid of that. I am afraid Böhm lied, that you are breaking your promise to us for nothing."

She turned away. Not much chance Mateo would feel like getting over yesterday if he heard about Anne's mistake, then of course he'd be ten times worse when they found out she'd gone. Enough. She was done explaining herself to these men. Another hour and then her job as peacemaker, mother, confidant and nanny was over. They could sort themselves out. She walked back toward the bus.

"Madame, I'm so sorry." The girl was scampering at her side, like a puppy.

Nancy looked down at her; such a fragile little thing. How old was she? No more than eighteen. Only a year or so older than Nancy had been when she fled her home. And God knows Nancy had made enough mistakes then, only she'd had the luxury of not running away during a war.

LIBERATION

"It's my fault, Anne. I should have taken you through the security protocols last night. Rolls looks good, though." Anne smiled. "My officers are coming in for a briefing, maybe they'll forgive you when they eat them."

50

They liked the plan, she could see that. Gaspard was the king of the roadside ambush, and Fournier had developed a way with plastic which had taken out a dozen small bridges and two key factories since D-Day, but they all liked the idea of a proper battle.

Still, they were angry at her. About Anne, about Denden, and so they tried to suppress their pleasure at the idea. Christ, it was like dealing with schoolboys. Anne came in with the rolls. She'd managed to filch some butter from the general store. The smell was divine. They leaped on it. Mateo couldn't even wait to butter his, just biting down through the crust and casting his eyes up to heaven. Yeah, they'd forgive anything now. Men.

Nancy spread the butter slowly, getting ready to savor it. Tardivat pointedly ignored the plate, pointing at the map instead.

"If we can find a route here, and I know a tracker there I trust. We'll be able to use the higher ground to fire down on them. Turn that whole section of road into a killing field."

It was a good idea. She set down her roll for a second. "How many men would we need?"

Mateo grunted. She looked at him, wondering if he had some issue with the plan. He had his hand on his throat and his skin was red and livid.

"Mateo, shit, are you choking? Greedy bastard. Hit him on his back, Gaspard, give him a drink of water."

Gaspard laughed, and clapped him on the back. The coughing increased and a bubbling pool of drool gathered at the corner of Mateo's mouth. He started scrabbling at his throat, then coughed again. Blood spattered across the map.

"Fuck!" Gaspard shouted and grabbed the water cup, trying to force it between Mateo's lips, but Mateo pushed him away, staggered to his feet and out of the bus, then collapsed.

"It's poison!" Fournier said following, and dropped on his knees beside Mateo.

Footsteps thundered down the path, and a group including the other Spanish lads emerged, guns at the ready, to see their friend and brother thrashing on the grass. Mateo convulsed.

"Role him on his side!" Nancy said. She crouched down next to him, putting her hand under his head.

He stared at her, his eyes filled with panic; the blood from his mouth streamed over her wrist. She stroked his hair, tried to meet his gaze, but his eyes were darting all over. She could not tell if he knew her. She said his name again and again, quietly, clearly.

His body convulsed again, then stiffened, the muscles on the side of his neck stood out like ropes and he gave a wet, rattling gasp. His eyes went blank. It was impossible. It was true.

Nancy stood up. From behind the Spanish boys and the others Anne was watching them. Nancy started to run. The girl turned and darted into the forest, west up the slope toward the promontory. Nancy moved fast, unthinking. Anne was crying, yelping as she ran and Nancy gained on her steadily, her heart pumping hard but with no doubt as to the outcome. The girl had nowhere to go.

Anne broke through the trees on the promontory and just managed to stop herself on the edge of the rock face, her arms windmilling. She stumbled backward onto the rough grass, then rolled over to see Nancy blocking her retreat. She slid back toward the edge on her belly.

"I'm not going to hurt you, Anne."

Nancy took a step forward; Anne slithered back again. God, the terror on her face. The wild animal terror. Nancy took a long breath.

"You didn't want to hurt us, did you? Someone made you do this?"

Anne blinked, but Nancy thought she caught a tiny nod.

"I understand...I understand. Now, just come back from the edge. Let's talk, you and me. I won't hurt you."

Anne's eyes were crazed, darting left and right.

"Anne, I won't let any one else hurt you either, I give you my word."

Nancy edged closer, put out her hand. And this time Anne took it.

The poisoned bread was burning in a covered camp fire. The men watched Nancy march Anne between them and into the bus. She saw the look in Tardivat's eyes as they passed. He was asking her a question and she didn't know the answer yet.

The blood-spattered map was still on the table. Nancy left it there.

"Tell me everything."

The girl was shaking, hard, like someone with a fever.

"Come on, Anne, the better angels of my nature say we can solve our problems with talking, so talk."

"The man from the Gestapo...he said it was my duty. That I was special."

Böhm. Of course it was him.

"When?" Nancy asked.

Anne looked around as if she was expecting the officer in question to pop out from behind one of the seats.

"When did he tell you this? Last night?"

"He came to the café, minutes after you left. After your friend took you to his barn. We all knew he'd been renting it from M. Boutelle. I remember I was still crying. He was very interested when I told him my name, that we'd spoken. He was kind. The Germans are trying to build a better world. The Jews and foreigners are trying to stop them. He said it was because of women like you... You forced the Germans to do things they didn't want to do. Like burn down farms. He said if you and your men were gone, there would be peace. He said many things. He gave me the stuff to put in your food. He sent me after you."

Someone must have spotted Nancy before she'd even got to the bar. She had a fleeting image of the man passing them in the street.

"He said he'd protect my family! That I must be brave for them! He said he'd protect me!"

Nancy could feel the anger bubbling in her veins. She'd seen herself in this girl.

"He can't. Only I can do that, Anne." Anne. "Did you tell him what I said about the book?" Anne shook her head, confused. Böhm had known already what Nancy's favorite book was. "And Böhm told you to say you had run away from your mother?"

A nod.

"You know how he got that information?" Nancy said at last. "He got it from torturing my husband, you Nazi bitch."

She grabbed hold of Anne's arm, dragging her out of the bus. She tried to resist, crying and screeching, grabbing onto the old seats, the edge of the door, but she was weak and Nancy had grown strong.

"You said you wouldn't hurt me!" she screamed as Nancy threw her onto the floor at Tardivat's feet.

He hauled her upright, grabbed hold of her right arm; Rodrigo gripped her left.

"I guess that makes us both lying cunts," Nancy spat the words out.

What had Böhm done to Henri to make him give up all those small secrets of the past? Her family, her favorite book. She felt the dry heat of her old hiding place under the porch in Sydney, reading by the light which shone in bright bars through the floorboards. The threat of her mother's footsteps above.

Nancy unholstered her pistol, and offered it to Juan. "She murdered your brother."

He shook his head. "She's just a girl."

Anne sank down between the men holding her. "Let me go, I'm sorry, I'm sorry... You'll never see me again..."

"Tardi?"

"I cannot."

"Fine."

Nancy lifted the gun. Anne's head snapped up and she stared into Nancy's eyes.

"He's dead! Your husband. Major Böhm said to his captain it was a shame he hadn't lasted longer, as he'd been so helpful." Nancy began to squeeze the trigger and the girl's face distorted into a vicious grimace. "*Heil Hit—*"

Nancy fired twice. The girl's body jerked in Tardi's arms and they dropped her. Nancy re-holstered the gun and stalked off into the woods, leaving the men to clear up the mess.

She went straight up to the promontory and made it to the edge before she fell to her knees. Her hands were shaking again. She needed a moment, just a moment. Her mind would not give it to her. Henri was dead. Tardi was right, Böhm had lied. She could hear the rattle of blood in Mateo's throat, she could feel Anne's thin wrist in her grip, she could see the girl's final look of murderous rage.

There could be no peace now, not for her. Buckmaster and his type thought peace was just the end of fighting, the German army rolled up neatly, the French free and grateful. The end is near, Nancy! He was a fool. They were all fools. This hell had no end, just different colors and flavors.

The rope Denden had used to show her how to hang over the cliff was still there. Just ordinary rope, like the one the Germans had used to make nooses for the one-armed farmer and his wife. Nancy rose, picked it up. One end was still firmly attached to the tree. They were at peace now. That was peace. Not in heaven, not hell, just a place of silence where you did not have to think, to remember.

Nancy made a loop.

No love, no hate. No bullies, no propaganda, no children desperate with loathing for revenge. No rage, no guilt. No Henri.

She fitted the rope around herself.

She must look a sight. Instinct is a powerful thing. She took the compact from her pocket, flicked it open and looked at herself, wiping the corner of her mouth as she caught her own gaze.

The rage and disgust lifted her in a wave, and she threw it, Buckmaster's sweet little goodbye, hope-you-don't-get-tortured-and-starved-to-death gift hard over the edge of the cliff—then she gave chase and threw herself forward into the void.

And was caught.

Her feet on the crumbling edge, her arms forward like a sky-diver, the rope around her waist taut. The knot gave a little and she jerked forward an inch. It made her smile. Perhaps it would give. *Come on, God, if you're there. I'm easy pickings.* Perhaps she and all her sudden talent for death would disappear into the clear air of the Cantal and her flesh would feed the trees and rot away her sin.

But the rope held and she stared down and out into the valley. She thought of Böhm. That curious gentle smile that told her he was content with his world. He was in Montluçon now, at his desk, signing his forms. This prisoner dies, that village to be burned to the ground, these men to be beaten till their own mothers wouldn't know them, these to be crammed into a stinking cattle cart and carried off to Germany. *He* wasn't in hell. How could that be? She shifted her weight and lifted her arms high.

She was mistress of the void. She would bring hell to him.

51

Tardivat hated the idea, of course. His first impulse had been to comfort her, offer sympathy, having understood what it meant to have Anne throw Henri's death in her face. When she told him her intentions had changed, but not her destination, he stalked off, but not before telling her it was a suicidal, idiotic thing to do, a waste of resources and men.

"We will come, *mon colonel*," Rodrigo said. "Me and Juan. I won't let this go unavenged."

"Exactly!" Denden said, hitting the table so the dirty cups rattled. Anne's cup. "This is just revenge! Revenge for Mateo, revenge for your husband."

"What the fuck is wrong with that?" Nancy said, opening a case of grenades and passing belts of them to the two Spaniards.

"Your mission here is supposed to be for all of us," Denden replied. "For everyone the Nazis have killed, and for every life they intend to take. That's what you were trained for."

René scratched his ear. "I don't care why she's killing them as long as the Nazis end up dead. I'm in."

Denden tried again. "You're playing his game, Nancy."

"Enough!" Nancy shot him a dark look. "Gentlemen, I appreciate your concern; you don't have to come. But I will not, *cannot* let this stand." She turned to Juan. "Be ready in an hour. You too, René."

"Can I bring my toys?" René blinked at her.

"Sure."

"Yes! Come on, boys. Let's gather up some more volunteers."

Denden watched through the window as René bounced off across the camp.

"He's mad. You know that, Nancy?"

She shrugged. "We're all mad now. You have the latest instructions from London, Denden." She handed him the notes she had made the day before, in those delicate hours when she thought she could save Henri. "What's due to the families of the fighters is in here. Coordinates for possible drops and locations of the arms caches. Usual codes. You know what to do if I don't make it back."

He slipped it into his back pocket and got slowly to his feet, the bruises he had taken the previous day making him move like an old man. "I know. But make it back."

When he had gone Nancy picked up her red satin cushion and used the nail scissors to pick apart the seam at the back, then felt around in the stuffing. There were perhaps a dozen pills; they looked like pearls in the gloom of the bus. Cyanide. The plan had been to sew one into the seams of each of her shirts, an insurance policy against the Gestapo. Of course, no one at SOE had told them to kill themselves if they were taken. The pills were simply presented, very politely, as an option. Can't stand the torture? Want the rape and the beatings to stop? Can't live with the shame of having betrayed your people? Don't want to risk giving them up? Take one of Doctor Buckmaster's patent cures and worry no more.

The rumor at Beaulieu was that people didn't take them, but somehow having the option of ending things made the horror a little easier to bear. Maybe, but she knew suicide would never be her way, never be a comfort, no matter what happened. She reached into her bag again and pulled out a half bottle of cologne. Another gift from Baker Street. She unscrewed the atomizer and tipped the pills in, then watched as the fatal tablets dissolved, turning that pretty, expensive scent poisonous.

The tide really was turning. The madam in Montluçon agreed to take Nancy to headquarters for only a thousand francs and her wedding ring. They talked in the kitchen of her quiet little house in the back streets. Nancy was surprised at how easily she handed the ring over. It was just a trinket now. She wanted Henri, not that little band of gold.

"And a paper," the madam added.

"What paper, Madame Juliette?" Nancy had insisted on getting a dress as part of the bargain, and was trying it on now, admiring herself in the full-length mirror. It was cunningly cut, full length in dark blue cotton, but it brushed Nancy's curves. Just the right level of suggestion without being too obvious on the street.

"You must sign this. With your real name."

Nancy turned from the mirror to see Madame Juliette had been busy writing something.

"What is it?"

Madame Juliette held herself very upright in her chair. "I am leaving the town to stay with my sister in Clermont, now, the moment we have done what we need to do. The Germans are losing. When they lose, the people will say I collaborated. This paper says I have been a very good friend of the Resistance."

Nancy looked at her. Sleek and well fed. No doubt her clients had been feeding her little extras from the day the Germans arrived in Montluçon. Interesting. Fournier's men said the fighters who had arrived at their camp since D-Day smelled of mothballs and farmers who had refused them help last year now trekked for hours to offer them delicacies from their fields. Even with the reprisals, they knew in the end the Germans would be gone. Accounts would be called in.

Nancy took her pen and as she signed, against all the rules that had been drummed into them at Beaulieu, "Nancy Fiocca, née Wake," she heard Juliette release a shuddering sigh.

"I shall take you to the gatehouse," she said. "None of my girls are in tonight, but I am not the only whoremonger in town, Madame. Other girls might be entertaining the officers."

"That's their bad luck," Nancy replied and handed back the pen. She'd let Madame Juliette run, but that didn't mean every collaborator in town was going to be handled gently. "You have the paper. Take me there."

52

Juliette led her past the main door and into a side street. The Gestapo headquarters, a former hotel, faced onto the busy square near the train station, and every day the populace of Montluçon could see the officers in their SS uniforms, their black leather coats, welcoming in the town council members for meetings and briefings. The people watched them, and passed by as quickly as they could. Before the war, taxis and private cars dropped businessmen and tourists in front of the elegant portico, but their luggage as well as all the food and linen flowing in and out of the hotel was taken into the yard at the rear. Now it was via that yard the real business of the Gestapo happened—the vans rolling in at all times of the day and night, the guards ticking off lists as men, women and children, dumb with fear, were lifted down like livestock and hustled in through the old service doors and down into the cells.

And this way too came the pleasures the officers enjoyed—the luxury goods plucked from cellars, shops and abandoned villas, and the women. Four sentries guarded the gateway into the yard: two on raised platforms, which gave them a view of the yard itself and the road leading to it, and two others ready to lift the barrier and check the names on their lists. The sentry stared hard at Nancy, and she lowered her eyes, afraid he'd caught the flash of hatred in them. She could feel darkness in her blood and bones so poisonous she was sure she could kill this man with a touch of her fingertip.

"She's not the usual girl," the sentry said. "Captain Hesse normally likes them a bit plumper than this piece."

Nancy felt his eyes slither over her.

"Sophie is sick," Juliette said. She sounded bored, irritated. A born actress, Nancy thought, but then maybe whores had to be. "Captain Hesse said this girl would do. Now, you want to keep him waiting?"

The sentry shrugged and made a note on his logbook. "Chicken for the captain's table," it said.

Juliette was gone, back into the night at once. The sentry put out his hand, clicked his fingers and Nancy handed him her bag. He opened it. Lipstick. Scent. A couple of foil-wrapped condoms. Then he handed it back with a sniff and led her from the gate to the service door. Nancy wasn't the first SOE officer to come this way. She thought about what she had heard of Maurice Southgate, the man captured just before she dropped into France. She thought of the two wireless operators who had disappeared through these doors into the fog and darkness at the same time and wondered if they were still alive somewhere in a camp. She thought of Henri and clenched her fists, driving her nails into her palms.

A noticeboard was bolted to the wall just inside the door. Nancy looked at it sideways, just long enough to see Fournier's picture and her own, and the ridiculous money now being offered to deliver them to this very building. The sentry didn't glance at it, just led her, thumping in his heavy boots, up the narrow service stairs and then out into the part of the building designed for the guests of the hotel, and now the officers. Heavy wood paneling was punctuated with huge mirrors and electric lights glowed under stained-glass shades. Nancy walked between an infinite number of images of herself. The sentry became an army and so did she, their footsteps now muffled by the thick carpets.

He pushed open a door, nodded her in with a sneer. Five men

looked up from the table. None of them Böhm. Her instinct had been correct. He was pure SS and would never corrupt his flesh with a French whore. These men looked up at her with greedy surprise.

Another girl was already here, a blonde, sitting on the knee of an officer who didn't look more than twenty, blushing to the tip of his ears as she caressed the back of his neck and wriggled a little on his lap, making the older men laugh.

The captain nearest Nancy reached out and put his arm around her waist, pulling her toward him, running his other hand over her breasts and down her front, then pushing his hand up her skirt, inserting a finger between the top of her stocking and the flesh of her thigh. He didn't even look up at her face.

"Sweet stranger, how kind of Madame Juliette to give us something fresh."

Nancy lifted the cap from his head and put it on, then leaned forward to kiss the top of his balding pate.

"Fresh and strong, sir," she said breathily, pressing closer to him. His fingers strayed up to the cotton of her knickers and the other men chuckled. "Another drink?"

He let her move away to the side table where a carafe of red wine stood, surrounded by a dozen glasses. One of the other officers was growing impatient with the youth. He moved up his chair and began kissing the girl's neck, kneading her breasts with his fat fingers while she giggled and groaned and squirmed on the boy's lap. They were all red in the face, sweaty with building desire, impatient. They couldn't take their eyes off the blonde.

Nancy poured the contents of her scent bottle into the wine and swilled it round in the decanter before filling the glasses and setting them on the table in front of each officer, then resumed her place next to her fat-fingered friend and lifting her own glass.

"The Führer!" she said. Even in their present state, their

conditioning kicked in. Each man grabbed his glass, and raised it before drinking, repeating the toast, even if they couldn't look away from the girl panting on the boy's lap.

Nancy felt the wine touch her lips; aware of the urge to drink herself, take it down to the dregs, but resisting. Böhm was somewhere in this building, waiting for her.

All credit to the SOE, things happened very quickly now. Her fat-fingered friend began to pant, his hand to his throat. One of the others stood up, took two stumbling paces to the door, then fell onto the red and blue rug laid over the polished parquet and began to fit.

Nancy's officer looked up at her face for the first time, his fleshy face registering shock, rage and finally, Nancy noticed with great satisfaction, recognition. He fumbled for his pistol, and Nancy didn't even try to stop him, just pulled the commando knife from his belt and cut his throat.

The girl scrambled away into the corner of the room, too shocked to scream, covering her face with her hands. Nancy undid the belt from her officer, now slumped on the table in front of her, and did it up around her own waist. It sat on her hips like the belt of a western gunslinger. The boy was already dead. The last officer managed to raise his gun, but he was vomiting at the same time, and fell sideways onto the floor before he managed to squeeze off a shot.

Nancy stepped over his thrashing body and pulled back the curtains at the window and, with the light behind her, waved into the darkness. Not exactly a subtle signal, but it didn't need to be.

The darkness, the void, had her now. It was Nietzsche these moronic sadistic shits liked, wasn't it? That line, "If you stare into the abyss, the abyss stares back at you"? She'd always thought it sounded a bit weak, the sort of thing that drunk journalists said to each other in Parisian bars when they were boasting about all the dangerous men they had encountered. But she got it now. She was the abyss, she had drunk it into herself in those moments after she had shot Böhm's spy, and now the abyss wasn't just looking back at these mad men—it was coming to swallow them up.

53

The roar of an engine up the road and the guards scrambled to their guns, but too slow. The quiet of the streets had been of expectation, not peace. The van, stolen from the gendarme station, smashed into the courtyard, Juan leaped from the cab and took out the sentry who had escorted her in, while Rodrigo stood on the running plate and took out the left machine-gun post with a blast from his Bren. Juan was already running up the shallow steps to the right firing from his hip. Nancy watched, smiling, as René stood and fired the bazooka straight into the back door.

The building shook and the remaining glasses rattled on the sideboard behind Nancy. The girl squealed. Half a dozen more men charged in behind the van through the broken barrier, and four of them took positions in the high guard posts. The insistent regular burst of fire from the captured machine guns met the half-dressed guards stumbling out of the shattered back door.

Nancy stepped back over the corpses of the officers, checked the pistol and her ammunition, then stepped out into the hall. It was just like training, those walks in Inverness where the instructors pulled their levers and targets dropped down in front of you, out of the bushes, from behind doorways. Nancy shot from her hip, double taps, one, two, clearing out two sentries as they turned the corner into the paneled corridor. A sleepy-looking captain stumbled out of one of the rooms, still hooking his thin steel rimmed glasses behind his ears and blinking in confusion. He froze when he saw her, then raised his hands, started to speak. Nancy fired twice into the center of his chest and the force of the bullets knocked him back into the room. She crossed the corridor and glanced down at him. His lips were still moving, but she couldn't hear his secrets any more than she had heard the secrets of that French boy she had watched dying on the street in Marseille. His eyes blinked behind his glasses. She shot him through his forehead and walked away. Another Nazi eaten by the void. She holstered her side arm and took out her knife.

The Germans were all focused on the assault at the rear, so half of the sentries she encountered had their backs to her. It made killing them almost too easy. The knife was becoming slippery in her hand, so she wiped her palm and its hilt on her dress, humming the Partisan song. She walked down the grand staircase as if she was meeting her husband for drinks in the hotel bar. Little men in gray-green, scurrying about. She heard a yell and a burst of gunfire from the direction of the kitchens. Some of the men were in the headquarters with her then. She had to move briskly. Ground floor. Offices.

A sergeant, urging his men through to the rear of the building, turned and found her facing him. He reacted quickly, knowing he had no time to reach for his gun or knife, and rammed his fist at her.

She caught the blow on her left forearm, felt the flesh and bone of her body shudder, then drove her knife into his belly, slicing upward. This knife was almost as good as her own Fairbairn-Sykes number. London had sent her out a replacement for the one she'd lost almost immediately. Thanks, Uncle Bucky.

The manager's office. Of course that would be his, with its triple-locked safe and tall windows over the courtyard garden, which lay in the center of the hotel buildings. The door opened as she approached, and another young officer, this one with almost white-blond hair, emerged, a heavy-looking trunk of papers in his arms. He was speaking over his shoulder to someone in the room. She shot him in the face. She wasn't sure if it was because she thought the box in his arms might deflect a bullet or just because she wanted to.

She stepped over his body and into the room. There he was, Major Böhm, looking exactly as he had in Marseille when they had last met, right down to the smile of polite surprise. He was standing by the neatly arranged bookcases as if choosing one for his night-time reading.

"Mrs. Fiocca! You have come to make another inquiry about your husband, I take it? I am afraid you are not here to make the deal we spoke of in Courçais, given the manner of your arrival." He shook his head slightly. "I confess I am surprised. I felt sure you would trade your life for Henri's after all you have put him through."

He was speaking in English and she replied in the same language, the words feeling strange and awkward in her mouth.

"Anne told me you had murdered him."

Böhm looked deeply saddened. "I understand. No, no, Madame Fiocca. Why would I kill someone so useful?"

Henri. She could see him as if he were in front of her, his dinner jacket slung over his shoulder. She holstered her revolver.

"He's told me so much about you."

Nancy's head spun. Her rich, sustaining rage was now caught up and confused with love, with hope. "Is he here?"

"No. But he's in a safe place though. Very safe."

Enough. She would cut the truth out of Böhm's black heart. She launched herself at him, her knife raised to slash across his face. Her line of attack was obvious. He took a step back so his back was against the desk and caught her wrist as she came into the strike and held it in his right hand. His left arm locked around her waist, stopping her pulling free. The blade shook, their strengths balanced between them.

"He wouldn't know you now, of course," Böhm said through gritted teeth. "You're not Nancy Wake any more, are you?" She willed the blade forward, it shivered closer to his skin. "Or maybe you've discovered your true nature at last. You're just what your mother said you were. A punishment to those who love you. Ugly, dirty, sin and waste of skin."

The image of Böhm and Henri sitting together in a room, like confiding friends. Discussing what Nancy's mother had said to her, the poison she had dripped into Nancy's bloodstream every day until Nancy had run. And kept running.

"*Mon colonel!*" It was René looking for her, shouting from the lobby. "SS reinforcements arriving. Let's go!"

There was another explosion from the lobby of the headquarters and Böhm thrust her away from him. She stumbled, went down on her knees and when she looked up again he had his revolver in his hand, aiming at her head.

"Better he does not see you as you really are."

She bared her teeth at him. He grunted, as if amused, and kept the gun steadily pointing at her head.

She heard René call for her again.

"Do you know what this symbol means?" he asked.

She let her gaze flick down. The carpet on which she was kneeling, spattered with the blood of the man she had killed in the doorway, was patterned with swastikas, but not in black and red—they were spinning in rows of green and gold.

"It's Tibetan in origin," Böhm continued. "It represents the sun. The Supreme Masculine. The Führer reminds us of that so we all strive to please him. He is our father. And how old were you when your father left? What would he think of his little girl now?" Again, that polite smile. "You've killed your men, you know. You let a spy give away your position then pull out twenty of your best fighting men for a suicide raid here? I ordered an attack on your camp at Chaudes-Aigues as soon as reports of Anne's signal came in."

The door burst open. René, revolver at the ready. Böhm turned toward him, but before René could fire, Nancy sprang across the carpet, her knife in her hand, and slashed at Böhm's face.

"Fuck!" René yelled, just managing to jerk the muzzle of his revolver upward so the bullet, already speeding from the chamber, shattered the window rather than burying itself in Nancy's back.

Nancy caught him across his cheekbone, and the force of her attack made him stagger sideways, striking his wrist against the edge of the desk so his gun spun from his grip. He screamed, hand to the wound. The blood leaked immediately through his fingers and onto his collar. She came at him again, but René caught her around the waist lifting her away bodily, carrying her out of the room as she howled with rage.

"Now, Nancy!" He screamed at her, setting her down in the hall and shoving her in the small of the back toward the lobby. "Playtime's over!"

Smoke, bodies. René threw grenades ahead of them to clear their path, pulling her sideways to shield her from the explosion. The mirrors shattered, the wood paneling splintering, the long after-hiss and rumble of masonry and plaster and a dense gray cloud of smoke and dust surrounding them. René dragged her forward again and she stumbled over a gut-shot soldier still twitching at her feet. The lobby. René rolled another grenade toward the double doors of the front entrance, and as it blew her hearing was knocked out, replaced by a high-pitched, insistent whine.

René pulled her through the burning doors into the street, then picked her up again, throwing her into the back of a flat-bed truck, its cold metal floor already slick with blood. Franc was slumped beside her, back against the cab, trying to hold his insides in with this hands. She snatched his Bren off his lap and fired short bursts at the few Germans trying to pursue. They fell or scattered, looking for cover. Only when they reached the outskirts of Montluçon did she look at Franc again. He was still, staring sightless back at the hell they had left behind them.

54

The French workmen had just finished hammering sheets of plywood over the shattered window when Captain Rohrbach came into Böhm's office, giving the room the gloom of late afternoon, though it was still not yet 9 a.m.

The body of the corporal had been removed, but the blood-stained rug was still in place. Rohrbach glanced down at it as he came in, watching his step.

"Thirty-eight dead, sir."

Rohrbach had volunteered himself to serve as Böhm's new principal assistant eight hours earlier, and so far was doing a good job, gathering information, interviewing witnesses and arranging work parties to make the building safe while Böhm had his wound treated, and examined his new face in his shaving mirror.

Böhm himself had found Heller's body in the upstairs corridor. His protégé had been shot twice in the chest and once through his forehead. Executed by Mrs. Fiocca herself as she made her bloody way from the officers' meeting room to his office. Heller's death hurt and surprised him, not only because Böhm appreciated his junior officer's capacity for hard work, his intelligence, but also because so many men like him, men on whom the Reich had planned to build its glorious future, had been lost. And lost to the stubborn, senseless Resistance of degenerates like Mrs. Fiocca and their subhuman allies in the east.

Böhm resolved to ask his wife to visit Heller's family when she had the opportunity. It was fitting for them to mourn together with his people both the man and what he represented.

Böhm dismissed the workmen—they shuffled out without speaking—before he spoke to Rohrbach again.

"And the Maquis camp?" Böhm asked. He spoke lightly, but the answer would make all the difference as to whether he could paint the events of yesterday as a success or not.

"The base itself was utterly destroyed by the bombings in the early evening," Rohrbach replied. "The snatch squads who went in before the ground troops managed to capture a number of fighters alive, and their information led to the discovery of several significant stashes of weapons in the surrounding area."

The snatch squads were an innovation of Böhm's, eagerly adopted by Commander Schultz of the Waffen-SS troops who led the raid. He was all too aware of the frustrations of chasing parachute drops. Better to let the Resistance tidy it all away, then seize their supplies by the truckload when they thought they were secure. Good.

"And the ground assault?"

Commander Schultz had also agreed that an attack in darkness would give the SS a tactical advantage. In daylight the Resistance's knowledge of the terrain gave them an undeniable edge. Darkness reduced it. Another suggestion of Böhm's.

"Final numbers are not confirmed, but current estimates are some hundred Maquisards dead, many more wounded and all the fighters dispersed," Rohrbach said, a glimmer of satisfaction on his face. "But Commander Schultz was badly injured by a wounded fighter as he toured the remains of the camp. He is unlikely to survive."

"That is a loss," Böhm replied quietly.

Böhm's wound had been cleaned, stitched and bandaged. Now it stung. Strange that by studying abroad he had reached adulthood without the dueling scars deemed so important to the manhood of many in the older German universities, but he had one now. Mrs. Fiocca had given him a perfect example, slicing his cheekbone.

"Your opinion of the action, Rohrbach?"

Rohrbach started with surprise, but to his credit took a moment to consider and answered crisply.

"An unqualified success, sir. The Waffen-SS proved more than a match for the Maquis this time. We were, perhaps, lucky that the White Mouse chose to stage her raid today, leaving the camp without some of its best fighters." Böhm thought briefly of Heller. Rohrbach was getting into his stride now. "It is shocking that some of the officers here were bypassing basic security however to satisfy distasteful appetites." He produced a sheet from the files under his arm. "I suggest the following changes to security protocols."

Böhm scanned the sheet as it was laid on his table. Perfectly sensible. He would include some of the points in his own report. Yes, last night had been a victory, though for one moment as that maddened woman threw herself across the room at him, her knife in her hand, he had doubted it.

55

Nancy's raiding party returned in time to at least offer a distraction and keep some of the escape routes open down the valley, but as the hours unspooled the scale of the loss became clear. Several of the larger arms stashes gone, their field hospital and its supplies, Nancy's bus and the storehouse all destroyed. And the men lost.

Nancy's gear had been in the truck and she'd changed out of her whore's outfit and back into slacks and boots as soon as they returned and realized the camp was under attack. They were only just clear of it when machine-gun fire hit the tank. She felt the heat of it on her face, like a blush of shame. It became Franc's funeral pyre and when she and René returned to the spot just before first light, they buried his charred remains by the road and marked the spot with a cross of stones.

As dawn broke, the survivors from the camp were walking in scattered groups through the forests on both sides of the river, avoiding the roads and taking meandering twisting routes to the fallback position near Aurillac. Occasionally, a Henschel would pass overhead, firing random machine-gun bursts into the foliage hoping to hit one or other of the groups. They missed. When Nancy and René reached the fallback, Tardivat and Fournier could hardly look at her. It was different to the aftermath of the attack on Gaspard's camp. No one was celebrating, telling blossoming stories of their heroism and daring. The air stank with defeat, and the whispers among the men were all about the lost weapons, the likely reprisals on the villages near where they were found, how the civilian population of Montluçon would suffer for the attack on the Gestapo headquarters.

Nancy set herself up in the corner of a half-ruined barn, and Fournier and Tardivat slept there too, exhausted and talking to each other only in low voices while Nancy stared at the wall and said little to anyone. She thought of Henri—what she might do to get him back, to find out if he were really alive or dead. Once Denden made it to the fallback they could radio requests for resupply, and perhaps in a few days she would return to Böhm, offer herself up on a plate. She needed to make this right first though. She had left them to fend for themselves hours after finding a spy in their camp. The dull ache of not knowing what was happening to Henri, which had become a familiar companion since the day of his arrest, had become an ever-present agony since that night in Courçais. It had driven her mad, and that madness had cost her men dearly. And they knew it.

It was two days before she saw Denden again. He was at the back of a ragged group led by Gaspard. When she saw Denden's face, she was afraid he was wounded, so ashen was he with fatigue and grief.

"The radio's gone, Nancy." It was the first thing he said to her when they found her in the barn. "I destroyed it when I thought we were going to be overrun."

"So now you have nothing," Gaspard said, sitting down heavily opposite her on the earth floor. "Without your rich men in London, you have nothing. No food, no guns, and *no soldiers.*"

She looked up and around the group, the last of her senior officers. They looked broken, disappointed.

"You should have been here," Gaspard said, making sure she knew. "You let that little bitch give away our position then went on your crazy mission, taking our best men from their posts when we needed them the most."

No one, not Tardivat, not Fournier, not even Denden tried to disagree.

"Fine. I'm nothing. I'm shit," she said, without heat. "But we still have a job to do. That army group..."

Denden started to pull off his boots, wincing hard as he did. "That job's canceled, Nancy. We're back on the usual harry-the-Germans missions, or we would be if we hadn't just had our men and weapons scattered."

"One hundred dead, two hundred wounded..." Gaspard continued.

"Oh, for heaven's sake, Gaspard," Denden screamed at him. "She gets the fucking point."

Gaspard turned toward him and Nancy wondered if they were finally going to kill each other here and now and save Böhm the job. Gaspard attacking Denden, Nancy fighting Gaspard, Fournier fighting her. But though Gaspard opened his mouth to speak, to sling something hateful at Denden, he stopped. Even he was too broken to fight with any spirit today. She'd broken them all.

She put her head in her hands, then felt a touch on her shoulder. She looked up. It was Tardivat; he offered her a water bottle. She took it and thanked him. He didn't reply. She had to fix this, she had to. It was more important than her own hurt, more important, today, in this moment, than Henri. She wanted to stop, to curl up and die as the realization hit her. She had no easy way out; there was no slipping off and arriving like a martyr in Böhm's office for her now. This was her job; this was what had to be done.

"Do you still have the code book, Denden?"

He nodded, not looking at her.

"Then I'll go and get us a radio. You said something about a spare in Saint-Amand? Used to belong to that girl who got picked up in March?"

"You'll never make it," Gaspard said, getting to his feet. "I'm going to see to my men."

Denden waited until Gaspard had marched out of the barn before he replied. "Yes. I stopped for a drink with my motorbike friend there. Bruno from the café in the square where we were said he had a spare set hidden away. But we have no vehicle, Nancy. The trucks are all gone."

"A bicycle then," she said firmly.

"But Saint-Amand is more than a hundred kilometers away."

"A bit less over the hills." She didn't need the lost maps to tell her that. She knew the roads and paths round here almost as well as Gaspard. Denden, Fournier and Tardivat exchanged cautious glances.

"I can get you the bicycle," Fournier said at last.

"But why do you have to go, Nancy?" Denden asked. "Can't you send one of the boys? You need to find which of our arms depots are still secure, resupply the men from there as best you can."

"Do you still have my notebook, Denden?"

He reached into his back pocket, showed it to her.

"Then you can handle all that. You and Fournier and Tardivat. But I can get through checkpoints. No one else here can."

He shoved the notebook back into her pocket, reached for her hands. "Nancy, your face is everywhere."

"They don't see my face when I go through checkpoints! They see a housewife. Look, I know I've been a goddamn fool. I fucked it up; I have to fix it."

She plunged her hands into her bag and pulled out the dress she had worn in the Gestapo raid. It was stiff with dried blood. "Tardi, can you make this into something respectable? Dress me as a war widow? God, what I wouldn't give for the material from that nightdress now."

Tardivat lit a cigarette. "I still have a parachute in my pack."

"Can you do it, Tardi?"

He flinched when she said his name.

"Yes. I can do it, *mon colonel*. It will take me till morning. You

302

should sleep, wash. You look like a witch out of fairy stories, not a housewife."

He took the bloody rag of a dress from her and walked out of the barn. She watched him go, thinking of that nightdress. He had made it as a gesture of his admiration, of fellowship and friendship, and she had lost it. Lost it and got men killed. She needed it back.

Fournier got up too, touched Denden on the shoulder. "We should begin at once, Denis."

Denden nodded. "One moment," he said, then waited until Fournier had slouched out of the barn. "Did you kill Böhm?" he asked. "I know about the offer he made in Courçais now, what Anne said."

That made it easier somehow. "No. And he said Henri is still alive, but I know I need to fix this now, Denden. I can't go looking for him until we are done."

He stood up, touched her shoulder. "I'm sorry, Nancy."

"Did Jules survive? I haven't seen him."

He looked away from her. "He did, but he daren't speak to me after Gaspard...Just get some sleep."

Then he was gone too.

She woke next morning aching from the cold ground and the bruises she had picked up in the raid. The dress was lying next to her. She went to wash in one of the icy tributaries that ran from the mountains and into the river in the valley below. Someone had told her once it took hundreds of years for the rain to work its way through the soil and then emerge again, purified and enriched in these springs. She worked the blood out of her nail beds and scrubbed her skin pink, then put on the dress Tardivat had washed and repaired, made more decent and plain with his harvested parachute silks. It was a little too big for her now, but Tardi had provided a sash, similar to ones she'd seen women wearing in Chaudes-Aigues—a very French attempt to make starvation fashionably acceptable. She smoothed her hair behind her ears and put on her shoes. Not her army boots, not her heels, but the mid-level low and feeble things made out of cardboard she wore when she needed to get through ordinary checkpoints.

The men, scattered around the clearing over their morning cooking fires, glanced at her in surprise. They had grown used to seeing her in slacks and army tunic, and her sudden reappearance as an ordinary Frenchwoman shocked them. Denden and Tardi were waiting by the barn, an iron-frame bike between them.

"Fournier delivered this for you," Denden said as she approached, trying to sound cheery. But Fournier hadn't stayed to see her off, Nancy thought. "And I've found these." He handed her a pair of reading glasses. "I picked them up in case mine got smashed, and I've been trying to remember the name of the square with the café and Bruno…but I can't recall it for the life of me."

He started describing the square, the way the light patterned the walls of the buildings in the afternoon and the qualities of the hospitality he'd enjoyed there, till Nancy just put her hand on his arm and he ground to a halt.

"I'll find it, Denden."

He was scared for her, she realized, under all the chatter. Tardi pushed himself off the wall and fished something out of his pocket. A crucifix on a chain. He showed it to her, then without saying anything, fastened it around her neck. For just a second she thought it was burning her skin, but no, the metal was just cold.

"Are you a Christian, Tardi?" she asked.

He didn't look her in the eye, but his voice didn't sound angry. "I have tried to be; I have not always succeeded. But if you are to look like a war widow…They would ask God's help."

56

Focus, Nancy. It was market day in Saint-Amand and the crowd might give her a little cover, but it also meant there were plenty of eyes on the street to recognize her. Those damned posters. She put on the glasses that Denden had given her; they gave the world a slightly pinched look, but they did not blind her. Between that and the rather poor dress, and the not very fashionable hat, most men's eyes glided over her.

The crowd was thin, and at each corner of the main square German soldiers lounged against the gray walls. She went through Denden's description of the friendly café again in her mind. A small square, he'd said. Near to the river with a chestnut tree in the middle. Not this one then, with the church on one side and the town hall on the other, and high up the hill.

She stopped at a stall to fill her string bag with a few gray-market potatoes and a mangy-looking cabbage. Now she was just a woman on her way back home from market. She fetched her bike and pushed it past the soldiers on the south of the square. Not looking at them, not *not* looking either. She was invisible to them.

The road sloped down steeply toward the river, the narrow pavements empty now and the houses shuttered and cold. She looked right and left, searching for some sign of this square. Had Denden said anything about the view that would help her to know which way to turn when she reached the river? She'd have to guess. Left, then, if she couldn't find it she'd put on a little dumb show of patting her pockets and fussing. Just an ordinary shopper who'd left something behind on one of her errands and had to turn back.

The river was full of summer rain, churning under the ancient stone arches of the bridge. She smiled at it. It was too narrow for a jeep full of soldiers to cross, so the Resistance wouldn't have to blow it up. Perhaps it would survive another five hundred years. She paused as if to admire the view. On the other side of the river was a towpath and a band of woodland; to the right and on this side the towpath was squeezed between the water and an old stretch of city wall.

Left it was then. Christ she was glad she hadn't had to operate in a town. She had almost rotted to death in the damp of the woods until the guys found her the bus, but at least she hadn't had to live day after day under the half-shuttered eyes of all these buildings, having to guess at the whisperings, compromises and collaborations going on behind the closed doors.

She passed two broken-down-looking warehouses and stole a glance back up toward the church. A shimmer of green among the timbered house fronts of an old square caught her eye; she turned up the path and found herself in Denden's square.

It was just as he had described it, a cartoon of small-town France, the high buildings leaning into one another, and one side occupied by the flank of an old seminary. The tree in the center of the square looked ancient too, gnarled and thick, but still sending forth fresh greenery into the summer air. The leaves shook and whispered in the breeze and she thought of the thousands of troops pouring into northern France, the individual men that made up the landing force, the fresh surge of hope.

She leaned her bicycle up against the wall in one of the narrow alleys leading off the square and hooked her bag over her arm. The café was open, but she had no passwords, no codes, and the charming young man Denden had spoken of, Bruno, had probably been shipped off to work in Germany or disappeared into the hills. She walked in.

It was a pretty mean little place: half a dozen tables and the zinc bar; three customers, all old men, and the barman. He was a great slab of a fellow, heavy armed and red faced. Did he look too well fed to be honest? She thought of the black-market men she had known in Marseille. Any one of them could have slit your throat for a hundred francs, but they were too bloody minded, too independent to deal with the Nazis. It was the men in suits with briefcases and polished shoes you had to look out for.

She asked for a brandy and when she had paid for it, drank it off and set her glass on the bar.

"Does Bruno still work here? An old friend of his asked me to pass on a message."

The barman polished a glass with a dirty towel. "Give me the message, I'll get it to him next time I see him. If I see him."

She looked straight at him. "Maybe I'll wait. See if he turns up."

He shrugged, then said a bit too casually, "If it's about the bike he's selling, it's out back. You can come see it if you like."

The last thing Nancy wanted to see was another bloody bike—she could barely move as it was and she was sure her ankle was bleeding.

"That's it!" she said brightly.

The yard at the back of the bar did have an old bike in it, which they bent over as they talked in case someone was watching from the overlooking buildings. Nancy fiddled with the seat and made a face.

"Bruno was picked up by the Gestapo two weeks ago," the barman said, "and I can't swear one of those old guys in my place isn't on their payroll. I've known them both twenty years, but who can tell these days?"

Nancy folded her arms, still staring at the bike. "I heard Bruno had a spare radio set. We lost ours."

The barman stood back, lifted his hands and shook his head

hard enough to make his jowls wobble, as if refusing an unreasonable price. "Not a hope, Madame. Not here. But I know they have a spare in Châteauroux, or at least they did a week ago."

"That's eighty kilometers away!"

"Nearest one I know of." A black cat emerged from the woodpile and rubbed against his legs. He bent down and scratched its ears. "One of their operators tried to run from a checkpoint, got shot in the back. You want Emmanuel, or at least that's what they call him. British fella."

No one had told Nancy about an operative called Emmanuel operating near Châteauroux. Fair enough—London wasn't going to chat with them about agents in adjacent networks unless they needed to.

"Can you give me the address?"

He did and, shooing the cat away from the door, led her back out through the main bar. Nancy called out a cheery promise to talk to her friend about Bruno's bike, and went to the narrow back alley where she had left her own.

Eighty kilometers away and she could barely put one foot in front of the other as it was. She looked at her ankle: yes, definitely bleeding. Eighty bloody kilometers, with an address and a name but no papers for the region and swarms of trigger-happy Gestapo all over the place. Then somehow, the ride back into the mountains.

"It has to be done, and you have to do it."

Christ, she was losing it. She'd said that out loud. At least she hadn't said it in English. She clambered painfully back onto the bike and pushed off.

57

Nancy missed the mountains now, all those twisting back roads surrounded by good cover where the Germans were no longer willing to explore thanks to the work of her men. Between Saint-Amand and Châteauroux the Boche were out in force and didn't look that bloody nervous at all. She managed to duck two checkpoints, seeing them in time to turn off her route without attracting attention, but the third one had set themselves up on a sharp bend on the back road between Maron and Diors. She ran straight into them, and of course, as they were off the main road they were bored, and she, teetering along on her bike after twelve hours in the saddle was a welcome distraction.

"Your papers, Madame! Where are you going?"

She stared up at him, saying nothing, her eyes wide. She could probably kill this one, a blow to the throat just like the one she had used on the guard at the transmitter station, but he had two friends with him, one already with his hand on his revolver. She was unarmed. Take out the corporal with the first guard's gun, hope the third one panicked and she had time to shoot him too, or rush him and go for his eyes? Perhaps a twenty percent chance.

So she burst into tears.

"Sir, please sir, you have to let me through. I don't have papers. My mother is looking after my little boy in Châteauroux while I work and I heard he is sick!"

The guard shook his head. He looked old for his rank. Old enough to have children himself and a wife who worried about them.

"Please, sir! He is only five years old, his name is Jacques and he is such a good little boy, but my mother sent to say he is so poorly and asking for his mummy." Perhaps it was the exhaustion, but Nancy had a clear vision of the sick child, his frightened grandmother, the tiny drafty flat where they were living. She was sobbing, and she meant it. She pointed at the scraggy vegetables in her shopping bag.

"Dear Madame Carrell, my boss's wife, gave me these to make him soup, and Monsieur, he said, 'Dearest Paulette, you must go to little Jacques, we can manage without you for a day if we must, but your child might die without his mother's love!' "

Her voice rose in a wail, and the corporal looked over his shoulder at the other two men. They looked baffled. Nancy called out the name of her fictitious son between sobs a couple of times, watching for her opportunity to crush his Adam's apple if it didn't work.

He cleared his throat and patted her on her shoulder.

"Now then, my dear. I'm sure little Jacques will be fine. You go along now."

Nancy got her feet back on the pedals even as she was pouring out her equally effusive thanks. She'd given herself hiccups.

"I shall pray for you, Monsieur!" she managed, then teetered off.

The town was low and sprawling, the center a snarl of twisting alleyways around an open central square. She had to stop and ask directions twice, and both times saw suspicion and fear on the faces of the people she spoke to. None of the patrols she saw stopped her, but the afternoon was advancing and in a couple of hours the number of people on the streets would shrink and she would become more noticeable.

At Beaulieu they had always told the students that if they noticed a patrol, French or German, apparently watching them the best thing to do was approach them. Ask for a match, the time. It made you immediately less suspicious. But Nancy didn't dare get that close. In the distance she might still look like just another Frenchwoman, but close to they'd smell the blood and sweat on her, see the exhaustion on her face. The warm afternoon sun cast long shadows between the buildings, so she kept to them as much as she could, making herself small.

She found the street at last, in one of the shabbier corners of town. She wheeled her bike round the back, leaving it at the end of the lane, and approached through the yard, like a friend. She knocked, then stood back a little from the door so anyone twitching the lace curtains aside or peering through the slatted shutters could see her. It was a tiny place. One room on top of another, basically.

She felt someone watching her, she was sure of it, and she could only hope it was this Emmanuel, not some Gestapo thug with a revolver in his hand. The seconds ticked by. Perhaps no one was home. Any decent agent in a town of this size would have two or three safe houses. Perhaps she would just curl up behind the garbage pile and go to sleep, wait to see who got to her first, friend or foe. Sounded good.

"You have got to be fucking kidding me." A familiar voice.

The door opened a couple of inches and Nancy found herself looking at the freckled face of the redhead, Marshall, from Inverness. The last time she'd seen him he'd been tied to the flag pole outside the main barracks building with his trousers round his ankles, gagged with the bandages Nancy had used to bind up her chest on her PT runs.

She almost turned round and walked away. This man would

never help her, not after she'd humiliated him twice. Perhaps there was a God after all and this was His last little joke, throwing this man and their history in her path at the moment her hope, her strength was at its lowest ebb.

But she didn't even have the strength to move.

One. Two. Three. She had nothing to say, nowhere to go.

After an age, he opened the door fully and stepped back. She followed him automatically, into the low grubby kitchen and closed it behind her.

"Marshall," she said quietly. "I need a radio for my Maquis in Cantal. We just got hit hard and need resupply now. I was told you had a spare set."

He sat down heavily on a wooden chair by the kitchen table and stared up at her. She could feel his rage, his hatred in the air like the static charge before a storm.

"You evil little bitch. You think you can just turn up here after what you did and make demands? I'll turn you into the Gestapo myself."

She sat down opposite him. She couldn't trust her legs to hold her up any longer anyway. "Do what you want. Get a message to London for my men though. Drop site code name Magenta should be operational still. If they can drop supplies there, there's a chance my men will get to them before the Germans."

She put her head in her hands and waited. He didn't move, didn't leave, didn't speak. She thought of Tardivat, of Fournier, of Jean-Clair and Franc. They were worth one last effort. Surely.
Come on, Nancy.

"This isn't about you and me, Marshall, this is about the war. Your problem with me can wait until after the Nazis are over and done with."

If ever you needed proof there was no God, here it was. After what she had done, after what she had cost her men following her own very bloody personal vendetta against Böhm, any functioning deity would have smote her on the spot for the hypocrisy of that little speech. Wait for it . . . and . . . No. No thunderbolt. No shattering light or demons dragging her to hell. Just Marshall, staring at her.

"You set me back a month with that little stunt. I only made it back to France the week before D-Day."

How was it possible for a human being to be as tired as she was now, and still be talking, moving?

"Oh, cry me a river! After the crap you put me through, you got off easy. I should have shoved that rose up your arse, not tucked it behind your ear." So much for diplomacy. *Count your breaths, Nancy.* "Do you need me to apologize, Marshall? Fine. I'm sorry. Even if we do both know you deserved it. Now help me."

She shifted in the chair, trying to find a more comfortable position and failed. A bolt of pain tore through her legs. She could feel the raw skin tearing on her inner thighs, and her back spasmed. She closed her eyes until it passed, and when she opened them again, Marshall was watching her.

"Where did you come from?"

"We regrouped near Aurillac, I came over the mountain to get to Saint-Amand. My contact there couldn't help me, and sent me on to you."

"You got a truck along those roads without being shot?" He raised his eyebrows.

"We lost all our motor transport in the attack. I came on my bike."

He stood up suddenly and Nancy thought he might be about to strike her, but he didn't. Instead he opened the door of a ratty dresser and took out a bottle and a couple of dusty glasses. Red wine. The cure of every ill known to man or woman. He filled the glasses and they drank them off. The rough alcohol hit her stomach as a soft explosion of warmth in her belly.

"The set is here and you can have it," he said at last. "And I'm transmitting tonight, so I can send your message to Baker Street. What pass phrase do you want them to use?"

She thought. Denden would find an ordinary radio somewhere so they could listen to *Ici Londres*, even if without a transmitter he was unable to talk back.

"Tell them to say, 'Hélène has had tea with friends.'" Denden would recognize her code name and if they heard that it would put them on the lookout for a drop at least.

He grunted, refilled their glasses, then looked at his watch. "It's safer to travel by night round here, even with the curfew. There's a bed upstairs. You can rest for a couple of hours."

A truce then. Good.

"Thank you," she said.

He nodded and pointed upstairs. She finished her glass, and began the slow painful climb up the short flight to the second floor. She hadn't felt this beaten up since her first day of parachute training. Marshall had pushed her off the platform into the lake that day, made her look like a bloody idiot.

She opened the door at the top of the stairs and sat down on the edge of the bed, feeling the relief and exhaustion sweep over her like soft waves over the shingle of a Mediterranean shore. She stared at her feet. *Take your shoes off, Nancy*, a voice in her head said firmly. She considered. No, don't take your shoes off. From the squelch of blood as she moved her toes she could feel that her heels were torn to ribbons, and she did not want to spend all her precious rest time bandaging them up. The shoes stayed on. She did still have a big silk handkerchief, the remains of the parachute, in her pocket though. She pulled it out, then ripped it in two before she pulled her skirt up to her waist and looked at the bloody mess of her upper thighs. She tied one half of her handkerchief around the top of each leg, shifting back and forth on the bed. The material was cool and though it wasn't much of a bandage, at least it would stop the wounds rubbing up against each other as she slept.

She began to lean back, her eyes already closed, when she heard the back door open and voices, low and urgent, then running footsteps up the stairs. *No, No. Go away.*

Marshall burst into the room. "Change of plans, Wake."

"Just kill me," she said.

"Don't think I'm not tempted," he replied. He was pulling an old armoire out of its alcove on the other side of the room. "Get off your arse and help me with this if you want the radio."

Charming. She got up, staggered over, grabbed the other end and shoved.

"What's happening, Marshall?"

"One of the friendly gendarmes just popped by. Seems some maniac took out Gestapo headquarters in Montluçon. Our local boys have got the wind up and are squeezing everyone hard before we do the same thing to them. Someone's going to give them this address eventually."

He squeezed into the gap behind the armoire and felt along the wall, then pulled a knife from his belt and cut away a section of the wallpaper. Nancy watched it fall back and he reached into the hole between the beams and pulled free the radio. Well, she hoped it was the radio—a brown leather solid case, like an oversized briefcase. "You have to go now."

"Straps?" she said.

He opened the bottom of the armoire and tossed a couple of rolls of buckled webbing onto the bed. Nancy fastened them onto the loops on the case as he shoved the wardrobe back into position. Outside a horn beeped twice.

"They're coming," Marshall said. "You armed?"

"No."

A sudden popping of small arms outside, then shouts in German.

Nancy went to the front window. "Four Gestapo, three Milice with them. Two more of them taking off after your lookout."

"Leave, Wake." He had split open the mattress and was pulling out a belt of grenades like a magician pulling handkerchiefs out of his closed fist.

"No, give me a revolver. You know I can shoot. We can take these men and both get away." She put out her hand.

He fixed the belt around his waist.

"We wouldn't have a hope. Go now before the house is surrounded." He saw her hesitate and leaned forward, resting his forehead on the edge of the mattress. "Nancy, I was scared. In Inverness. When I saw who you were, I thought you'd tell them I'd been a coward coming out of France. But I'm not scared now." He got up again. "There. Now sod off, will you?"

Fists began to hammer at the front door.

Nancy picked up the set and attached it like a backpack across her shoulders. She almost fell under the weight of it. Marshall lifted the front window, pulled the pin on his grenade and dropped it down into the street.

"Look out!"

Then the thunderous clap of the explosion. The house shook and on the street someone screamed like a rabbit in a snare. Bullets started to pepper the window frame, cracking the wood into splinters.

Marshall staggered backward but didn't fall.

"Marshall?"

"It's nothing," he said. "Get going."

Boots on the ground floor. More shouts. Marshall pulling the pin on another grenade.

She felt her hands on the frame of the back window. Hauled it up and climbed through, then twisted round, hung down and let herself drop into the yard. The back door opened as she sprinted toward the rear gate.

"Stop! Stop or I'll shoot!"

She didn't stop. The bullet hissed by her ear, and she swung out into the back street. Nobody there yet. Behind her she heard a third grenade, another rippling crackle of gunfire. No point turning back. No point waiting. Marshall was a rat in a trap, and she had to clear the area before the Gestapo or the Milice called in more reinforcements. Her bike was just where she had left it. She climbed on and the pain made her gasp. Then she started to ride.

58

Dusk was closing in and Nancy had managed maybe two miles—pathetic really—when she thought they'd got her. Lights shone on the road in front, perhaps five hundred yards ahead. So, they'd put out roadblocks even on these back ways. Her first thought was to stash the bike, find cover well away from the road and wait. Then she heard barking behind her, stopped pedaling and turned and looked. Torches bounced across the fields like marsh lights as far as she could see on both sides of the road—and they had dogs.

She needed help and she had no friends left. Then she spotted a farmhouse, perhaps a hundred yards off the road. In the dusk she could just make out a lighted window. Time to make new friends.

The woman took one look at her and tried to close the door on her, but Nancy leaned her weight against it, shoved one foot in and then groaned in agony as it was squeezed between the frame and the door.

"Oh, I'm so sorry!" the woman said.

Nancy blinked, and looked at her properly. She was a girl really, early twenties. Her hair was clean and neatly tied in a bun, and her cotton house frock, though faded, had been pressed. The ideal pretty French farmer's wife.

"Please let me in," Nancy said. "For France, let me in."

Then she saw the crucifix around the woman's neck and

touched the one around her own neck which Tardi had given her.

"One Christian to another."

What clear skin she had, no makeup at all. Nancy could see her fear and doubt, then a slight firming of that thin jaw as she made up her mind.

"You can hide in the cellar." The door was opened.

Nancy tumbled through, a kitchen, a staircase. The woman was opening a trapdoor under the stairs and Nancy found herself shooed down a short ladder and into complete darkness. She felt the tramped earth beneath her feet. It smelled of apples and straw. A little light leaked in through the slats of the trapdoor over her head. *Just* over her head. It was a low cellar, not enough room to stand up. She crawled into the corner under the ladder, undid the strap around her waist and felt the release and burn as her shoulders lost the weight of the radio. It thunked down the inch or two onto the earth floor, then like an echo she heard the thump at the front door of the little farmhouse. She drew up her knees, wrapped her arms around them. The light flickered above as the young woman went to answer the door again. Nancy waited, trying not to breathe.

"Good evening."

"Good evening, Madame. We're looking for a woman. A very dangerous woman." A German voice. One of the Gestapo officers. "One of my men saw a woman approaching your house, moments ago."

The woman's voice was calm. "That was me, I imagine. I popped out to check the chickens were in for the night. Foxes, you know."

She was playing up her accent a bit, Nancy noticed.

"Nevertheless, Madame…I hope you won't mind if we conduct a brief search."

"I have nothing to hide." Her voice contained just the right note of restrained irritation.

The boots came into the kitchen, followed by the tap of the woman's clogs.

"What's down there?"

"Food. When we have any."

He was right over her.

"If you could open it up, Madame."

Nancy stopped breathing. The trapdoor lifted and the treacherous light illuminated the square of earth at the bottom of the ladder.

"I'll just take a look. If you'd stand over there, please."

A torch beam flicked on and began exploring the corners farthest from Nancy, a couple of crates, some half-empty hessian sacks.

The stairs to the upper story creaked and the torch whipped out of the cellar.

"Who is that?" the German said, his voice loud with alarm. Nancy heard the snap of leather as he unholstered his pistol.

"Maman?" The voice of a child, a girl. "What is happening? Who is that man?"

Her mother responded in soothing tones. "It's fine, dear, go back to bed." Then she continued, a fresh thread of indignation trembling through her voice. "I think you should leave, you're scaring my daughter."

The man said nothing.

"Unless you think my four-year-old child is a dangerous woman?"

A cough, then the sound of the gun being returned to its holster.

"No, Madame. Please do contact us if you see or hear anything suspicious however."

"Of course."

The footsteps retreated, and as the front door opened and closed again, Nancy took in a long slow breath. A phrase floated through her mind. *Kindred spirits are not so scarce as I used to think.* She smiled. She remembered the thrill of hope she had felt reading those words under her mother's porch, between those other narrow beams of light.

The woman spoke upstairs, clear, conversational.

"I hope you haven't died of fright down there. Perhaps you should wait a little before you come up, in case they come back. I shall get some supper ready. My name is Celeste, by the way."

Pretty name, Nancy thought, then fell into a fitful doze.

Nancy didn't even realize she'd been asleep until the creak of the trapdoor opening woke her. She picked up the radio—bloody thing still weighed a ton—and clambered, her legs cramped and shaking, up into the kitchen.

The table was laid for two. Nancy sat down, very carefully, and watched as Celeste ladled stew into white china bowls, then, sitting down herself, began to cut up a fresh loaf. Nancy's mouth watered.

"Do start, Madame."

Nancy did not need to be asked twice. The food was delicious, chicken and gravy, carrots and pearl onions, the bread light and airy. Bliss. Utter bloody bliss.

"So, you are a very dangerous woman?" Celeste said, starting on her own supper at a more sedate pace. "Never mind, it's best I don't know. I just hope you're giving as good as you're obviously getting."

Nancy nodded, still chewing, then swallowed happily. "Where is your husband?"

"I am a widow," Celeste replied. "My husband Guy was killed during the invasion."

"I'm sorry."

Celeste did not reply at once, and the click of their spoons against the china plates was the only sound in the room.

"I manage. But it is very difficult to keep up with the farm. One does what one must. For the children."

The floorboard on the stairs creaked, and Nancy spun round, wondering if, for one foul moment, this whole thing, the kind welcome, the food, was just a cruel joke and the Gestapo were still in the house. It was the little girl who had disturbed the Germans' original search. She was whip thin, long black hair almost down to her waist. She wore a pale blue nightgown and carried a teddy bear, swinging it by the paw from one hand.

"Maman?"

"Go to bed at once, Maria!"

The little girl thrust out her bottom lip. "But I am hungry, and I'm not tired."

Celeste held up her hand. "You have been fed. Bed. At once."

Maria threw down her teddy bear so it bounced down to the bottom of the staircase, then stamped angrily back up the stairs. Above them a door slammed.

Celeste went and picked up the toy, dusting him off and then sitting him in the rocking chair by the fire. Nancy could imagine the girl creeping guiltily downstairs to find him at dawn and her relief when she found he had not been too uncomfortable overnight.

"A very dangerous woman," Nancy said with a smile.

Celeste returned to her chair and picked up her spoon again. "I hope so. I hope she stays fierce. It is so hard to bring up a little one by myself. She thinks I'm a tyrant, but I'm just trying to survive."

Nancy had an image of her mother, a familiar one, turning from the food cupboards in the kitchen as Nancy came home from school, banging the door, dropping her coat on the floor and starting to shout at her. For the first time, though, she noticed how empty that food cupboard looked, how worn and faded her mother's clothes.

She felt her throat tighten. "You are a good mother."

LIBERATION

Celeste nodded, taking the compliment as her due. "Are you finished? Give me your dress and I shall wash it while you clean yourself up and see to your wounds. While it dries you can sleep a little, then be on your way."

59

The fresh bandages on her thighs lasted about fifteen miles, but by the time the road started to climb upward, they had twisted and rolled, leaving the flesh exposed again. The ones around her ankles lasted another five. One. Two. One. Two. Pushing down with one foot and then the other, inching forward along the rough country track, deeply shadowed by oak trees. The air was cool, but the forest seemed strangely quiet, stripped of birdsong, and there was no breeze to make the leaves stir and whisper. All Nancy could hear was her own breath.

Too steep. If the road had been flat, she could have built a rhythm, and then perhaps the pain would have dulled with its regular repetition, but the rough climbing ground made that impossible. Each turn of the wheels was a new torment. The straps from the radio set dug into her shoulders and the skin on her back where the edge of the case rested against her was slowly rubbing raw. And she still had God knew how many miles to go, almost all of them up.

Her thoughts came in short loops and flashes. Henri reading the newspaper at breakfast before the war broke out, setting down his coffee cup. The moment in the shadowed moonlight when Antoine blew his brains out. The secretary at the Free French Forces Headquarters. Böhm, holding his hand to his bleeding face. One. Two. One…Two…She knew a junction was coming up, the moment this track joined one of the metaled roads. There would be patrols. She'd be able to turn off it again after a mile or so, but while she was on it she'd be vulnerable.

The air was getting warm now, even under the shade of the trees. She turned onto the main road and the gradient increased a little. The blood from her thighs ran like rivulets of sweat down the inside of her leg. She glanced up. The sun was already past its zenith, and she had left the farm before dawn, so what was that—seven hours riding now? It felt like five minutes and an eternity.

Behind her she heard the drone of a petrol engine. Shit. That meant Germans.

She wiped the sweat out of her eyes and looked right and left. The banks rose steeply on each side of her, and the ditch at the side of the road was shallow and overgrown. She just had to keep going and hope that whoever was coming up behind her wasn't looking for a woman with a case strapped to her back. But she needed to look ordinary, like a woman who had only gone a couple of miles, who was just on her way into the next village. *Lift up your head, Nancy. Straighten your shoulders, Nancy. Smile. Look like you're having fun.* The pain shivered through her. The engine noise increased and they were on her, and passing her by, a flash of dark green, canvas, huge wheels, a low cloud of dust kicked up by the tires. She kept looking forward, head up.

One. Two. Three wagons. They didn't even slow down, just pulled out a little so they didn't knock her off the road. The last one was full of German troops, in their gray helmets and greenish tunics, crammed onto benches facing each other. The private at the back on the right-hand side, a boy in his late teens, smiled at her and raised his hand, a small private wave. She smiled back, and kept smiling until they disappeared out of sight around the next curve.

The track that led her off the main road again was rough, just earth in some places, gravel in others, with sudden pools of mud. It climbed then fell, climbed and fell. The bike wobbled and bounced over potholes dug by summer rain and grooves cut by horse-drawn carts. The daylight began to fade, and then it was only a matter of time. A twist of the path between fields, a steeper downward gradient than usual toward a wide and shallow stream, and a thick branch knocked loose in one of the sudden summer storms, not yet cleared away.

The front wheel caught and she was thrown forward over the handlebars. For a moment she was flying forward and sideways and too slow to do anything to save herself. She landed hard on her left side and the air was knocked out of her.

For a second or two, perhaps, she lost consciousness; it was difficult to tell given her mind had been a sort of dead white nothingness for hours. It was so peaceful here, lying on the earth. She could just hear the stream a hundred yards farther down the hill, and as the earth cooled, the air finally stirred the leaves very gently, like a hand through water.

"Nancy."

There he was. Had he been away? She was so glad he was home.

"Nancy."

Of course, he'd come back late in the afternoon yesterday, earlier than she'd expected, and he laughed at her, the way she threw herself into his arms, wrapped her legs around his waist. They hadn't even made it upstairs, making love on the fancy sofa in the sitting room, hardly undressing, such was the immediate, absolute urgency.

"Nancy, my darling."

Then where had they gone? The Hotel du Louvre et Paix, of course, by the harbor, where they could dine on the terrace and watch the boats coming and going as the last light faded, the fishermen carrying their baskets of lobsters straight into the kitchen where the chef waited to prepare Henri and Nancy's supper. Had they been dancing? Ah, yes the Metropole! The barman there really understood that mixing a cocktail was an art. Nancy couldn't help laughing, to see him so serious, but oh my, the drinks he could make, and they always had the best bands. Nancy had seen Rita Hayworth there once, and Maurice Chevalier twice.

"Listen to me, Nancy."

Back home, purring up the hill in Henri's favorite sports car, his hand always steady on the wheel no matter how much he'd drunk. She loved to see a man drive. Then making love again. In bed, this time, and drifting off to sleep in his arms under the cool white sheets.

"Nancy, you have to get up."

She half opened her eyes. He was standing between her and the French windows that led onto the balcony; the lace curtains were billowing behind him in waves. Strange, Nancy couldn't feel the breeze. How handsome he was, her Henri. How kind to her.

"I don't want to, Henri darling, don't make me," she said.

He just kept looking at her. Why was he sad? How could he be sad on such a beautiful day?

"Open your eyes, Nancy."

"I..."

His eyes were still kind, but his voice grew firm. "I mean it, Nancy. Open your eyes."

She did. Marseille was gone. Henri was gone. She was lying in the dark on a path in the Auvergne, a radio strapped to her back, blood drying between her legs, her muscles cramping, her ribs bruised to hell, crazy with thirst. And now someone was crying, great racking sobs, a terrible, heart-wrenching sound. She listened, amazed, for a full minute before she realized it was her.

Henri, I fucked up. I fucked everything up. I'm so sorry. I was so stupid. I just... I didn't know. The trees and the earth and the dark air said nothing. *The things I have seen, Henri! The things I have done. I've killed men, got men killed. That girl, Jesus, what am I? Fuck, the Germans have killed children because of what I've done.*

Eventually, the sobbing died away. Nothing had changed. She was still here, in occupied France. The dead were still dead and the living were waiting for her.

She pushed herself up on her knees, then, staggering under the weight of the radio, onto her feet, picked up the bicycle.

Fournier let go a stream of frightened obscenities when he saw her. The lookouts a hundred yards down the track had tried to help and had been told to fuck off, so they'd contented themselves with walking either side of her as she reached the cook house and barracks they'd set up in a deserted farm, half a mile from the barn where she'd left them, shepherding her on her way and making sure she didn't hit any of the booby traps they'd set along the path.

For a moment it looked as if she was just going to keep going right through the camp, as if she'd forgotten how to even stop, but Tardivat grabbed the handles of the bike and held it. She looked at him, eyes dull and confused.

"For Christ's sake, someone help her!" he shouted.

Fournier sprinted over and tried to lift her from the seat, but she pushed him away. It was a feeble push, but he stood back a pace, arms wide as she slowly climbed off. Her dress was torn and dirty, streaked with blood.

Denden carefully lifted the radio from her shoulders, slipping her arms free. Then she collapsed. Fournier caught her and carried her, gently as a bridegroom, to the farmhouse, shouting over his shoulder for a medic.

60

"Nancy, wake up!"

Not Henri's voice. That was how she knew she wasn't dead. That and the pain.

"Denden?"

"Yes, my only love, it's me. How are you? Can you move?"

She opened her eyes and cautiously pulled herself up on her elbows. The pain was different. Dull, throbbing, rather than bolts of agony. She realized she was wearing a thin cotton shirt, a pretty clean one too. Her thighs and ankles were bandaged and she was lying on a thick layer of blankets in a wooden cot in a small square room. Wooden floors, no glass in the windows. Bright sunshine and Denden sitting on a three-legged stool by her head.

"Good. You're alive," Denden said with a deep sigh of relief. "I thought you were just going to slip into a very picturesque coma and we'd end up having to bury you here. I have already started work on a very touching eulogy."

She smiled. "How long have I been out?"

"A little more than two days, if you ignore the occasional semi-lucid moment when you woke up enough to take a drink and ask if Henri was here yet."

Nancy noticed a paperback book on the floor beside him, a pitcher of water.

"Have you been playing nursemaid, Denden?"

He crossed his ankles. "When I haven't been tapping away in a frenzy at my splendid new radio. London has made two drops to our new sites since you got back, the darlings, packed with all sorts of goodies. Including the rather fancy antiseptic creams the doctor and I have been rubbing all over the remains of your lovely skin. How does it feel?"

She thought. "Like cold water on a hot day. Since when do we have a doctor?"

"His name is Tanant. He's come up to join us full time."

Nancy nodded. Tanant was one of the sympathetic medical men whom Gaspard had "kidnapped" on D-Day to help with the wounded, a gray man in late middle age who had moved with calm and speed among those horrors. He was most welcome.

Nancy put out her hand, and Denden held her wrist as she swung her legs over the edge of the bed and sat up properly. Little flickers of fire ran through her muscles and when she put her hand to her neck she found another bandage on her shoulder.

"And the war?"

"Oh, that!" Denden said, handing her a glass and pouring a mix of water and wine into it. "Do you want the good news or the bad news?"

"Just tell me." She took a long swallow.

"Very well. The Germans are on the run, and the Allies have landed in the south." He reached forward and put a hand on her knee. "Marseille has been liberated, but before you ask, no, we have no news about anyone the Gestapo might have still been holding there." She took another drink. "So, Das Reich are desperately trying to get back to Germany before the Ruskies overrun the Fatherland and take revenge for all the shit the Nazis pulled when they invaded. It will not be pretty."

He paused and rubbed the back of his neck, looking at her sideways.

"Denden…"

"Well, if you must know, London would like us...they are rather insistent in fact, to stop a battalion of SS getting back to Germany. They suggest forcing them to 'a permanent halt' in Cosne-d'Allier. They think we have three days."

A battalion? Jesus.

"Oh yes, and they have a Panzer tank or two with them."

"I don't suppose they explained what they meant by 'permanent halt,' did they?"

Denden refilled her glass. "Reading between the lines, which is tough to do in code and a signal spiky with interference, they know perfectly well we can't take prisoners, so the implication is if we have to kill them all even after they've surrendered, they won't look too hard for the mass grave. Or we can hold them if we want until the Americans come sweeping in and handle the official cleanup."

Nancy gave him back her glass and tried to stand up. A fresh Catherine wheel of pain shot off around her nervous system, but she didn't fall over. For the first time she noticed her working clothes, slacks, tunic hanging from the back of the door. Did they get a laundry maid up here as well as a doctor?

She tottered over, and giving Denden a look which said, pretty clearly, *I shall dress myself thank you very much*, asked, "And what do the men say to this exciting suggestion from London?"

Denden sniffed. "The only person who is really happy is René because he's been dying to fire his bazookas at a Panzer. The others are...inclined to be surly. It's nearly over. They want to go home. Why risk dying and never seeing your family again when the Germans are beaten? Actually, I don't think Tardivat cares any more. Fournier could go either way. Did you know his father ran a garage in Clermont? He wants to go back there. And Gaspard has apparently done taking orders from London now he's been resupplied. Oh, and he's promoted himself again. He's a general now."

Nancy shrugged on her tunic, and found a clean pair of socks in the pocket.

"Colonel Wake! Why are you putting your boots on?"

"Time to rally the troops. And if Gaspard has awarded himself a promotion, I think I shall too, so that's Field Marshal Wake to you."

Gaspard did not approve of her new title, but she didn't give him much time to think about it. The moment she walked out of the farmhouse in her fresh uniform like Christ risen from the dead, she had them.

Fournier took one look at her, then crossed the yard to stand at her side. Tardivat followed, and as he passed in front of her, winked. Gaspard wasn't coming over easy though.

"We are done! France is free!" he yelled at her when she announced her new rank and their orders. "The Germans are leaving! Why should we stand in the way? That was the whole fucking idea!"

The men behind him shifted nervously. The urge to go home and the urge to fight back, especially now they had new weapons in their hands again, were at war within them. She guessed the urge to fight was still stronger.

"On their own terms?" she said, straight at Gaspard, but loud enough for them all to hear. "Is that what you want? They come here, take your land, kill your people, and you're just going to sit back and let the Americans and British get rid of them for you? Let them leave with their tanks and troops like they are on a parade? Wave them through so they can go fight the Russians after everything *they* have been through? What sort of men are you?"

She dropped the pretense she was talking to him, held out her arms.

"Gaspard's right, I can't make you stay. Know this, though: if you quit, France may achieve peace for a time, but you'll never be at peace with yourselves. You can go home safely, but can you look your wives, your daughters in the face knowing you let the Germans walk over your land without striking a blow? Those Americans and British fighting to free your country, will you go whining to your mothers saying you wanted to go home? Or will you give them back their pride in their men? Will you give the women of France who have suffered and fought alongside you that gift? Give them back their belief. Deliver them their liberation!"

Then they started to cheer.

61

Over the next twenty-four hours Tardivat drove her between the scattered camps and she gave the same speech, or versions of it, a dozen times. By the time the men started to gather at a chateau on the hill just outside Cosne-d'Allier, they were back to full strength.

Denden brought them the latest intelligence from London while they were eating canned rations round the fire in the Great Hall. They'd left the farmhouse the day before, and designated this chateau, a fine seventeenth-century building still hung with tapestries, their headquarters and rallying point.

The Germans who'd looted the place had done a half-hearted sort of job, taking down some of the pictures and smashing up some of the chairs, but the massive oak dining table had been too heavy to move.

Denden paused as he came in, looking around at the fluttering shadows in the high-beamed ceiling, the elaborate carvings around the fireplace. "Got to say, this is much nicer than that buggy little hovel of yours on the plateau, Fournier," he said.

Fournier smiled and shook his head.

"What have you got, Denden?" Nancy asked, and he walked over to her and handed her the papers.

She scanned them briefly then put them on the table so the others—Juan, Gaspard, Fournier and Tardivat—could all see.

Gaspard sniffed. "Tomorrow then."

Nancy nodded. "Brief your lads, gentlemen. And try and make them get some rest."

Denden found her in her chamber at three in the morning, looking out from the leaded windows down the hill toward Cosne-d'Allier.

"My lady!"

"Not a bad billet, is it?" she replied, turning away from the moonlit view. "But I can't sleep. The bed is too soft."

Denden sat on it, bouncing up and down so the springs squeaked. "Fancy a drink? I hear rumors the Germans couldn't get into the wine cellar, and you and I are rather good at locks. I'm sure the owner wouldn't mind."

"Not tonight, Denden. Though if you want to find some charming young man to party with, don't let me stop you."

He made a huffing noise, then fell backward on the bed.

"Does terrible things to my libido, knowing there's an action coming in the morning. Can't really enjoy the curious young men if I keep thinking of them getting shot the next day." He folded his hands behind his head. "Is this plan of yours going to work?"

She leaned against the window and crossed her arms. "I don't know, Denden. It's a long shot. You haven't forgotten your role, I hope."

"No, darling. I'm all set to be utterly heroic. Then, if any of us survive I'll break open the cellar and find a nice new friend all flush with victory."

She wasn't sure she believed him. She'd noticed how he still looked at Jules when he thought no one could see him. She lay down on the bed next to him, and he put his arm around her shoulder, gathering her onto his chest.

"Nancy?"

He was stroking her hair.

"What is it?"

"There was something else in the intelligence, something I kept to myself," he said, then hesitated.

She bit her lip. "Major Böhm," she whispered.

"Yes, dearie. Seems this battalion is the remains of a number of units and the word from London is that all the local Gestapo officers are traveling back to Germany with them." He drew in breath to say something more, but she put her hand on his chest, stopping him.

"It's all right, Denden. I won't run off again. Not until this is done. Then I'll find him."

He kissed the top of her head. "Good. We need you."

They didn't say any more and eventually she could tell by his breathing he had fallen into a doze. Nancy could not, and watched the soft shadows cast by the moon chase each other around the room until it was time to get up. To begin.

62

I t was the German people who had failed. They had not had the necessary will, had not deserved the leader that had been sent to them. Böhm was crushed into the back of a Kübelwagen, rattling back toward his thankless country, surrounded by exactly the sort of spineless generals and other senior officers who had betrayed the Führer. It was cruel that decent military men like Commander Schultz were killed while soft-bellied, soft-minded men like these survived. Their medals clinked as the wagon jolted slowly along the road.

Ridiculous to travel in this way. He might be of some assistance in Berlin, but he was stuck with the survivors of two ragged battalions and they were forced to move at the crawling pace of the men and the half-dozen Panzer tanks. How had the Allies won? How could the British and Americans not see that their interests and Germany's were aligned? It was obvious they had to join together to defeat the Jewish-Marxist conspirators who had taken over Russia, and instead those nations, full of decent racial stock, had joined hands with a bunch of semi-human Slavs. It was disgusting, disappointing, outrageous. How had they managed to survive, to fight when they were forced to scavenge for weapons among their own dead? Nothing he had learned studying psychology at Cambridge with the brightest minds of his generation had prepared him for their capacity for suffering. Everything he knew told him that they should have broken months ago, that the

French, whom they had treated with forbearance as long as possible, should have accepted and celebrated them; that the English, with their respect for good breeding and advanced thinking on eugenics and racial purity should have joined hands with them from the start. Yet they had not.

He imagined what he would do if he ever met one of the German generals who had command in the east: spit in his face, tear off his epaulets, splatter his pathetic unworthy brains all over the road.

He was staring at a colonel on the facing bench, imagining this image with a pleasing quiver—his rage at least distracted him from the cheek wound Wake had given him which refused to heal—when the man suddenly coughed and blood began to run from the corner of his mouth. He looked surprised, then hurt, as if the victim of some small social slight, then he slumped forward and Böhm saw the bullet hole in the canvas.

The truck jolted to a full stop and Böhm heard the mewl of bullets in the air. Outside orders were being shouted. He ignored his companions and pushed his way to the back of the wagon and jumped down onto the road.

"Take cover, men!" he shouted at the confused infantry, only now in a haze of exhaustion realizing they were being fired upon. They began to scatter off the main road, but the banks were steep, the ditches shallow.

"Use the vehicles for cover! Watch for where the shooting is coming from before you return fire."

Three feet from him a sergeant leading his squad out of the firing line took a bullet in the throat and staggered past Böhm, trying to stop the wound with his hand. Böhm stepped aside to avoid the arterial spray.

A hundred yards behind him he heard a burst of light machine-gun fire and saw three men writhing in the ditch. He jogged up to the very front of the column where the tank commander and the colonel supposedly in charge of this shit show of an operation were fighting, yelling at each other in full view of the men.

"What the hell are you doing?" Böhm said sharply. "Why have we stopped?"

The tank commander saluted. "The colonel insists we counter-attack, sir, and assist the wounded."

Böhm turned on the colonel. Weak chin, dark hair. Poor stock. He'd never be allowed in the SS.

"This is an ambush, Colonel. Do not let the enemy choose the ground on which to fight. Push on into the town at once. The Allied forces are a day behind us; we must cross this bridge before the Maquis blow it if we have any hope of taking part in the defense of the Fatherland."

The colonel grew red in the face. "I will not run from a bunch of peasants who have got their hands on a few light arms!"

Just behind them they heard a sudden roar and the flatly echoing clap of a rocket being launched. They spun around, shielding their eyes, as the wagon in the center of the column exploded into flames.

"It seems the peasants have bazookas too, Colonel," Böhm snapped.

The colonel turned away from him. "Forward! Forward at once! Into the town!"

The tank commander scrambled back into his Panzer and Böhm heard him screaming the same order into his radio. The column jerked into urgent motion. One of the tanks in the middle of the column behind them began shouldering the flaming wagon out of the way as men, their clothes and hair aflame, still struggled out of it. As the other wagons moved forward, the infantry jogged at their sides.

Böhm followed the colonel into his staff car. The colonel shot him a foul look, but waited until Böhm had slammed the door before he ordered his man to drive on.

*

Denden had been up in the bell tower since before dawn, gazing down on the quiet square below him. It was a pretty enough place: the road from Montluçon wound up to it through wooded valleys to the south, disgorging into a market place surrounded by solid three-story buildings in a mix of stone and half-timbering. The ground floors were the shopfronts of the little town, the grocer's store and the butcher's, the ironmonger's and the bars. All shuttered today. The modest, classical frontage of the town hall watched from the northern edge of the square, the steps worn by generations climbing them to register births, marriages, deaths, fetch their papers and ration cards. The door today was locked.

Back from the square, the artisans and textile workers had their workshops and homes, and then the houses began to thin, turning into small farms. The town was fringed with orchards. The church, rebuilt in pale stone a hundred or so years earlier by a local pig-farmer-turned-railway entrepreneur, occupied the north-east corner of the square. The religious authority of the town watched over its people in respectful partnership with the secular town hall, shoulder to shoulder with the main road passing between them and then over the bridge.

When Denden swung his binoculars to the north, he could see Gaspard and Rodrigo checking the charges along the handsome stone bridge which crossed the river. It was wider than most of the river crossings in the region. The pig farmer had built this too, his gift, to replace the ancient narrow crossing which had served the little town for three hundred years. It was the only bridge within twenty miles left that would allow a tank to pass. The pig farmer had, in his forward-thinking generosity, painted a target on the place.

Nancy had sent men into the town to evacuate the civilians as soon as she'd got the final information from London. Not everyone had gone though. The mayor, who had been turning a blind eye to Maquis activity in the area for two years, had insisted on being given a rifle and a place to stand, and had bought half a dozen gendarmes with him. He was under Tardivat's command behind a row of sandbags at the corner of the town hall. Some other inhabitants had stayed to guard their property, and a number of young women had volunteered to care for the injured at the chateau or in the town hall. The rest of the population, though, had gathered up their children, taken what food and water they could carry and walked up into the hills, not knowing what would be left of their lives when the day was over.

Denden saw the column first as a glint of light on a windshield farther down the valley. Gradually the great fat snake of it came into view. He counted tanks, and swallowed. Five of the bastard things. Shit. The infantrymen looked to be marching in good order too. He had hoped they'd look a bit more beaten up. Christ, there were a lot of them.

He took out his hip flask and took a long pull.

"Jules, give Field Marshal Wake the following details, will you?" He rattled off his estimates of troop numbers, the wagons and tank count. "Then you'd better find your place."

It was like Nancy to have assigned Jules the role of messenger between them. They had not spoken much while waiting for the convoy to appear in the valley, just slightly awkward nonsense. But Denden had felt Jules beginning to soften, heard the note of regret in his voice. It helped even as it hurt, and Denden was thankful to him and to Nancy for it.

Jules stood up. "Good luck, Denis," he said. It had been Captain Rake up to now.

"And to you, Jules," Denden replied. "Be well." Jules dashed down the winding stairs from the belfry without saying anything more, and Denden found he had to blink a couple of times to clear his vision.

He was just in time to see the column shudder to a halt, half a mile outside town.

"No, no…" he said softly. "Run to Mummy and Daddy, dear hearts."

A sudden blur of flames. René had managed to get into first position with his toys. Good.

"Come on, into town," Denden said again. "Not nice out there, is it, my dears? Come on."

A minute passed, then the column jerked forward, faster this time. Denden put down the glasses and picked up a flag—well, the tattered remains of Nancy's red satin cushion salvaged from the bus and now tied to a stick—and stuck it through the louvered windows.

Nancy had been staring at that bloody bell tower for an hour even before they heard the boom of the explosion and the distant rattle of gunfire. Then the red flag.

"Showtime, boys," she shouted.

The exit from the square between the church and town hall was blocked by a wall of sandbags—on the west guarded by a troop under Tardivat, on the east by Nancy's men. She rested her Lee-Enfield on top of the sandbag wall and wet her lips, tasting the soft tang of V for Victory by Elizabeth Arden.

They weren't stupid. A tank rumbled into the square first, the growl of its engine deafening, the scale of it in the market square impossible. In its shadow came a flood of infantry. One of René's protégés stood up to the west of the bridge and fired his bazooka into its tracks while the rest of them laid down covering fire, picking off the infantry and driving them back into cover.

The charge exploded, throwing two of the infantry into the air, but the tank trundled forward.

"Shit!" Juan was firing and reloading steadily beside her. "How is it still moving?"

A second tank rumbled into the square and came alongside the first. For a moment the two monsters paused in the center of the square around a hundred feet in front of them. Behind them surged a fresh swarm of infantry. They pushed forward again. Nancy was betting they wouldn't shell their positions and risk making the road and bridge impassable. Didn't mean they wouldn't just roll over them though.

René's protégé stood up again.

"Good luck," Nancy whispered. *Reload, pick your target, fire. Reload, pick your target, fire.* She brought down one NCO, waving his men forward just in front of the tank. He went down and the tank rolled over him.

A rush of air and the explosion of the bazooka. She watched the charge bounce under the tank and explode, blinding her. When she could see again, it was stopped, and black smoke was pouring from the turret, the hatch opened and two of the crew struggled out, choking. She took down one. The first tank was still coming straight at them, and the square was still filling with infantry, firing at them from behind the tanks, the market cross. No matter how many they took down, more surged from behind and the main body of them, led by the first tank, bore down inexorably on their position. Holes were appearing in their ranks.

"Fall back!" Nancy yelled, swapping her rifle for her Bren and firing short, controlled bursts. The Germans would be sending flanking parties through the back streets and round to their rear by now and she'd only got a few scattered guns hiding in houses off the square to hold them off.

Juan stumbled and fell, his shoulder shot through.

Nancy looked to the west. Tardivat was pulling back too. The Germans were swarming over his sandbag defenses and the Maquis were fighting hand to hand, the stubborn bastards. Nancy grabbed Juan's collar, pulling him backward, still firing from her hip, cutting down the men in front of her. Everything was training now. Sound and light, instinct serving her, her conscious mind blanked out by noise. The tank was almost on them, and the third was lumbering into the square.

Juan was shouting at her. "GO!"

She released his collar and headed for the corner of the church without looking back. Damn, they *were* coming through the side streets. She pulled at the door of the bell tower. A sergeant, his face pocked with scars, came up suddenly on her blind side, and the machine gun jammed. He charged her. She allowed the Bren to swing on its strap, pulled her knife and sidestepped, letting him run onto its slashing edge as she twisted it across his throat.

Then through the door and up the tight spiral stairs. She slipped, her boots wet with Juan's blood, her hands with the German's, then threw herself forward again. The noise was deafening; the tank coughed out a shell and it exploded among the sandbags, sending clouds of earth into the sky and shaking the foundations of the tower.

She scrambled through the trapdoor and into the belfry, her lungs screaming and her muscles on fire. Denden was waiting for her, binoculars in hand. He turned.

"Down!"

She didn't think, just flattened herself on the dusty and ill-fitting planks. Denden pulled his side arm and fired, one, two. She heard a gasp and twisted round in time to see a soldier standing above her, the front of his tunic blossoming with a dark damp stain. Her heart lurched and she kicked out, catching his shin and sending him back down the stairs, then slammed down the trapdoor. How had she not heard him?

"Seal it!" Denden shouted at her.

Move, Nancy. She grabbed the waiting sandbag Jules and Denden had dragged up the tower at dawn and shoved it on top of the trapdoor.

"Alone at last," Denden said with a crooked smile.

She took the binoculars from him. "Thank you."

He didn't reply. Just nodded and looked back out into the square. She lifted the binoculars to her eyes, trying to take it all in. Below her she saw the bodies of the Maquis slumped over the sandbags.

"Come on, Gaspard, you son of a bitch," she muttered, squeezing the field glasses until her knuckles turned white. His men were spread on both sides of the close approach to the bridge on the town side. The last line of defense.

"Do it. Blow the charge."

Böhm and the colonel had abandoned the car and taken up a position on a high slope to the west of the town. Junior officers scrambled up the banks toward them, or away with the colonel's orders.

The colonel was in an increasingly good mood. "A rather ragtag attempt to hold the bridge," he said. "A lucky shot with the bazooka, and brave men, of course, but under-supplied and under-manned. I think we have you to thank for that, Böhm, do we not?"

Böhm did not reply, continuing to watch the action through his binoculars.

"I understand," the colonel continued as if Böhm had simply not understood, "that you laid the groundwork for a very successful raid near Chaudes-Aigues. Marvelous. Scattered them to the four winds. I hear they were so desperate for resupply a woman went to Châteauroux for a new radio!"

Böhm lowered his glasses, looked at him. "Did she get it?"

The colonel shrugged. "I believe so, but the locals were quite sure she never made it out of town again. Hadn't you heard?"

"Communications have been somewhat disrupted since the Allies invaded the south," he replied. Could it be her? She was quite mad when he saw her in Montluçon. Too crazed to charm her way through the countryside with a radio on her back. It could not be her.

"They will blow the bridge," Böhm said.

The colonel laughed politely. "No, no. If they had sufficient explosives they'd have blown it before we arrived! This little defense is proof they can't take it down." He tilted his head to one side. "Though even if they had, we'd have been able to construct an adequate crossing in half a day. Heaven knows we have enough men, and enough timber available! The river is relatively shallow here."

The thoughts began to turn in Böhm's head. If it had been her who fetched the radio...

"When did the woman get the radio?"

"The report came in a week ago. Ha!"

"What?" Böhm shifted his view.

"That little puff on the bridge, just clearing. Poor bastards only had enough explosive to open an envelope. The bridge is intact and they're running for their lives."

Böhm watched as a small group of men ran across the bridge, the German forces swelling behind them. One Frenchman fell forward onto the road.

The colonel raised his voice. "Get everyone moving please, I want the whole column across that bridge in half an hour. Push on. See if the damaged tank is repairable and report back to me."

Böhm could feel it in his blood. This unease. He scanned the square, the lightly defended sandbag emplacements, the pathetic charge on the bridge. They hadn't even managed to set it in the place where it had the best chance of doing some real damage. It was like they weren't even trying. The raid on Wake's camp had been a success, a great success, but he'd been sure there were a thousand men in those hills, and they'd found fewer than a hundred bodies.

They weren't even trying...

Something caught his eye, a flag stuck through the louvers of the bell tower.

"It's a trap!"

The colonel's face twisted into an expression of polite

skepticism. The Germans poured into the middle of the town, no longer firing, their guns at their sides. Two tanks were on the bridge itself, the three others waiting their turn in the square. A squad of engineers were already examining the damaged one. In the square. Böhm felt his stomach clench. The tanks could fire round 180 degrees, but if there were men on the upper stories of those buildings with more bazookas they were vulnerable.

"Get your men out! Withdraw!" he screamed in the colonel's face.

It was already too late.

Nancy watched Gaspard blow the fake charge and then run; the man next to him went down. Damn. Damn. Damn.

"Nancy! It's working!"

Denden pulled on her arm and she swung her binoculars back to the square. It was crushed with troops now. Two tanks were pulling out onto the bridge, infantry surging around them.

"Wait!" she said.

"But Nancy…"

"Wait, Denden."

The second tank ground its gears and pulled out over the water as the fifth and final Panzer entered the square. The Kübel-wagens were backed up behind it, blocking the road.

"Now!"

Denden launched himself onto the bell rope and the deep-throated clang rang out across the town.

All hell broke loose.

The third-floor windows all around the square burst open and the Maquis who had been waiting inside started pouring fire down onto the crowd of German soldiers below. At the same moment the bridge exploded, a chain of blasts that shook the tower, showering dust down on them. Denden yelled with delight. A great fountain of dirt and stone rocketed skyward, and a choking cloud was blown back into the square.

As the dust cleared over the river, Nancy saw that the bridge was gone. In the riverbed the two tanks lay on their sides in the fast-flowing water, surrounded by struggling men. From his redoubts on the far side of the bank, Gaspard fired down at the Germans in the water. The few who had made it across had already dropped their weapons and were standing on the bank, too scared to help their drowning comrades, their hands in the air.

Denden yelped again. Bazooka rounds exploded round the three Panzers. The gun turret of one swung round and fired into the ground floor of the butcher's shop. A shattering, tumbling, punching of falling masonry and the house crumbled into the square, collapsing onto the German troops packed below. They started screaming at the tank commander. Then, as two more bazooka rounds from the opposite side of the square hit the tank, they rolled back from it like a wave. Smoke poured through the slits in the armor. René had got to his second position, then.

The screaming was getting louder. Infantrymen were throwing themselves against the walls, flinging their rifles down as if they had burned their hands. Others launched themselves forward on the ground. Nancy looked south. Fournier was folding up the rear of the column, gathering the stragglers and wagons who hadn't yet made it into the town. She could see it was him by his walk. His Bren was held loosely across his chest, his rifle on his back, and he was chatting to the man beside him. The stragglers all had their hands in the air, and their weapons littered the roadside.

"That's enough." She whispered it. Then blinked, and shook her head. "Denden, that's enough. They are done."

He held the rope and the tolling ceased. The gunfire turned from a storm to an occasional ripple. A final scattering of cracks. Then silence. They shifted the sandbag off the trapdoor, and

Nancy walked down the spiral stairs slowly, awkwardly. She'd started bleeding from her ankles again and only now did the pain find a way to get through the fog of her brain. She hadn't spotted any men she recognized as Gestapo in the square. Perhaps they were in the wagons? Or perhaps the intel was wrong. God, this hellish pull and push of doubt and hope.

Denden followed her. They ignored the body on the stairs and the other by the door and stepped out into the square, their backs to the river. Tardivat was already separating out the officers, tasking his boys to collect the Germans' weapons. The Maquis poured out of the houses, their guns trained on the cowering troops. Tardivat strolled over to them.

"Congratulations, Field Marshal Wake," he said.

Nancy's eyes traveled over the bodies, some Maquis, many, many more German infantry caught in that killing field. She still couldn't spot any Gestapo men. How long had it lasted? Three minutes? Five?

"Once they are disarmed, organize burial parties," she said. "Did the mayor make it?"

Tardi nodded.

"Good. Talk to him about where they should be buried. Put the officers in the police cells or take them to the chateau—"

"Nancy! Behind you!" Fournier's voice.

She spun round. A major. He had reared up from the river like an ugly ghost, his side arm raised, ten feet from her. So this is where I die then, Nancy thought. Thank God I got to see these bastards beaten first.

A single shot. Nancy flinched but felt no pain. Had the idiot managed to miss from this range? No. His right eye had disappeared. He fell forward, dead before he hit the ground. Nancy heard the sound of a hundred weapons being lifted, bolts sliding back—the Maquis were aiming their guns at the trembling prisoners, and she ran forward, arms raised.

"No!" Nancy shouted. "Lads, I'm fine! Look at me! We did it!"

Everything was on a knife edge. Their blood was up and there wasn't a man among them who hadn't seen a friend's farm burned, had a relative disappear. They all knew the stories of the women and children killed, the wild brutality of the Gestapo in these last months. But no. Not now. They couldn't beat the Germans and then become them.

She clambered on top of a tank where they could all see her. *Come on, Nancy. Just once more. Find the words.* She spread her arms wide.

"Men of the Maquis! Listen to me! These men are your prisoners. You have won, you have won your liberation. France is free. The troops who took your country are at your feet, begging for mercy. Be men!" *Please listen. Please, please, by all that is holy, please listen.* This day had to be a victory, a day to celebrate, not a massacre of prisoners to shame them in the years to come. "Listen to me! Be better than ordinary men! Be men of the Maquis."

One. Two. Then slowly, one at a time, they lowered their guns. To her right, a German private, a boy of seventeen at most, started to cry, and another older man looking up at a Maquis gun next to him put his arm around his shoulders. The muzzle was pointed away from him again.

She looked around, to the other side of the river, where the shot that had saved her life had come from. There was Gaspard, rifle at his side. He raised his hand in greeting.

63

M ost of the prisoners had been billeted through the town and in the castle itself, disarmed and in small groups with each house guarded by Maquisards that Nancy trusted not to get drunk and take a bloody revenge before the Allies arrived. Still nothing on any Gestapo men, though perhaps they were hiding among the ordinary soldiers. She would find out soon. She would look every one of them in the eye before the Americans arrived. First she had to make sure that peace held, that the day of victory did not slide into slaughter at darkness.

Nancy and Fournier went back to the Great Hall of the chateau and, with a bottle of brandy on the table in front of them, worked through the arrangements for the next weeks. They had already had deputations from some of the towns and villages in the area asking representatives of their group to take part in ceremonies of thanksgiving for their liberation. Denden was in some far-off corner of the tower, sending and receiving messages and updates in a frenzy of Morse.

"We go to the villages that were victims of reprisals first," Nancy said. "Then the home towns of the men who died."

She pulled a notebook from her tunic pocket.

"What is that?" Fournier asked. "I thought you gave your notes to Captain Rake."

"My book of the dead," Nancy replied, handing it to him and then refilling her glass. "Names, addresses. That I kept with me."

Fournier took it like a holy object and put it in his own pocket, then finished his own glass. "I'll make a tour in town. Check everything is in order. Good night, Field Marshal."

"Good night."

But Nancy didn't go to bed. She had to work out a plan to gather up all the weapons and explosives she could, empty the remaining caches of arms before some kid found them and come up with some system to distribute the remaining cash she had from London to the men and the families of those who had not survived. Then she would make her search.

An urgent step in the corridor made her lift her head. Jules.

"Madame Nancy, we have picked up the colonel who commanded the column. Tardivat has him locked up in the pantry."

"That's fine, Jules. What else?"

"The colonel had a Gestapo man with him. Denis told me... if I heard of any Gestapo I should tell you, only you. But I think some of the men have found out. He's in the stables."

She shot to her feet and was out of the room before he had even finished speaking, hand on her side arm.

Half a dozen Maquisards were there, arguing with the two guards, who stood aside as she approached.

"Lads," she said lightly, "go get some sleep. And check yourself for wounds. Keep them clean. Be a bit fucking tragic if you died of blood poisoning now, wouldn't it? Leave this one to me."

It worked. The little crowd melted away and the guards shot her grateful looks. She lit a lantern from the one hanging in the courtyard. Would this man know what had happened to Henri? She was afraid she'd answer a blank look with a bullet. Could any of them remember how many people they'd killed? She opened the door, shutting it behind her before lifting the lamp. The stables smelled of fresh hay and leather. The Gestapo man was propped up against the door of one of the stalls, his ankles and wrists bound and a feed sack over his head. Nancy remembered how that felt. She hung the lantern on a hook to her side.

The shock, when she pulled the sack off his head and saw Böhm blinking up at her, was brutal. Another of God's little bombshells. He knew. She was going to get her answer and suddenly she was afraid, afraid for the first time in her life. It was as if the floor had disappeared underneath her and it took all her strength to stay standing.

She had taken out her side arm and pressed the barrel to the side of his head before her conscious mind even recognized him.

"Is Henri alive?" she said. She imagined the bullet in slow motion spinning in the barrel then shattering his skull, plowing through the soft matter of his brain, the long spurt of blood and bone that would fly across the straw beside him.

He watched her. Then, seeing she would wait for an answer, he reached with his bound wrists into the side pocket of his tunic.

"I will tell you. But do this one thing for me." His fingers caught the edge of a letter and plucked it free. "Get this to my daughter. Give me your word."

"Fine."

He lifted his bound hands and she took the envelope, shoved it into the pocket of her slacks, still holding the revolver to his head.

"Now tell me. Is Henri alive?"

"The answer is in your pocket. That's a farewell letter to my child. Because I know that you're going to execute me, just as I did your husband many weeks ago. He was killed, shortly after a visit from his father and sister. Life has a cruel symmetry."

The image of Böhm's brains splattering all over the straw was so clear she was surprised to discover that she had not already pulled the trigger.

Böhm was staring up at her, and for the first time since she had met him, he looked...confused.

"Do it, Madame Fiocca. I murdered your husband. I ordered

his torture. I tormented him for weeks. He suffered terribly, you know. Then I tortured you, with a chance to save him. I know what that did to you, Madame Fiocca. I saw it. You have already tried to kill me once; why are you hesitating now?"

She heard the desperation in his voice. She uncocked her revolver and returned it to the holster on her hip.

"No, Böhm. You will stand trial. I'd like very much to kill you, but that would be selfish of me, don't you think? There are plenty of other widows, mothers, fathers and husbands who need answers from you. I'm going to hand you over to the Americans."

He knitted his fingers together, but Nancy could see they were trembling. She picked up the lantern and left him alone in the dark.

64

Dear Fraulein Böhm,

My name is Nancy Wake, and I am an agent working with the Maquis in southern France. We have just captured your father and are going to hand him over to the American authorities. He asked me to send this letter to you. I do not know what he has written, but I imagine it's something about how he sacrificed his life for the dream of a Greater Germany and how he was willing to do difficult things to protect you and your future.

Your father is a monster. A stunted man and for all his learning, he knows nothing of human life, of love. I saw the regime he served before the war, and saw nothing but cruelty and posturing brutality pretending to be strength. That is not strength, it is weakness trying to disguise itself, lashing out to hide its own lacerating fear. He will tell you he is a patriot, I guess. I know he is a coward.

He tortured and murdered my husband. He killed my friends. He is not a hero to be welcomed home. He and his kind have caused untold suffering to millions of women like me, to millions of little girls like you, and I think we are only just beginning to learn the true horror of what they have done behind this mask of science and patriotism.

You are young. You do not bear responsibility for this suffering, but in the next few years you will have a choice to make. To be angry and afraid for your whole life, and shut your eyes to the truth. Or to be strong, to face it and become part of building a different future.

Yours,

Nancy Wake

65

The Americans arrived late the next morning and scooped up the prisoners with cheerful efficiency. They also left crates of supplies, food mostly, but a good amount of fuel too, for the returning townsfolk of Cosne-d'Allier and a couple of structural engineers who were tasked with rebuilding the bridge Gaspard had just blown up. News that Paris was liberated reached them mid-afternoon.

Once the prisoners were gone, including Böhm, the tension in the town began to dissipate and by the early afternoon the mayor was said to be organizing a party. Every member of the Maquis had a girl on his arm and flowers in his buttonhole and the owner of the chateau arrived, not to throw them out on the street, but to break open the wine cellar and share out the contents.

When she'd shaken hands with the Americans and gone through the latest instructions from London, Nancy withdrew to her chamber and tried to sleep. She had known Henri was dead. Known it for months now really, and since the bike ride it had felt like a certainty, but she had not faced it, really stared it down, until Böhm had told her last night. It left her empty. She had said goodbye, begun her grieving without even knowing it.

"No moping, Field Marshal!" Denden bounced into the room as dusk approached, his face pink and his grin wolfish and pleased.

She pulled herself up onto her elbows. "Made up with Jules again, Denden?"

His smile faltered. "To a degree. We are friends again, but he daren't..."

"I shouldn't have asked, I'm sorry."

He shook his head. "Don't be. It is his choice. Now be a good girl and brush your hair. I have a little surprise for you."

She struggled out of bed and found her brush and her lipstick. Shame about that compact she had hurled into the void. Maybe Buckmaster would give her another one if she asked nicely. She examined herself in the spotted mirror over the dressing table, wondering how often the lady of the manor had peered into it, arranging her diamonds round her neck. The reflection she saw looked surprisingly like Nancy Wake.

"Denden, was it luck?"

"Was what luck, sweetie?" he replied.

"That shot in the bell tower when you took out the man about to kill me. You always got such terrible marks at marksmanship, but I saw you take the shot. Textbook. Not to mention an impressive reaction time."

He shrugged. "You know I hate guns. I had to make that clear to the instructors. Doesn't mean I can't shoot straight in the right circumstances."

"Thank you."

He watched her put down her brush, then grabbed her by the hand and led her out of the room and down the grand staircase, pulling her arm so hard that she had to protest, then shoved her out onto the front steps, holding her shoulders as he stood slightly behind her.

"You already thanked me. Now come along."

Fournier, Juan, René, Tardivat and Gaspard were waiting on the steps. Juan had his arm in a sling, and Gaspard had put on a suit. Even with the eyepatch, he looked like a prosperous middle-aged businessman, the sort who would open the door for the ladies on the way into a decent restaurant in Montluçon and leave a good tip, which, Nancy realized, was probably what he was. She remembered some rumor about an electronics shop he used to run. He was carrying a large bouquet, fresh flowers from the gardens of Cosne-d'Allier. He presented them to Nancy, thrusting them a little awkwardly at her with a bow.

"*Alors*, Madame Nancy," he said.

She took the flowers and shook his hand. Gaspard blushed then put his hand out to Denden.

Denden shook it briefly. "Now, let's get this party started, shall we?"

Gaspard cleared his throat and yelled. "Field Marshal Wake, we salute you!"

So it began.

Troops of Maquis, some carrying French flags, some with banners of their villages and towns, began to march from the rear of the chateau and draw up in ranks in front of her. They did it pretty well too, despite a bit of shoving and laughter, and they kept coming. Tens, then hundreds of men drawing themselves up in front of the steps until the courtyard was packed. The breeze pulled at the flags making them snap and flutter.

Denden leaned forward and whispered in her ear. "And after this, drinks!"

Gaspard stepped forward. "Three cheers for the Field Marshal!"

The noise almost knocked her off her feet.

The Great Hall was packed. They hung up the flags around the beams, managed to shift the huge oak table and bring in new ones, then for hours the Maquis and their guests ate, drank and sang the national anthems of the Allies, or versions of them. They slurped their wine and blushed when the matrons of the town cuffed their ears and corrected their table manners, grew sentimental, then started singing again. The boys around Nancy at the top table were discussing their plans for the future. Tardivat and Fournier planned to rejoin the regular army, Gaspard was thinking about going into politics, and Denden declared sourly he was buggering off to Paris as soon as possible to see exactly how liberated they actually were. René astonished them all by declaring he was going to Paris too, to fulfill his dream of writing books for children and, once he and Denden had sworn they would share digs on Montmartre, was describing in great detail the plot of his first masterpiece about a little white Australian mouse who came to Paris for a series of exciting adventures. While he was rejecting some of Denden's increasingly obscene story ideas, Nancy recognized a familiar figure at the back of the hall.

"Garrow!"

She left the others and all but ran into his arms. He held her tightly for a moment, then pushed her away so he could look at her properly. He was dressed in civilian clothes, looking like an English tourist on a motoring tour. All tweed and brogues.

"When did you get here?" she asked.

"Not long ago, Captain Wake. And no, I am not going to address you as Field Marshal."

Nancy pouted and he laughed.

"I came to give you the word from London. Bloody good show, in Buckmaster's own words."

"Thank you," she replied, meaning it.

Garrow grew more serious. "Look, Nancy, can you get away for a couple of days? From what I can see you've got everything in order here and I have the car. I thought you might like to come back to Marseille with me. We can leave in the morning."

Nancy looked around the room—the men flush with victory, these men she had led, cared for, fought with, who had fought alongside her. Another rendition of the Marseillaise began, and they were all on their feet and belting it out so the walls shook. There would never be a better time.

"Can we leave now?"

He patted her on the shoulder. "I'll fetch the car."

When she found him again out on the drive, Denden was in the back seat, his pack by his side. "Paris can wait, dearie. I'm coming too."

66

They made good time, even if the route was a meandering one, requiring them to constantly retrace their steps to avoid destroyed bridges and wreckage on the roads, and to wait for columns of American and British troops to pass by. It gave them time to catch up. Philippe had been found alive, just, in a camp north of Paris. Marshall too had somehow survived, making it out of the house with three bullet wounds by crawling through the attics of his neighbors. Garrow did not dwell on the losses.

At last they were in the outskirts of the city, then in the suburbs, and before she was ready for it, on Nancy's own street. Now Garrow was bringing the car to a halt opposite her home. He let her and Denden out, told them he had paperwork to deal with and would be back in an hour, then drove away. Having exchanged the briefest of greetings with the fishmonger and his wife and a couple of other curious neighbors, Nancy approached her old home. The garden was overgrown, and the door was locked.

"Shall I pick it?" Denden asked, watching her.

She shook her head and dug her fingers into the dry soil of the pot holding a fading bay tree at the top of the steps. She fitted it into the lock. Turned it. Pushed open the door and walked inside. Denden followed her.

The air smelled stale.

Denden gasped. "I'm sorry, Nancy."

LIBERATION

It was a shell. Whoever had lived in it after she'd left had stripped everything on their way out: the pictures and books Henri had chosen with such care, even Nancy's fancy coffee table. She could imagine it now, tied to the roof of some German officer's car, abandoned on the road somewhere between here and the Swiss border. What they couldn't take, they'd trashed. Rubbish and waste was piled in the corners, rotting food stank up the kitchen. Upstairs they found only empty rooms, the curtains torn down, and someone had tried to start a fire at the top of the stairs.

"Bastards," Denden said.

Nancy felt nothing. Now Henri was dead, it was just a set of walls.

Someone knocked at the front door and they went down together. Maybe Garrow had realized she wouldn't want so long to sit in this wreck of a place where she had once been so happy. She opened the door. It was not Garrow.

"Claudette!"

"Madame!" She was flushed and panting. "Your neighbors told me you had come home."

As soon as Denden realized it was someone she knew, he went and sat on the stairs, his face as somber and still as she had ever seen it.

Nancy's maid had aged ten years in less than eighteen months. With a deep pang she noticed the scarf around Claudette's head. Someone must have accused her of having an affair with a German, of collaborating, and they'd punished her for it. Nancy had seen it happening in one of the towns they had passed through on their way here, women stripped to their underwear in the square, their heads shaved while the crowd jeered. She'd seen Milice hanging from the lampposts in another, cardboard signs saying TRAITOR around their necks, and wondered how many of the men and women passing by had done a little light collaborating of their own. Enough. The Germans were gone. But things happen in war.

"Come in, Claudette." The maid hesitated on the step. "Claudette, I know Henri is dead, so if you are worried about telling me that, there's no need."

Claudette's shoulders dropped a little. "I didn't know if you had heard...I...I don't want to come in, Madame. But I had to tell you something. Before anyone else did. A man from the Gestapo came to my mother's house, two, three days after you left."

Nancy leaned against the door frame, folded her arms. "A tall man? Mid-forties with blond hair? Liked to talk about his education in England?"

Claudette nodded.

"His name is Böhm, I know him. What happened?"

Claudette couldn't look at her. She stared at her worn shoes and spoke quickly. "He wanted to know about you, Madame. Wanted to know everything about you. I couldn't tell him anything about your friends who came to the house, but he didn't seem to want to know about that. He wanted to know about you, so I...I told him everything I could remember, everything I had heard. About how your father left and you disliked your mother, and how you ran away, and your favorite books and bars and everything else I could think of." She sniffed and knocked away her tears with the back of her hand. "I was so scared, and for my mother and my little brother too."

Nancy took a long, slow breath. So he had learned all of that from her clever little maid. None of it from Henri.

"I am so sorry, Madame."

Nancy could feel the back of her eyes growing hot. That image which had so hurt her, of Henri telling Böhm all her secrets, had been a lie. Henri had endured, and said nothing. Böhm had got everything he had just by frightening this young girl. She felt a deep fierce pulse of pride in her husband.

"I understand, Claudette."

She couldn't say any more right now, and started to shut the door, but Claudette put her hand against the panel of stained glass, stopping her.

"I have something for you."

Nancy waited impatiently while Claudette rummaged in her handbag.

"Monsieur Fiocca sent it to my mother's address in Saint-Julien. We kept it in the hope you would come home safely."

An envelope, addressed to Nancy Fiocca in Henri's handwriting.

Nancy stared at it, trembling between Claudette's fingers. She managed to take it from her and with a whispered thank you, finally closed the door. She went and sat by Denden on the stairs, and when she couldn't manage to open the envelope, he took it from her, broke the seal, took out and handed the single folded sheet back to her in silence.

Dear Nancy,

They granted me a letter, hopefully it finds you and finds you well. I don't have much time before they take me, so I must be brief. How to sum up our life together? I could tell you I love you. And I do. I could tell you every second with you was worth a thousand years in this place. And it was. But you've always been a woman of action, so I'll just tell you what I did. Nan, they offered me a last meal, and I requested one thing, a glass of 1928 Krug. Böhm has just brought it to me himself. I toast your health with it, my darling girl.

I am not afraid. Your happiness is what I most desire in this world, your name will be the last word I speak.

All my love, always, Henri

For the second time since she had come to France she cried, sobbed until her ribs ached, but this time Denden had his arm around her, and held her tight until the worst of it was over.

*

When Garrow returned, they were still sitting together on the stairs like children waiting for a parent to come home. Nancy got to her feet, put the letter carefully in her pocket and opened the door for him.

Garrow glanced inside and made a face. "Damn. Sorry you didn't get a better homecoming, old girl."

Behind her Denden stood up too and picked up their packs from the hall.

"It's just a house, Garrow," Nancy said. "I shall sell it. Go back to Paris. Go to all the bars with Denden and René for a while. I don't think I could face living here any more anyway."

"We'll keep you entertained," Denden said, coming past her onto the step.

Garrow thrust his hands into his pockets and hunched his shoulders. "It's not pretty, Nancy, but do you want to have a look around the town? As I have the car? Then I can drive you both back to your boys in the morning. You know every village in the Auvergne will want to throw you a party. They'll need to see you there."

She glanced at Denden and he nodded.

Nancy joined them on the step, shutting the door behind her. She could do that. Take a longer farewell, see her men settled back into civilian life.

"And after that I can probably get you both jobs in Paris, if you'd like it," Garrow went on. "Something dull at the embassy shoving paper about, but God knows there's going to be a lot to do, sorting out this mess."

"It'll make a change from the circus," Denden said dryly. "Count me in, Garrow, if it pays well enough to keep me in brandy."

They walked back to the car. Denden slid into the back seat and Garrow opened the door for her, a sudden return to some sort of pre war gallantry, and they began a slow journey through the scarred city.

LIBERATION

The cathedral looked as if it had escaped the worst, high above the bombed-out harbor, still keeping watch, full of the prayers of the fishermen and their wives. On the water one or two of their little boats were picking their way through the wreckage of larger vessels, off to gather in the nets as the daylight drained from the great expanse of the sky.

Sorting out this mess would take a generation, Nancy thought, leaning out of the window as Garrow drove steadily on, her chin in her hand. Now began the slow, painful work of rebuilding, of creating a solid foundation of remembrance, and of forgetting. The hellish business of rewriting the laws, reestablishing the norms, rebuilding the goodwill, the respect and charity which shore up peace. It would be dull work and full of compromise, nothing like the horror and excitement of her life in the Auvergne.

Garrow shifted gears and the car purred as he turned up the road on the edge of the Old Quarter. On one of the heaps of spoil, an old lady and a little girl were collecting the bricks which had not been shattered into a rusty wheelbarrow, which they could use to rebuild. At the bottom of the heap were neat stacks of those already rescued.

"Garrow, stop the car will you?"

He did, and she climbed out.

"What are we doing, Nancy?"

She shielded her eyes from the evening sun and pointed at the two figures at work.

"I want to help them."

She began to clamber up the heap of rubble.

Garrow twisted round to Denden in the back seat. "Now what do we do?"

Denden was watching her, silhouetted against the hazy blue sky as she greeted the old woman and the child, then stooped to gather up the bricks.

Denden got out of the car with a sigh, and Garrow killed the engine and did the same. Denden squinted into the sun, then reached into his top pocket for a pair of sunglasses. He put them on before he replied. "You know what we do now. We follow her, of course."

They walked up the slope to join her.

Historical Note

For the sake of our story we have changed dates, altered the timeline of events, invented some episodes, omitted some individuals and created composite characters out of others. Out of respect for Nancy, the people she fought with and their families, however, we want to give readers an outline of some of the changes we have made, and recommend further reading for anyone who would like to know more.

Nancy was born in Wellington, New Zealand, in 1912. Her parents separated after the family moved to Australia. A gift from her maternal aunt allowed Nancy to travel first to America, then London, then Paris, where she worked as a journalist for the Hearst Newspaper Group. She was disgusted by the anti-semitic violence she saw on assignment in Vienna and Berlin and swore to fight the Nazis whenever she had the chance.

She met wealthy industrialist Henri Fiocca while on holiday in the south of France in 1936. She was in England when war was declared but returned to France immediately and she and Henri married on November 30, 1939, not in January 1943 when the Old Port of Marseille was destroyed, an event she watched from a distance. From the beginning of the war Nancy acted as a courier and moved refugees and escaped prisoners along the Pat O'Leary and Ian Garrow escape routes, earning the nickname the White Mouse from the Germans for her ability to slip through checkpoints. She also arranged and funded the escape of Ian Garrow from prison after he was captured. When challenged about the money for the bribe, she did make a formal complaint to the post office and claimed she'd used it to pay her bar bill.

Having heard the Gestapo were following her and tapping her phone, she fled Marseille and was for weeks trapped in France trying to escape over the Pyrenees. She did jump from a moving train under fire, losing all her money, jewels and papers in the process. Henri Fiocca was picked up by the Gestapo some time after Nancy left Marseille. They did torture him for information on Nancy which he refused to give in spite of the pleas of his family and he was murdered by the Gestapo on October 16, 1943. Nancy only learned of his death after the liberation.

Having finally reached England and been refused by the Free French, Nancy was accepted into the S.O.E. with Garrow's help. She met Denis Rake during her training and she and Violette Szabo debagged an instructor and flew his pants from a flagpole. She did break in to the offices of one training base to read her report card (with another friend, not Denis), but as it was good, she didn't alter it. She was dropped into France in the Spring of 1944. With her then and throughout the war was John Hind Farmer, codenamed Hubert, who also worked closely with the Maquis until liberation. They were met by Henri Tardivat who became a lifelong friend. In her biography she tells the story of overhearing Gaspard (Émile Coulaudon) and his men plotting to kill her and how having faced him and his men down, she and Hubert left to work with Henri Fournier instead, meeting up with Denis and his radio some days later. Nancy and Gaspard developed a good working relationship later in the war. He was made a Chevalier of the Légion d'honneur as were Tardivat, Denis and Nancy herself. She also worked closely with Antoine Llorca (Laurent) and René Dusacq (Bazooka), and many others.

On D-Day itself Nancy was picking up René Dusacq from a safe house in Montluçon. She did blow up various bridges during her time in France, though not the Garabit Viaduct, which readers who know the region will recognize from the description in this novel. The timeline of events—Nancy getting her bus, the attack on Gaspard's camp and so on—has also been altered. Nancy did kill with her bare hands, narrowly avoid assassination, lead men in combat and order a female spy shot. Her men would only obey the order to execute the woman when Nancy made it clear she was willing to do so herself. Nancy did participate in a raid on Gestapo Headquarters led by Henri Tardivat. She did not enter the building and poison the officers first. She regarded her epic bike ride (some five hundred kilometers in seventy-two hours) as one of her greatest achievements of the war, managing as a result to get a vital message to London via a Free French operator that they needed a new radio set and codes. The Maquis did give her a march past to celebrate her birthday on August 30, 1944, five days after the liberation of Paris. Nancy also led numerous actions against the Germans, captured fleeing German troops and saw them safely delivered to U.S. forces. The authors have represented and dramatized those actions in the battle of Cosne-d'Allier, though the battle itself is our invention.

Having tortured and murdered her husband in Marseille, the Gestapo actively hunted Nancy throughout her time in France. They plastered her image across the Auvergne, offered increasingly huge rewards for her capture and regularly sent spies to try and infiltrate the Maquis. Böhm is a dramatized version of those efforts. Though he is an invention, the atrocities carried out by the Nazis against individuals and entire villages in occupied France are not.

Whatever we have invented or altered the authors would like to note that the astonishing bravery, leadership and character of Nancy Wake is without doubt greater than any one novel can hold.

Nancy Wake was married to her second husband, John Farmer, for forty years and lived with him in Australia for most of that time. After his death she returned to Europe and died in 2011 in London. As she had requested, her ashes were scattered near the village of Verneix, five miles from Montluçon.

Nancy wrote her own biography, *The White Mouse,* as did Denis Rake, *Rake's Progress.* Maurice Buckmaster also wrote a remarkable account of the S.O.E., *They Fought Alone*, which is still in print. Russell Braddon's biography of Nancy, *Nancy Wake,* has been a consistent bestseller since publication. In *Search of the Maquis: Rural Resistance in Southern France,* by H. R. Edward, is an excellent scholarly study in English of what happened in the region where Nancy served; and *Behind the Lines: The Oral History of Special Operations in World War II,* by Russell Miller, is a fascinating collection of testimony from many other brave agents working behind enemy lines.

Darby Kealey & Imogen Robertson
Los Angeles and London, 2019

Imogen Kealey is the pseudonym of Darby Kealey and Imogen Robertson.

Darby Kealey is a writer and producer, based in Los Angeles. His credits include the critically acclaimed series *Patriot* for Amazon, as well as a number of film and television projects currently in development. His feature script *Liberation* was nominated for the 2017 Blacklist. He has an MFA in screenwriting from UCLA and a BA in politics from UC Santa Cruz.

Imogen Robertson is a writer of historical fiction. Now based in London, she was born and brought up in Darlington and read Russian and German at Cambridge. Before becoming a writer, she directed for TV, film, and radio. She is the author of several novels, including the Crowther and Westerman series. Imogen has been shortlisted for the CWA Historical Dagger three times (2011, 2013, and 2014), as well as for its most prestigious award, the Dagger in the Library. She has also written *King of Kings,* a collaboration with the legendary international bestseller Wilbur Smith.